THE REGENT

A FIVE TOWNS STORY OF ADVENTURE IN LONDON

BY

ARNOLD BENNETT

METHUEN & CO. LTD.
36 ESSEX STREET W.C.
LONDON

First Published in 1913

WORKS BY ARNOLD BENNETT

NOVELS

A Man from the North
Anna of the Five Towns
Leonora
A Great Man
Sacred and Profane Love
Whom God Hath Joined
Buried Alive
The Old Wives' Tale
The Glimpse
Helen with the High Hand
Clayhanger
The Card
Hilda Lessways

FANTASIAS

The Grand Babylon Hotel
The Gates of Wrath
Teresa of Watling Street
The Loot of Cities
Hugo
The Ghost
The City of Pleasure

SHORT STORIES

Tales of the Five Towns
The Grim Smile of the Five Towns
The Matador of the Five Towns

BELLES-LETTRES

Journalism for Women
Fame and Fiction
How to Become an Author
The Truth About an Author
The Reasonable Life
How to Live on Twenty-Four Hours a Day
The Human Machine
Literary Taste
The Feast of St Friend
Those United States
The Plain Man and His Wife

DRAMA

Polite Farces
Cupid and Common Sense
What the Public Wants
The Honeymoon
The Great Adventure

CONTENTS

CHURNET VALLEY BOOKS

1 King Street, Leek, Staffordshire ST13 5NW 01538 399033

© Churnet Valley Books 2006
ISBN 1 904546 43 9 (978 1-904546-43-6)

The Grand Theatre, Hanley, the Empire Music Hall in *The Regent*

INTRODUCTION

Even before its publication in 1913 Arnold Bennett was confidently predicting that *The Regent* would be a popular success. Writing to his agent, J. B. Pinker, in April 1912, Bennett asserted: 'You may take it positively from me that this book is all right. I have read nearly all of it aloud to friends, with enormous success' (*Letters* I, 168). His friends would not have had long to wait to hear successive instalments. Bennett's journal for 11th April 1912 records: 'To-day at 3.30 I finished 'The Regent', 78,200 words, written in two months less three days' (*Journals* II, 46). Its speed of composition was matched by an equally speedy early publication history, with its appearance in serial form in both England and America in late 1912 prior to book publication in September 1913. Sales figures and press reviews accounted the book a commercial and a critical success.

Initial euphoria over the appearance of any book is no guarantee of the long-term critical attention necessary for regular reprinting and new editions. From the appearance of F. J. Harvey Darton's first book length study of Bennett in 1918 to John Lucas's 1974 *Arnold Bennett. A Study of His Fiction*, *The Regent* has been dismissed as a minor roman à clef, with Machin read as a thinly disguised mouthpiece for Bennett. Whilst it is true that the fictional Machin of both *The Regent* and its predecessor *The Card* (1911) shares some characteristics with Bennett, these relate mainly to uncontentious biographical details such as date of birth. Read in sequence the two novels may suggest a near seamless transition of the hero from the commercial and social limitations of his provincial roots to his successful entry into the cosmopolitan world of global and financial capital. This reading takes its cue from a restricted interpretation of Bennett's sub-title to the novel, *A Five Towns Story of Adventure in London*, in which the cheeky chappy from the provinces outwits his supposedly smarter and more sophisticated town cousins. In the process it loses sight of just how often the narrator parts company with the conventional views of his hero, preferring to debate a detailed and insightful recording of the changing Edwardian aesthetic.

A critical predilection for the romantic nature of the '*Adventure*' is in danger of neglecting the '(ad)venture' or speculation of exported provincial capital for cosmopolitan business and finance. *The Regent* contributes to that early twentieth century literary topography showing the mobility of both human and financial capital involved in the construction of an aesthetic wedded to modernity and the increasing hegemony of market society. Critics from Darton to Lucas have failed to discuss this aspect of Bennett's careful literary engagement of an Edwardian cultural milieu that his contemporary readers and reviewers applauded. Theirs was almost the last word on *The Regent* until Eleanor Stewart-Tanguy published a serious and sustained analysis of Bennett's use of theatre as trope in her 2003 essay 'Theatre and Theatricality in Arnold Bennett's Novels from *A Man from the North* to *The Regent*.' Exploring the novel's text as a well-staged parody of the theatre industry, she is able to acknowledge its contribution towards establishing

THE REGENT

Edwardian cultural values as a frame of reference for the long-running dialectic with Modernism.

When Bennett raises the curtain on his story he is precise in dating its beginnings in 1910: '(It was in the autumn of the great gambling year, 1910.)' This opening becomes significant in retrospect because it is the year chosen by Virginia Woolf to date her perceived crucial fracture between the Edwardians and the Georgians. Woolf's 1924 Hogarth Press essay, *Mr. Bennett and Mrs. Brown*, suggested, 'that on or about December 1910 human character changed... All human relations have shifted - those between masters and servants, husbands and wives, parents and children. And when human relations change there is at the same time a change in religion, conduct, politics and literature'(4-5). Bennett is condemned as an Edwardian novelist whose literary 'tools are the wrong ones for us to use' (18).

The problem with this argument is that Bennett's novels do explore the interaction between institutional social movements and human nature - *The Regent* itself nuances politics, literature and the aesthetics of the new drama. Even more problematic for Woolf's summary dismissal of Bennett's outmoded literary tools is his use of them precisely to defend Bloomsbury's own avant-garde values at a time when public opinion was culturally conservative. The hero of *The Regent*, Edward Henry Machin, would have been in London when Roger Fry's exhibition 'Monet and the Post-Impressionists,' promoting new French paintings and sculptures, opened at the Grafton Galleries. If Machin had read Bennett's *New Age* (December 1910) review of this show he might have been encouraged to have at least seen what all the fuss was about, secure in the knowledge that his authorial provincial parent thought better of its cosmopolitan cultured repercussions than did many Londoners: 'Its authenticity is admitted by all those who have kept themselves fully awake. And in twenty years London will be signing an apology for its guffaw' (reprinted in Samuel Hynes, 242-244). Had Machin read to the review's conclusion he might have felt a sense of personal unease for his fictional future, given Bennett's readiness to concede that the techniques of post-impressionist painting might in time change the nature of fiction:

> Noting in myself that a regular contemplation of these pictures inspires a weariness of all other pictures that are not absolutely first-rate, giving them a disconcerting affinity to the tops of chocolate boxes or 'art' photographs I have permitted myself to suspect that supposing some writer were to come along and say in words what these men have done in paint, I might conceivably be disgusted with nearly the whole of modern fiction, and I might have to begin again. (Hynes, 244)

Bennett's words were prophetic, for the consequences of 1914-1918 were that both artists and politicians would have to 'begin again' to reconstruct both their cultural and their economic worlds. *The Regent* may be read as a cultural text summarising and debating the status of the popular art of music-hall and the aesthetic status of experimental avant-garde theatre, against the background of a socio-economic status quo represented by vested landed interests and a scarcely perceptible, but gathering, political momentum for change. A year after its publication

THE REGENT

Britain was at war and the Edwardian world so clearly delineated in *The Regent* would be destroyed. In the post-war world of the arts *The Regent* may appear a minor casualty of World War I, but its critical reappraisal offers valuable insights into a world which was lost and the cultural mores that underlay its functioning.

Bennett's novels may have been regarded as the gold standard of the publishing industry in 1913 but as a writer (and private investor) he was aware of the frenetic activity in world stock activities that heralded globalisation and the removal of domestic economic certainties. *The Regent* brings home to the capital city of Empire the rapaciousness of imperialism's exploitation of the Belgian Congo of Joseph Conrad's *The Heart of Darkness* (1899). Throughout the novel all Machin's speculations in London are contingent upon stock-market fluctuations linked to colonial commodity production. Thus Machin, by telephoning twice to his stockbrokers in Manchester, 'had just made the sum of three hundred and forty-one pounds in a purely speculative transaction concerning Rubber Shares. (It was in the autumn of... 1910)' (1). The opening of the novel establishes that the aesthetic debates to follow have their origin in a material reality linking the provinces (Manchester/Stoke-on-Trent) to the metropolis (London) and to the imperial economic hinterland.

The rapidly dwindling stock of rubber trees in the Congo led to frantic efforts to find new sources, accompanied by continuing inhuman treatment of the indigenous workers in the Amazon and the West Indies. In the year *The Regent* begins, the price of rubber reached an all time high and investors, including Machin, scrambled to take up new issues of shares in the flotation of the emergent rubber companies in South-East Asia. Bennett may well have seen the cartoon in *The Illustrated London News* for 5th March 1910, showing frenzied dealings in rubber shares, or read the 19th April *Daily Mirror*'s report of a rubber share buying at the Chartered Bank when police were called in to control the crowds and where one man was trampled underfoot. There is, then, a global perspective to *The Regent* that almost unknowingly exposes metropolitan domestic imperialist culture as dependent upon territorial acquisition and exploitation.

If Bennett was alert to the speculation in rubber shares, and international markets, he certainly had an insider's knowledge of the psychology of Machin. There can be little doubt that Machin is the author's alter ego. Throughout the novel there is a creative tension between character and narrator resulting in Machin/Bennett expressing a range of mutually exclusive views on the form, content and accessibility of dramatic presentations. Lucas's critical error is to impart the notion of the intentional fallacy into Bennett's text, whereas I would argue that Machin allows Bennett to express views that would be personal anathema but which are crucial to a debate about materialism versus aestheticism. Bennett himself makes clear his view on the nature of this debate in a 1909 essay 'Middle-Class' (reprinted in *Books and Persons*). Initially Bennett aligns himself with Machin as being born below the middle class but 'by the help of God and strict attention to business I [and Machin] have gained the right of entrance into it' (90). Whereas Machin is happy with his acquired middle class designation, Bennett develops a 'profound and instinctive hostility to this class' (90). He despises its materialism: 'They deliberately gaze into shop windows in order to discover an outlet for their money' (90). He despairs of its aesthetic ignorance: 'Blind to nearly every form of beauty, they scorn art... It prefers the novelist among artists because the novel gives the longest success from ennui at least expenditure of money and effort' (93). Yet the astute commercial author is aware that it is the Machins of the world who provide for his existence and whose materialism must not be blatantly affronted by the author's aestheticism: 'If you happen to be a literary artist, it makes you think - the reflection that when you dine you eat the bread unwillingly furnished by the enemies of art and of progress!' (100). It is within the textual space created by the division between Machin's naïve perspective and the narrator's accumulated wisdom that the reader is invited to reflect upon the poetics of Edwardian drama.

Nevertheless, when the novel begins there is a psychic harmony between the provincial fictional Machin and his cosmopolitan author. Bennett mischievously encourages a reading of Machin as a character in search of his author, with an explicit act of narrative identity theft so blatant as to suggest metafictional intent: ' ...this very successful man of the world of the Five Towns, having been born on the 27th May 1867, had reached the age of forty-three and a half years!' (1) These are Bennett's biographical details. The initial similarity goes deeper, for we read that despite his monetary success Machin 'did not feel so jolly! He was surprised, he was even a little hurt, to discover by introspection that monetary gain was not necessarily accompanied by felicity... 'I must be getting older,' he reflected' (1). Intriguing, then, to consult Bennett's *Journals* for the autumn 1910 and to read how closely he has transferred his situation and feelings:

Thursday, September 22nd
Also I made a mess of another water-colour.
Hence depression, though my affairs are prospering as they never prospered before. Which shows how little content has to do with prosperity.

(Journal, Vol I, 384)

And things were little better a week later:

Friday, September 30th
I began to foresee a comparative failure for 'Clayhanger' in England, and then also in America ... I was still gloomy this morning. I hated to go on with my play .... I notice that a British paper, announcing 'Cupid and Commonsense' for next week there, thinks fit to explain that the author 'A.B.' is a novelist of repute. *This at the age of 43, after having written what I have written* [italics added].

(Journal, Vol I, 385-6)

Publishing *The Author's Craft* a year after *The Regent*, Bennett could have been describing his technique in the latter when he wrote 'First-class fiction is, and must be, in the final resort, autobiographical' (61). When, however, he goes on to write, 'Upon occasion some human being may entrust him with confidences extremely precious for his craft. But such windfalls are so rare as to be negligible'(62), we realise that for Bennett the exploration of his own psyche represents a windfall as productive as that of rubber shares for plot development in *The Regent*. The materialist Machin remains in a state of creative tension with the aesthetically sensitive Bennett throughout the novel. At the novel's end Machin is ill at home and the doctor's diagnosis is 'nerves' caused by his involvement in the world of theatre and succeeding against the odds in making money from art.

We have an evocative picture of popular culture and the provincial music-hall in Bennett's essay 'The Hanbridge Empire' which appeared in *The Nation* in 1910. And it is with Machin's 1910 visit to the Empire Music Hall, Hanbridge, that Bennett delivers one of his great set pieces. (Bennett's 'Empire Music Hall' was The Grand Theatre, Hanley, on the corner of Trinity Street and Foundry Street. Fire destroyed much of the building in the early 1930s, although it still stands today as a building in search of a function.) When Machin first enters the Empire his thoughts are stolidly provincial and materialistic, with his measure of theatrical success being the cash taken in the auditorium, rather than the quality of performance mounted on the stage. Provincial pride swells even before the curtain rises: 'He had said to himself, full of honest pride in the Five Towns: 'This music-hall, admitted by the press to be one of the finest in the provinces, holds over two thousand five hundred people' (30). The entrepreneur in him begins 'instinctively to calculate the amount of money in the house' (30). Prefaced by purely economic considerations, neither Machin nor the reader is prepared for the dazzling performance on stage/page that is Bennett's sustained passage of prose in praise of popular culture.

The curtain rises on 'a restaurant of quiet aspect, into which entered a waiter bearing a pile of plates some two feet high' (32). He is joined by a second waiter and it is immediately apparent that both are drunk and that their two piles of plates are unstable. Two smartly dressed diners take their seats and calmly watch the increasingly tottering waiters. The conditions for the classic slapstick routine are now in place. 'The popular audience, with that quick mental grasp for which popular audiences are renowned, soon perceived that the table was in close proximity to a lofty sideboard, and that on either hand of the sideboard were two chairs, upon which the two waiters were trying to climb in order to deposit their plates on the topmost shelf of the sideboard' (33). The tension mounts through a series of closely averted catastrophes, performed with the heightened awareness of slow-motion technique, until the inevitable climax involving waiters and diners in an avalanche of smashed plates. General mayhem then ensues as waiters and customers begin a competitive orgy of destruction until:

> The waiters arose, and, opening the sideboard, disclosed many hundreds of unsuspected plates of all kinds, ripe for smashing. Niagaras of plates surged on to the stage. All four performers revelled and wallowed in smashed plates. New supplies of plates were constantly being supplied from strange concealments, and finally the tables and chairs were broken to pieces, and each object on the walls was torn down and flung in bits onto the general gorgeous debris, to the top of which clambered the violet hat, necklace and yellow petticoat, brandishing one single little plate, whose life had been miraculously spared. Shrieks of joy in that little plate played over the din like lightning in a thunderstorm. And the curtain fell.' (35)

The uniquely valuable documentary nature of this

piece deserves anthologising in any collection of music-hall writing. The music-hall appeared in the margins of literary fiction prior to Bennett, noticeably in the novels and stories of George Moore and George Gissing, but it had never been accorded that starring role played by mainstream theatre/drama from *Mansfield Park* onwards. Bennett's four-page celebration of popular culture predates such modernist exploration of the genre as T. S. Eliot's view of the music-hall as a site of popular performing arts seen as tribal ritual, and Virginia Woolf's attempt to reunite performers and audience in the commonality of the traditional English pageant with 'something drawn from the crowd in the penny seats and not yet dead in ourselves' (Woolf, 'Anon', quoted in Esty, 103). Given the level of critically false antipathy engendered by the Bennett/Realism versus Woolf/Modernism binary, it is perhaps a measure of the artistic unity between the two to reflect that in key passages in *The Regent* and Woolf's 1941 *Between the Acts*, there is a commonality of purpose in the depiction of music-hall and pageant. As Jed Esty writes: 'The pageant-novel redirects attention from the 'theatre of the brain' to a more public and communal theatre ... Woolf draws on pageantry as a traditional form that is still viable in modern England' (103). The recalcitrant vulgarity of music-hall lives on in Woolf's hereditary village idiot whose fluidity of temporal and spatial movement maintains the 'contact between artist and audience in a post-metropolitan English culture' (103).

Bennett's music-hall is 'still viable' because it re-enacts those traditions, such as clog dancing and pottery production/destruction, that are central to respectively the cultural and economic life of a perceived enclosed provincial domain. In reality provincial life had already been both openly and surreptitiously invaded by global values and images. Indeed, when Bennett reported on his visit to the Hanbridge Empire he metaphorically joined Hanbridge to a circuit of power controlled from the capital: 'It was as though some deity of ten thousand syndicated halls was controlling the show from some throne studded with electric switches in Shaftesbury Avenue' ('Hanbridge Empire', 279). When Machin enters the Empire he is disappointed not to be recognised as a local celebrity. His anonymity is seen as '[m]ore proof that the Five Towns was a vast and seething concentration of cities, and no longer a mere district where everybody knew everybody' (32). Bennett's Five Towns in a state of identity crisis in the face of global ties has been documented in Kurt Koenigsberger's 'Elephants in the Labyrinth of Empire: Modernism and the Menagerie in *The Old Wives' Tale*'. In the light of his reading it would be reasonable to read the Empire Theatre as itself a sign of those Imperial ties 'approach[ing] the provincial as an integral part of the total fabric of modern life' (132). This music-hall is not only the repository of the collective history of an industrial community/audience in which the plate smashing is a provincial mnemonic ritual but also a naming of extraneous cultural and political influences that have helped shape the provincial consciousness.

In realistic provincial terms broken plates meant jobs; the destruction of plates combined the cathartic release of laughter with a sober reflection on economic life: 'Judge, therefore, the simple but terrific satisfaction of a Five Towns audience in the hugeness of the calamity... every plate smashed means a demand for a new plate and increased prosperity for the Five Towns' (34). Thus roused, the audience enacts a scene of popular near hysteria eerily proleptic of events only a year off: 'The audience was now a field of artillery which nothing could silence' (34/5). In global terms it is also pertinent that the audience is, in due course, silenced by the dimming of the house lights as 'the cinematograph began its restless twinkling' (41). In locating film within the programmatic make-up of music-hall, Bennett marks the point at which music-hall began its decline in the face of the rapid expansion of film-making and cinematic exhibitions and the increasing importation of films from America and Continental Europe. Certainly Bennett was to return to cinema as textual location in *The Price of Love,* but by the time of its publication in 1914 the cinema auditorium had become a site of atomisation and private seduction rather than of commonality and openly shared pleasures. D.H. Lawrence's 1920 *The Lost Girl* also makes important reference to the competition between popular live performance and film. Ann Ardis's essay 'Delimiting Modernism and the Literary Field: D.H. Lawrence and *The Lost Girl'* centres on the relationship with Bennett's and Lawrence's work with particular emphasis on the 'historically specific characterization of nickelodeon vaudeville cinema and travelling music hall theatre...'(128). Both writers help the cultural historian to focus on literary representations of the transition from music-hall to cinema. Whilst it is generally acknowledged that Lawrence drew upon *Anna of the Five Towns* in depicting his heroine, the music-hall/film link between *The Lost Girl* and *The Regent* has gone unremarked.

Also unremarked is the industrial/provincial intertextual link between *The Regent* and the work of a writer much admired by Bennett, George Moore. Bennett published an essay in *Fame and Fiction* in 1901 in which he praised Moore's work in general and *A Mummer's Wife* in particular as 'one of the supreme novels of the century' (257). Bennett further acknowledged his debt to the book in a 1920 letter to Moore, writing, 'I wish to tell you that it was the first chapters of *A Mummer's Wife* which opened my eyes to the romantic nature of the district that I had blindly inhabited for over twenty years. You are indeed the father of all my Five Towns books' (*Letters* III, 139). The fourth of the opening chapters alluded to by Bennett describes a visit to a potbank by Dick Lennox, a touring company actor-manager, and his intended sexual conquest, Kate Ede. It is a lengthy and technically accurate passage of some ten pages and may be read as the literary precursor to Henry Mynor and Anna Tellwright's tour of Mynor's works in *Anna of the Five Towns*. Moore based his fictional Powell and Jones's Hanley works on the potbank of Bishop & Stonier's Church Works. Whereas the Mynor's factory is still very much active as Burgess, Dorling & Leigh, the Potteries Shopping Arcade now occupies the old Bishop & Stonier site.

Lennox prefaces his attempted seduction with an image of Hanley as a theatre, 'We're on the stage, the footlights run round here, and the valley is the pit ...' (64), before bringing it to a farcical conclusion that bears more than a passing resemblance to Bennett's carnivalesque plate-throwing scene. Hero and heroine find themselves alone in the storeroom, surrounded by crockery:

.... but that moment, happening to tread on her skirt, her feet slipped. He made a desperate effort to sustain her, but her legs had gone between his.

The crash was tremendous. A pile of plates three feet high was sent spinning, a row of salad-bowls was over, and then with a heavy stagger Mr. Lennox went down into a dinner-service, sending the soup-tureen rolling gravely into the next room. (81)

Bennett transforms Moore's private dramatic farce into public performance where an entire audience is willingly seduced. At Bishop & Stonier the broken crockery is dismissed as mere inconvenience, whereas at the Empire it is positively applauded, so that 'the stage-manager came before the curtain and guaranteed that two thousand four hundred plates had been broken' (35). Incidentally, intending Potteries flâneurs might wish to know that Bennett's fictional theatre and Moore's fictional pottery occupied sites in central Hanley almost literally within plate throwing distance of each other.

Machin's move from plate smashing to poetic drama is developed in Stewart-Tanguy's essay in a section subtitled 'A Parody of the Theatre Industry':

He is spotted from a box [at The Empire] by a famous American playwright and actor, and the rest of the novel, which takes place in London, describes how Machin, through a series of scams and careful business negotiations, makes himself manager of the new theatre... Through the character of Machin Bennett is mocking what he saw as the pretensions of the avant-garde who tried to transform Edwardian theatre, whether aspiring to the poetic or the intellectual. (132)

THE REGENT

Stewart-Tanguy further examines Machin's jaundiced view of the acting profession in 'contrast to the idealistic adoring view of performers that Richard [Larch] has in *A Man from the North*' (133). In essence, we are given a picture that 'points to the unreliability, unpredictability and instability of the theatre world which Bennett himself had experienced at first hand' (133).

Bennett's knowledge of London theatre shows itself in two distinct areas of *The Regent*. The more mundane concern is Bennett's running commentary on the abysmal state of theatre architecture. Himself a successful playwright, with no fewer than five plays produced on the London stage between 1908 and the time of *The Regent*'s publication in 1913, Bennett had a vested interest in the physical condition of London theatres. Machin's conversation with the architect Mr. Alloyd, whom he will commission to build the Regent theatre, fairly represents Bennett's professional critical stance:

> I should like to meet an architect who had thoroughly got it into his head that when people pay for seats to see a play they want to be able to see it, and not just get a look at it now and then over other people's heads and round corners of boxes and things. In most theatres that I've been in the architects seemed to think that iron pillars and wooden heads are transparent. Either that, or the architects were rascals! Same with hearing! The pit costs half-a-crown, and you don't pay half-a-crown to hear glasses rattled in a bar or motor-omnibuses rushing down the street. I was never yet in a London theatre where the architect had really understood that what the people in the pit wanted to hear was the play and nothing but the play. (152-153)

THE REGENT

When built, the Regent owes its novelty as much to its unprecedented audience-friendly design as to the nature of the productions mounted. Machin inspects the new theatre and is satisfied that '[e]very seat in the narrow and high-pitched gallery ... had a perfect and entire view of the proscenium opening' (260). Such fictional innovation derives directly from Bennett's 1911 tour of America. The resulting travel book, *Your United States*, reports his joy in finding that 'American theatrical architects have made a great discovery - namely, that every member of the audience goes to the play with a desire to be able to see and hear what passes on the stage' (138). When the fictional Machin eventually reaches New York he is manipulated by Bennett, the ventriloquist, into mouthing his master's words: ' 'This is my sort of place!' ' (293).

The provincial entrepreneur, Machin, is very much in the forefront of a general expansion of theatre building in the early twentieth century. Bennett himself notes in his 1908 'Preface. The Crisis in the Theatre' to his play *Cupid and Commonsense*, 'a few years and Shaftesbury Avenue will be lined with theatres from end to end!' (8). During the period covered by the Regent's construction - 1910 to 1911 - no fewer than five new London theatres were built. However farcical *The Regent*'s plot, it turns upon a very literal concrete material base. Indeed, Chris Baldick's study *The Modern Movement 1910-1940* looks at the literary importance of architecture 'as a vocation, as a business, and as the form of art most intimately connected with everyday life ...' (177) in the fiction of John Galsworthy, Lawrence, Woolf and Bennett. Baldick makes the point, in relation to *Clayhanger*, that '[b]uildings serve as fixed points or milestones all the better to measure human mobility in its dynamics of expansion and aspiration' (178). This insight is an important sub-text to Machin's ambition to move beyond the economic boundaries of provincialism and to leave a solid metropolitan monument to his homegrown reputation as a 'Card'.

How appropriate, in terms of Bennett's own youthful frustration at the unreasonable demands made upon his free time by the conventions of chapel attendance, that his alter ego's theatre was to be built upon the site of an old chapel. History in 1910 was seen to be on Machin/Bennett's side with the chapel becoming vacant as 'ownership had slipped from the nerveless hand of a dying sect of dissenters...' (149). From Methodism to musicals would have been music to Bennett's ears. He did, however, have a further target of secular power in his critical gaze at this point. In the 'Preface. The Crisis in the Theatre' Bennett reports upon conversations with leaseholders of theatres noting, 'what struck me most was the bitterness of lessees against landlords. 'It's the ground-landlord that is crushing us to death' ' (10). *The Regent* develops this theme when, in the course of Machin's Machiavellian efforts to obtain the lease for his theatre site, Bennett launches an attack that goes well beyond the London upper class with its grip on the leasehold system and the ownership of whole streets. In a passage of some bitterness that would not have been out of context in, say, Lawrence's depiction of the industrial Midlands of *Lady Chatterley's Lover*, Bennett bestrides the provincial/metropolitan divide to condemn unregulated unearned income:

THE REGENT

In the provinces, besides castles, forests and moors, Lord Woldo owned many acres of land under which was coal, and he allowed enterprising persons to dig deep for this coal, and often explode themselves to death in the adventure, on the understanding that they paid him sixpence for every ton of coal brought to the surface, whether they made any profit on it or not. This arrangement was called 'Mining rights'... (169)

Bennett writes about the year 1910 when a wave of unofficial strikes in the coal and rail industries heralded the potent arrival of organised labour. It was also the year following Lloyd George's 'People's Budget,' proposing a series of increased taxes upon the income of such large landowners as Bennett's fictional Lord Woldo. But *The Regent* goes further in a prescient prediction of social upheaval to come and the 1926 General Strike:

He [Lord Woldo] was the representative of an old order going down in the unforeseeable welter of twentieth-century politics. Numbers of thoughtful students of English conditions spent much of their time in wondering what would happen one day to the Lord Woldos of England. And when a really great strike came, and a dozen ex-artisans met in a private room of a West End hotel, and decided, without consulting Lord Woldo or the Prime Minister or anybody, that the commerce of the country should be brought to a standstill ... (169)

This is Bennett the political analyst and putative socialist. The febrile sense of pre-war unease in *The Regent* may have reached a wider audience in the form of Bennett's sugar-coated plot than with a more overtly political text.

THE REGENT

Politics also enter *The Regent* backstage with the appearance of Isabel Joy and her Militant Suffragette Society. Again, Bennett touches on controversial contemporary political events - November 1910 witnessed the first violent clash between police and Suffragettes demonstrating outside the Houses of Parliament. Indeed, Machin may well have had first-hand knowledge, if not of the actual clash, of its political fall-out. As with *The Lion's Share*, published in 1916, Bennett appears to find it commercially convenient to cloak his political radicalism in the costume of comedy. That his contribution to the debate on the suffrage movement in *The Regent* and *The Lion's Share* did not go unacknowledged and unappreciated is apparent in, for example, Rebecca West's review of the latter in the *Daily News and Leader* which concluded: 'One greatly admires Mr. Bennett for making his small but spirited contribution to the theory of feminism so excellent and rich a story of adventure' (*Young Rebecca*, 324). West wrote perceptive reviews of several of Bennett's works and these are collected in Jane Marcus's *The Young Rebecca. Writings of Rebecca West 1911-1917*.

Bennett's 'spirited contribution' to the suffrage movement in *The Regent* is to cast a leading suffragette, Isabel Joy, in the play that opens Machin's new theatre. Isabel was deliberately courting arrest and publicity to raise funds and Machin engages her, not because she can act, but because her high newsworthy profile would help rescue the sinking box office receipts at his new theatre. This is Bennett the astute commentator on the contemporary scene, aware of Edwardian celebrity crossover from politics to show business. Margaret D.

THE REGENT

Stetz's *Gender and the London Theatre 1880-1920* provides ample documentation to justify Bennett's appropriation of the suffrage movements as box office guarantor:

> Whether radicals or reformers, turn-of-the-century activists in the British suffrage movements all agreed that theatre could be a potent weapon in their struggles. It could cheer and divert fellow suffragists, as did the charming one-act farce *How the Vote Was Won* by Cicely Hamilton and Christopher St. John [Christabel Marshall]. It could reach and persuade audiences that might otherwise be indifferent to the cause or ignorant of its logic. And it could also serve as an effective means of fundraising. Because so many professional actresses endorsed the call for women's suffrage - they were, after all, workers and taxpayers who understood why they deserved political representation - the quality of benefit performances could often be quite high. (102)

When Isabel Joy appears at *The Regent* it is to 'a crammed and half-delirious auditorium' (314). The celebrity effect spills beyond the auditorium so that 'Piccadilly Circus thronged with a multitude of loafers who were happy in the mere spectacle of Isabel Joy's name glowing on an electric sign' (314 -315).

It is interesting to reflect that in creating Isabel Joy Bennett would have been very much aware of a real-life counterpart in the person of Elizabeth Robins, herself a leading suffrage campaigner, novelist and actress. Bennett had seen her on stage as early as 1896, reviewing her performance in Ibsen's *Little Eyolf* in his 'Music and Mummery' column in *Woman*, 2nd December 1896. That she went on to make as marked an impression upon him as did Isabel Joy on her first-night audience is apparent from

Bennett's ability to recall her on-stage appearance when the names of her fellow actors had faded from his memory. Writing his *Evening Standard* 'Books and Persons' column in 1928 he is 'reminded of another emotional experience which ranks in my memory with any experience resulting from the perusal of a book. Namely, a performance of *Hedda Gabler*, in the last century... I can recall the name of the actress who played Hedda - Elizabeth Robins... Unforgettable!' (139). In creating Isabel Joy in the political image of Robins, Bennett quietly makes the point, developed more stridently in Woolf's *Three Guineas*, that physical strength is not the only, or most valid, source of political power: 'She looked as though a moderate breeze would have overthrown her, but she also looked, to the enlightened observer, as though she would recoil before no cruelty and no suffering in pursuit of her vision. The blind dreaming force behind her apparent frailty would strike terror into the heart of any man intelligent enough to understand it' (298). Bennett here appends a programme note predicting the social and political upheavals of post-war British society.

The drama too was changing in 1910. The Azure Society's private one-night production of the poetic play 'The Orient Pearl' in Chapter VIII of *The Regent* is representative of a movement towards experimental fringe theatre and, not surprisingly, somewhat baffling to a devotee of 'The Hanbridge Empire' and of undemanding dramatic fare. In 1910 the 'widening division ...between minority art and majority entertainment was most visibly entrenched in the theatre... The 'New Drama' of the Edwardian period had offered impressive challenges to the timidity and triviality of the commercial stage ...' (Baldick, 114-115). Whilst Bennett's alter ego, Machin, is alone in being bewildered by the new drama, and yet inclined to question his critical credentials - '...his cold indifference was so conspicuous.... And the dreadful thought crossed his mind... 'Are the ideas of the Five Towns wrong? Am I a provincial after all?' '(223) - Bennett himself was sympathetic towards ideas to revitalise the theatre. In his 'Preface' he criticises the conservatism of theatrical management and espouses the values of the Stage Society ('Azure Society') set up to promote the work of Bernard Shaw and Harley Granville-Barker. *The Regent* includes a detailed description of stage scenery and lighting (221-222) that reads as the fictional recreation of the work of the innovative designer Gordon Craig for the new Art Theatre. Bennett, the critic and playwright, is well able to appreciate that Machin's production of 'The Orient Pearl' 'combined in the highest degree the poetry of Mr. W. B. Yeats with the critical intellectuality of Mr. Bernard Shaw, [and] was an excellent augury for London's dramatic future ...' (240-241). His alter ego, Machin, however, is incapable of critical judgement beyond that conveyed by healthy box office receipts.

If Bennett successfully depicts avant-garde theatre and its specialised outlets with his picture of the Azure Society, he is mimetically accurate in his account of the first night of 'The Orient Pearl'. Machin sheds his own personality to become a textually overweight double doppelganger of Henry James and Oscar Wilde. Unable to face the tension inside the theatre, Machin feels the need to escape. 'His breast had to expand in the boundless prairie of Piccadilly Circus. His legs had to walk. His arms had to swing. Now he crossed the

Circus again to his own pavement and gazed like a stranger at his own posters' (272). Machin's behaviour mirrors that of James at the first night of his *Guy Domville* when he fled St. James's Theatre and 'came out into the cold night and threaded his way through the line of carriages. He walked down the short street leading into St. James's Square, anxious, disturbed, overcome with fear' (Edel, 96). When Machin realises that the last act is over, he echoes James's very real fears: 'And then suddenly several preoccupied men strode rapidly out of the theatre, buttoning their coats, and vanished phantom-like... Critics, on their way to destruction!' (273). Bennett himself, along with Shaw and H. G. Wells, was one of those critics rushing from James's play to file his copy. Bennett's review of *Guy Domville*, which appeared in *Woman* (16th January 1895, p.7), was one of the less hostile responses. But clearly his experience of being part of a hostile audience was to serve him well in his fictional representation of that intense, self-absorbed world.

'The Orient Pearl' proved to be the sort of success of which James could only dream. While absenting himself from his own play, James sat in the Haymarket theatre watching Oscar Wilde's hit *An Ideal Husband*. By an uncanny feat of literary multi-ventriloquism, when Machin gives his curtain-call speech, he repeats Wilde's 1892 witticisms to his first-night audience at *Lady Windermere's Fan*. His 'I congratulate you. This evening you - have succeeded!' (277) is an echo of Wilde's '...your appreciation has been *most* intelligent. I congratulate you on the great success of your performance...' (quoted in Ellman, 346). Bennett goes further in directing Machin - 'And as he raised his hand it occurred to him that his hand held a cigarette' -

to mimic Wilde's stage mannerism whereby he 'responded to curtain calls with... a cigarette in his fingers' (Ellman, 347). Given this level of borrowing it is perhaps a little surprising to find that Wilde is not on Bennett's list of required reading in *Literary Taste*: 'The following authors are omitted, I think justifiably: - Hallam ... Oscar Wilde ...' (121). Questions of fair play apart, this ludic James/Wilde intertextuality is evidence of the literary nature of Bennett's text, an aspect of its cosmopolitan knowingness all too easily relegated to the wings by the comic business on the main stage.

There is one final irony. Bennett, the provincial clerk who fled to London, lived in France, toured America and travelled throughout Europe, denies any such cosmopolitan conversion to his fictional alter ego. For critics such as Lucas, Machin never left Bursley, for he erroneously refers to him as Denry throughout his commentary - a name unseen/unheard throughout the text except in the confines of the family home. For *The Regent* is indeed two texts, the suspect, artificial, disingenuous world of the metropolis viewed through Machin's down-to-earth provincial eyes, and the glittering, sophisticated, vital world of intellectual London and beyond, viewed through Bennett's knowing cosmopolitan eyes. With only two further Five Towns novels to come it is as though Bennett himself is beginning to disown his Potteries inheritance. While Bennett prepares to embrace fully a cosmopolitan life-style, inclusive of literary fame and commercial success, made possible by such Five Towns texts as *The Old Wives' Tale* and *Clayhanger*, his alter ego is dismissed to a perceived provincial future of self-satisfied sentimental nostalgia: 'I've done with London. The Five

THE REGENT

Towns are good enough for me' (318). In 1913, however, the political, cultural and economic forces of the capital and its global hinterland were weakening provincial borders. Indeed, Machin's naïve smugness is about to be shattered, not only by the changes consequent upon the events of 1910, but also by a war that will send many a provincial far from home, never to return.

JOHN SHAPCOTT
Chairman, Arnold Bennett Society

Acknowledgements

Thanks are long overdue to Oliver Harris who not only introduced me to the serious pleasures of literary intellectual life during my MA studies at Keele University but who was also instrumental in guiding my thesis on Jack Kerouac, jazz and improvisation into the pages of *The Journal of American Studies*. The interpretative skills acquired at Keele's School of American Studies have proved invaluable in my study of Bennett's neglected texts. Kurt Koenigsberger, Case Western Reserve University, Ohio, has been an unfailingly generous and careful reader of my recent work, with the result that any errors of fact or interpretation that may remain are the result of my own obstinacy. Kurt's skilful mix of historical analysis and incisive critical commentary in his own work on *The Old Wives' Tale* and *Clayhanger* provide an inspirational model for a new wave of Bennett scholarship. I am also grateful to Scott McCracken, University of Keele, for finding time in a busy schedule to read my *Regent* piece in draft and convince me to modify an altogether too defensive stance towards some of Bennett's critics. Thanks also to Scott I have had the pleasure of sampling again the joys of intellectual discourse at Keele seminars. Finally, thanks to my wife Linda whose frequent, but patient, retyping of my appalling handwriting has probably given her a greater familiarity with *The Regent* than anyone could reasonably wish.

THE REGENT

BIBLIOGRAPHY

Ardis, Ann.	'Delimiting Modernism and the Literary Field: D.H. Lawrence and *The Lost Girl*'. Lynne Hapgood and Nancy L Paxton, edited. *Outside Modernism. In Pursuit of the English Novel, 1900-30.* London: Routledge & Kegan Paul, 2000.
Baldick, Chris.	*The Modern Movement. 1910-1940.* Oxford: Oxford U.P., 2004.
Bennett, Arnold.	*Fame and Fiction. An Enquiry into Certain Popularities.* London: Grant Richards, 1901.
	'Preface. The Crisis in the Theatre' in *Cupid and Commonsense. A Play in Four Acts.* London: New Age Press, 1909.
	'The Hanbridge Empire' in *Paris Nights and Other Impressions of Places and People.* London: Hodder & Stoughton, 1913.
	Literary Taste. How to Form it. London: Hodder & Stoughton, 1909.
	Your United States. New York: Harper & Brothers, 1912.
	The Regent; A Five Towns Story of Adventure in London. Leek. Churnet Valley Books, 2006.
	Books and Persons. Being Comments on a Past Epoch 1908-1911. London: Chatto & Windus, 1917.
	The Journals of Arnold Bennett 1911-1921. Edited by Newman Flower. London: Cassell and Company, 1932.
	Letters of Arnold Bennett. Letters to J. B. Pinker. Edited by James Hepburn. London: Oxford U.P., 1966.
	Letters of Arnold Bennett. 1889-1915. Edited by James Hepburn. London: Oxford U.P., 1968.
Darton, F.J. Harvey.	*Arnold Bennett.* New York: Henry Holt, 1913.
Edel, Leon, ed.	*Guy Domville.* Henry James. London: Rupert Hart-Davis, 1961.
Ellman, Richard.	*Oscar Wilde.* London: Hamish Hamilton, 1987.
Esty, Jed.	*A Shrinking Island. Modernism and National Culture in England.* Princeton: Princeton U.P., 2004.
Hynes, Samuel, edited.	*The Author's Craft and Other Critical Writings of Arnold Bennett.* Lincoln: Nebraska U.P., 1968.
Koenigsberger, Kurt.	'Elephants in the Labyrinth of Empire: Modernism and the Menagerie in *The Old Wives' Tale*' in *Twentieth Century Literature* Vol. 49. 2.
Lucas, John.	*Arnold Bennett. A Study of his Fiction.* London: Methuen, 1974.
Marcus, Jane.	*The Young Rebecca. Writings of Rebecca West 1911-1917.* London: Macmillan, 1982.
Moore, George.	A Mummer's Wife. New York: Bretano's, 1925.
Stewart-Tanguy, Eleanor.	'Theatre and Theatricality in Arnold Bennett's Novels from *A Man from the North to The Regent*' in *Cahiers Victoriens et Edouardiens*, 59, April 2004.
Stetz, Margaret D.	*Gender and the London Theatre 1880-1920.* High Wycombe: Rivendale Press, 2004.
Woolf, Virginia.	*Mr. Bennett and Mrs. Brown.* London: Hogarth Press, 1924.

The Theatre Royal, Hanley, the Queen's Theatre
in George Moore's *A Mummer's Wife*

THE REGENT

PART I

CHAPTER I

DOG-BITE

I

" AND yet," Edward Henry Machin reflected as at
six minutes to six he approached his own dwelling
at the top of Bleakridge, " and yet—I don't feel so jolly
after all!"

The first two words of this disturbing meditation had
reference to the fact that, by telephoning twice to his
stockbrokers at Manchester, he had just made the sum
of three hundred and forty-one pounds in a purely
speculative transaction concerning Rubber Shares.
(It was in the autumn of the great gambling year, 1910.)
He had simply opened his lucky and wise mouth at the
proper moment, and the money, like ripe, golden fruit,
had fallen into it, a gift from benign heaven, surely a
cause for happiness! And yet—he did not feel so jolly!
He was surprised, he was even a little hurt, to discover
by introspection that monetary gain was not necessarily accompanied by felicity. Nevertheless, this
very successful man of the world of the Five Towns,
having been born on the 27th of May 1867, had reached
the age of forty-three and a half years!

" I must be getting older," he reflected.

He was right. He was still young, as every man of

forty-three will agree, but he was getting older. A few years ago a windfall of three hundred and forty-one pounds would not have been followed by morbid self-analysis; it would have been followed by unreasoning, instinctive elation, which elation would have endured at least twelve hours.

As he disappeared within the reddish garden wall which sheltered his abode from the publicity of Trafalgar Road, he half hoped to see Nellie waiting for him on the famous marble step of the porch, for the woman had long, long since invented a way of scouting for his advent from the small window in the bathroom. But there was nobody on the marble step. His melancholy increased. At the midday meal he had complained of neuralgia, and hence this was an evening upon which he might fairly have expected to see sympathy charmingly attired in the porch. It is true that the neuralgia had completely gone. " Still," he said to himself with justifiable sardonic gloom, " how does she know my neuralgia's gone? She doesn't know."

Having opened the front-door (with the thinnest, neatest latch-key in the Five Towns), he entered his home and stumbled slightly over a brush that was lying against the sunk door-mat. He gazed at that brush with resentment. It was a dilapidated hand-brush. The offensive object would have been out of place, at nightfall, in the lobby of any house. But in the lobby of his house—the house which he had planned a dozen years earlier, to the special end of minimizing domestic labour, and which he had always kept up to date with the latest devices—in his lobby the spectacle of a vile, outworn hand-brush at tea-time amounted to a scandal. Less than a fortnight previously he had purchased and presented to his wife a marvellous electric vacuum-cleaner, surpassing all former vacuum-cleaners. You simply attached this machine by a cord to the wall, like a dog, and waved it in mysterious passes over the floor, like a fan, and the house was clean! He was as proud of this machine as though he had invented it, instead of having merely bought it; every day he inquired about its feats, expecting enthusiastic replies as a sort of reward for his own keenness: and be it said that he had had enthusiastic replies.

And now this obscene hand-brush!

As he carefully removed his hat and his beautiful new Melton overcoat (which had the colour and the soft smoothness of a damson), he animadverted upon the astounding negligence of women. There were Nellie (his wife), his mother, the nurse, the cook, the maid—five of them; and in his mind they had all plotted together—a conspiracy of carelessness—to leave the inexcusable tool in his lobby for him to stumble over. What was the use of accidentally procuring three hundred and forty-one pounds?

Still no sign of Nellie, though he purposely made a noisy rattle with his ebon walking-stick. Then the maid burst out of the kitchen with a tray and the principal utensils for high tea thereon. She had a guilty air. The household was evidently late. Two steps at a time he rushed upstairs to the bathroom, so as to be waiting in the dining-room at six precisely, in order, if possible, to shame the household and fill it with remorse and unpleasantness. Yet ordinarily he was not a very prompt man, nor did he delight in giving pain. On the contrary, he was apt to be casual, blithe and agreeable.

The bathroom was his peculiar domain, which he was always modernizing, and where his talent for the ingenious organization of comfort, and his utter indifference to æsthetic beauty, had the fullest scope.

By universal consent admitted to be the finest bath-room in the Five Towns, it typified the whole house. He was disappointed on this occasion to see no untidy trace in it of the children's ablution; some transgres-sion of the supreme domestic law that the bathroom must always be free and immaculate when father wanted it would have suited his gathering humour. As he washed his hands and cleansed his well-trimmed nails with a nail-brush that had cost five shillings and sixpence, he glanced at himself in the mirror, which he was splashing. A stoutish, broad-shouldered, fair, chubby man, with a short bright beard and plenteous bright hair! His neck-tie pleased him; the elegance of his turned-back wristbands pleased him; and he liked the rich down on his forearms.

He could not believe that he looked forty-three and a half. And yet he had recently had an idea of shaving off his beard, partly to defy time, but partly also (I must admit) because a friend had suggested to him, wildly, perhaps—that if he dispensed with a beard his hair might grow more sturdily. . . . Yes, there was one weak spot in the middle of the top of his head, where the crop had of late disconcertingly thinned! The hairdresser had informed him that the symptom would vanish under electric massage, and that, if he doubted the *bona-fides* of hairdressers, any doctor would testify to the value of electric massage. But now Edward Henry Machin, strangely discouraged, inex-plicably robbed of the zest of existence, decided that it was not worth while to shave off his beard. Nothing was worth while. If he was forty-three and a half, he was forty-three and a half! To become bald was the common lot. Moreover, beardless, he would need the service of a barber every day. And he was absolutely persuaded that not a barber worth the name could be found in the Five Towns. He actually went to Manchester—thirty-six miles—to get his hair cut. The operation never cost him less than a sovereign and half a day's time. . . . And he honestly deemed himself to be a fellow of simple tastes! Such is the effect of the canker of luxury. Happily he could afford these simple tastes, for, although not rich in the modern significance of the term, he paid income tax on some five thousand pounds a year, without quite convincing the Surveyor of Taxes that he was an honest man.

He brushed the thick hair over the weak spot, he turned down his wristbands, he brushed the collar of his jacket, and lastly, his beard; and he put on his jacket—with a certain care, for he was very neat. And then, reflectively twisting his moustache to military points, he spied through the smaller window to see whether the new high hoarding of the football-ground really did prevent a serious observer from descrying wayfarers as they breasted the hill from Hanbridge. It did not. Then he spied through the larger window upon the yard, to see whether the wall of the new rooms which he had lately added to his house showed any further trace of damp, and whether the new chauffeur was washing the new motor car with all his heart. The wall showed no further trace of damp, and the new chauffeur's bent back seemed to symbolize an extreme conscientiousness.

Then the clock on the landing struck six and he hurried off to put the household to open shame.

II

NELLIE came into the dining-room two minutes after her husband. As Edward Henry had laboriously counted these two minutes almost second by second on the dining-room clock, he was very tired of waiting. His secret annoyance was increased by the fact that Nellie took off her white apron in the doorway and flung it hurriedly on to the table-tray which, during the progress of meals, was established outside the dining-room door. He did not actually witness this operation of undressing, because Nellie was screened by the half-closed door; but he was entirely aware of it. He disliked it, and he had always disliked it. When Nellie was at work, either as a mother or as the owner of certain fine silver ornaments, he rather enjoyed the wonderful white apron, for it suited her temperament; but as the head of a household with six thousand pounds a year at its disposal, he objected to any hint of the thing at meals. And to-night he objected to it altogether. Who could guess from the homeliness of their family life that he was in a position to spend a hundred pounds a week and still have enough income left over to pay the salary of a town clerk or so? Nobody could guess; and he felt that people ought to be able to guess. When he was young he would have esteemed an income of six thousand pounds a year as necessarily implicating feudal state, valets, castles, yachts, family solicitors, racing-stables, county society, dinner-calls and a drawling London accent. Why should his wife wear an apron at all? But the sad truth was that neither his wife nor his mother ever *looked* rich, or even endeavoured to look rich. His mother would carry an eighty-pound sealskin as though she had picked it up at a jumble sale, and his wife put such simplicity into the wearing of a hundred-and-eighty pound diamond ring that its expensiveness was generally quite wasted.

And yet, while the logical male in him scathingly condemned this feminine defect of character, his private soul was glad of it, for he well knew that he would have been considerably irked by the complexities and grandeurs of high life. But never would he have admitted this.

Nellie's face, as she sat down, was not limpid. He understood naught of it. More than twenty years had passed since they had first met—he and a wistful little creature—at a historic town-hall dance. He could still see the wistful little creature in those placid and pure features, in that buxom body; but now there was a formidable, capable and experienced woman there too. Impossible to credit that the wistful little creature was thirty-seven! But she was! Indeed, it was very doubtful if she would ever see thirty-eight again. Once he had had the most romantic feelings about her. He could recall the slim flexibility of her waist, the timorous melting invitation of her eyes. And now. . . . Such was human existence!

She sat up erect on her chair. She did not apologize for being late. She made no inquiry as to his neuralgia. On the other hand, she was not cross. She was just neutral, polite, cheerful, and apparently conscious of perfection. He strongly desired to inform her of the exact time of day, but his lips would not articulate the words.

"Maud," she said with divine calm to the maid who bore in the baked York ham under its silver canopy, "you haven't taken away that brush that's in the passage."

(Another illustration of Nellie's inability to live up to six thousand pounds a year; she would always refer to the hall as the " passage! ")

" Please'm, I did, m'm," replied Maud, now as conscious of perfection as her mistress. " He must have took it back again."

" Who's ' he? ' " demanded the master.

" Carlo, sir." Upon which triumph Maud retired.

Edward Henry was dashed. Nevertheless, he quickly recovered his presence of mind and sought about for a justification of his previous verdict upon the negligence of five women.

" It would have been easy enough to put the brush where the dog couldn't get at it," he said. But he said this strictly to himself. He could not say it aloud. Nor could he say aloud the words " neuralgia," " three hundred and forty-one pounds," any more than he could say " late."

That he was in a peculiar mental condition is proved by the fact that he did not remark the absence of his mother until he was putting her share of baked ham on to a plate.

He thought: " This is a bit thick, this is! " meaning the extreme lateness of his mother for the meal. But his only audible remark was a somewhat impatient banging down of the hot plate in front of his mother's empty chair.

In answer to this banging Nellie quietly began:

" Your mother—"

(He knew instantly, then, that Nellie was disturbed about something or other. Mother-in-law and daughter-in-law lived together under one roof in perfect amity. Nay, more, they often formed powerful and unscrupulous leagues against him. But whenever Nellie was disturbed, by no matter what, she would say " your mother " instead of merely " mother! " It was an extraordinary subtle, silly and effective way of putting him in the wrong.)

" Your mother is staying upstairs with Robert."

Robert was the eldest child, aged eight.

" Oh! " breathed Edward Henry. He might have

inquired what the nurse was for; he might have inquired how his mother meant to get her tea. But he refrained, adding simply, " What's up now? "

And in retort to his wife's " your," he laid a faint emphasis on the word " now," to imply that those women were always inventing some fresh imaginary woe for the children.

" Carlo's bitten him—in the calf," said Nellie, tightening her lips.

This, at any rate, was not imaginary.

" The kid was teasing him as usual, I suppose? " he suggested.

" That I don't know," said Nellie. " But I know we must get rid of that dog."

" Serious? "

" Of course we must," Nellie insisted, with an inadvertent heat, which she immediately cooled.

" I mean the bite."

" Well—it's a bite right enough."

" And you're thinking of hydrophobia, death amid horrible agony, and so on."

" No, I'm not," she said stoutly, trying to smile.

But he knew she was. And he knew also that the bite was a trifle. If it had been a good bite she would have made it enormous; she would have hinted that the dog had left a chasm in the boy's flesh.

" Yes, you are," he continued to twit her, encouraged by her attempt at a smile.

However, the smile expired.

" I suppose you won't deny that Carlo's teeth may have been dirty? He's always nosing in some filth or other," she said challengingly, in a measured tone of sagacity. " And there may be blood-poisoning."

" Blood fiddlesticks! " exclaimed Edward Henry.

Such a nonsensical and infantile rejoinder deserved

no answer, and it received none. Shortly afterwards
Maud entered and whispered that Nellie was wanted
upstairs. As soon as his wife had gone Edward Henry
rang the bell.

"Maud," he said, "bring me the *Signal* out of my
left-hand overcoat pocket."

And he defiantly finished his meal at leisure, with
the news of the day propped up against the flower-pot,
which he had set before him instead of the dish of ham.

III

LATER, catching through the open door fragments of
a conversation on the stairs which indicated that his
mother was at last coming down for tea, he sped like a
threatened delinquent into the drawing-room. He
had no wish to encounter his mother, though that
woman usually said little.

The drawing-room, after the bathroom, was Edward
Henry's favourite district in the home. Since he could
not spend the whole of his time in the bathroom—and
he could not!—he wisely gave a special care to the
drawing-room, and he loved it as one always loves that
upon which one has bestowed benefits. He was proud
of the drawing-room, and he had the right to be. The
principal object in it, at night, was the electric chandelier, which would have been adequate for a lighthouse.
Edward Henry's eyes were not what they used to be;
and the minor advertisements in the *Signal*—which
constituted his sole evening perusals—often lacked
legibility. Edward Henry sincerely believed in light
and heat; he was almost the only person in the Five
Towns who did. In the Five Towns people have fires
in their grates—not to warm the room, but to make the

room bright. Seemingly they use their pride to keep themselves warm. At any rate, whenever Edward Henry talked to them of radiators, they would sternly reply that a radiator did not and could not brighten a room. Edward Henry had made the great discovery that an efficient chandelier will brighten a room better even than a fire, and he had gilded his radiator. The notion of gilding the radiator was not his own; he had seen a gilded radiator in the newest hotel at Birmingham, and had rejoiced as some peculiar souls rejoice when they meet a fine line in a new poem. (In concession to popular prejudice Edward Henry had firegrates in his house, and fires therein during exceptionally frosty weather; but this did not save him from being regarded in the Five Towns as in some ways a peculiar soul.) The effulgent source of dark heat was scientifically situated in front of the window, and on ordinarily cold evenings Edward Henry and his wife and mother, and an acquaintance if one happened to come in, would gather round the radiator and play bridge or dummy whist.

The other phenomena of the drawing-room which particularly interested Edward Henry were the Turkey carpet, the four vast easy-chairs, the sofa, the imposing cigar-cabinet and the mechanical piano-player. At one brief period he had hovered a good deal about the revolving bookcase containing the *Encyclopædia* (to which his collection of books was limited), but the frail passion for literature had not survived a struggle with the seductions of the mechanical piano-player.

The walls of the room never drew his notice. He had chosen, some years before, a patent washable kind of wall-paper (which could be wiped over with a damp cloth), and he had also chosen the pattern of the paper, but it is a fact that he could spend hours in any room without even seeing the pattern of its paper. (In the same way his wife's cushions and little draperies and bows were invisible to him, though he had searched for and duly obtained the perfect quality of swansdown which filled the cushions.)

The one ornament of the walls which attracted him was a large and splendidly-framed oil-painting of a ruined castle, in the midst of a sombre forest, through which cows were strolling. In the tower of the castle was a clock, and this clock was a realistic timepiece, whose fingers moved and told the hour. Two of the oriel windows of the castle were realistic holes in its masonry; through one of them you could put a key to wind up the clock, and through the other you could put a key to wind up the secret musical box, which played sixteen different tunes. He had bought this handsome relic of the Victorian era (not less artistic, despite your scorn, than many devices for satisfying the higher instincts of the present day) at an auction sale in the Strand, London. But it, too, had been supplanted in his esteem by the mechanical piano-player.

He now selected an example of the most expensive cigar in the cigar-cabinet and lighted it as only a connoisseur can light a cigar, lovingly; he blew out the match lingeringly, with regret, and dropped it and the cigar's red collar with care into a large copper bowl on the centre table, instead of flinging it against the Japanese umbrella in the fireplace. (A grave disadvantage of radiators is that you cannot throw odds and ends into them.) He chose the most expensive cigar because he wanted comfort and peace. The ham was not digesting very well.

Then he sat down and applied himself to the property advertisements in the *Signal*, a form of sensational serial which usually enthralled him—but not tonight. He allowed the paper to lapse on to the floor, and then rose impatiently, rearranged the thick dark blue curtains behind the radiator, and finally yielded to the silent call of the mechanical piano-player. He quite knew that to dally with the piano-player while smoking a high-class cigar was to insult the cigar. But he did not care. He tilted the cigar upwards from an extreme corner of his mouth, and through the celestial smoke gazed at the titles of the new music rolls which had been delivered that day, and which were ranged on the top of the piano itself.

And while he did so he was thinking:

" Why in thunder didn't the little thing come and tell me at once about that kid and his dog-bite? I wonder **why** she didn't! She seemed only to mention it by accident. I wonder why she didn't bounce into the bathroom and tell me at once? "

But it was untrue that he sought vainly for an answer to this riddle. He was aware of the answer. He even kept saying over the answer to himself:

" She's made up her mind I've been teasing her a bit too much lately about those kids and their precious illnesses. And she's doing the dignified. That's what she's doing! She's doing the dignified! "

Of course, instantly after his tea he ought to have gone upstairs to inspect the wounded victim of dogs. The victim was his own child, and its mother was his wife. He knew that he ought to have gone upstairs long since. He knew that he ought now to go, and the sooner the better! But somehow he could not go; he could not bring himself to go. In the minor and major crises of married life there are not two partners, but four; each partner has a dual personality; each partner is indeed two different persons, and one of these fights against the other, with the common result of a fatal inaction.

The wickeder of the opposing persons in Edward Henry, getting the upper hand of the more virtuous, sniggered. "Dirty teeth, indeed! Blood-poisoning, indeed! Why not rabies, while she's about it? I guarantee she's dreaming of coffins and mourning coaches already!"

Scanning nonchalantly the titles of the music rolls, he suddenly saw: "Funeral March. Chopin."

"She shall have it," he said, affixing the roll to the mechanism. And added: "Whatever it is!"

For he was not acquainted with the Funeral March from Chopin's Pianoforte Sonata. His musical education had, in truth, begun only a year earlier—with the advertisements of the "Pianisto" mechanical player. He was a judge of advertisements, and the "Pianisto" literature pleased him in a high degree. He justifiably reckoned that he could distinguish between honest and dishonest advertising. He made a deep study of the question of mechanical players, and deliberately came to the conclusion that the Pianisto was the best. It was also the most costly. But one of the conveniences of having six thousand pounds a year is that you need not deny yourself the best mechanical player because it happens to be the most costly. He bought a Pianisto, and incidentally he bought a superb grand piano and exiled the old cottage piano to the nursery.

The Pianisto was the best, partly because, like the vacuum-cleaner, it could be operated by electricity, and partly because, by means of certain curved lines on the unrolling paper, and of certain gun-metal levers and clutches, it enabled the operator to put his secret ardent soul into the music. Assuredly it had given

Edward Henry a taste for music. The whole world of musical compositions was his to conquer, and he conquered it at the rate of about two great masters a month. From Handel to Richard Strauss, even from Palestrina to Debussy, the achievements of genius lay at his mercy. He criticized them with a freedom that was entirely unprejudiced by tradition. Beethoven was no more to him than Arthur Sullivan—indeed, was rather less. The works of his choice were the " Tannhäuser " overture, a potpourri of Verdi's " Aida," Chopin's Study in Thirds (which ravished him), and a selection from "The Merry Widow" (which also ravished him). So that on the whole it may be said that he had a very good natural taste.

He at once liked Chopin's Funeral March. He entered profoundly into the spirit of it. With the gun-metal levers he produced in a marvellous fashion the long tragic roll of the drums, and by the manipulation of a clutch he distilled into the chant at the graveside a melancholy sweetness that rent the heart. The later crescendoes were overwhelming. And as he played there, with the bright blaze of the chandelier on his fair hair and beard, and the blue cigar smoke in his nostrils, and the effluence of the gilded radiator behind him, and the intimacy of the drawn window-curtains and the closed and curtained door folding him in from the world, and the agony of the music grieving his artistic soul to the core—as he played there he grew gradually happier and happier, and the zest of existence seemed to return. It was not only that he felt the elemental, unfathomable satisfaction of a male who is sheltered in solitude from a pack of women that have got on his nerves. There was also the more piquant assurance that he was behaving in a very sprightly manner. How long was it since he had accomplished anything worthy of his ancient reputation as a " card," as " the " card of the Five Towns? He could not say. But now he knew that he was being a card again. The whole town would smile and forgive and admire if it learnt that—

Nellie invaded the room. She had resumed the affray.

" Denry! " she reproached him, in an uncontrolled voice. " I'm ashamed of you! I really am! " She was no longer doing the dignified. The mask was off and the unmistakable lineaments of the outraged mother appeared. That she should address him as " Denry " proved the intensity of her agitation. Years ago, when he had been made an alderman, his wife and his mother had decided that " Denry " was no longer a suitable name for him, and had abandoned it in favour of " Edward Henry."

He ceased playing.

" Why? " he protested, with a ridiculous air of innocence. " I'm only playing Chopin. Can't I play Chopin? "

He was rather surprised and impressed that she had recognized the piece for what it was. But of course she did, as a fact, know something about music, he remembered, though she never touched the Pianisto.

" I think it's a pity you can't choose some other evening for your funeral marches! " she exclaimed.

" If that's it," said Edward Henry like lightning, " why did you stick me out you weren't afraid of hydrophobia? "

" I'll thank you to come upstairs," she replied with warmth.

" Oh, all right, my dear! All right! " he cooed.

And they went upstairs in a rather solemn procession.

IV

NELLIE led the way to the chamber known as
" Maisie's room," where the youngest of the Machins
was wont to sleep in charge of the nurse who, under
the supervision of the mother of all three, had dominion
over Robert, Ralph and their little sister.

The first thing that Edward Henry noticed was the
screen which shut off one of the beds. The unfurling
of the four-fold screen was always a sure sign that
Nellie was taking an infantile illness seriously. It was
an indication to Edward Henry of the importance of
the dog-bite in Nellie's esteem.

When all the chicks of the brood happened to be
simultaneously sound the screen reposed, inconspicu-
ous, at an angle against a wall behind the door; but
when pestilence was abroad, the screen travelled from
one room to another in the wake of it, and, spreading
wide, took part in the battle of life and death.

In an angle of the screen, on the side of it away from
the bed and near the fire (in times of stress Nellie would
not rely on radiators) sat old Mrs Machin, knitting.
She was a thin, bony woman of sixty-nine years, and as
hard and imperishable as teak. So far as her son knew
she had only had two illnesses in her life. The first
was an attack of influenza, and the second was an attack
of acute rheumatism, which had incapacitated her for
several weeks.

Edward Henry and Nellie had taken advantage of
her helplessness, then, to force her to give up her
barbaric cottage in Brougham Street and share per-
manently the splendid comfort of their home. She
existed in their home like a philosophic prisoner-of-war
at the court of conquerors, behaving faultlessly, behav-

ing magnanimously in the melancholy grandeur of her
fall, but never renouncing her soul's secret independ-
ence, nor permitting herself to forget that she was on
foreign ground.

When Edward Henry looked at those yellow and
seasoned fingers, which by hard manual labour had
kept herself and him in the young days of his humble
obscurity, and which during sixty years had not been
idle for more than six weeks in all, he grew almost
apologetic for his wealth.

They reminded him of the day when his total resources were five pounds—won in a wager, and of the
day when he drove proudly about behind a mule
collecting other people's rents, and of the glittering days
when he burst in on her from Llandudno with over a
thousand gold sovereigns in a hat-box—product of his
first great picturesque coup—imagining himself to be
an English Jay Gould.

She had not blenched, even then. She had not
blenched since. And she never would blench. In
spite of his gorgeous position and his unique reputation,
in spite of her well-concealed but notorious pride in
him, he still went in fear of that ageless woman, whose
undaunted eye always told him that he was still the lad
Denry, and her inferior in moral force. The curve of
her thin lips seemed ever to be warning him that with
her pretensions were quite useless, and that she saw
through him and through him to the innermost grottoes
of his poor human depravity.

He caught her eye guiltily.

" Behold the Alderman ! " she murmured with
grimness.

That was all. But the three words took thirty
years off his back, snatched the half-crown cigar out of
his hand and reduced him again to the raw, hungry boy

of Brougham Street. And he knew that he had sinned gravely in not coming upstairs very much earlier.

" Is that you, father? " called the high voice of Robert from the back of the screen.

He had to admit to his son that it was he.

The infant lay on his back in Maisie's bed, while his mother sat lightly on the edge of nurse's bed near by.

" Well, you're a nice chap! " said Edward Henry, avoiding Nellie's glance, but trying to face his son as one innocent man may face another—and not perfectly succeeding. He never could feel like a real father, somehow.

" My temperature's above normal," announced Robert, proudly, and then added with regret, " but not much! "

There was the clinical thermometer—instrument which Edward Henry despised and detested as being an inciter of illnesses—in a glass of water on the table between the two beds.

" Father! " Robert began again.

" Well, Robert? " said Edward Henry, cheerfully. He was glad that the child was in one of his rare loquacious moods, because the chatter not only proved that the dog had done no serious damage—it also eased the silent strain between himself and Nellie.

" Why did you play the Funeral March, father? " asked Robert, and the question fell into the tranquillity of the room rather like a bomb that had not quite decided whether or not to burst.

For the second time that evening Edward Henry was dashed.

" Have you been meddling with my music rolls? "

" No, father. I only read the labels."

This child simply read everything.

" How did you know I was playing a funeral march? " Edward Henry demanded.

" Oh, *I* didn't tell him! " Nellie put in, excusing herself before she was accused. She smiled benignly, as an angel-woman, capable of forgiving all. But there were moments when Edward Henry hated moral superiority and Christian meekness in a wife. Moreover, Nellie somewhat spoiled her own effect by adding, with an artificial continuation of the smile, " You needn't look at *me !* "

Edward Henry considered the remark otiose. Though he had indeed ventured to look at her, he had not looked at her in the manner which she implied.

" It made a noise like funerals and things," Robert explained.

" Well, it seems to me *you've* been playing a funeral march," said Edward Henry to the child.

He thought this rather funny, rather worthy of himself, but the child answered with ruthless gravity and a touch of disdain (for he was a disdainful child, without bowels):

" I don't know what you mean, father." The curve of his lips (he had his grandmother's lips) appeared to say: " I wish you wouldn't try to be silly, father." However, youth forgets very quickly, and the next instant Robert was beginning once more, " Father! "

" Well, Robert? "

By mutual agreement of the parents the child was never addressed as " Bob " or " Bobby," or by any other diminutive. In their practical opinion a child's name was his name, and ought not to be mauled or dismembered on the pretext of fondness. Similarly, the child had not been baptized after his father, or after any male member of either the Machin or the

Cotterill family. Why should family names be per-
petuated merely because they were family names? A
natural human reaction, this, against the excessive
sentimentalism of the Victorian era!

" What does ' stamped out ' mean? " Robert inquired.

Now Robert, among other activities, busied himself
in the collection of postage stamps, and in consequence
his father's mind, under the impulse of the question,
ran immediately to postage stamps.

" Stamped out? " said Edward Henry, with the air
of omniscience that a father is bound to assume.
" Postage stamps are stamped out—by a machine—
you see."

Robert's scorn of this explanation was manifest.

" Well," Edward Henry, piqued, made another
attempt, " you stamp a fire out with your feet." And
he stamped illustratively on the floor. After all, the
child was only eight.

" I knew all that before," said Robert, coldly.
" You don't understand."

" What makes you ask, dear? Let us show father
your leg." Nellie's voice was soothing.

" Yes," Robert murmured, staring reflectively at
the ceiling. " That's it. It says in the *Encyclopædia*
that hydrophobia is stamped out in this country—by
Mr Long's muzzling order. Who is Mr Long? "

A second bomb had fallen on exactly the same spot
as the first, and the two exploded simultaneously. And
the explosion was none the less terrible because it was
silent and invisible. The tidy domestic chamber was
strewn in a moment with an awful mass of wounded
susceptibilities. Beyond the screen the *nick-nick* of
grandmother's steel needles stopped and started again.
It was characteristic of her temperament that she should

recover before the younger generations could recover. Edward Henry, as befitted his sex, regained his nerve a little earlier than Nellie.

" I told you never to touch my *Encyclopædia*," said he, sternly. Robert had twice been caught on his stomach on the floor with a vast volume open under his chin, and his studies had been traced by vile thumb-marks.

" I know," said Robert.

Whenever anybody gave that child a piece of un-solicited information he almost invariably replied, " I know."

" But hydrophobia! " cried Nellie. " How did you know about hydrophobia? "

" We had it in spellings last week," Robert ex-plained.

" The deuce you did! " muttered Edward Henry.

The one bright facet of the many-sided and gloomy crisis was the very obvious truth that Robert was the most extraordinary child that ever lived.

" But when on earth did you get at the *Encyclopædia*, Robert? " his mother exclaimed, completely at a loss.

" It was before you came in from Hillport," the wondrous infant answered. " After my leg had stopped hurting me a bit."

" But when I came in nurse said it had only just happened! "

" Shows how much *she* knew! " said Robert, with contempt.

" Does your leg hurt you now? " Edward Henry inquired.

" A bit. That's why I can't go to sleep, of course."

" Well, let's have a look at it." Edward Henry attempted jollity.

" Mother's wrapped it all up in boracic wool."

The bed-clothes were drawn down and the leg gradually revealed. And the sight of the little soft leg, so fragile and defenceless, really did touch Edward Henry. It made him feel more like an authentic father than he had felt for a long time. And the sight of the red wound hurt him. Still, it was a beautifully clean wound, and it was not a large wound.

" It's a clean wound," he observed judiciously. In spite of himself he could not keep a certain flippant harsh quality out of his tone.

" Well, I've naturally washed it with carbolic," Nellie returned sharply.

He illogically resented this sharpness.

" Of course he was bitten through his stocking? "

" Of course," said Nellie, re-enveloping the wound hastily, as though Edward Henry was not worthy to regard it.

" Well, then, by the time they got through the stocking the animal's teeth couldn't be dirty. Everyone knows that."

Nellie shut her lips.

" Were you teasing Carlo? " Edward Henry demanded curtly of his son.

" I don't know."

Whenever anybody asked that child for a piece of information he almost invariably replied, " I don't know."

" How—you don't know? You must know whether you were teasing the dog or not! " Edward Henry was nettled.

The renewed spectacle of his own wound had predisposed Robert to feel a great and tearful sympathy for himself. His mouth now began to take strange shapes and to increase magically in area, and beads appeared in the corners of his large eyes.

" I—I was only measuring his tail by his hind leg," he blubbered and then sobbed.

Edward Henry did his best to save his dignity.

" Come, come! " he reasoned, less menacingly. " Boys who can read *Encyclopædias* mustn't be cry-babies. You'd no business measuring Carlo's tail by his hind leg. You ought to remember that that dog's older than you." And this remark, too, he thought rather funny, but apparently he was alone in his opinion.

Then he felt something against his calf. And it was Carlo's nose. Carlo was a large, very shaggy and un-kempt Northern terrier, but owing to vagueness of his principal points, due doubtless to a vagueness in his immediate ancestry, it was impossible to decide whether he had come from the north or the south side of the Tweed. This ageing friend of Edward Henry's, sur-mising that something unusual was afoot in his house, and having entirely forgotten the trifling episode of the bite, had unobtrusively come to make inquiries.

" Poor old boy! " said Edward Henry, stooping to pat the dog. " Did they try to measure his tail with his hind leg? "

The gesture was partly instinctive, for he loved Carlo; but it also had its origin in sheer nervousness, in sheer ignorance of what was the best thing to do. However, he was at once aware that he had done the worst thing. Had not Nellie announced that the dog must be got rid of? And here he was fondly caressing the bloodthirsty dog! With a hysterical movement of the lower part of her leg Nellie pushed violently against the dog—she did not kick, but she nearly kicked—and Carlo, faintly howling a protest, fled.

Edward Henry was hurt. He escaped from be-tween the beds and from that close, enervating domestic atmosphere where he was misunderstood by women and disdained by infants. He wanted fresh air; he wanted bars, whiskies, billiard-rooms and the society of masculine men-about-town. The whole of his own world was against him.

As he passed by his knitting mother she ignored him and moved not. She had a great gift of holding aloof from conjugal complications.

On the landing he decided that he would go out at once into the major world. Half-way down the stairs he saw his overcoat on the hall-stand beckoning to him and offering release.

Then he heard the bedroom door and his wife's footsteps.

" Edward Henry! "

" Well? "

He stopped and looked up inimically at her face, which overhung the banisters. It was the face of a woman outraged in her most profound feelings, but amazingly determined to be sweet.

" What do you think of it? "

" What do I think of what? The wound? "

" Yes."

" Why, it's simply nothing. Nothing at all. You know how that kid always heals up quick. You won't be able to find the wound in a day or two."

" Don't you think it ought to be cauterized at once? "

He moved on downwards.

" No, I don't. I've been bitten three times in my life by dogs. And I was never cauterized."

" Well, I *do* think it ought to be cauterized." She raised her voice slightly as he retreated from her. " And I shall be glad if you'll call in at Dr Stirling's and ask him to come round."

He made no reply, but put on his overcoat and his hat and took his stick. Glancing up the stairs he saw Nellie was now standing at the head of them, under the electric light there, and watching him. He knew that she thought he was cravenly obeying her command. She could have no idea that before she spoke to him he had already decided to put on his overcoat and hat and take his stick and go forth into the major world. However, that was no affair of his.

He hesitated a second. Then the nurse appeared out of the kitchen, with a squalling Maisie in her arms, and ran upstairs. Why Maisie was squalling, and why she should have been in the kitchen at such an hour instead of in bed, he could not guess. But he could guess that if he remained one second longer in that exasperating minor world he would begin to smash furniture. And so he quitted it.

V

IT was raining slightly, but he dared not return to the house for his umbrella. In the haze and wet of the shivering October night the clock of Bleakridge Church glowed like a fiery disc suspended in the sky, and, mysteriously hanging there, without visible means of support, it seemed to him somehow to symbolize the enigma of the universe and intensify his inward gloom. Never before had he had such feelings to such a degree. It is scarcely an exaggeration to say that never before had the enigma of the universe occurred to him. The side gates clicked as he stood hesitant under the shelter of the wall, and a figure emerged from his domain. It was Bellfield, the new chauffeur, going across to his home in the little square in front of the church. Bell-

field touched his cap with an eager and willing hand,
as new chauffeurs will.

" Want the car, sir? . . . Setting in for a wet
night! "

" No, thanks."

It was a lie. He did want the car. He wanted the
car so that he might ride right away into a new and
more interesting world, or at any rate into Hanbridge,
centre of the pleasures, the wickedness and the commerce of the Five Towns. But he dared not have the
car. He dared not have his own car. He must slip
off noiseless and unassuming. Even to go to Dr
Stirling's he dared not have the car. Besides, he could
have walked down the hill to Dr Stirling's in three
minutes. Not that he had the least intention of going
to Dr Stirling's. No! His wife imagined that he was
going. But she was mistaken. Within an hour,
when Dr Stirling had failed to arrive, she would doubtless telephone and get her Dr Stirling. Not, however,
with Edward Henry's assistance!

He reviewed his conduct throughout the evening.
In what particular had it been sinful? In no
particular. True, the accident to the boy was a misfortune, but had he not borne that misfortune lightly,
minimized it and endeavoured to teach others to bear
it lightly? His blithe humour ought surely to have
been an example to Nellie! And as for the episode of
the funeral march on the Pianisto, really, really, the
tiresome little thing ought to have better appreciated
his whimsical drollery!

But Nellie was altered; he was altered; everything
was altered. He remembered the ecstasy of their
excursion to Switzerland. He remembered the rapture
with which, on their honeymoon, he had clasped a new
opal bracelet on her exciting arm. He could not

possibly have such sensations now. What was the
meaning of life? Was life worth living? The fact
was—he was growing old. Useless to pretend to himself that it was not so. Both he and she were growing
old. Only, she seemed to be placidly content, and he
was not content. And more and more the domestic
atmosphere and the atmosphere of the district fretted
and even annoyed him. To-night's affair was not
unique. But it was a culmination. He gazed pessi-
mistically north and south along the slimy expanse of
Trafalgar Road, which sank northwards in the direction
of Dr Stirling's, and southwards in the direction
of joyous Hanbridge. He loathed and despised
Trafalgar Road. What was the use of making three
hundred and forty-one pounds by a shrewd speculation? None. He could not employ three hundred
and forty-one pounds to increase his happiness. Money
had become futile for him. Astounding thought!
He desired no more of it! He had a considerable income from investments, and also at least four thousand
a year from the Five Towns Universal Thrift Club, that
wonderful but unpretentious organization which now
embraced every corner of the Five Towns—that gorgeous invention for profitably taking care of the pennies
of the working-classes—that excellent device, his own,
for selling to the working-classes every kind of goods at
credit prices after having received part of the money in
advance!

"I want a change!" he said to himself, and threw
away his cigar.

After all, the bitterest thought in his heart was,
perhaps, that, on that evening he had tried to be a
" card," and, for the first time in his brilliant career as
a " card," had failed. He, Henry Machin, who had
been the youngest Mayor of Bursley years and years

ago, he, the recognized amuser of the Five Towns, he, one of the greatest " characters " that the Five Towns had ever produced! He had failed of an effect!

He slipped out on to the pavement and saw, under the gas-lamp, on the new hoarding of the football ground, a poster intimating that during that particular week there was a gigantic attraction at the Empire Music Hall at Hanbridge. According to the posters there was a gigantic attraction every week at the Empire, but Edward Henry happened to know that this week the attraction was indeed somewhat out of the common. And to-night was Friday, the fashionable night for the bloods and the modishness of the Five Towns. He looked at the church clock and then at his watch. He would be in time for the " second house," which started at nine o'clock. At the same moment an electric tram-car came thundering up out of Bursley. He boarded it and was saluted by the conductor. Remaining on the platform he lit a cigarette and tried to feel cheerful. But he could not conquer his depression.

" Yes," he thought, " what I want is change—and a lot of it, too! "

CHAPTER II

THE BANK-NOTE

I

ALDERMAN MACHIN had to stand at the back, and somewhat towards the side, of that part of the auditorium known as the Grand Circle at the Empire Music Hall, Hanbridge. The attendants at the entrance, and in the lounge, where the salutation " Welcome " shone in electricity over a large cupid-surrounded mirror, had compassionately and yet exultingly told him that there was not a seat left in the house. He had shared their exultation. He had said to himself, full of honest pride in the Five Towns: " This music-hall, admitted by the press to be one of the finest in the provinces, holds over two thousand five hundred people. And yet we can fill it to overflowing twice every night! And only a few years ago there wasn't a decent music-hall in the entire district! "

The word " Progress " flitted through his head.

It was not strictly true that the Empire was or could be filled to overflowing twice every night, but it was true that at that particular moment not a seat was unsold; and the aspect of a crowded auditorium is apt to give an optimistic quality to broad generalizations. Alderman Machin began instinctively to calculate the amount of money in the house, and to wonder whether there would be a chance for a second music-hall in the dissipated town of Hanbridge. He also wondered why the idea of a second music-hall in Hanbridge had never occurred to him before.

The Grand Circle was so called because it was grand. Its plush fauteuils cost a shilling, no mean price for a community where seven pounds of potatoes can be bought for sixpence, and the view of the stage therefrom was perfect. But the Alderman's view was far from perfect, since he had to peer as best he could between and above the shoulders of several men, each apparently, but not really, taller than himself. By constant slight movements, to comply with the movements of the rampart of shoulders, he could discern fragments of various advertisements of soap, motor-cars, whisky, shirts, perfume, pills, bricks and tea—for the drop-curtain was down. And, curiously, he felt obliged to keep his eyes on the drop-curtain and across the long intervening vista of hats and heads and smoke to explore its most difficult corners again and again, lest when it went up he might not be in proper practice for seeing what was behind it.

Nevertheless, despite the marked inconveniences of his situation, he felt brighter, he felt almost happy in this dense atmosphere of success. He even found a certain peculiar and perverse satisfaction in the fact that he had as yet been recognized by nobody. Once or twice the owners of shoulders had turned and deliberately glared at the worrying fellow who had the impudence to be all the time peeping over them and between them; they had not distinguished the fellow from any ordinary fellow. Could they have known that he was the famous Alderman Edward Henry Machin, founder and sole proprietor of the Thrift Club, into which their wives were probably paying so much a week, they would most assuredly have glared to another tune, and they would have said with pride afterwards: " That chap Machin o' Bursley was standing behind me at the Empire to-night! " And though

Machin is amongst the commonest names in the Five
Towns, all would have known that the great and admired Denry was meant. . . . It was astonishing that
a personage so notorious should not have been instantly
" spotted " in such a resort as the Empire. More
proof that the Five Towns was a vast and seething
concentration of cities, and no longer a mere district
where everybody knew everybody!

The curtain rose, and as it did so a thunderous,
crashing applause of greeting broke forth; applause
that thrilled and impressed and inspired; applause
that made every individual in the place feel right glad
that he was there. For the curtain had risen on
the gigantic attraction, which many members of the
audience were about to see for the fifth time that week;
in fact, it was rumoured that certain men of fashion,
whose habit was to refuse themselves nothing, had
attended every performance of the gigantic attraction
since the second house on Monday.

The scene represented a restaurant of quiet aspect,
into which entered a waiter bearing a pile of plates
some two feet high. The waiter being intoxicated the
tower of plates leaned this way and that as he staggered
about, and the whole house really did hold its breath
in the simultaneous hope and fear of an enormous and
resounding smash. Then entered a second intoxicated
waiter, also bearing a pile of plates some two feet high,
and the risk of destruction was thus more than doubled
—it was quadrupled, for each waiter, in addition to the
risks of his own inebriety, was now subject to the
dreadful peril of colliding with the other. However,
there was no catastrophe.

Then arrived two customers, one in a dress suit and
an eyeglass, and the other in a large violet hat, a
diamond necklace and a yellow satin skirt. The

which customers, seemingly well used to the sight of
drunken waiters tottering to and fro with towers of
plates, sat down at a table and waited calmly for
attention. The popular audience, with that quick
mental grasp for which popular audiences are so renowned, soon perceived that the table was in close
proximity to a lofty sideboard, and that on either hand
of the sideboard were two chairs, upon which the two
waiters were trying to climb in order to deposit their
plates on the topmost shelf of the sideboard. The
waiters successfully mounted the chairs and successfully
lifted their towers of plates to within half an inch of the
desired shelf, and then the chairs began to show signs
of insecurity. By this time the audience was stimu-
lated to an ecstasy of expectation, whose painful-
ness was only equalled by its extreme delectability.
The sole unmoved persons in the building were
the customers awaiting attention at the restaurant
table.

One tower was safely lodged on the shelf. But
was it? It was not! Yes? No! It curved; it
straightened; it curved again. The excitement was
as keen as that of watching a drowning man attempt
to reach the shore. It was simply excruciating. It
could not be borne any longer, and when it could not
be borne any longer the tower sprawled irrevocably
and seven dozen plates fell in a cascade on the violet
hat, and so with an inconceivable clatter to the floor.
Almost at the same moment the being in the dress-
suit and the eyeglass, becoming aware of phenomena
slightly unusual even in a restaurant, dropped his eyeglass, turned round to the sideboard and received the
other waiter's seven dozen plates in the face and on the
crown of his head.

No such effect had ever been seen in the Five Towns,

and the felicity of the audience exceeded all previous felicities. The audience yelled, roared, shrieked,
gasped, trembled, and punched itself in a furious passion
of pleasure. They make plates in the Five Towns.
They live by making plates. They understand plates.
In the Five Towns a man will carry not seven but
twenty-seven dozen plates on a swaying plank for eight
hours a day up steps and down steps, and in doorways
and out of doorways, and not break one plate in seven
years! Judge, therefore, the simple but terrific satisfaction of a Five Towns audience in the hugeness of the
calamity. Moreover, every plate smashed means a
demand for a new plate and increased prosperity for
the Five Towns. The grateful crowd in the auditorium of the Empire would have covered the stage
with wreaths, if it had known that wreaths were used
for other occasions than funerals; which it did not
know.

Fresh complications instantly ensued, which cruelly
cut short the agreeable exercise of uncontrolled laughter.
It was obvious that one of the waiters was about to fall.
And in the enforced tranquillity of a new dread every
dyspeptic person in the house was deliciously conscious
of a sudden freedom from indigestion due to the agreeable exercise of uncontrolled laughter, and wished
fervently that he could laugh like that after every meal.
The waiter fell; he fell through the large violet hat and
disappeared beneath the surface of a sea of crockery.
The other waiter fell too, but the sea was not deep
enough to drown a couple of them. Then the
customers, recovering themselves, decided that they
must not be outclassed in this competition of havoc,
and they overthrew the table and everything on it, and
all the other tables and everything on all the other
tables. The audience was now a field of artillery

which nothing could silence. The waiters arose, and, opening the sideboard, disclosed many hundreds of unsuspected plates of all kinds, ripe for smashing. Niagaras of plates surged on to the stage. All four performers revelled and wallowed in smashed plates. New supplies of plates were constantly being produced from strange concealments, and finally the tables and chairs were broken to pieces, and each object on the walls was torn down and flung in bits on to the gorgeous general debris, to the top of which clambered the violet hat, necklace and yellow petticoat, brandishing one single little plate, whose life had been miraculously spared. Shrieks of joy in that little plate played over the din like lightning in a thunderstorm. And the curtain fell.

It was rung up fifteen times, and fifteen times the quartette of artists, breathless, bowed in acknowledgment of the frenzied and boisterous testimony to their unique talents. No singer, no tragedian, no comedian, no wit could have had such a triumph, could have given such intense pleasure. And yet none of the four had spoken a word. Such is genius.

At the end of the fifteenth call the stage-manager came before the curtain and guaranteed that two thousand four hundred plates had been broken.

The lights went up. Strong men were seen to be wiping tears from their eyes. Complete strangers were seen addressing each other in the manner of old friends. Such is art.

"Well, that was worth a bob, that was!" muttered Edward Henry to himself. And it was. Edward Henry had not escaped the general fate. Nobody, being present, could have escaped it. He was enchanted. He had utterly forgotten every care.

"Good evening, Mr Machin," said a voice at his

side. Not only he turned but nearly everyone in the vicinity turned. The voice was the voice of the stout and splendid managing director of the Empire, and it sounded with the ring of authority above the rising tinkle of the bar behind the Grand Circle.

" Oh! How d'ye do, Mr Dakins? " Edward Henry held out a cordial hand, for even the greatest men are pleased to be greeted in a place of entertainment by the managing director thereof. Further, his identity was now recognized.

" Haven't you seen those gentlemen in that box beckoning to you? " said Mr Dakins, proudly deprecating complimentary remarks on the show.

" Which box? "

Mr Dakins' hand indicated a stage-box. And Henry, looking, saw three men, one unknown to him, the second, Robert Brindley, the architect, of Bursley, and the third, Dr Stirling.

Instantly his conscience leapt up within him. He thought of rabies. Yes, sobered in the fraction of a second, he thought of rabies. Supposing that, after all, in spite of Mr Long's Muzzling Order, as cited by his infant son, an odd case of rabies should have lingered in the British Isles, and supposing that Carlo had been infected . . . ! Not impossible . . . ! Was it providential that Dr Stirling was in the auditorium?

" You know two of them? " said Mr Dakins.

" Yes."

" Well, the third's a Mr Bryany. He's manager to Mr Seven Sachs." Mr Dakins' tone was respectful.

" And who's Mr Seven Sachs? " asked Edward Henry, absently. It was a stupid question.

He was impressively informed that Mr Seven Sachs was the arch-famous American actor-playwright, now nearing the end of a provincial tour, which had surpassed all records of provincial tours, and that he would be at the Theatre Royal, Hanbridge, next week. Edward Henry then remembered that the hoardings had been full of Mr Seven Sachs for some time past.

" They keep on making signs to you," said Mr Dakins, referring to the occupants of the stage-box.

Edward Henry waved a reply to the box.

" Here! I'll take you there the shortest way," said Mr Dakins.

II

" WELCOME to Stirling's box, Machin! " Robert Brindley greeted the alderman with an almost imperceptible wink. Edward Henry had encountered this wink once or twice before; he could not decide precisely what it meant; it was apt to make him reflective. He did not dislike Robert Brindley, his habit was not to dislike people; he admitted Brindley to be a clever architect, though he objected to the " modern " style of the fronts of his houses and schools. But he did take exception to the man's attitude towards the Five Towns, of which, by the way, Brindley was just as much a native as himself. Brindley seemed to live in the Five Towns like a highly-cultured stranger in a savage land, and to derive rather too much sardonic amusement from the spectacle of existence therein. Brindley was a very special crony of Stirling's, and had influenced Stirling. But Stirling was too clever to submit unduly to the influence. Besides, Stirling was not a native; he was only a Scotchman, and Edward Henry considered that what Stirling thought of the district did not matter. Other details about Brindley which Edward Henry deprecated were his necktie, which, for Edward Henry's taste, was too flowing, his scorn of the Pianisto (despite the man's tremendous interest in music) and his incipient madness on the subject of books—a madness shared by Stirling. Brindley and the doctor were for ever chattering about books—and buying them.

So that, on the whole, Dr Stirling's box was not a place where Edward Henry felt entirely at home. Nevertheless, the two men, having presented Mr Bryany, did their best, each in his own way, to make him feel at home.

" Take this chair, Machin," said Stirling, indicating a chair at the front.

" Oh! I can't take the front chair! " Edward Henry protested.

" Of course you can, my dear Machin! " said Brindley, sharply. " The front chair in a stage-box is the one proper seat in the house for you. Do as your doctor prescribes."

And Edward Henry accordingly sat down at the front, with Mr Bryany by his side, and the other two sat behind. But Edward Henry was not quite comfortable. He faintly resented that speech of Brindley's. And yet he did feel that what Brindley had said was true, and he was indeed glad to be in the front chair of a brilliant stage-box on the grand tier, instead of being packed away in the nethermost twilight of the Grand Circle. He wondered how Brindley and Stirling had managed to distinguish his face among the confusion of faces in that distant obscurity; he, Edward Henry, had failed to notice them, even in the prominence of their box. But that they had distinguished him showed how familiar and striking a figure he was. He wondered, too, why they should have invited him to hob-nob with them. He was not of their set. Indeed, like many very eminent men, he was not to any degree in anybody's set. Of one thing he was sure—because he had read it on the self-conscious faces of all three of them—namely, that they had been discussing him. Possibly he had been brought up for Mr Bryany's inspection as a major lion and character of the district. Well, he did not mind that; nay, he enjoyed that. He could feel Mr Bryany covertly looking him over. And he thought: " Look, my boy! I make no charge." He smiled and nodded to one or two people who with pride saluted him from the stalls. . . . It was meet that he should be visible there on that Friday night!

" A full house! " he observed, to break the rather awkward silence of the box, as he glanced round at the magnificent smoke-veiled pageant of the aristocracy and the democracy of the Five Towns, crowded together, tier above gilded tier, up to the dim roof where ragged lads and maids giggled and flirted while waiting for the broken plates to be cleared away and the moving pictures to begin.

" You may say it! " agreed Mr Bryany, who spoke with a very slight American accent. " Dakins positively hadn't a seat to offer me. I happened to have the evening free. It isn't often I do have a free evening. And so I thought I'd pop in here. But if Dakins hadn't introduced me to these gentlemen my seat would have had to be a standing one."

" So that's how they got to know him, is it? " thought Edward Henry.

And then there was another short silence.

" Hear you've been doing something striking in rubber shares, Machin? " said Brindley at length.

Astonishing how these things got abroad!

" Oh! very little, very little! " Edward Henry laughed modestly. " Too late to do much! In another fortnight the bottom will be all out of the rubber market."

" Of course I'm an Englishman "— Mr Bryany began.

" Why ' of course '? " Edward Henry interrupted him.

" Hear! Hear! Alderman. Why ' of course '? " said Brindley, approvingly, and Stirling's rich laugh was heard. " Only it does just happen," Brindley added, " that Mr Bryany did us the honour to be born in the district."

" Yes! Longshaw," Mr Bryany admitted, half proud and half apologetic. " Which I left at the age of two."

" Oh, Longshaw! " murmured Edward Henry with a peculiar inflection.

Longshaw is at the opposite end of the Five Towns from Bursley, and the majority of the inhabitants of Bursley have never been to Longshaw in their lives, have only heard of it, as they hear of Chicago or Bangkok. Edward Henry had often been to Longshaw, but, like every visitor from Bursley, he instinctively regarded it as a foolish and unnecessary place.

" As I was saying," resumed Mr Bryany, quite unintimidated, " I'm an Englishman. But I've lived eighteen years in America, and it seems to me the bottom will soon be knocked out of pretty nearly all the markets in England. Look at the Five Towns! "

" No, don't, Mr Bryany! " said Brindley. " Don't go to extremes! "

" Personally, I don't mind looking at the Five Towns," said Edward Henry. " What of it? "

" Well, did you ever see such people for looking twice at a five-pound note? "

Edward Henry most certainly did not like this aspersion on his native district. He gazed in silence at Mr Bryany's brassy and yet simple face, and did not like the face either.

And Mr Bryany, beautifully unaware that he had failed in tact, continued: " The Five Towns is the most English place I've ever seen, believe me! Of course it has its good points, and England has her good points; but there's no money stirring. There's no field for speculation on the spot, and as for outside investment, no Englishman will touch anything that really—is—good." He emphasized the last three words.

" What d'ye do yeself, Mr Bryany? " inquired Dr Stirling.

" What do I do with my little bit? " cried Mr Bryany. " Oh! I know what to do with my little bit. I can get ten per cent. in Seattle and twelve to fifteen in Calgary on my little bit; and security just as good as English railway stock—*and* better! "

The theatre was darkened and the cinematograph began its restless twinkling.

Mr Bryany went on offering to Edward Henry, in a suitably lowered voice, his views on the great questions of investment and speculation, and Edward Henry made cautious replies.

" And even when there *is* a good thing going at home," Mr Bryany said, in a wounded tone, " what Englishman'd look at it? "

" I would," said Edward Henry with a blandness that was only skin-deep. For all the time he was cogitating the question whether the presence of Dr Stirling in the audience ought or ought not to be regarded as providential.

" Now, I've got the option on a little affair in London," said Mr Bryany, while Edward Henry glanced quickly at him in the darkness. " And can I get anybody to go into it? I can't."

" What sort of a little affair? "

" Building a theatre in the West End."

Even a less impassive man than Edward Henry would have started at the coincidence of this remark. And Edward Henry started. Twenty minutes ago he had been idly dreaming of theatrical speculation, and now he could almost see theatrical speculation shimmering before him in the pale shifting rays of the cinematograph that cut through the gloom of the mysterious auditorium.

" Oh! " And in this new interest he forgot the enigma of the ways of Providence.

" Of course, you know, I'm in the business," said Mr Bryany. " I'm Seven Sachs's manager." It was as if he owned and operated Mr Seven Sachs.

" So I heard," said Edward Henry, and then remarked with mischievous cordiality, " and I suppose these chaps told you I was the sort of man you were after. And you got them to ask me in, eh, Mr Bryany? "

Mr Bryany gave an uneasy laugh, but seemed to find naught to say.

" Well, what *is* your little affair? " Edward Henry encouraged him.

" Oh, I can't tell you now," said Mr Bryany. " It would take too long. The thing has to be explained."

" Well, what about to-morrow? "

" I have to leave for London by the first train in the morning."

" Well, some other time? "

" After to-morrow will be too late."

" Well, what about to-night? "

" The fact is, I've half promised to go with Dr Stirling to some club or other after the show. Otherwise we might have had a quiet, confidential chat in my

rooms over at the Turk's Head. I never dreamt—"
Mr Bryany was now as melancholy as a greedy lad who
regards rich fruit at arm's length through a plate-glass
window, and he had ceased to be patronizing.

" I'll soon get rid of Stirling for you," said Edward
Henry, turning instantly towards the doctor. The
ways of Providence had been made plain to Edward
Henry. " I say, doc! " But the doctor and Brindley
were in conversation with another man at the open door
of the box.

" What is it? " said Stirling.

" I've come to fetch you. You're wanted at my
place."

" Well, you're a caution! " said Stirling.

" Why am I a caution? " Edward Henry smoothly
protested. " I didn't tell you before because I didn't
want to spoil your fun."

Stirling's mien was not happy.

" Did they tell you I was here? " he asked.

" You'd almost think so, wouldn't you? " said
Edward Henry in a playful, enigmatic tone. After all,
he decided privately, his wife was right; it was better
that Stirling should see the infant. And there was also
this natural human thought in his mind; he objected
to the doctor giving an entire evening to diversions
away from home—he considered that a doctor, when
not on a round of visits, ought to be for ever in his
consulting-room, ready for a sudden call of emergency.
It was monstrous that Stirling should have proposed,
after an escapade at the music-hall, to spend further
hours with chance acquaintances in vague clubs!
Half the town might fall sick and die while the doctor
was vainly amusing himself. Thus the righteous lay-
man in Edward Henry!

" What's the matter? " asked Stirling.

" My eldest's been rather badly bitten by a dog, and the missis wants it cauterized."

" Really? "

" Well, you bet she does! "

" Where's the bite? "

" In the calf."

The other man at the door having departed Robert Brindley abruptly joined the conversation at this point.

" I suppose you've heard of that case of hydrophobia at Bleakridge? " said Brindley.

Edward Henry's heart jumped.

" No, I haven't! " he said anxiously. " What is it? "

He gazed at the white blur of Brindley's face in the darkened box, and he could hear the rapid clicking of the cinematograph behind him.

" Didn't you see it in the *Signal* ? "

" No."

" Neither did I," said Brindley.

At the same moment the moving pictures came to an end, the theatre was filled with light, and the band began to play " God Save the King." Brindley and Stirling were laughing. And, indeed, Brindley had scored, this time, over the unparalleled card of the Five Towns.

" I make you a present of that," said Edward Henry. " But my wife's most precious infant has to be cauterized, doctor," he added firmly.

" Got your car here? " Stirling questioned.

" No. Have you? "

" No."

" Well, there's the tram. I'll follow you later. I've some business round this way. Persuade my wife not to worry, will you? "

And when a discontented Dr Stirling had made his excuses and adieux to Mr Bryany, and Robert Brindley had decided that he could not leave his crony to travel by tram-car alone, and the two men had gone, then Edward Henry turned to Mr Bryany.

" That's how I get rid of the doctor, you see! "

" But *has* your child been bitten by a dog? " asked Mr Bryany, acutely perplexed.

" You'd almost think so, wouldn't you? " Edward Henry replied, carefully non-committal. " What price going to the Turk's Head now? "

He remembered with satisfaction, and yet with misgiving, a remark made to him, a judgment passed on him, by a very old woman very many years before. This discerning hag, the Widow Hullins by name, had said to him briefly, " Well, you're a queer 'un! "

III

WITHIN five minutes he was following Mr Bryany into a small parlour on the first floor of the Turk's Head—a room with which he had no previous acquaintance, though, like most industrious men of affairs in metropolitan Hanbridge, he reckoned to know something about the Turk's Head. Mr Bryany turned up the gas—the Turk's Head took pride in being a " hostelry," and, while it had accustomed itself to incandescent mantles (on the ground floor), it had not yet conquered a natural distaste for electricity—and Edward Henry saw a smart dispatch-box, a dress-suit, a trouser-stretcher and other necessaries of theatrical business life at large in the apartment.

" I've never seen this room before," said Edward Henry.

" Take your overcoat off and sit down, will you? " said Mr Bryany, as he turned to replenish the fire from a bucket. " It's my private sitting-room. Whenever I am on my travels I always take a private sitting-room. It pays, you know. . . . Of course I mean if I'm alone. When I'm looking after Mr Sachs, of course we share a sitting-room."

Edward Henry agreed lightly:

" I suppose so."

But the fact was that he was much impressed. He himself had never taken a private sitting-room in any hotel. He had sometimes felt the desire, but he had not had the " face "—as they say down there—to do it. To take a private sitting-room in a hotel was generally regarded in the Five Towns as the very summit of dashing expensiveness and futile luxury.

" I didn't know they had any private sitting-rooms in this shanty," said Edward Henry.

Mr Bryany, having finished with the fire, fronted him, shovel in hand, with a remarkable air of consummate wisdom, and replied:

" You can generally get what you want, if you insist on having it, even in this ' shanty.' "

Edward Henry regretted his use of the word " shanty." Inhabitants of the Five Towns may allow themselves to twit the historic and excellent Turk's Head, but they do not extend the privilege to strangers. And in justice to the Turk's Head it is to be clearly stated that it did no more to cow and discourage travellers than any other provincial hotel in England. It was a sound and serious English provincial hotel, and it linked century to century.

Said Mr Bryany:

" 'Merica's the place for hotels."

" Yes, I expect it is."

" Been to Chicago? "

" No, I haven't."

Mr Bryany, as he removed his overcoat, could be seen politely forbearing to raise his eyebrows.

" Of course you've been to New York? "

Edward Henry would have given all he had in his pockets to be able to say that he had been to New York. But by some inexplicable negligence he had hitherto omitted to go to New York, and being a truthful person (except in the gravest crises) he was obliged to answer miserably:

" No, I haven't."

Mr Bryany gazed at him with amazement and compassion, apparently staggered by the discovery that there existed in England a man of the world who had contrived to struggle on for forty years without perfecting his education by a visit to New York.

Edward Henry could not tolerate Mr Bryany's look. It was a look which he had never been able to tolerate on the features of anybody whatsoever. He reminded himself that his secret object in accompanying Mr Bryany to the Turk's Head was to repay Mr Bryany— in what coin he knew not yet—for the aspersions which at the music-hall he had cast upon England in general and upon the Five Towns in particular, and also to get revenge for having been tricked into believing, even for a moment, that there was really a case of hydrophobia at Bleakridge. It is true that Mr Bryany was innocent of this deception, which had been accomplished by Robert Brindley, but that was a detail which did not trouble Edward Henry, who lumped his grievances together—for convenience.

He had been reflecting that some sentimental people, unused to the ways of paternal affection in the Five Towns, might consider him a rather callous father; he had been reflecting, again, that Nellie's suggestion of blood-poisoning might not be as entirely foolish as feminine suggestions in such circumstances too often are. But now he put these thoughts away, reassuring himself against hydrophobia anyhow, by the recollection of the definite statement of the *Encyclopædia*. Moreover, had he not inspected the wound—as healthy a wound as you could wish for?

And he said in a new tone, very curtly:

" Now, Mr Bryany, what about this little affair of yours? "

He saw that Mr Bryany accepted the implied rebuke with the deference properly shown by a man who needs something towards the man in possession of what he needs. And studying the fellow's countenance, he decided that, despite its brassiness and simple cunning, it was scarcely the countenance of a rascal.

" Well, it's like this," said Mr Bryany, sitting down opposite Edward Henry at the centre table, and reaching with obsequious liveliness for the dispatch-box.

He drew from the dispatch-box, which was lettered " W. C. B.," first a cut-glass flask of whisky with a patent stopper, and then a spacious box of cigarettes.

" I always travel with the right sort," he remarked, holding the golden liquid up to the light. " It's safer and it saves any trouble with orders after closing-time. . . . These English hotels, you know—! "

So saying he dispensed whisky and cigarettes, there being a siphon and glasses, and three matches in a match-stand, on the table.

" Here's looking! " he said, with raised glass.

And Edward Henry responded, in conformity with the changeless ritual of the Five Towns:

" I looks! "

And they sipped.

Whereupon Mr Bryany next drew from the dispatch-box a piece of transparent paper.

" I want you to look at this plan of Piccadilly Circus and environs," said he.

Now there is a Piccadilly in Hanbridge; also a Pall Mall and a Chancery Lane. The adjective " metropolitan," applied to Hanbridge, is just.

" London? " questioned Edward Henry, " I understood London when we were chatting over there." With his elbow he indicated the music-hall, somewhere vaguely outside the room.

" London," said Mr Bryany.

And Edward Henry thought:

" What on earth am I meddling with London for? What use should I be in London? "

" You see the plot marked in red? " Mr Bryany proceeded. " Well, that's the site. There's an old chapel on it now."

" What do all these straight lines mean? " Edward Henry inquired, examining the plan. Lines radiated from the red plot in various directions.

" Those are the lines of vision," said Mr Bryany. " They show just where an electric sign at the corner of the front of the proposed theatre could be seen from. You notice the site is not in the Circus itself—a shade to the north." Mr Bryany's finger approached Edward Henry's on the plan, and the clouds from their cigarettes fraternally mingled. " Now you see by those lines that the electric sign of the proposed theatre would be visible from nearly the whole of Piccadilly Circus, parts of Lower Regent Street, Coventry Street and even Shaftesbury Avenue. You see what a site it is—absolutely unique."

Edward Henry asked coldly:

" Have you bought it? "

" No," Mr Bryany seemed to apologize. " I haven't exactly bought it. But I've got an option on it."

The magic word " option " wakened the drowsy speculator in Edward Henry. And the mere act of looking at the plan endowed the plot of land with reality! There it was! It existed!

" An option to buy it? "

" You can't buy land in the West End of London," said Mr Bryany, sagely. " You can only lease it."

" Well, of course! " Edward Henry concurred.

" The freehold belongs to Lord Woldo, now aged six months."

" Really! " murmured Edward Henry.

" I've got an option to take up the remainder of the lease, with sixty-four years to run, on the condition I put up a theatre. And the option expires in exactly a fortnight's time."

Edward Henry frowned and then asked:

" What are the figures? "

" That is to say," Mr Bryany corrected himself, smiling courteously, " I've got half the option."

" And who's got the other half? "

" Rose Euclid's got the other half."

At the mention of the name of one of the most renowned star-actresses in England, Edward Henry excusably started.

" Not *the*—? " he exclaimed.

Mr Bryany nodded proudly, blowing out much smoke.

" Tell me," asked Edward Henry, confidentially, leaning forward, " where do those ladies get their names from? "

" It happens in this case to be her real name," said Mr Bryany. " Her father kept a tobacconist's shop in Cheapside. The sign was kept up for many years, until Rose paid to have it changed."

" Well, well! " breathed Edward Henry, secretly

thrilled by these extraordinary revelations. " And so you and she have got it between you? "

Mr Bryany said:

" I bought half of it from her some time ago. She was badly hard up for a hundred pounds and I let her have the money." He threw away his cigarette half-smoked, with a free gesture that seemed to imply that he was capable of parting with a hundred pounds just as easily.

" How did she *get* the option? " Edward Henry inquired, putting into the query all the innuendo of a man accustomed to look at great worldly affairs from the inside.

" How did she get it? She got it from the late Lord Woldo. She was always very friendly with the late Lord Woldo, you know." Edward Henry nodded. " Why, she and the Countess of Chell are as thick as thieves! You know something about the Countess down here, I reckon? "

The Countess of Chell was the wife of the supreme local magnate.

Edward Henry answered calmly, " We do."

He was tempted to relate a unique adventure of his youth, when he had driven the Countess to a public meeting in his mule-carriage, but sheer pride kept him silent.

" I asked you for the figures," he added, in a manner which requested Mr Bryany to remember that he was the founder, chairman and proprietor of the Five Towns Universal Thrift Club, one of the most successful business organizations in the Midlands.

" Here they are! " said Mr Bryany, passing across the table a sheet of paper.

And as Edward Henry studied them he could hear Mr Bryany faintly cooing into his ear: " Of course

Rose got the ground-rent reduced. And when I tell you that the demand for theatres in the West End far exceeds the supply, and that theatre rents are always going up. . . . When I tell you that a theatre costing £25,000 to build can be let for £11,000 a year, and often £300 a week on a short term . . . ! " And he could hear the gas singing over his head. . . . And also, unhappily, he could hear Dr Stirling talking to his wife and saying to her that the bite was far more serious than it looked, and Nellie hoping very audibly that nothing had " happened " to him, her still absent husband . . . ! And then he could hear Mr Bryany again:

" When I tell you . . ."

" When you tell me all this, Mr Bryany," he interrupted with that ferocity which in the Five Towns is regarded as mere directness, " I wonder why the devil you want to sell your half of the option—if you *do* want to sell it. Do you want to sell it? "

" To tell you the truth," said Mr Bryany, as if up to that moment he had told naught but lies, " I do."

" Why? "

" Oh, I'm always travelling about, you see. England one day—America the next." (Apparently he had quickly abandoned the strictness of veracity.) " All depends on the governor's movements! I couldn't keep a proper eye on an affair of that kind."

Edward Henry laughed:

" And could I? "

" Chance for you to go a bit oftener to London," said Mr Bryany, laughing too. Then, with extreme and convincing seriousness, " You're the very man for a thing of that kind. And you know it! "

Edward Henry was not displeased by this flattery.

" How much? "

" How much? Well, I told you frankly what I paid. I made no concealment of that, did I now? Well, I want what I paid. It's worth it! "

" Got a copy of the option, I hope! "

Mr Bryany produced a copy of the option.

" I am nothing but an infernal ass to mix myself up in a mad scheme like this," said Edward Henry to his soul, perusing the documents. " It's right off my line, right bang off it . . . ! But what a lark ! " But even to his soul he did not utter the remainder of the truth about himself, namely: " I should like to cut a dash before this insufferable patronizer of England and the Five Towns."

Suddenly something snapped within him and he said to Mr Bryany:

" I'm on! "

Those words and no more!

" You are? " Mr Bryany exclaimed, mistrusting his ears.

Edward Henry nodded.

" Well, that's business anyway! " said Mr Bryany, taking a fresh cigarette and lighting it.

" It's how we do business down here," said Edward Henry, quite inaccurately; for it was not in the least how they did business down there.

Mr Bryany asked, with a rather obvious anxiety:

" But when can you pay? "

" Oh, I'll send you a cheque in a day or two." And Edward Henry in his turn took a fresh cigarette.

" That won't do! That won't do! " cried Mr Bryany. " I absolutely must have the money to-morrow morning in London. I can sell the option in London for eighty pounds—I know that."

" You must have it? "

" Must! "

They exchanged glances. And Edward Henry, rapidly acquiring new knowledge of human nature on the threshold of a world strange to him, understood that Mr Bryany, with his private sitting-room and his investments in Seattle and Calgary, was at his wits' end for a bag of English sovereigns, and had trusted to some chance encounter to save him from a calamity. And his contempt for Mr Bryany was that of a man to whom his bankers are positively servile.

" Here! " Mr Bryany almost shouted. " Don't light your cigarette with my option! "

" I beg pardon! " Edward Henry apologized, dropping the document which he had creased into a spill. There were no matches left on the table.

" I'll find you a matcn! "

" It's of no consequence," said Edward Henry, feeling in his pockets. Having discovered therein a piece of paper he twisted it and rose to put it to the gas.

" Could you slip round to your bank and meet me at the station in the morning with the cash? " suggested Mr Bryany.

" No, I couldn't," said Edward Henry.

" Well, then, what—? "

" Here, you'd better take this," the " Card," reborn, soothed his host and, blowing out the spill which he had just ignited at the gas, he offered it to Mr Bryany.

" What? "

" This, man! "

Mr Bryany, observing the peculiarity of the spill, seized it and unrolled it—not without a certain agitation.

He stammered:

" Do you mean to say it's genuine? "

" You'd almost think so, wouldn't you? " said

Edward Henry. He was growing fond of this reply, and of the enigmatic, playful tone that he had invented for it.

" But—"

" We may, as you say, look twice at a fiver," continued Edward Henry. " But we're apt to be careless about hundred-pound notes in this district. I daresay that's why I always carry one."

" But it's burnt! "

" Only just the edge. Not enough to harm it. If any bank in England refuses it, return it to me and I'll give you a couple more in exchange. Is that talking? "

" Well, I'm dashed! " Mr Bryany attempted to rise, and then subsided back into his chair. " I am simply and totally dashed! " He smiled weakly, hysterically.

And in that instant Edward Henry felt all the sweetness of a complete and luscious revenge.

He said commandingly:

" You must sign me a transfer. I'll dictate it! "

Then he jumped up.

" You're in a hurry? "

" I am. My wife is expecting me. You promised to find me a match." Edward Henry waved the unlit cigarette as a reproach to Mr Bryany's imperfect hospitality.

IV

THE clock of Bleakridge Church, still imperturbably shining in the night, showed a quarter to one when he saw it again on his hurried and guilty way home. The pavements were drying in the fresh night wind and he had his overcoat buttoned up to the neck. He was absolutely solitary in the long, muddy perspective of

Trafalgar Road. He walked because the last tram-car was already housed in its shed at the other end of the world, and he walked quickly because his conscience drove him onwards. And yet he dreaded to arrive, lest a wound in the child's leg should have maliciously decided to fester in order to put him in the wrong. He was now as apprehensive concerning that wound as Nellie herself had been at tea-time.

But, in his mind, above the dark gulf of anxiety, there floated brighter thoughts. Despite his fears and his remorse as a father, he laughed aloud in the deserted street when he remembered Mr Bryany's visage of astonishment upon uncreasing the note. Indubitably he had made a terrific and everlasting impression upon Mr Bryany. He was sending Mr Bryany out of the Five Towns a different man. He had taught Mr Bryany a thing or two. To what brilliant use had he turned the purely accidental possession of a hundred-pound note! One of his finest inspirations—an inspiration worthy of the great days of his youth! Yes, he had had his hour that evening, and it had been a glorious one. Also, it had cost him a hundred pounds, and he did not care; he would retire to bed with a net gain of two hundred and forty-one pounds instead of three hundred and forty-one pounds—that was all!

For he did not mean to take up the option. The ecstasy was cooled now and he saw clearly that London and theatrical enterprises therein would not be suited to his genius. In the Five Towns he was on his own ground; he was a figure; he was sure of himself. In London he would be a provincial, with the diffidence and the uncertainty of a provincial. Nevertheless, London seemed to be summoning him from afar off, and he dreamt agreeably of London as one dreams of the impossible East.

As soon as he opened the gate in the wall of his property he saw that the drawing-room was illuminated and all the other front rooms in darkness. Either his wife or his mother, then, was sitting up in the drawing-room. He inserted a cautious latch-key into the door and entered the silent home like a sinner. The dim light in the hall gravely reproached him. All his movements were modest and restrained. No noisy rattling of his stick now!

The drawing-room **door** was slightly ajar. He hesitated, and then, nerving himself, pushed against it.

Nellie, with lowered head, was seated at a table, mending, the image of tranquillity and soft resignation. A pile of children's garments lay by her side, but the article in her busy hands appeared to be an undershirt of his own. None but she ever reinforced the buttons on his linen. Such was her wifely rule, and he considered that there was no sense in it. She was working by the light of a single lamp on the table, the splendid chandelier being out of action. Her economy in the use of electricity was incurable, and he considered that there was no sense in that either.

She glanced up, with a guarded expression that might have meant anything.

He said:

" Aren't you trying your eyes? "

And she replied:

" Oh, no! "

Then, plunging, he came to the point:

" Well, doctor been? "

She nodded.

" What does he say? "

" It's quite all right. He did nothing but cover up the place with a bit of cyanide gauze."

Instantly, in his own esteem, he regained perfection

as a father. Of course the bite was nothing! Had he not said so from the first? Had he not been quite sure throughout that the bite was nothing?

" Then why did you sit up? " he asked, and there was a faint righteous challenge in his tone.

" I was anxious about you. I was afraid—"

" Didn't Stirling tell you I had some business? "

" I forget—"

" I told him to, anyhow. . . . Important business."

" It must have been," said Nellie, in an inscrutable voice.

She rose and gathered together her paraphernalia, and he saw that she was wearing the damnable white apron. The close atmosphere of the home enveloped and stifled him once more. How different was this exasperating interior from the large jolly freedom of the Empire Music Hall, and from the whisky, cigarettes and masculinity of that private room at the Turk's Head!

" It was! " he repeated grimly and resentfully. " Very important! And I'll tell you another thing. I shall probably have to go to London."

He said this just to startle her.

" It will do you all the good in the world," she replied angelically, but unstartled. " It's just what you need! " And she gazed at him as though his welfare and felicity were her sole preoccupation.

" I meant I might have to stop there quite a while," he insisted.

" If you ask me," she said, " I think it would do us all good."

So saying, she retired, having expressed no curiosity whatever as to the nature of the very important business in London.

For a moment, left alone, he was at a loss. Then, snorting, he went to the table and extinguished the lamp. He was now in darkness. The light in the hall showed him the position of the door.

He snorted again. "Oh, very well then!" he muttered. " If that's it! . . . I'm hanged if I don't go to London! . . . I'm hanged if I don't go to London! "

CHAPTER III

WILKINS'S

I

THE early adventures of Alderman Machin of Bursley at Wilkins's Hotel, London, were so singular, and to him so refreshing, that they must be recounted in some detail.

He went to London by the morning express from Knype, on the Monday week after his visit to the music-hall. In the meantime he had had some correspondence with Mr Bryany, more poetic than precise, about the option, and had informed Mr Bryany that he would arrive in London several days before the option expired. But he had not given a definite date. The whole affair, indeed, was amusingly vague; and, despite his assurances to his wife that the matter was momentous, he did not regard his trip to London as a business trip at all, but rather as a simple freakish change of air. The one certain item in the whole situation was that he had in his pocket a quite considerable sum of actual money, destined—he hoped, but was not sure—to take up the option at the proper hour.

Nellie, impeccable to the last, accompanied him in the motor to Knype, the main-line station. The drive, superficially pleasant, was in reality very disconcerting to him. For nine days the household had talked in apparent cheerfulness of father's visit to London, as though it were an occasion for joy on father's behalf, tempered by affectionate sorrow for his absence. The official theory was that all was for the best in the best of all possible homes, and this theory was admirably maintained. And yet everybody knew — even to Maisie—that it was not so; everybody knew that the master and the mistress of the home, calm and sweet as was their demeanour, were contending in a terrific silent and mysterious altercation, which in some way was connected with the visit to London.

So far as Edward Henry was concerned he had been hoping for some decisive event—a tone, gesture, glance, pressure—during the drive to Knype, which offered the last chance of a real concord. No such event occurred. They conversed with the same false cordiality as had marked their relations since the evening of the dog-bite. On that evening Nellie had suddenly transformed herself into a distressingly perfect angel, and not once had she descended from her high estate. At least daily she had kissed him — what kisses! Kisses that were not kisses! Tasteless mockeries, like non-alcoholic ale! He could have killed her, but he could not put a finger on a fault in her marvellous wifely behaviour; she would have died victorious.

So that his freakish excursion was not starting very auspiciously. And, waiting with her for the train on the platform at Knype, he felt this more and more. His old clerk, Penkethman, was there to receive certain final instructions on Thrift Club matters, and the sweetness of Nellie's attitude towards the ancient man, and the ancient man's naïve pleasure therein, positively maddened Edward Henry. To such an extent that he began to think: " Is she going to spoil my trip for me? "

Then Brindley came up. Brindley, too, was going to London. And Nellie's saccharine assurances to Brindley that Edward Henry really needed a change just about completed Edward Henry's desperation. Not even the uproarious advent of two jolly wholesale grocers, Messieurs Garvin & Quorrall, also going to London, could effectually lighten his pessimism.

When the train steamed in, Edward Henry, in fear, postponed the ultimate kiss as long as possible. He allowed Brindley to climb before him into the second-class compartment, and purposely tarried in finding change for the porter; and then he turned to Nellie and stooped. She raised her white veil and raised the angelic face. They kissed—the same false kiss—and she was withdrawing her lips. . . . But suddenly she put them again to his for one second, with a hysterical, clinging pressure. It was nothing. Nobody could have noticed it. She herself pretended that she had not done it. Edward Henry had to pretend not to notice it. But to him it was everything. She had relented. She had surrendered. The sign had come from her. She wished him to enjoy his visit to London.

He said to himself:

" Dashed if I don't write to her every day! "

He leaned out of the window as the train rolled away and waved and smiled to her, not concealing his sentiments now; nor did she conceal hers as she replied with exquisite pantomime to his signals. But if the train had not been rapidly and infallibly separating them the reconciliation could scarcely have been thus open. If for some reason the train had backed into the station and ejected its passengers, those two would have covered up their feelings again in an instant. Such is human nature in the Five Towns.

When Edward Henry withdrew his head into the compartment Brindley and Mr Garvin, the latter standing at the corridor door, observed that his spirits had shot up in the most astonishing manner, and in their blindness they attributed the phenomenon to Edward Henry's delight in a temporary freedom from domesticity.

Mr Garvin had come from the neighbouring compartment, which was first-class, to suggest a game at bridge. Messieurs Garvin & Quorrall journeyed to London once a week and sometimes oftener, and, being traders, they had special season-tickets. They travelled first-class because their special season-tickets were first-class. Brindley said that he didn't mind a game, but that he had not the slightest intention of paying excess fare for the privilege. Mr Garvin told him to come along and trust in Messieurs Garvin & Quorrall. Edward Henry, not nowadays an enthusiastic card-player, enthusiastically agreed to join the hand, and announced that he did not care if he paid forty excess fares. Whereupon Robert Brindley grumbled enviously that it was "all very well for millionaires"! . . . They followed Mr Garvin into the first-class compartment, and it soon appeared that Messrs Garvin & Quorrall did, in fact, own the train, and that the London and North Western Railway was no more than their washpot.

"Bring us a cushion from somewhere, will ye?" said Mr Quorrall, casually, to a ticket-collector who entered.

And the resplendent official obeyed. The long cushion, rapt from another compartment, was placed on the knees of the quartette, and the game began. The ticket-collector examined the tickets of Brindley and Edward Henry, and somehow failed to notice that they were of the wrong colour. And at this proof of their influential greatness Messieurs Garvin & Quorrall were both secretly proud.

The last rubber finished in the neighbourhood of

Willesden, and Edward Henry, having won eighteen-pence halfpenny, was exuberantly content, for Messrs Garvin, Quorrall and Brindley were all renowned card-players. The cushion was thrown away and a fitful conversation occupied the few remaining minutes of the journey.

" Where do you put up? " Brindley asked Edward Henry.

" Majestic," said Edward Henry. " Where do you? "

" Oh! Kingsway, I suppose."

The Majestic and the Kingsway were two of the half-dozen very large and very mediocre hotels in London which, from causes which nobody, and especi-ally no American, has ever been able to discover, are particularly affected by Midland provincials " on the jaunt! " Both had an immense reputation in the Five Towns.

There was nothing new to say about the Majestic and the Kingsway, and the talk flagged until Mr Quorrall mentioned Seven Sachs. The mighty Seven Sachs, in his world-famous play, " Overheard," had taken precedence of all other topics in the Five Towns during the previous week. He had crammed the theatre and half emptied the Empire Music Hall for six nights; a wonderful feat. Incidentally, his fifteen hundredth appearance in " Overheard " had taken place in the Five Towns, and the Five Towns had found in this fact a peculiar satisfaction, as though some deep merit had thereby been acquired or rewarded. Seven Sachs's tour was now closed, and on the Sunday he had gone to London, *en route* for America.

" I heard *he* stops at Wilkins's," said Mr Garvin.

" Wilkins's your grandmother! " Brindley essayed to crush Mr Garvin.

" I don't say he *does* stop at Wilkins's," said Mr Garvin, an individual not easy to crush; " I only say I heard as he did."

" They wouldn't have him! " Brindley insisted firmly.

Mr Quorrall at any rate seemed tacitly to agree with Brindley. The august name of Wilkins's was in its essence so exclusive that vast numbers of fairly canny provincials had never heard of it. Ask ten well-informed provincials which is the first hotel in London and nine of them would certainly reply, the Grand Babylon. Not that even wealthy provincials from the industrial districts are in the habit of staying at the Grand Babylon! No! Edward Henry, for example, had never stayed at the Grand Babylon, no more than he had ever bought a first-class ticket on a railroad. The idea of doing so had scarcely occurred to him. There are certain ways of extravagant smartness which are not considered to be good form among solid wealthy provincials. Why travel first-class (they argue) when second is just as good and no one can tell the difference once you get out of the train? Why ape the tricks of another stratum of society? They like to read about the dinner-parties and supper-parties at the Grand Babylon; but they are not emulous and they do not imitate. At their most adventurous they would lunch or dine in the neutral region of the grill-room at the Grand Babylon. As for Wilkins's, in Devonshire Square, which is infinitely better known among princes than in the Five Towns, and whose name is affectionately pronounced with a " V " by half the monarchs of Europe, few industrial provincials had ever seen it. The class which is the backbone of England left it serenely alone to royalty and the aristocratic parasites of royalty.

" I don't see why they shouldn't have him," said Edward Henry, as he lifted a challenging nose in the air.

" Perhaps you don't, Alderman! " said Brindley.

" *I* wouldn't mind going to Wilkins's," Edward Henry persisted.

" I'd like to see you," said Brindley, with curt scorn.

" Well," said Edward Henry, " I'll bet you a fiver I do." Had he not won eighteenpence halfpenny, and was he not securely at peace with his wife?

" I don't bet fivers," said the cautious Brindley. " But I'll bet you half-a-crown."

" Done! " said Edward Henry.

" When will you go? "

" Either to-day or to-morrow. I must go to the Majestic first, because I've ordered a room and so on."

" Ha! " hurtled Brindley, as if to insinuate that Edward Henry was seeking to escape from the consequences of his boast.

And yet he ought to have known Edward Henry. He did know Edward Henry. And he hoped to lose his half-crown. On his face and on the faces of the other two was the cheerful admission that tales of the doings of Alderman Machin, the great local card, at Wilkins's—if he succeeded in getting in—would be cheap at half-a-crown.

Porters cried out " Euston! "

II

It was rather late in the afternoon when Edward Henry arrived in front of the façade of Wilkins's. He came in a taxi-cab, and though the distance from the

Majestic to Wilkins's is not more than a couple of miles, and he had had nothing else to preoccupy him after lunch, he had spent some three hours in the business of transferring himself from the portals of the one hotel to the portals of the other. Two hours and three-quarters of this period of time had been passed in finding courage merely to start. Even so, he had left his luggage behind him. He said to himself that, first of all, he would go and spy out Wilkins's; in the perilous work of scouting he rightly wished to be unhampered by impedimenta; moreover, in case of repulse or accident, he must have a base of operations upon which he could retreat in good order.

He now looked on Wilkins's for the first time in his life, and he was even more afraid of it than he had been while thinking about it in the vestibule of the Majestic. It was not larger than the Majestic; it was perhaps smaller; it could not show more terra-cotta, plate-glass and sculptured cornice than the Majestic. But it had a demeanour . . . and it was in a square which had a demeanour. . . . In every window-sill—not only of the hotel, but of nearly every mighty house in the Square—there were boxes of bright blooming flowers. These he could plainly distinguish in the October dusk, and they were a wonderful phenomenon—say what you will about the mildness of that particular October! A sublime tranquillity reigned over the scene. A liveried keeper was locking the gate of the garden in the middle of the Square as if potentates had just quitted it and rendered it for ever sacred. And between the sacred shadowed grove and the inscrutable fronts of the stately houses there flitted automobiles of the silent and expensive kind, driven by chauffeurs in pale grey or dark purple, who reclined as they steered, and who were supported on their left sides by footmen who reclined as they contemplated the grandeur of existence.

Edward Henry's taxi-cab in that Square seemed like a homeless cat that had strayed into a dog-show.

At the exact instant, when the taxi-cab came to rest under the massive portico of Wilkins's, a chamberlain in white gloves bravely soiled the gloves by seizing the vile brass handle of its door. He bowed to Edward Henry and assisted him to alight on to a crimson carpet. The driver of the taxi glanced with pert and candid scorn at the chamberlain, but Edward Henry looked demurely aside, and then in abstraction mounted the broad carpeted steps.

" What about poor little me? " cried the driver, who was evidently a ribald socialist, or at best a republican.

The chamberlain, pained, glanced at Edward Henry for support and direction in this crisis.

" Didn't I tell you I'd keep you? " said Edward Henry, raised now by the steps above the driver.

" Between you and me, you didn't," said the driver.

The chamberlain, with an ineffable gesture, wafted the taxi-cab away into some limbo appointed for waiting vehicles.

A page opened a pair of doors, and another page opened another pair of doors, each with eighteen century ceremonies of deference, and Edward Henry stood at length in the hall of Wilkins's. The sanctuary, then, was successfully defiled, and up to the present nobody had demanded his credentials! He took breath.

In its physical aspects Wilkins's appeared to him to resemble other hotels—such as the Majestic. And so far he was not mistaken. Once Wilkins's had not resembled other hotels. For many years it had deliberately refused to recognize that even the nineteenth century had dawned, and its magnificent antique discomfort had been one of its main attractions to the elect. For the elect desired nothing but their own privileged society in order to be happy in a hotel. A hip-bath on a blanket in the middle of the bedroom floor richly sufficed them, provided they could be guaranteed against the calamity of meeting the unelect in the corridors or at *table d'hôte*. But the rising waters of democracy—the intermixture of classes—had reacted adversely on Wilkins's. The fall of the Emperor Maximilian of Mexico had given Wilkins's sad food for thought long, long ago, and the obvious general weakening of the monarchical principle had most considerably shaken it. Came the day when Wilkins's reluctantly decided that even it could not fight against the tendency of the whole world, and then, at one superb stroke, it had rebuilt and brought itself utterly up-to-date.

Thus it resembled other hotels. (Save, possibly, in the reticence of its advertisements! The Majestic would advertise bathrooms as a miracle of modernity, just as though common dwelling-houses had not possessed bathrooms for the past thirty years. Wilkins's had superlative bathrooms, but it said nothing about them. Wilkins's would as soon have advertised two hundred bathrooms as two hundred bolsters; and for the new Wilkins's a bathroom was not more modern than a bolster.) Also, other hotels resembled Wilkins's. The Majestic, too, had a chamberlain at its portico and an assortment of pages to prove to its clients that they were incapable of performing the simplest act for themselves. Nevertheless, the difference between Wilkins's and the Majestic was enormous; and yet so subtle was it that Edward Henry could not immediately detect where it resided. Then he understood. The difference between Wilkins's and the Majestic resided in the theory which underlay its manner. And the theory was that every person entering its walls was of royal blood until he had admitted the contrary.

Within the hotel it was already night.

Edward Henry self-consciously crossed the illuminated hall, which was dotted with fashionable figures. He knew not whither he was going, until by chance he saw a golden grille with the word " Reception " shining over it in letters of gold. Behind this grille, and still further protected by an impregnable mahogany counter, stood three young dandies in attitudes of graceful ease. He approached them. The fearful moment was upon him. He had never in his life been so genuinely frightened. Abject disgrace might be his portion within the next ten seconds.

Addressing himself to the dandy in the middle he managed to articulate:

" What have you got in the way of rooms? "

Could the Five Towns have seen him then, as he waited, it would hardly have recognized its " card," its character, its mirror of aplomb and inventive audacity, in this figure of provincial and plebeian diffidence.

The dandy bowed.

" Do you want a suite, sir? "

" Certainly! " said Edward Henry. Rather too quickly, rather too defiantly; in fact, rather rudely! A *habitué* would not have so savagely hurled back in the dandy's teeth the insinuation that he wanted only one paltry room.

However, the dandy smiled, accepting with meekness Edward Henry's sudden arrogance, and consulted a sort of pentateuch that was open in front of him.

No person in the hall saw Edward Henry's hat fly up into the air and fall back on his head. But in the imagination of Edward Henry this was what his hat did.

He was saved. He would have a proud tale for Brindley. The thing was as simple as the alphabet. You just walked in and they either fell on your neck or kissed your feet.

Wilkins's, indeed!

A very handsome footman, not only in white gloves but in white calves, was soon supplicating him to deign to enter a lift. And when he emerged from the lift another dandy—in a frock-coat of Paradise—was awaiting him with obeisances. Apparently it had not yet occurred to anybody that he was not the younger son of some aged king.

He was prayed to walk into a gorgeous suite, consisting of a corridor, a noble drawing-room (with portrait of His Majesty of Spain on the walls), a large bedroom with two satin-wood beds, a small bedroom and a bathroom, all gleaming with patent devices in porcelain and silver that fully equalled those at home.

Asked if this suite would do, he said it would, trying as well as he could to imply that he had seen better. Then the dandy produced a note-book and a pencil and impassively waited. The horrid fact that he was unelect could no longer be concealed.

"E. H. Machin, Bursley," he said shortly; and added: "Alderman Machin." After all, why should he be ashamed of being an Alderman?

To his astonishment the dandy smiled very cordially, though always with profound respect.

"Ah! yes!" said the dandy. It was as though he

had said: " We have long wished for the high patronage of this great reputation." Edward Henry could make naught of it.

His opinion of Wilkins's went down.

He followed the departing dandy up the corridor to the door of the suite in an entirely vain attempt to inquire the price of the suite per day. Not a syllable would pass his lips. The dandy bowed and vanished. Edward Henry stood lost at his own door, and his wandering eye caught sight of a pile of trunks near to another door in the main corridor. These trunks gave him a terrible shock. He shut out the rest of the hotel and retired into his private corridor to reflect. He perceived only too plainly that his luggage, now at the Majestic, never could come into Wilkins's. It was not fashionable enough. It lacked elegance. The lounge-suit that he was wearing might serve, but his luggage was totally impossible. Never before had he imagined that the aspect of one's luggage could have the least importance in one's scheme of existence. He was learning, and he frankly admitted that he was in an incomparable mess.

III

AT the end of an extensive stroll through and round his new vast domain, he had come to no decision upon a course of action. Certain details of the strange adventure pleased him—as, for instance, the dandy's welcoming recognition of his name; that, though puzzling, was a source of comfort to him in his difficulties. He also liked the suite; nay, more, he was much impressed by its gorgeousness, and such novel complications as the forked electric switches, all of which he turned on, and the double windows, one within the other, appealed to the domestic expert in him; indeed, he at once had the idea of doubling the window of the best bedroom at home; to do so would be a fierce blow to the Five Towns Electric Traction Company, which, as everybody knew, delighted to keep everybody awake at night and at dawn by means of its late and its early tram-cars.

However, he could not wander up and down the glittering solitude of his extensive suite for ever. Something must be done. Then he had the notion of writing to Nellie; he had promised himself to write her daily; moreover, it would pass the time and perhaps help him to some resolution.

He sat down to a delicate Louis XVI. desk, on which lay a Bible, a Peerage, a telephone-book, a telephone, a lamp and much distinguished stationery. Between the tasselled folds of plushy curtains that pleated themselves with the grandeur of painted curtains in a theatre, he glanced out at the lights of Devonshire Square, from which not a sound came. Then he lit the lamp and unscrewed his fountain-pen.

" My dear wife—"

That was how he always began, whether in storm or sunshine. Nellie always began, " My darling husband," but he was not a man to fling " darlings " about. Few husbands in the Five Towns are. He thought " darling," but he never wrote it, and he never said it, save quizzingly.

After these three words the composition of the letter came to a pause. What was he going to tell Nellie? He assuredly was not going to tell her that he had engaged an unpriced suite at Wilkins's. He was not going to mention Wilkins's. Then he intelligently perceived that the note-paper and also the envelope mentioned Wilkins's in no ambiguous manner. He tore up the sheet and searched for plain paper.

Now on the desk there was the ordinary hotel stationery, mourning stationery, cards, letter-cards and envelopes for every mood; but not a piece that was not embossed with the historic name in royal blue. The which appeared to Edward Henry to point to a defect of foresight on the part of Wilkins's. At the gigantic political club to which he belonged, and which he had occasionally visited in order to demonstrate to himself and others that he was a clubman, plain stationery was everywhere provided for the use of husbands with a taste for reticence. Why not at Wilkins's also?

On the other hand, why should he *not* write to his wife on Wilkins's paper? Was he afraid of his wife? He was not. Would not the news ultimately reach Bursley that he had stayed at Wilkins's? It would. Nevertheless, he could not find the courage to write to Nellie on Wilkins's paper.

He looked around. He was fearfully alone. He wanted the companionship, were it only momentary, of something human. He decided to have a look at the flunkey, and he rang a bell.

Immediately, just as though wafted thither on a magic carpet from the Court of Austria, a gentleman-in-waiting arrived in the doorway of the drawing-room, planted himself gracefully on his black silk calves, and bowed.

"I want some plain note-paper, please."

"Very good, sir." Oh! Perfection of tone and of mien!

Three minutes later the plain note-paper and envelopes were being presented to Edward Henry on a salver. As he took them he looked inquiringly at the gentleman-in-waiting, who supported his gaze with an impenetrable, invulnerable servility. Edward Henry, beaten off with great loss, thought: "There's nothing doing here just now in the human companionship line," and assumed the mask of a hereditary prince.

The black calves carried away their immaculate living burden, set above all earthly ties.

He wrote nicely to Nellie about the weather and the journey and informed her also that London seemed as full as ever, and that he might go to the theatre but he wasn't sure. He dated the letter from the Majestic.

As he was finishing it he heard mysterious, disturbing footfalls in his private corridor, and after trying for some time to ignore them, he was forced by a vague alarm to investigate their origin. A short, middle-aged, pallid man, with a long nose and long moustaches, wearing a red-and-black-striped sleeved waistcoat and a white apron, was in the corridor. At the Turk's Head such a person would have been the boots. But Edward Henry remembered a notice under the bell, advising visitors to ring once for the waiter, twice for the chambermaid, and three times for the valet. This, then, was the valet. In certain picturesque details of costume Wilkins's was coquettishly French.

" What is it? " he demanded.

" I came to see if your luggage had arrived, sir. No doubt your servant is bringing it. Can I be of any assistance to you? "

The man thoughtfully twirled one end of his moustache. It was an appalling fault in demeanour; but the man was proud of his moustache.

" The first human being I've met here! " thought Edward Henry, attracted too by a gleam in the eye of this eternal haunter of corridors.

" His servant! " He saw that something must be done, and quickly! Wilkins's provided valets for emergencies, but obviously it expected visitors to bring their own valets in addition. Obviously existence without a private valet was inconceivable to Wilkins's.

" The fact is," said Edward Henry, " I'm in a very awkward situation." He hesitated, seeking to and fro in his mind for particulars of the situation.

" Sorry to hear that, sir."

" Yes, a very awkward situation." He hesitated again. " I'd booked passages for myself and my valet on the *Minnetonka*, sailing from Tilbury at noon to-day, and sent him on in front with my stuff, and at the very last moment I've been absolutely prevented from sailing! You see how awkward it is! I haven't a thing here."

" It is indeed, sir. And I suppose *he's* gone on, sir? "

" Of course he has! He wouldn't find out till after she sailed that I wasn't on board. You know the crush and confusion there is on those big liners just before they start." Edward Henry had once assisted, under very dramatic circumstances, at the departure of a Transatlantic liner from Liverpool.

" Just so, sir! "

" I've neither servant nor clothes! " He considered that so far he was doing admirably. Indeed, the tale could not have been bettered, he thought. His hope was that the fellow would not have the idea of consulting the shipping intelligence in order to confirm the departure of the *Minnetonka* from Tilbury that day. Possibly the *Minnetonka* never had sailed and never would sail from Tilbury. Possibly she had been sold years ago. He had selected the first ship's name that came into his head. What did it matter?

"My man," he added to clinch—the proper word "man" had only just occurred to him—"my man can't be back again under three weeks at the soonest."

The valet made one half-eager step towards him.

"If you're wanting a temporary valet, sir, my son's out of a place for the moment—through no fault of his own. He's a very good valet, sir, and soon learns a gentleman's ways."

"Yes," said Edward Henry, judiciously. "But could he come at once? That's the point." And he looked at his watch, as if to imply that another hour without a valet would be more than human nature could stand.

"I could have him round here in less than an hour, sir," said the hotel-valet, comprehending the gesture. "He's at Norwich Mews—Berkeley Square way, sir."

Edward Henry hesitated.

"Very well, then!" he said commandingly. "Send for him. Let me see him."

He thought:

"Dash it! I'm at Wilkins's—I'll be *at* Wilkins's!"

"Certainly, sir! Thank you very much, sir."

The hotel-valet was retiring when Edward Henry called him back.

"Stop a moment. I'm just going out. Help me on with my overcoat, will you?"

The man jumped.

"And you might get me a tooth-brush," Edward Henry airily suggested. "And I've a letter for the post."

As he walked down Devonshire Square in the dark

he hummed a tune; certain sign that he was self-conscious, uneasy, and yet not unhappy. At a small but expensive hosier's in a side street he bought a shirt and a suit of pyjamas, and also permitted himself to be tempted by a special job line of hair-brushes that the hosier had in his fancy department. On hearing the powerful word " Wilkins's," the hosier promised with passionate obsequiousness that the goods should be delivered instantly.

Edward Henry cooled his excitement by an extended stroll, and finally re-entered the outer hall of the hotel at half-past seven, and sat down therein to see the world. He knew by instinct that the boldest lounge-suit must not at that hour penetrate further into the public rooms of Wilkins's.

The world at its haughtiest was driving up to Wilkins's to eat its dinner in the unrivalled restaurant, and often guests staying at the hotel came into the outer hall to greet invited friends. And Edward Henry was so overfaced by visions of woman's brilliance and man's utter correctness that he scarcely knew where to look—so apologetic was he for his grey lounge-suit and the creases in his boots. In less than a quarter of an hour he appreciated with painful clearness that his entire conception of existence had been wrong, and that he must begin again at the beginning. Nothing in his luggage at the Majestic would do. His socks would not do, nor his shoes, nor the braid on his trousers, nor his cuff-links, nor his ready-made white bow, nor the number of studs in his shirt-front, nor the collar of his coat. Nothing! Nothing! To-morrow would be a full day.

He ventured apologetically into the lift. In his private corridor a young man respectfully waited, hat in hand, the paternal red-and-black waistcoat by his side for purposes of introduction. The young man was wearing a rather shabby blue suit, but a rich and distinguished overcoat that fitted him ill. In another five minutes Edward Henry had engaged a skilled valet, aged twenty-four, name Joseph, with a testimonial of efficiency from Sir Nicholas Winkworth, Bart., at a salary of a pound a week and all found.

Joseph seemed to await instructions. And Edward Henry was placed in a new quandary. He knew not whether the small bedroom in the suite was for a child, or for his wife's maid, or for his valet. Quite probably it would be a sacrilegious defiance of precedent to put a valet in the small bedroom. Quite probably Wilkins's had a floor for private valets in the roof. Again, quite probably, the small bedroom might be, after all, specially destined for valets! He could not decide, and the most precious thing in the universe to him in that crisis was his reputation as a man-about-town in the eyes of Joseph.

But something had to be done.

" You'll sleep in this room," said Edward Henry, indicating the door. " I may want you in the night."

" Yes, sir," said Joseph.

" I presume you'll dine up here, sir," said Joseph, glancing at the lounge-suit.

His father had informed him of his new master's predicament.

" I shall," said Edward Henry. " You might get the menu."

IV

HE had a very bad night indeed—owing, no doubt, partly to a general uneasiness in his unusual surroundings, and partly also to a special uneasiness caused by the propinquity of a sleeping valet; but the main origin of it was certainly his dreadful anxiety about the question of a first-class tailor. In the organization of his new life a first-class tailor was essential, and he was not acquainted with a first-class London tailor. He did not know a great deal concerning clothes, though quite passably well dressed for a provincial, but he knew enough to be sure that it was impossible to judge the merits of a tailor by his signboard, and therefore that if, wandering in the precincts of Bond Street, he entered the first establishment that " looked likely," he would have a good chance of being " done in the eye." So he phrased it to himself as he lay in bed. He wanted a definite and utterly reliable address.

He rang the bell. Only, as it happened to be the wrong bell, he obtained the presence of Joseph in a roundabout way, through the agency of a gentleman-in-waiting. Such, however, is the human faculty of adaptation to environment that he was merely amused in the morning by an error which, on the previous night, would have put him into a sweat.

" Good morning, sir," said Joseph.

Edward Henry nodded, his hands under his head as he lay on his back. He decided to leave all initiative to Joseph. The man drew up the blinds, and closing the double windows at the top opened them very wide at the bottom.

" It is a rainy morning, sir," said Joseph, letting in vast quantities of air from Devonshire Square.

Clearly, Sir Nicholas Winkworth had been a breezy master.

" Oh! " murmured Edward Henry.

He felt a careless contempt for Joseph's flunkeyism. Hitherto he had had the theory that footmen, valets and all male personal attendants were an inexcusable

excrescence on the social fabric. The mere sight of
them often angered him, though for some reason he
had no objection whatever to servility in a nice-looking
maid—indeed, rather enjoyed it. But now, in the
person of Joseph, he saw that there were human or
half-human beings born to self-abasement, and that,
if their destiny was to be fulfilled, valetry was a necessary institution. He had no pity for Joseph, no shame
in employing him. He scorned Joseph; and yet his
desire, as a man-about-town, to keep Joseph's esteem,
was in no way diminished!

" Shall I prepare your bath, sir? " asked Joseph,
stationed in a supple attitude by the side of the
bed.

Edward Henry was visited by an idea.

" Have you had yours? " he demanded like a pistol-
shot.

Edward Henry saw that Sir Nicholas had never
asked that particular question.

" No, sir."

" Not had your bath, man! What on earth do
you mean by it? Go and have your bath at
once! "

A faint sycophantic smile lightened the amazed
features of Joseph. And Edward Henry thought:
" It's astonishing, all the same, the way they can read
their masters. This chap has seen already that I'm a
card. And yet how? "

" Yes, sir," said Joseph.

" Have your bath in the bathroom here. And be
sure to leave everything in order for me."

" Yes, sir."

As soon as Joseph had gone Edward Henry jumped
out of bed and listened. He heard the discreet Joseph
respectfully push the bolt of the bathroom door. Then

he crept with noiseless rapidity to the small bedroom and was aware therein of a lack of order and of ventilation. The rich and distinguished overcoat was hanging on the brass knob at the foot of the bed. He seized it, and, scrutinizing the loop, read in yellow letters: " *Quayther & Cuthering, 47 Vigo Street, W.*" He knew that Quayther & Cuthering must be the tailors of Sir Nicholas Winkworth, and hence first-class.

Hoping for the best, and putting his trust in the general decency of human nature, he did not trouble himself with the problem: was the overcoat a gift or an appropriation? But he preferred to assume the generosity of Sir Nicholas rather than the dishonesty of Joseph.

Repassing the bathroom door he knocked loudly on its glass.

" Don't be all day! " he cried. He was in a hurry now.

An hour later he said to Joseph:

" I'm going down to Quayther & Cuthering's."

" Yes, sir," said Joseph, obviously much reassured.

" Nincompoop! " Edward Henry exclaimed secretly. " The fool thinks better of me because my tailors are first-class."

But Edward Henry had failed to notice that he himself was thinking better of himself because he had adopted first-class tailors.

Beneath the main door of his suite, as he went forth, he found a business card of the West End Electric Brougham Supply Agency. And downstairs, solely to impress his individuality on the hall-porter, he showed the card to that vizier with the casual question:

" These people any good? "

" An excellent firm, sir."

" What do they charge? "

" By the week, sir? "

He hesitated. " Yes, by the week."

" Twenty guineas, sir."

" Well, you might telephone for one. Can you get it at once? "

" Certainly, sir."

The vizier turned towards the telephone in his lair.

" I say—" said Edward Henry.

" Sir? "

" I suppose one will be enough? "

" Well, sir, as a rule, yes," said the vizier, calmly. " Sometimes I get a couple for one family, sir."

Though he had started jocularly, Edward Henry finished by blenching. " I think one will do. . . . I may possibly send for my own car."

He drove to Quayther & Cuthering's in his electric brougham and there dropped casually the name of Winkworth. He explained humorously his singular misadventure of the *Minnetonka,* and was very successful therewith—so successful, indeed, that he actually began to believe in the reality of the adventure himself, and had an irrational impulse to dispatch a wireless message to his bewildered valet on board the *Minnetonka.*

Subsequently he paid other fruitful visits in the neighbourhood, and at about half-past eleven the fruit was arriving at Wilkins's in the shape of many parcels and boxes, comprising diverse items in the equipment of a man-about-town, such as tie-clips and Innovation trunks.

Returning late to Wilkins's for lunch he marched jauntily into the large brilliant restaurant and commenced an adequate repast. Of course he was still wearing his mediocre lounge-suit (his sole suit for another two days), but somehow the consciousness that Quayther & Cuthering were cutting out wondrous garments for him in Vigo Street stiffened his shoulders and gave a mysterious style to that lounge-suit.

At lunch he made one mistake and enjoyed one very remarkable piece of luck.

The mistake was to order an artichoke. He did not know how to eat an artichoke. He had never tried to eat an artichoke, and his first essay in this difficult and complex craft was a sad fiasco. It would not have mattered if, at the table next to his own, there had not been two obviously experienced women, one ill-dressed, with a red hat, the other well-dressed, with a blue hat; one middle-aged, the other much younger; but both very observant. And even so, it would scarcely have mattered had not the younger woman been so slim, pretty and alluring. While tolerably careless of the opinion of the red-hatted, plain woman of middle-age, he desired the unqualified approval of the delightful young thing in the blue hat. They certainly interested themselves in his manœuvres with the artichoke, and their amusement was imperfectly concealed. He forgave the blue hat, but considered that the red hat ought to have known better. They could not be princesses, nor even titled aristocrats. He supposed them to belong to some baccarat-playing county family.

The piece of luck consisted in the passage down the restaurant of the Countess of Chell, who had been lunching there with a party, and whom he had known

locally in more gusty days. The Countess bowed stiffly
to the red hat, and the red hat responded with eager
fulsomeness. It seemed to be here as it no longer was
in the Five Towns; everybody knew everybody! The
red hat and the blue might be titled, after all, he
thought. Then, by sheer accident, the Countess
caught sight of himself and stopped dead, bringing
her escort to a standstill behind her. Edward Henry
blushed and rose.

" Is it *you*, Mr Machin? " murmured the still lovely
creature warmly.

They shook hands. Never had social pleasure so
thrilled him. The conversation was short. He did
not presume on the past. He knew that here he was
not on his own ashpit, as they say in the Five Towns.
The Countess and her escort went forward. Edward
Henry sat down again.

He gave the red and the blue hats one calm glance,
which they failed to withstand. The affair of the
artichoke was for ever wiped out.

After lunch he went forth again in his electric
brougham. The weather had cleared. The opulent
streets were full of pride and sunshine. And as he
penetrated into one shop after another, receiving kow-
tows, obeisances, curtsies, homage, surrender, resignation, submission, he gradually comprehended that
it takes all sorts to make a world, and that those
who are called to greatness must accept with dignity
the ceremonials inseparable from greatness. And
the world had never seemed to him so fine, nor
any adventure so diverting and uplifting as this
adventure.

When he returned to his suite his private
corridor was piled up with a numerous and excessively attractive assortment of parcels. Joseph

took his overcoat and hat and a new umbrella and placed an easy-chair conveniently for him in the drawing-room.

" Get my bill," he said shortly to Joseph as he sank into the gilded fauteuil.

" Yes, sir."

One advantage of a valet, he discovered, is that you can order him to do things which to do yourself would more than exhaust your moral courage.

The black-calved gentleman-in-waiting brought the bill. It lay on a salver and was folded, conceivably so as to break the shock of it to the recipient.

Edward Henry took it.

" Wait a minute," he said.

He read on the bill: " Apartments, £8. Dinner, £1, 2s. od. Breakfast, 6s. 6d. Lunch, 18s. Half Chablis, 6s. 6d. Valet's board, 10s. Tooth-brush, 2s. 6d."

" That's a bit thick, half-a-crown for that tooth-brush! " he said to himself. " However—"

The next instant he blenched once more.

" Gosh! " he privately exclaimed as he read: " Paid driver of taxi-cab, £2, 3s. 6d."

He had forgotten the taxi. But he admired the *sang-froid* of Wilkins's, which paid such trifles as a matter of course, without deigning to disturb a guest by an inquiry. Wilkins's rose again in his esteem.

The total of the bill exceeded thirteen pounds.

" All right," he said to the gentleman-in-waiting.

" Are you leaving to-day, sir? " the being permitted himself to ask.

" Of course I'm not leaving to-day! Haven't I hired an electric brougham for a week? " Edward Henry burst out. " But I suppose I'm entitled to know how much I'm spending! "

The gentleman-in-waiting humbly bowed and departed.

Alone in the splendid chamber Edward Henry drew out a swollen pocket-book and examined its crisp, crinkly contents, which made a beauteous and a reassuring sight.

" Pooh! " he muttered.

He reckoned he would be living at the rate of about fifteen pounds a day, or five thousand five hundred a year. (He did not count the cost of his purchases, because they were in the nature of a capital expenditure.)

" Cheap! " he muttered. " For once I'm about living up to my income! "

The sensation was exquisite in its novelty.

He ordered tea, and afterwards, feeling sleepy, he went fast asleep.

He awoke to the ringing of the telephone-bell. It was quite dark. The telephone-bell continued to ring.

" Joseph! " he called.

The valet entered.

" What time is it? "

" After ten o'clock, sir."

" The deuce it is! "

He had slept over four hours!

" Well, answer that confounded telephone."

Joseph obeyed.

" It's a Mr Bryany, sir, if I catch the name right," said Joseph.

Bryany! For twenty-four hours he had scarcely thought of Bryany or the option either.

" Bring the telephone here," said Edward Henry.

The cord would just reach to his chair.

" Hello! Bryany! Is that you? " cried Edward Henry, gaily.

And then he heard the weakened voice of Mr Bryany in his ear:

" How d'ye do, Mr Machin? I've been after you for the better part of two days, and now I find you're staying in the same hotel as Mr Sachs and me! "

" Oh! " said Edward Henry.

He understood now why, on the previous day, the dandy introducing him to his suite had smiled a welcome at the name of Alderman Machin, and why Joseph had accepted so naturally the command to take a bath. Bryany had been talking. Bryany had been recounting his exploits as a card.

The voice of Bryany in his ear continued:

" Look here! I've got Miss Euclid here and some friends of hers. Of course she wants to see you at once. Can you come down? "

" Er—" He hesitated.

He could not come down. He would have no evening wear till the next day but one.

Said the voice of Bryany:

" What? "

" I can't," said Edward Henry. " I'm not very well. But listen. All of you come up to my rooms here and have supper, will you? Suite 48."

" I'll ask the lady," said the voice of Bryany, altered now, and a few seconds later: " We're coming."

" Joseph," Edward Henry gave orders rapidly, as he took off his coat and removed the pocket-book from it. " I'm ill, you understand. Anyhow, not well. Take this," handing him the coat, " and bring me the new dressing-gown out of that green cardboard box from Rollet's—I think it is. And then get the supper menu. I'm very hungry. I've had no dinner."

Within sixty seconds he sat in state, wearing a

grandiose yellow dressing-gown. The change was accomplished just in time. Mr Bryany entered, and not only Mr Bryany but Mr Seven Sachs, and not only these, but the lady who had worn a red hat at lunch.

" Miss Rose Euclid," said Mr Bryany, puffing and bending.

CHAPTER IV

ENTRY INTO THE THEATRICAL WORLD

I

ONCE, on a short visit to London, Edward Henry had paid half-a-crown to be let into a certain enclosure with a very low ceiling. This enclosure was already crowded with some three hundred people, sitting and standing. Edward Henry had stood in the only unoccupied spot he could find, behind a pillar. When he had made himself as comfortable as possible by turning up his collar against the sharp winds that continually entered from the street, he had peered forward, and seen in front of his enclosure another and larger enclosure also crowded with people, but more expensive people. After a blank interval of thirty minutes a band had begun to play at an incredible distance in front of him, extinguishing the noises of traffic in the street. After another interval an oblong space rather further off even than the band suddenly grew bright, and Edward Henry, by curving his neck first to one side of the pillar and then to the other, had had tantalizing glimpses of the interior of a doll's drawing-room and of male and female dolls therein.

He could only see, even partially, the inferior half of the drawing-room—a little higher than the heads of the dolls—because the rest was cut off from his vision by the lowness of his own ceiling.

The dolls were talking, but he could not catch

clearly what they said, save at the rare moments when an omnibus or a van did not happen to be thundering down the street behind him. Then one special doll had come exquisitely into the drawing-room, and at the sight of her the five hundred people in front of him, and numbers of other people perched hidden beyond his ceiling, had clapped fervently and even cried aloud in their excitement. And he, too, had clapped fervently, and had muttered " Bravo! " This special doll was a marvel of touching and persuasive grace, with a voice—when Edward Henry could hear it— that melted the spine. This special doll had every elegance and seemed to be in the highest pride of youth.

At the close of the affair, as this special doll sank into the embrace of a male doll from whom she had been unjustly separated, and then straightened herself, deliciously and confidently smiling, to take the tremendous applause of Edward Henry and the rest, Edward Henry thought that he had never assisted at a triumph so genuine and so inspiring.

Oblivious of the pain in his neck, and of the choking, foul atmosphere of the enclosure, accurately described as the Pit, he had gone forth into the street with a subconscious notion in his head that the special doll was more than human, was half divine. And he had said afterwards, with immense satisfaction, at Bursley: " Yes, I saw Rose Euclid in ' Flower of the Heart.' "

He had never set eyes on her since.

And now, on this day at Wilkins's, he had seen in the restaurant, and he saw again before him in his private parlour, a faded and stoutish woman, negligently if expensively dressed, with a fatigued, nervous, watery glance, an unnatural, pale-violet complexion, a

wrinkled skin and dyed hair; a woman of whom it
might be said that she had escaped grandmotherhood,
if indeed she had escaped it, by mere luck—and he was
point-blank commanded to believe that she and Rose
Euclid were the same person.

It was one of the most shattering shocks of all his
career, which nevertheless had not been untumultuous.
And within his dressing-gown—which nobody remarked upon—he was busy picking up and piecing
together, as quickly as he could, the shivered fragments
of his ideas.

He literally did not recognize Rose Euclid. True,
fifteen years had passed since the night in the pit!
And he himself was fifteen years older. But in his
mind he had never pictured any change in Rose Euclid.
True, he had been familiar with the enormous renown
of Rose Euclid as far back as he could remember taking
any interest in theatrical advertisements! But he had
not permitted her to reach an age of more than about
thirty-one or two. Whereas he now perceived that
even the exquisite doll in paradise that he had gloated
over from his pit must have been quite thirty-five—
then. . . .

Well, he scornfully pitied Rose Euclid! He blamed
her for not having accomplished the miracle of eternal
youth. He actually considered that she had cheated
him. " Is this all? What a swindle! " he thought,
as he was piecing together the shivered fragments of his
ideas into a new pattern. He had felt much the same
as a boy, at Bursley Annual Wakes once, on entering a
booth which promised horrors and did not supply them.
He had been " done " all these years. . . .

Reluctantly he admitted that Rose Euclid could
not help her age. But, at any rate, she ought to have
grown older beautifully, with charming dignity and

vivacity—in fact, she ought to have contrived to be old and young simultaneously. Or, in the alternative, she ought to have modestly retired into the country and lived on her memories and such money as she had not squandered. She had no right to be abroad.

At worst, she ought to have *looked* famous. And, because her name and fame and photographs as an emotional actress had been continually in the newspapers, therefore she ought to have been refined, delicate, distinguished and full of witty and gracious small-talk. That she had played the heroine of " Flower of the Heart " four hundred times, and the heroine of " The Grenadier " four hundred and fifty times, and the heroine of " The Wife's Ordeal " nearly five hundred times, made it incumbent upon her, in Edward Henry's subconscious opinion, to possess all the talents of a woman of the world and all the virgin freshness of a girl. Which shows how cruelly stupid Edward Henry was in comparison with the enlightened rest of us.

Why (he protested secretly), she was even tongue-tied!

" Glad to meet you, Mr Machin," she said awkwardly, in a weak voice, with a peculiar gesture as she shook hands. Then, a mechanical, nervous giggle; and then silence!

" Happy to make your acquaintance, sir," said Mr Seven Sachs, and the arch-famous American actor-author also lapsed into silence. But the silence of Mr Seven Sachs was different from Rose Euclid's. He was not shy. A dark and handsome, tranquil, youngish man, with a redoubtable square chin, delicately rounded at the corners, he strikingly resembled his own figure on the stage; and moreover, he seemed to regard silence as a natural and proper condition. He simply stood, in a graceful posture, with his muscles at ease, and waited. Mr Bryany, behind, seemed to be reduced in stature, and to have become apologetic for himself in the presence of greatness.

Still, Mr Bryany did say something.

Said Mr Bryany:

" Sorry to hear you've been seedy, Mr Machin! "

" Oh, yes! " Rose Euclid blurted out, as if shot. " It's very good of you to ask us up here."

Mr Seven Sachs concurred, adding that he hoped the illness was not serious.

Edward Henry said it was not.

" Won't you sit down, all of you? " said Edward Henry. " Miss—er—Euclid—"

They all sat down except Mr Bryany.

" Sit down, Bryany," said Edward Henry. " I'm glad to be able to return your hospitality at the Turk's Head."

This was a blow for Mr Bryany, who obviously felt it, and grew even more apologetic as he fumbled with assumed sprightliness at a chair.

" Fancy your being here all the time! " said he. " And me looked for you everywhere—"

" Mr Bryany," Seven Sachs interrupted him calmly, " have you got those letters off? "

" Not yet, sir."

Seven Sachs urbanely smiled. " I think we ought to get them off to-night."

" Certainly," agreed Mr Bryany with eagerness, and moved towards the door.

" Here's the key of my sitting-room," Seven Sachs stopped him, producing a key.

Mr Bryany, by a mischance catching Edward Henry's eye as he took the key, blushed.

In a moment Edward Henry was alone with the two silent celebrities.

"Well," said Edward Henry to himself, "I've let myself in for it this time—no mistake! What in the name of common sense am I doing here?"

Rose Euclid coughed and arranged the folds of her dress.

"I suppose, like most Americans, you see all the sights," said Edward Henry to Seven Sachs—the Five Towns is much visited by Americans. "What do you think of my dressing-gown?"

"Bully!" said Seven Sachs, with the faintest twinkle. And Rose Euclid gave the mechanical, nervous giggle.

"I can do with this chap," thought Edward Henry.

The gentleman-in-waiting entered with the supper menu.

"Thank heaven!" thought Edward Henry.

Rose Euclid, requested to order a supper after her own mind, stared vaguely at the menu for some moments, and then said that she did not know what to order.

"Artichokes?" Edward Henry blandly suggested.

Again the giggle, followed this time by a flush! And suddenly Edward Henry recognized in her the entrancing creature of fifteen years ago! Her head thrown back, she had put her left hand behind her and was groping with her long fingers for an object to touch. Having found at length the arm of another chair, she drew her fingers feverishly along its surface. He vividly remembered the gesture in "Flower of the Heart." She had used it with terrific effect at every grand emotional crisis of the play. He now recognized even her face!

"Did Mr Bryany tell you that my two boys are

coming up?" said she. " I left them behind to do
some telephoning for me."

"Delighted!" said Edward Henry. "The more
the merrier!"

And he hoped that he spoke true.

But her two boys!

"Mr Marrier—he's a young manager. I don't
know whether you know him; very, very talented.
And Carlo Trent."

"Same name as my dog," Edward Henry indis-
creetly murmured—and his fancy flew back to the
home he had quitted; and Wilkins's and everybody in
it grew transiently unreal to him.

"Delighted!" he said again.

He was relieved that her two boys were not her offspring. That, at least, was something gained.

"*You* know—the dramatist," said Rose Euclid,
apparently disappointed by the effect on Edward
Henry of the name of Carlo Trent.

"Really!" said Edward Henry. "I hope he won't
mind me being in a dressing-gown."

The gentleman-in-waiting, obsequiously restive,
managed to choose the supper himself. Leaving, he
reached the door just in time to hold it open for the
entrance of Mr Marrier and Mr Carlo Trent, who were
talking with noticeable freedom and emphasis, in an
accent which in the Five Towns is known as the " haw
haw," the "lah-di-dah" or the "Kensingtonian"
accent.

II

WITHIN ten minutes, within less than ten minutes,
Alderman Edward Henry Machin's supper-party at
Wilkins's was so wonderfully changed for the better

that Edward Henry might have been excused for not recognizing it as his own.

The service at Wilkins's, where they profoundly understood human nature, was very intelligent. Somewhere in a central bureau at Wilkins's sat a psychologist, who knew, for example, that a supper commanded on the spur of the moment must be produced instantly if it is to be enjoyed. Delay in these capricious cases impairs the ecstasy and therefore lessens the chance of other similar meals being commanded at the same establishment. Hence, no sooner had the gentleman-in-waiting disappeared with the order than certain esquires appeared with the limbs and body of a table which they set up in Edward Henry's drawing-room, and they covered the board with a damask cloth and half covered the damask cloth with flowers, glasses and plates, and laid a special private wire from the skirting-board near the hearth to a spot on the table beneath Edward Henry's left hand, so that he could summon courtiers on the slightest provocation with the minimum of exertion. Then immediately brown bread-and-butter and lemons and red-pepper came, followed by oysters, followed by bottles of pale wine, both still and sparkling. Thus, before the principal dishes had even begun to frizzle in the distant kitchens, the revellers were under the illusion that the entire supper was waiting just outside the door. . . .

Yes, they were revellers now! For the advent of her young men had transformed Rose Euclid, and Rose Euclid had transformed the general situation. At the table, Edward Henry occupied one side of it, Mr Seven Sachs occupied the side opposite, Mr Marrier, the very, very talented young manager, occupied the side to Edward Henry's left, and Rose Euclid and Carlo Trent together occupied the side to his right.

Trent and Marrier were each about thirty years of
age.   Trent, with a deep voice, had extremely lustrous
eyes, which eyes continually dwelt on Rose Euclid in
admiration.   Apparently, all she needed in this valley
was oysters and admiration, and she now had both in
unlimited quantities.

" Oysters are darlings," she said, as she swallowed
the first.

Carlo Trent kissed her hand, respectfully—for she
was old enough to be his mother.

" And you are the greatest tragic actress in the
world, Ra-ose! " said he in the Kensingtonian bass.

A few moments earlier Rose Euclid had whispered
to Edward Henry that Carlo Trent was the greatest
dramatic poet in the world.   She flowered now beneath
the sun of those dark lustrous eyes and the soft rain of
that admiration from the greatest dramatic poet in the
world.   It really did seem to Edward Henry that she
grew younger.   Assuredly she grew more girlish and
her voice improved.   And then the bottles began to
pop, and it was as though the action of uncorking wine
automatically uncorked hearts also.   Mr Seven Sachs,
sitting square and upright, smiled gaily at Edward
Henry across the gleaming table and raised a glass.
Little Marrier, who at nearly all times had a most
enthusiastic smile, did the same.   In the result five
glasses met over the central bed of chrysanthemums.
Edward Henry was happy.   Surrounded by enigmas—
for he had no conception whatever why Rose Euclid
had brought any of the three men to his table—he was
nevertheless uplifted.

As he looked about him, at the rich table, and at the
glittering chandelier overhead (albeit the lamps thereof
were inferior to his own), and at the expanses of soft
carpet, and at the silken-textured walls, and at the

THE THEATRICAL WORLD

voluptuous curtains, and at the couple of impeccable gentlemen in-waiting, and at Joseph, who knew his place behind his master's chair—he came to the justifiable conclusion that money was a marvellous thing, and the workings of commerce mysterious and beautiful. He had invented the Five Towns Thrift Club; working men and their wives in the Five Towns were paying their twopences and sixpences and shillings weekly into his club, and finding the transaction a real convenience—and lo! he was entertaining celebrities at Wilkins's.

For, mind you, they were celebrities. He knew Seven Sachs was a celebrity because he had verily seen him act—and act very well—in his own play, and because his name in letters a foot high had dominated all the hoardings of the Five Towns. As for Rose Euclid, could there be a greater celebrity? Such was the strange power of the popular legend concerning her that even now, despite the first fearful shock of disappointment, Edward Henry could not call her by her name without self-consciously stumbling over it, without a curious thrill. And further, he was revising his judgment of her, as well as lowering her age slightly. On coming into the room she had doubtless been almost as startled as himself, and her constrained muteness had been probably due to a guilty feeling in the matter of passing too open remarks to a friend about a perfect stranger's manner of eating artichokes. The which supposition flattered him. (By the way, he wished she had brought the young friend who had shared her amusement over his artichokes.) With regard to the other two men, he was quite ready to believe that Carlo Trent was the world's greatest dramatic poet, and to admit the exceeding talent of Mr Marrier as a theatrical manager. . . . In fact, unmistakable celebrities, one and all! He himself was a celebrity. A certain quality in the attitude of each of his guests showed clearly that they considered him a celebrity, and not only a celebrity but a card—Bryany must have been talking—and the conviction of this rendered him happy. His magnificent hunger rendered him still happier. And the reflection that Brindley owed him half-a-crown put a top on his bliss!

" I like your dressing-gown, Mr Machin," said Carlo Trent, suddenly, after his first spoonful of soup.

" Then I needn't apologize for it! " Edward Henry replied.

" It is the dressing-gown of my dreams," Carlo Trent went on.

" Well," said Edward Henry, " as we're on the subject, I like your shirt-front."

Carlo Trent was wearing a soft shirt. The other three shirts were all rigidly starched. Hitherto Edward Henry had imagined that a fashionable evening shirt should be, before aught else, bullet-proof. He now appreciated the distinction of a frilled and gently flowing breast-plate, especially when a broad purple eyeglass ribbon wandered across it. Rose Euclid gazed in modest transport at Carlo's chest.

" The colour," Carlo proceeded, ignoring Edward Henry's compliment, " the colour is inspiring. So is the texture. I have a woman's delight in textures. I could certainly produce better hexameters in such a dressing-gown."

Although Edward Henry, owing to an unfortunate hiatus in his education, did not know what a hexameter might be, he was artist enough to comprehend the effect of attire on creative work, for he had noticed that he himself could make more money in one necktie than in another, and he would instinctively take particular care in the morning choice of a cravat on days when he meditated a great coup.

" Why don't you get one? " Marrier suggested.

" Do you really think I could? " asked Carlo Trent, as if the possibility were shimmering far out of his reach like a rainbow.

" Rather! " smiled Marrier. " I don't mind laying a fiver that Mr Machin's dressing-gown came from Drook's in Old Bond Street." But instead of saying " Old " he said " Ehoold."

" It did," Edward Henry admitted.

Mr Marrier beamed with satisfaction.

" Drook's, you say," murmured Carlo Trent. " Old Bond Street," and wrote down the information on his shirt cuff.

Rose Euclid watched him write.

" Yes, Carlo," said she. " But don't you think we'd better begin to talk about the theatre? You haven't told me yet if you got hold of Longay on the 'phone."

" Of course we got hold of him," said Marrier. " He agrees with me that ' The Intellectual ' is a better name for it."

Rose Euclid clapped her hands.

" I'm so glad! " she cried. " Now what do *you* think of it as a name, Mr Machin—' The Intellectual Theatre '? You see it's most important we should settle on the name, isn't it? "

It is no exaggeration to say that Edward Henry felt a wave of cold in the small of his back, and also a sinking away of the nevertheless quite solid chair on which he sat. He had more than the typical Englishman's sane distrust of that morbid word ' Intellectual.' His attitude towards it amounted to active dislike. If ever he used it, he would on no account use it alone;

he would say, " Intellectual and all that sort of thing! " with an air of pushing violently away from him everything that the phrase implied. The notion of baptizing a theatre with the fearsome word horrified him. Still, he had to maintain his nerve and his repute. So he drank some champagne, and smiled nonchalantly as the imperturbable duellist smiles while the pistols are being examined.

" Well—" he murmured.

" You see," Marrier broke in, with the smile ecstatic, almost dancing on his chair. " There's no use in compromise. Compromise is and always has been the curse of this country. The unintellectual drahma is dead—dead. Naoobody can deny that. All the box-offices in the West are proclaiming it—"

" Should you call your play intellectual, Mr Sachs? " Edward Henry inquired across the table.

" I scarcely know," said Mr Seven Sachs, calmly. " I know I've played it myself fifteen hundred and two times, and that's saying nothing of my three subsidiary companies on the road."

" What *is* Mr Sachs's play ?" asked Carlo Trent, fretfully.

" Don't you know, Carlo? " Rose Euclid patted him. " ' Overheard.' "

" Oh! I've never seen it."

" But it was on all the hoardings! "

" I never read the hoardings," said Carlo. " Is it in verse? "

" No, it isn't," Mr Seven Sachs briefly responded. " But I've made over six hundred thousand dollars out of it."

" Then of course it's intellectual! " asserted Mr Marrier, positively. " That proves it. I'm very sorry I've not seen it either; but it must be intellectual.

The day of the unintellectual drahma is over. The people won't have it. We must have faith in the people, and we can't show our faith better than by calling our theatre by its proper name—'The Intellectual Theatre'!"

(" *His* theatre!" thought Edward Henry. "What's he got to do with it?")

" I don't know that I'm so much in love with your 'Intellectual,'" muttered Carlo Trent.

" *Aren't* you?" protested Rose Euclid, shocked.

" Of course I'm not," said Carlo. "I told you before, and I tell you now, that there's only one name for the theatre—'The Muses' Theatre!'"

" Perhaps you're right!" Rose agreed, as if a swift revelation had come to her. "Yes, you're right."

(" She'll make a cheerful sort of partner for a fellow," thought Edward Henry, "if she's in the habit of changing her mind like that every thirty seconds." His appetite had gone. He could only drink.)

" Naturally, I'm right! Aren't we going to open with my play, and isn't my play in verse? . . . I'm sure you'll agree with me, Mr Machin, that there is no real drama except the poetical drama."

Edward Henry was entirely at a loss. Indeed, he was drowning in his dressing-gown, so favourable to the composition of hexameters.

" Poetry . . . " he vaguely breathed.

" Yes, sir," said Carlo Trent. "Poetry."

" I've never read any poetry in my life," said Edward Henry, like a desperate criminal. "Not a line."

Whereupon Carlo Trent rose up from his seat, and his eyeglasses dangled in front of him.

" Mr Machin," said he with the utmost benevolence.

" This is the most interesting thing I've ever come across. Do you know, you're precisely the man I've always been wanting to meet? . . . The virgin mind. The clean slate. . . . Do you know, you're precisely the man that it's my ambition to write for? "

" It's very kind of you," said Edward Henry, feebly; beaten, and consciously beaten.

(He thought miserably:

" What would Nellie think if she saw me in this gang? ")

Carlo Trent went on, turning to Rose Euclid:

" Rose, will you recite those lines of Nashe? "

Rose Euclid began to blush.

" That bit you taught me the day before yesterday? "

" Only the three lines! No more! They are the very essence of poetry—poetry at its purest. We'll see the effect of them on Mr Machin. We'll just see. It's the ideal opportunity to test my theory. Now, there's a good girl! "

" Oh! I can't. I'm too nervous," stammered Rose.

" You can, and you must," said Carlo, gazing at her in homage. " Nobody in the world can say them as well as you can. Now! "

Rose Euclid stood up.

" One moment," Carlo stopped her. " There's too much light. We can't do with all this light. Mr Machin—do you mind? "

A wave of the hand and all the lights were extinguished, save a lamp on the mantelpiece, and in the disconcertingly darkened room Rose Euclid turned her face towards the ray from this solitary silk-shaded globe.

Her hand groped out behind her, found the table-cloth and began to scratch it agitatedly. She lifted her head. She was the actress, impressive and subjugating, and Edward Henry felt her power. Then she intoned:

> " Brightness falls from the air ;
> Queens have died young and fair ;
> Dust hath closed Helen's eye."

And she ceased and sat down. There was a silence.

" *Bravo !* " murmured Carlo Trent.

" Bra*vo !* " murmured Mr Marrier.

Edward Henry in the gloom caught Mr Seven Sachs's unalterable observant smile across the table.

" Well, Mr Machin? " said Carlo Trent.

Edward Henry had felt a tremor at the vibrations of Rose Euclid's voice. But the words she uttered had set up no clear image in his mind, unless it might be of some solid body falling from the air, or of a young woman named Helen, walking along Trafalgar Road, Bursley, on a dusty day, and getting the dust in her eyes. He knew not what to answer.

" Is that all there is of it? " he asked at length.

Carlo Trent said:

" It's from Thomas Nashe's ' Song in Time of Pestilence.' The closing lines of the verse are:

> " ' I am sick, I must die—
> Lord, have mercy on me !' "

" Well," said Edward Henry, recovering, " I rather like the end. I think the end's very appropriate."

Mr Seven Sachs choked over his wine, and kept on choking.

III

MR MARRIER was the first to recover from this blow to the prestige of poetry. Or perhaps it would be more honest to say that Mr Marrier had suffered no inconvenience from the *contretemps*. His apparent gleeful zest in life had not been impaired. He was a born optimist, of an extreme type unknown beyond the circumferences of theatrical circles.

"I *say*," he emphasized, "I've got an ideah. We ought to be photographed like that. Do you no end of good." He glanced encouragingly at Rose Euclid. "Don't you see it in the illustrated papers? 'A prayvate supper-party at Wilkins's Hotel. Miss Ra-ose Euclid reciting verse at a discussion of the plans for her new theatre in Piccadilly Circus. The figures, reading from left to right, are, Mr Seven Sachs, the famous actor-author, Miss Rose Euclid, Mr Carlo Trent, the celebrated dramatic poet, Mr Alderman Machin, the well-known Midlands capitalist,' and so on!" Mr Marrier repeated, "and so on."

"It's a notion," said Rose Euclid, dreamily.

"But how *can* we be photographed?" Carlo Trent demanded with irritation.

"Perfectly easy."

"Now?"

"In ten minutes. I know a photographer in Brook Street."

"Would he come at once?" Carlo Trent frowned at his watch.

"Rather!" Mr Marrier gaily soothed him, as he went over to the telephone. And Mr Marrier's bright, boyish face radiated forth the assurance that nothing in all his existence had more completely filled him with sincere joy than this enterprise of procuring a photograph of the party. Even in giving the photographer's number—he was one of those prodigies who remember infallibly all telephone numbers—his voice seemed to gloat upon his project.

(And while Mr Marrier, having obtained communication with the photographer, was saying gloriously into the telephone: " Yes, Wilkins's. No. Quite private. I've got Miss Rose Euclid here, and Mr Seven Sachs"— while Mr Marrier was thus proceeding with his list of star attractions, Edward Henry was thinking:

" ' *Her* new theatre '—now! It was ' his ' a few minutes back! . . . ' The well-known Midlands capitalist,' eh? Oh! Ah! ")

He drank again. He said to himself: " I've had all I can digest of this beastly balloony stuff." (He meant the champagne.) " If I finish the glass I'm bound to have a bad night." And he finished the glass, and planked it down firmly on the table.

" Well," he remarked aloud cheerfully. " If we're to be photographed, I suppose we shall want a bit more light on the subject."

Joseph sprang to the switches.

" Please! " Carlo Trent raised a protesting hand.

The switches were not turned. In the beautiful dimness the greatest tragic actress in the world and the greatest dramatic poet in the world gazed at each other, seeking and finding solace in mutual esteem.

" I suppose it wouldn't do to call it the Euclid Theatre? " Rose questioned casually, without moving her eyes.

" Splendid! " cried Mr Marrier from the telephone.

" It all depends whether there are enough mathematical students in London to fill the theatre for a run," said Edward Henry.

" Oh! D'you think so? " murmured Rose, surprised and vaguely puzzled.

At that instant Edward Henry might have rushed from the room and taken the night-mail back to the Five Towns, and never any more have ventured into the perils of London, if Carlo Trent had not turned his head, and signified by a curt, reluctant laugh that he saw the joke. For Edward Henry could no longer depend on Mr Seven Sachs. Mr Seven Sachs had to take the greatest pains to keep the muscles of his face in strict order. The slightest laxity with them—and he would have been involved in another and more serious suffocation.

" No," said Carlo Trent, " ' The Muses' Theatre ' is the only possible title. There is money in the poetical drama." He looked hard at Edward Henry, as though to stare down the memory of the failure of Nashe's verse. " I don't want money. I hate the thought of money. But money is the only proof of democratic appreciation, and that is what I need, and what every artist needs. . . . Don't you think there's money in the poetical drama, Mr Sachs? "

" Not in America," said Mr Sachs. " London is a queer place."

" Look at the runs of Stephen Phillips's plays! "

" Yes. . . . I only reckon to know America."

" Look at what Pilgrim's made out of Shakspere."

" I thought you were talking about poetry," said Edward Henry too hastily.

" And isn't Shakspere poetry? " Carlo Trent challenged.

" Well, I suppose if you put it in that way, he *is !* "

Edward Henry cautiously admitted, humbled. He was under the disadvantage of never having either seen or read "Shakspere." His sure instinct had always warned him against being drawn into "Shakspere."

"And has Miss Euclid ever done anything finer than Constance?"

"I don't know," Edward Henry pleaded.

"Why—Miss Euclid in ' King John '—"

"I never saw ' King John,' " said Edward Henry.

"*Do you mean to say*," expostulated Carlo Trent in italics, "*that you never saw Rose Euclid as Constance ?*"

And Edward Henry, shaking his abashed head, perceived that his life had been wasted.

Carlo, for a few moments, grew reflective and softer.

"It's one of my earliest and most precious boyish memories," he murmured, as he examined the ceiling. "It must have been in eighteen—"

Rose Euclid abandoned the ice with which she had just been served, and by a single gesture drew Carlo's attention away from the ceiling, and towards the fact that it would be clumsy on his part to indulge further in the chronology of her career. She began to blush again.

Mr Marrier, now back at the table after a successful expedition, beamed over his ice:

"It was your ' Constance ' that led to your friend-ship with the Countess of Chell, wasn't it, Ra-ose? You know," he turned to Edward Henry, " Miss Euclid and the Countess are virry intimate."

"Yes, I know," said Edward Henry.

Rose Euclid continued to blush. Her agitated hand scratched the back of the chair behind her.

"Even Sir John Pilgrim admits I can act Shakspere," she said in a thick mournful voice, looking at the cloth as she pronounced the august name of the head of the dramatic profession. "It may surprise you to know, Mr Machin, that about a month ago, after he'd quarrelled with Selina Gregory, Sir John asked me if I'd care to star with him on his Shaksperean tour round the world next spring, and I said I would if he'd include Carlo's poetical play, 'The Orient Pearl,' and he wouldn't! No, he wouldn't! And now he's got little Cora Pryde! She isn't twenty-two, and she's going to play Juliet! Can you imagine such a thing! As if a mere girl could play Juliet!"

Carlo observed the mature actress with deep satisfaction, proud of her, and proud also of himself.

"I wouldn't go with Pilgrim now," exclaimed Rose, passionately, "not if he went down on his knees to me!"

"And nothing on earth would induce me to let him have 'The Orient Pearl'!" Carlo Trent asseverated with equal passion. "He's lost that for ever!" he added grimly. "It won't be he who'll collar the profits out of that! It'll just be ourselves!"

"Not if he went down on his knees to me!" Rose was repeating to herself with fervency.

The calm of despair took possession of Edward Henry. He felt that he must act immediately—he knew his own mood, by long experience. Exploring the pockets of the dressing-gown which had aroused the longing of the greatest dramatic poet in the world, he discovered in one of them precisely the piece of apparatus he required—namely, a slip of paper suitable for writing. It was a carbon duplicate of the bill for the dressing-gown, and showed the word "Drook" in massive printed black, and the figures £4, 4s. in faint blue. He drew a pencil from his waistcoat and inscribed on the paper:

" Go out, and then come back in a couple of minutes and tell me someone wants to speak to me urgently in the next room."

With a minimum of ostentation he gave the document to Joseph, who, evidently well trained under Sir Nicholas, vanished into the next room before attempting to read it.

" I hope," said Edward Henry to Carlo Trent, " that this money-making play is reserved for the new theatre? "

" Utterly," said Carlo Trent.

" With Miss Euclid in the principal part? "

" Rather! " sang Mr Marrier. " Rather! "

" I shall never, never appear at any other theatre, Mr Machin! " said Rose, with tragic emotion, once more feeling with her fingers along the back of her chair. " So I hope the building will begin at once. In less than six months we ought to open."

" Easily! " sang the optimist.

Joseph returned to the room, and sought his master's attention in a whisper.

" What is it? " Edward Henry asked irritably. " Speak up! "

" A gentleman wishes to know if he can speak to you in the next room, sir."

" Well, he can't."

" He said it was urgent, sir."

Scowling, Edward Henry rose. " Excuse me," he said. " I won't be a moment. Help yourselves to the liqueurs. You chaps can go, I fancy." The last remark was addressed to the gentlemen-in-waiting.

The next room was the vast bedroom with two beds in it. Edward Henry closed the door carefully, and drew the *portière* across it. Then he listened. No sound penetrated from the scene of the supper.

" There *is* a telephone in this room, isn't there? " he said to Joseph. " Oh, yes, there it is! Well, you can go."

" Yes, sir."

Edward Henry sat down on one of the beds by the hook on which hung the telephone. And he cogitated upon the characteristics of certain members of the party which he had just left. " I'm a ' virgin mind,' am I? " he thought. " I'm a ' clean slate' ? Well! . . . Their notion of business is to begin by discussing the name of the theatre! And they haven't even taken up the option! Ye gods! ' Intellectual '! ' Muses '! ' The Orient Pearl.' And she's fifty—that I swear! Not a word yet of real business—not one word! He may be a poet. I daresay he is. He's a conceited ass. Why, even Bryany was better than that lot. Only Sachs turned Bryany out. I like Sachs. But he won't open his mouth. . . . ' Capitalist '! Well, they spoilt my appetite, and I hate champagne! . . . The poet hates money. . . . No, he ' hates the thought of money.' And she's changing her mind the whole blessed time! A month ago she'd have gone over to Pilgrim, and the poet too, like a house-a-fire! . . . Photographed indeed! The bally photographer will be here in a minute! . . . They take me for a fool! . . . Or don't they know any better? . . . Anyhow, I am a fool. . . . I must teach 'em summat!"

He seized the telephone.

" Hello!" he said into it. " I want you to put me on to the drawing-room of Suite No. 48, please. Who? Oh, me! I'm in the bedroom of Suite No. 48. Machin, Alderman Machin. Thanks. That's all right."

He waited. Then he heard Marrier's Kensingtonian voice in the telephone asking who he was.

" Is that Mr Machin's room? " he continued, imitating with a broad farcical effect the acute Kensingtonianism of Mr Marrier's tones. " Is Miss Ra-ose Euclid there? Oh! She is! Well, you tell her that Sir John Pilgrim's private secretary wishes to speak to her? Thanks. All right. *I'*ll hold the line."

A pause. Then he heard Rose's voice in the telephone, and he resumed:

" Miss Euclid? Yes. Sir John Pilgrim. I beg pardon! Banks? Oh, *Banks !* No, I'm not Banks. I suppose you mean my predecessor. He's left. Left last week. No, I don't know why. Sir John instructs me to ask if you and Mr Trent could lunch with him to-morrow at wun-thirty? What? Oh! at his house. Yes. I mean flat. Flat! I said flat. You think you could? "

Pause. He could hear her calling to Carlo Trent.

" Thanks. No, I don't know exactly," he went on again. " But I know the arrangement with Miss Pryde is broken off. And Sir John wants a play at once. He told me that! At once! Yes. ' The Orient Pearl.' That was the title. At the Royal first, and then the world's tour. Fifteen months at least in all, so I gathered. Of course I don't speak officially. Well, many thanks. Saoo good of you. I'll tell Sir John it's arranged. One-thirty to-morrow. Good-bye! "

He hung up the telephone. The excited, eager, effusive tones of Rose Euclid remained in his ears. Aware of a strange phenomenon on his forehead, he touched it. He was perspiring.

" I'll teach 'em a thing or two," he muttered.

And again:

" Serves her right. . . . Never, never appear at any other theatre, Mr Machin! ' . . . ' Bended knees! ' . . . ' Utterly! ' . . . Cheerful partners! Oh! cheerful partners! "

He returned to his supper-party. Nobody said a word about the telephoning. But Rose Euclid and Carlo Trent looked even more like conspirators than they did before; and Mr Marrier's joy in life seemed to be just the least bit diminished.

" So sorry! " Edward Henry began hurriedly, and, without consulting the poet's wishes, subtly turned on all the lights. " Now, don't you think we'd better discuss the question of taking up the option? You know, it expires on Friday."

" No," said Rose Euclid, girlishly. " It expires to-morrow. That's why it's so *fortunate* we got hold of you to-night."

" But Mr Bryany told me Friday. And the date was clear enough on the copy of the option he gave me."

" A mistake of copying," beamed Mr Marrier. " However, it's all right."

" Well," observed Edward Henry with heartiness, " I don't mind telling you that for sheer calm coolness you take the cake. However, as Mr Marrier so ably says, it's all right. Now I understand if I go into this affair I can count on you absolutely, and also on Mr Trent's services." He tried to talk as if he had been diplomatizing with actresses and poets all his life.

" A—absolutely! " said Rose.

And Mr Carlo Trent nodded.

" You Iscariots! " Edward Henry addressed them, in the silence of the brain, behind his smile. " You Iscariots! "

The photographer arrived with certain cases, and

at once Rose Euclid and Carlo Trent began instinctively to pose.

"To think," Edward Henry pleasantly reflected,
"that they are hugging themselves because Sir John
Pilgrim's secretary happened to telephone just while
I was out of the room!"

CHAPTER V

MR SACHS TALKS

I

IT was the sudden flash of the photographer's magnesium light, plainly felt by him through his closed lids, that somehow instantly inspired Edward Henry to a definite and ruthless line of action. He opened his eyes and beheld the triumphant group, and the photographer himself, victorious over even the triumphant, in a superb pose that suggested that all distinguished mankind in his presence was naught but food for the conquering camera. The photographer smiled indulgently, and his smile said: " Having been photographed by me, you have each of you reached the summit of your career. Be content. Retire! Die! Destiny is accomplished."

" Mr Machin," said Rose Euclid, " I do believe your eyes were shut! "

" So do I! " Edward Henry curtly agreed.

" But you'll spoil the group! "

" Not a bit of it! " said Edward Henry. " I always shut my eyes when I'm being photographed by flash-light. I open my mouth instead. So long as something's open, what does it matter? "

The truth was that only in the nick of time had he, by a happy miracle of ingenuity, invented a way of ruining the photograph. The absolute necessity for its ruin had presented itself to him rather late in the proceedings, when the photographer had already finished arranging the hands and shoulders of every-body in an artistic pattern. The photograph had to be spoilt for the imperative reason that his mother, though she never read a newspaper, did as a fact look at a picture-newspaper, *The Daily Film*, which from pride she insisted on paying for out of her own purse, at the rate of one halfpenny a day. Now *The Daily Film* specialized in theatrical photographs, on which it said it spent large sums of money: and Edward Henry in a vision had seen the historic group in a future issue of the *Film*. He had also, in the same vision, seen his mother conning the said issue, and the sardonic curve of her lips as she recognized her son therein, and he had even heard her dry, cynical, contemptuous exclamation: " Bless us! " He could never have looked squarely in his mother's face again if that group had appeared in her chosen organ! Her silent and grim scorn would have crushed his self-conceit to a miserable, hopeless pulp. Hence his resolve to render the photograph impossible.

" Perhaps I'd better take another one? " the photo-grapher suggested, " though I think Mr—er—Machin was all right." At the supreme crisis the man had been too busy with his fireworks to keep a watch on every separate eye and mouth of the assemblage.

" Of course I was all right! " said Edward Henry, almost with brutality. " Please take that thing away, as quickly as you can. We have business to attend to."

" Yes, sir," agreed the photographer, no longer victorious.

Edward Henry rang his bell, and two gentlemen-in-waiting arrived.

" Clear this table immediately! "

The tone of the command startled everybody except

the gentlemen-in-waiting and Mr Seven Sachs. Rose
Euclid gave vent to her nervous giggle. The poet and
Mr Marrier tried to appear detached and dignified, and
succeeded in appearing guiltily confused—for which
they contemned themselves. Despite this volition,
the glances of all three of them too clearly signified
" This capitalist must be humoured. He has an unlimited supply of actual cash, and therefore he has
the right to be peculiar. Moreover, we know that he
is a card." . . . And, curiously, Edward Henry himself was deriving great force of character from the
simple reflection that he had indeed a lot of money,
real available money, his to do utterly as he liked with
it, hidden in a secret place in that very room. " I'll
show 'em what's what! " he privately mused. " Celebrities or not, I'll show 'em! If they think they can
come it over me—! "

It was, I regret to say, the state of mind of a
bully. Such is the noxious influence of excessive
coin!

He reproached the greatest actress and the greatest
dramatic poet for deceiving him, and quite ignored
the nevertheless fairly obvious fact that he had first
deceived them.

" Now then," he began, with something of the
pomposity of a chairman at a directors' meeting, as
soon as the table had been cleared and the room emptied
of gentlemen-in-waiting and photographer and photo-
graphic apparatus, " let us see exactly where we
stand."

He glanced specially at Rose Euclid, who with
an air of deep business acumen returned the
glance.

" Yes," she eagerly replied, as one seeking after
righteousness. " *Do* let's see."

" The option must be taken up to-morrow. Good! That's clear. It came rather casual-like, but it's now clear. £4500 has to be paid down to buy the existing building on the land and so on. . . . Eh? "

" Yes. Of course Mr Bryany told you all that, didn't he? " said Rose, brightly.

" Mr Bryany did tell me," Edward Henry admitted sternly. " But if Mr Bryany can make a mistake in the day of the week he might make a mistake in a few noughts at the end of a sum of money."

Suddenly Mr Seven Sachs startled them all by emerging from his silence with the words:

" The figure is O.K."

Instinctively Edward Henry waited for more; but no more came. Mr Seven Sachs was one of those rare and disconcerting persons who do not keep on talking after they have finished. He resumed his tranquillity, he re-entered into his silence, with no symptom of self-consciousness, entirely cheerful and at ease. And Edward Henry was aware of his observant and steady gaze. Edward Henry said to himself: " This man is expecting me to behave in a remarkable way. Bryany has been telling him all about me, and he is waiting to see if I really am as good as my reputation. I have just got to be as good as my reputation! " He looked up at the electric chandelier, almost with regret that it was not gas. One cannot light one's cigarette by twisting a hundred-pound bank-note and sticking it into an electric chandelier. Moreover, there were some thousands of matches on the table. Still further, he had done the cigarette-lighting trick once for all. A first-class card must not repeat himself.

" This money," Edward Henry proceeded, " has

to be paid to Slossons, Lord Woldo's solicitors, to-morrow, Wednesday, rain or shine? " He finished the phrase on a note of interrogation, and as nobody offered any reply, he rapped on the table, and repeated, half-menacingly: " Rain or shine! "

" Yes," said Rose Euclid, leaning timidly forward and taking a cigarette from a gold case that lay on the table. All her movements indicated an earnest desire to be thoroughly business-like.

" So that, Miss Euclid," Edward Henry continued impressively, but with a wilful touch of incredulity, " you are in a position to pay your share of this money to-morrow? "

"Certainly! " said Miss Euclid. And it was as if she had said, aggrieved: " Can you doubt my honour? "

" To-morrow morning? "

" Ye-es."

" That is to say, to-morrow morning you will have £2250 in actual cash—coin, notes—actually in your possession? "

Miss Euclid's disengaged hand was feeling out behind her again for some surface upon which to express its emotion and hers.

" Well—" she stopped, flushing.

(" These people are astounding," Edward Henry reflected, like a god. " She's not got the money. I knew it! ")

" It's like this, Mr Machin," Marrier began.

" Excuse me, Mr Marrier," Edward Henry turned on him, determined if he could to eliminate the opti-mism from that beaming face. " Any friend of Miss Euclid's is welcome here, but you've already talked about this theatre as ' ours,' and I just want to know where you come in."

" Where I come in? " Marrier smiled, absolutely unperturbed. " Miss Euclid has appointed me general manajah."

" At what salary, if it isn't a rude question?"

" Oh! We haven't settled details yet. You see the theatre isn't built yet."

" True! " said Edward Henry. " I was forgetting! I was thinking for the moment that the theatre was all ready and going to be opened to-morrow night with ' The Orient Pearl.' Have you had much experience of managing theatres, Mr Marrier? I suppose you have."

" Eho yes! " exclaimed Mr Marrier. " I began life as a lawyah's clerk, but—"

" So did I," Edward Henry interjected.

" How interesting! " Rose Euclid murmured with fervency, after puffing forth a long shaft of smoke.

" However, I threw it up," Marrier went on.

" I didn't," said Edward Henry. " I got thrown out! "

Strange that in that moment he was positively proud of having been dismissed from his first situation! Strange that all the company, too, thought the better of him for having been dismissed! Strange that Marrier regretted that he also had not been dismissed! But so it was. The possession of much ready money emits a peculiar effluence in both directions—back to the past, forward into the future.

" I threw it up," said Marrier, " because the stage had an irresistible attraction for me. I'd been stage-manajah for an amateur company, you knaoo. I found a shop as stage-manajah of a company touring ' Uncle Tom's Cabin.' I stuck to that for six years, and then I threw that up too. Then I've managed one of Miss Euclid's provincial tours. And since I met our friend Trent I've had the chance to show what my ideas about play-producing really are. I fancy my production of Trent's one-act play won't be forgotten in a hurry. . . . You know—' The Nymph '? You read about it, didn't you? "

" I did not," said Edward Henry. " How long did it run? "

" Oh! It didn't run. It wasn't put on for a run. It was part of one of the Sunday night shows of the Play-Producing Society, at the Court Theatre. Most intellectual people in London, you know. No such audience anywhere else in the wahld! " His rather chubby face glistened and shimmered with enthusiasm. " You bet! " he added. " But that was only by the way. My real game is management—general management. And I think I may say I know what it is? "

" Evidently! " Edward Henry concurred. " But shall you have to give up any other engagement in order to take charge of The Muses' Theatre? Because if so—"

Mr Marrier replied:

" No."

Edward Henry observed:

" Oh! "

" But," said Marrier, reassuringly, " if necessary I would throw up any engagement—you understand me, any—in favour of The Intellectual Theatah—as I prefer to call it. You see, as I own part of the option—"

By these last words Edward Henry was confounded, even to muteness.

" I forgot to mention, Mr Machin," said Rose Euclid, very quickly. " I've disposed of a quarter of my half of the option to Mr Marrier. He fully agreed with me it was better that he should have a proper interest in the theatre."

" Why of course! " cried Mr Marrier, uplifted.

" Let me see," said Edward Henry, after a long breath, " a quarter. That makes it that you have to find £562, 10s. to-morrow, Mr Marrier."

" Yes."

" To-morrow morning—you'll be all right? "

" Well, I won't swear for the morning, but I shall turn up with the stuff in the afternoon, anyhow.   I've two men in tow, and one of them's a certainty."

" Which? "

" I don't know which," said Mr Marrier.   " How-evah, you may count on yours sincerely, Mr Machin."

There was a pause.

" Perhaps I ought to tell you," Rose Euclid smiled, " perhaps I ought to tell you that Mr Trent is also one of our partners.   He has taken another quarter of my half."

Edward Henry controlled himself.

" Excellent! " said he, with glee.   " Mr Trent's money all ready, too? "

" I am providing most of it—temporarily," said Rose Euclid.

" I see.   Then I understand you have your three quarters of £2250 all ready in hand."

She glanced at Mr Seven Sachs.

" Have I, Mr Sachs? "

And Mr Sachs, after an instant's hesitation, bowed in assent.

" Mr Sachs is not exactly going into the specula-tion, but he is lending us money on the security of our interests.   That's the way to put it, isn't it, Mr Sachs? "

Mr Sachs once more bowed.

And Edward Henry exclaimed:

" Now I really do see! "

He gave one glance across the table at Mr Seven Sachs, as who should say: " And have you too allowed yourself to be dragged into this affair? I really thought you were cleverer. Don't you agree with me that we're both fools of the most arrant description? " And under that brief glance Mr Seven Sachs's calm deserted him as it had never deserted him on the stage, where for over fifteen hundred nights he had withstood the menace of revolvers, poison, and female treachery through three hours and four acts without a single moment of agitation.

Apparently Miss Rose Euclid could exercise a siren's charm upon nearly all sorts of men. But Edward Henry knew one sort of men upon whom she could not exercise it—namely, the sort of men who are born and bred in the Five Towns. His instinctive belief in the Five Towns as the sole cradle of hard practical common sense was never stronger than just now. You might by wiles get the better of London and America, but not of the Five Towns. If Rose Euclid were to go around and about the Five Towns trying to do the siren business, she would pretty soon discover that she was up against something rather special in the way of human nature!

Why, the probability was that these three—Rose Euclid (only a few hours since a glorious name and legend to him), Carlo Trent, and Mr Marrier—could not at that moment produce even ten pounds between them! . . . And Marrier offering to lay fivers! . . . He scornfully pitied them. And he was not altogether without pity for Seven Sachs, who had doubtless succeeded in life by sheer accident and knew no more than an infant what to do with his too-easily-earned money.

II

" WELL," said Edward Henry, " shall I tell you what I've decided? "

" Please do! " Rose Euclid entreated him.

" I've decided to make you a present of my half of the option."

" But aren't you going in with us? " exclaimed Rose, horror-struck.

" No, madam."

" But Mr Bryany told us positively you were! He said it was all arranged! "

" Mr Bryany ought to be more careful," said Edward Henry. " If he doesn't mind he'll be telling a downright lie some day."

" But you bought half the option! "

" Well," said Edward Henry, reasoning. " What *is* an option? What does it mean? It means you are free to take something or leave it. I'm leaving it."

" But why? " demanded Mr Marrier, gloomier.

Carlo Trent played with his eyeglasses and said not a word.

" Why? " Edward Henry replied. " Simply because I feel I'm not fitted for the job. I don't know enough. I don't understand. I shouldn't go the right way about the affair. For instance, I should never have guessed by myself that it was the proper thing to settle the name of the theatre before you'd got the lease of the land you're going to build it on. Then I'm old-fashioned. I hate leaving things to the last moment; but seemingly there's only one proper moment in these theatrical affairs, and that's the very last. I'm afraid there'd be too much trusting in providence for my taste. I believe in trusting in providence, but I can't bear to see providence overworked. And I've never even tried to be intellectual, and I'm a bit frightened of poetry plays—"

" But you've not read my play! " Carlo Trent mutteringly protested.

" That is so," admitted Edward Henry.

" Will you read it? "

" Mr Trent," said Edward Henry, " I'm not so young as I was."

" We're ruined! " sighed Rose Euclid, with a tragic gesture.

" Ruined? " Edward Henry took her up smiling. " Nobody is ruined who knows where he can get a square meal. Do you mean to tell me you don't know where you're going to lunch to-morrow? " And he looked hard at her.

It was a blow. She blenched under it.

" Oh, yes," she said, with her giggle, " I know that."

(" Well you just don't! " he answered her in his heart. " You think you're going to lunch with John Pilgrim. And you aren't. And it serves you right! ")

" Besides," he continued aloud, " how can you say you're ruined when I'm making you a present of something that I paid £100 for? "

" But where am I to find the other half of the money —£2250? " she burst out. " We were depending absolutely on you for it. If I don't get it, the option will be lost, and the option's very valuable."

" All the easier to find the money then! "

" What? In less than twenty-four hours? It can't be done. I couldn't get it in all London."

" Mr Marrier will get it for you . . . one of his certainties! " Edward Henry smiled in the Five Towns manner.

" I *might*, you knaoo! " said Marrier, brightening to full hope in the fraction of a second.

But Rose Euclid only shook her head.

" Mr Seven Sachs, then? " Edward Henry suggested.

" I should have been delighted," said Mr Sachs, with the most perfect gracious tranquillity. " But I cannot find another £2250 to-morrow."

" I shall just speak to that Mr Bryany! " said Rose Euclid, in the accents of homicide.

" I think you ought to," Edward Henry concurred. " But that won't help things. I feel a little responsible, especially to a lady. You have a quarter of the whole option left in your hands, Miss Euclid. I'll pay you at the same rate as Bryany sold to me. I gave £100 for half. Your quarter is therefore worth £50. Well, I'll pay you £50."

" And then what? "

" Then let the whole affair slide."

" But that won't help me to my theatre! " Rose Euclid said, pouting. She was now decidedly less unhappy than her face pretended, because Edward Henry had reminded her of Sir John Pilgrim, and she had dreams of world-triumphs for herself and for Carlo Trent's play. She was almost glad to be rid of all the worry of the horrid little prospective theatre.

" I have bank-notes," cooed Edward Henry, softly.

Her head sank.

Edward Henry rose in the incomparable yellow dressing-gown and walked to and fro a little, and then from his secret store he produced a bundle of notes, and counted out five tens and, coming behind Rose, stretched out his arm, and laid the treasure on the table in front of her under the brilliant chandelier.

" I don't want you to feel you have anything against me," he cooed still more softly.

Silence reigned. Edward Henry resumed his chair, and gazed at Rose Euclid. She was quite a dozen years older than his wife, and she looked more than a dozen years older. She had no fixed home, no husband, no children, no regular situation. She accepted the homage of young men, who were cleverer than herself save in one important respect. She was always in and out of restaurants and hotels and express trains. She was always committing hygienic indiscretions. She could not refrain from a certain girlishness which, having regard to her years, her waist and her complexion, was ridiculous. His wife would have been afraid of her and would have despised her, simultaneously. She was coarsened by the continual gaze of the gaping public. No two women could possibly be more utterly dissimilar than Rose Euclid and the cloistered Nellie. . . . And yet, as Rose Euclid's hesitant fingers closed on the bank-notes with a gesture of relief, Edward Henry had an agreeable and kindly sensation that all women were alike, after all, in the need of a shield, a protection, a strong and generous male hand. He was touched by the spectacle of Rose Euclid, as naïve as any young lass when confronted by actual bank-notes; and he was touched also by the thought of Nellie and the children afar off, existing in comfort and peace, but utterly, wistfully, dependent on himself.

" And what about me? " growled Carlo Trent.

" You! "

The fellow was only a poet. He negligently dropped him five fivers, his share of the option's value.

Mr Marrier said nothing, but his eye met Edward Henry's, and in silence five fivers were meted out to

Mr Marrier also. . . . It was so easy to delight these persons who apparently seldom set eyes on real ready money.

" You might sign receipts, all of you, just as a matter of form," said Edward Henry.

A little later the three associates were off.

" As we're both in the hotel, Mr Sachs," said Edward Henry, " you might stay for a chat and a drink."

Mr Seven Sachs politely agreed.

Edward Henry accompanied the trio of worshippers and worshipped to the door of his suite, but no further, because of his dressing-gown. Rose Euclid had assumed a resplendent opera-cloak. They rang imperially for the lift. Lackeys bowed humbly before them. They spoke of taxi-cabs and other luxuries. They were perfectly at home in the grandeur of the hotel. As the illuminated lift carried them down out of sight, their smiling heads disappearing last, they seemed exactly like persons of extreme wealth. And indeed for the moment they were wealthy. They had parted with certain hopes, but they had had a windfall; and two of them were looking forward with absolute assurance to a profitable meal and deal with Sir John Pilgrim on the morrow.

" Funny place, London! " said the provincial to himself as he re-entered his suite to rejoin Mr Seven Sachs.

III

" WELL, sir," said Mr Seven Sachs, " I have to thank you for getting me out of a very unsatisfactory situation."

" Did you really want to get out of it? " asked Edward Henry.

Mr Sachs replied simply:

" I did, sir. There were too many partners for my taste."

They were seated more familiarly now in the drawing-room, being indeed separated only by a small table, upon which were glasses. And whereas on a night in the previous week Edward Henry had been entertained by Mr Bryany in a private parlour at the Turk's Head, Hanbridge, on this night he was in a sort repaying the welcome to Mr Bryany's master in a private parlour at Wilkins's, London. The sole difference in favour of Mr Bryany was that while Mr Bryany provided cigarettes and whisky, Edward Henry was providing only cigarettes and Vichy water. Mr Seven Sachs had said that he never took whisky; and though Edward Henry's passion for Vichy water was not quite ungovernable, he thought well to give rein to it on the present occasion, having read somewhere that Vichy water placated the stomach.

Joseph had been instructed to retire.

" And not only that," resumed Mr Seven Sachs, " but you've got a very good thing entirely into your own hands! Masterly, sir! Masterly! Why, at the end you positively had the air of doing them a favour! You made them believe you *were* doing them a favour."

" And don't you think I was? "

Mr Sachs reflected, and then laughed.

" You were," he said. " That's the beauty of it. But at the same time you were getting away with the goods! "

It was by sheer instinct, and not by learning, that Edward Henry fully grasped, as he did, the deep significance of the American idiom employed by Mr Seven

Sachs. He too laughed, as Mr Sachs had laughed. He was immeasurably flattered. He had not been so flattered since the Countess of Chell had permitted him to offer her China tea, meringues, and Berlin pancakes at the Sub Rosa tea-rooms in Hanbridge—and that was a very long time ago.

" You really *do* think it's a good thing? " Edward Henry ventured, for he had not yet been convinced of the entire goodness of theatrical enterprise near Piccadilly Circus.

Mr Seven Sachs convinced him—not by argument but by the sincerity of his gestures and tones. For it was impossible to question that Mr Seven Sachs knew what he was talking about. The shape of Mr Seven Sachs's chin was alone enough to prove that Mr Sachs was incapable of a mere ignorant effervescence. Everything about Mr Sachs was persuasive and confidence-inspiring. His long silences had the easy vigour of oratory, and they served also to make his speech peculiarly impressive. Moreover, he was a handsome and a dark man, and probably half a dozen years younger than Edward Henry. And the discipline of lime-light had taught him the skill to be forever graceful. And his smile, rare enough, was that of a boy.

" Of course," said he, " if Miss Euclid and the others had had any sense they might have done very well for themselves. If you ask me, the option alone is worth ten thousand dollars. But then they haven't any sense! And that's all there is to it."

" So you'd advise me to go ahead with the affair on my own? "

Mr Seven Sachs, his black eyes twinkling, leaned forward and became rather intimately humorous:

" You look as if you wanted advice, don't you? " said he.

"I suppose I do—now I come to think of it!" agreed Edward Henry, with a most admirable quizzicalness; in spite of the fact that he had not really meant to "go ahead with the affair," being in truth a little doubtful of his capacity to handle it.

But Mr Seven Sachs was, all unconsciously, forcing Edward Henry to believe in his own capacities; and the two as it were suddenly developed a more cordial friendliness. Each felt the quick lifting of the plane of their relations, and was aware of a pleasurable emotion.

"I'm moving onwards—gently onwards," crooned Edward Henry to himself. "What price Brindley and his half-crown now?" Londoners might call him a provincial, and undoubtedly would call him a provincial; he admitted, even, that he felt like a provincial in the streets of London. And yet here he was, "doing Londoners in the eye all over the place," and receiving the open homage of Mr Seven Sachs, whose name was the basis of a cosmopolitan legend.

And now he made the cardinal discovery, which marks an epoch in the life of every man who arrives at it, that world-celebrated persons are very like other persons. And he was happy and rather proud in this discovery, and began to feel a certain vague desire to tell Mr Seven Sachs the history of his career—or at any rate the picturesque portions of it. For he too was famous in his own sphere; and in the drawing-room of Wilkins's one celebrity was hob-nobbing with another! ("Put that in your pipe and smoke it, Mr Brindley!") Yes, he was happy, both in what he had already accomplished, and in the contemplation of romantic adventures to come.

And yet his happiness was marred—not fatally but quite appreciably—by a remorse that no amount of private argument with himself would conjure away. Which was the more singular in that a morbid tendency to remorse had never been among Edward Henry's defects! He was worrying, foolish fellow, about the false telephone-call in which, for the purpose of testing Rose Euclid's loyalty to the new enterprise, he had pretended to be the new private secretary of Sir John Pilgrim. Yet what harm had it done? And had it not done a lot of good? Rose Euclid and her youthful worshipper were no worse off than they had been before being victimized by the deceit of the telephone-call. Prior to the call they had assumed themselves to be deprived for ever of the benefits which association with Sir John Pilgrim could offer, and as a fact they were deprived for ever of such benefits. Nothing changed there! Before the call they had had no hope of lunching with the enormous Sir John on the morrow, and as a fact they would not lunch with the enormous Sir John on the morrow. Nothing changed there, either! Again, in no event would Edward Henry have joined the trio in order to make a quartet in partnership. Even had he been as convinced of Rose's loyalty as he was convinced of her disloyalty, he would never have been rash enough to co-operate with such a crew. Again, nothing changed!

On the other hand, he had acquired an assurance of the artiste's duplicity, which assurance had made it easier for him to disappoint her, while the prospect of a business repast with Sir John had helped her to bear the disappointment as a brave woman should. It was true that on the morrow, about lunch-time, Rose Euclid and Carlo Trent might have to live through a few rather trying moments, and they would certainly be very angry; but these drawbacks would

have been more than compensated for in advance by
the pleasures of hope.   And had they not between
them pocketed seventy-five pounds which they had
stood to lose?

Such reasoning was unanswerable, and his remorse
did not attempt to answer it.   His remorse was not
open to reason; it was one of those stupid, primitive
sentiments which obstinately persist in the refined
and rational fabric of modern humanity.

He was just sorry for Rose Euclid.

" Do you know what I did? " he burst out confidentially, and confessed the whole telephone-trick
to Mr Seven Sachs.

Mr Seven Sachs, somewhat to Edward Henry's
surprise, expressed high admiration of the device.

" A bit mean, though, don't you think? " Edward
Henry protested weakly.

" Not at all! " cried Mr Sachs.   " You got the goods
on her.   And she deserved it."

(Again this enigmatic and mystical word " goods "!
But he understood it.)

Thus encouraged, he was now quite determined to
give Mr Seven Sachs a brief episodic account of his
career.   A fair conversational opening was all he
wanted in order to begin.

" I wonder what will happen to her—ultimately? "
he said, meaning to work back from the ends of careers
to their beginnings, and so to himself.

" Rose Euclid? "

" Yes."

Mr Sachs shook his head compassionately.

" How did Mr Bryany get in with her? " asked
Edward Henry.

" Bryany is a highly peculiar person," said Mr
Seven Sachs, familiarly.   " He's all right so long as

you don't unstrap him. He was born to convince newspaper reporters of his own greatness."

" I had a bit of a talk with him myself," said Edward Henry.

" Oh, yes! He told me all about you."

" But *I* never told him anything about myself," said Edward Henry, quickly.

" No, but he has eyes, you know, and ears too. Seems to me the people of the Five Towns do little else of a night but discuss you, Mr Machin. *I* heard a good bit when *I* was down there, though I don't go about much when I'm on the road. I reckon I could write a whole biography of you."

Edward Henry smiled self-consciously. He was, of course, enraptured, but at the same time it was disappointing to find Mr Sachs already so fully informed as to the details of his career. However, he did not intend to let that prevent him from telling the story afresh, in his own manner.

" I suppose you've had your adventures, too," he remarked with nonchalance, partly from politeness but mainly in order to avoid the appearance of hurry in his egotism.

IV

" You bet I have! " Mr Seven Sachs cordially agreed, abandoning the end of a cigarette, putting his hands behind his head, and crossing his legs.

Whereupon there was a brief pause.

" I remember—" Edward Henry began.

" I daresay you've heard—" began Mr Seven Sachs, simultaneously.

They were like two men who by inadvertence had

attempted to pass through a narrow doorway abreast. Edward Henry, as the host, drew back.

" I beg your pardon! " he apologized.

" Not at all," said Seven Sachs. " I was only going to say you've probably heard that I was always up against Archibald Florance."

" Really! " murmured Edward Henry, impressed in spite of himself. For the renown of Archibald Florance exceeded that of Seven Sachs as the sun the moon, and was older and more securely established than it as the sun the moon. The renown of Rose Euclid was as naught to it. Doubtful it was whether, in the annals of modern histrionics, the grandeur and the romance of that American name could be surpassed by any renown save that of the incomparable Henry Irving. The retirement of Archibald Florance from the stage a couple of years earlier had caused crimson gleams of sunset splendour to shoot across the Atlantic and irradiate even the Garrick Club, London, so that the members thereof had to shade their offended eyes. Edward Henry had never seen Archibald Florance, but it was not necessary to have seen him in order to appreciate the majesty of his glory. No male in the history of the world was ever more photographed, and few have been the subject of more anecdotes.

" I expect he's a wealthy chap in his old age," said Edward Henry.

" Wealthy! " exclaimed Mr Sachs. " He's the richest actor in America, and that's saying in the world. He had the greatest reputation. He's still the handsomest man in the United States—that's admitted— with his white hair! They used to say he was the cruellest, but it's not so. Though of course he could be a perfect terror with his companies."

" And so you knew Archibald Florance? "

" You bet I did. He never had any friends—never —but I knew him as well as anybody could. Why, in San Francisco, after the show, I've walked with him back to his hotel, and he's walked with me back to mine, and so on and so on till three or four o'clock in the morning. You see, we couldn't stop until it happened that he finished a cigar at the exact moment when we got to his hotel door. If the cigar wasn't finished, then he must needs stroll back a bit, and before I knew where I was he'd be lighting a fresh one. He smoked the finest cigars in America. I remember him telling me they cost him three dollars apiece."

And Edward Henry then perceived another profound truth, his second cardinal discovery on that notable evening: namely, that no matter how high you rise, you will always find that others have risen higher. Nay, it is not until you have achieved a considerable peak that you are able to appreciate the loftiness of those mightier summits. He himself was high, and so he could judge the greater height of Seven Sachs; and it was only through the greater height of Seven Sachs that he could form an adequate idea of the pinnacle occupied by the unique Archibald Florance. Honestly, he had never dreamt that there existed a man who habitually smoked twelve-shilling cigars— and yet he reckoned to know a thing or two about cigars!

" I am nothing! " he thought modestly. Nevertheless, though the savour of the name of Archibald Florance was agreeable, he decided that he had heard enough for the moment about Archibald Florance, and that he would relate to Mr Sachs the famous episode of his own career in which the Countess of Chell and a mule had so prominently performed.

" I remember—" he recommenced.

" My first encounter with Archibald Florance was very funny," proceeded Mr Seven Sachs, blandly deaf. " I was starving in New York,—trying to sell a new razor on commission—and I was determined to get on to the stage. I had one visiting-card left—just one. I wrote ' Important ' on it, and sent it up to Wunch. I don't know whether you've ever heard of Wunch. Wunch was Archibald Florance's stage-manager, and nearly as famous as Archibald himself. Well, Wunch sent for me upstairs to his room, but when he found I was only the usual youngster after the usual job he just had me thrown out of the theatre. He said I'd no right to put ' Important ' on a visiting-card. ' Well,' I said to myself, ' I'm going to get back into that theatre somehow! ' So I went up to Archibald's private house —Sixtieth Street I think it was—and asked to see him, and I saw him. When I got into his room he was writing. He kept on writing for some minutes, and then he swung round on his chair.

" ' And what can I do for you, sir? ' he said.

" ' Do you want any actors, Mr Florance? ' I said.

" ' Are you an actor? ' he said.

" ' I want to be one,' I said.

" ' Well,' he said, ' there's a school round the corner.'

" ' Well,' I said, ' you might give me a card of introduction, Mr Florance.'

" He gave me the card. I didn't take it to the school. I went straight back to the theatre with it, and had it sent up to Wunch. It just said, ' Introducing Mr Sachs, a young man anxious to get on.' Wunch took it for a positive order to find me a place. The company was full, so he threw out one poor devil of a super to make room for me. Curious thing—old Wunchy got it into his head that I was a *protégé* of

Archibald's, and he always looked after me. What d'ye think about that? "

" Brilliant! " said Edward Henry. And it was! The simplicity of the thing was what impressed him. Since winning a scholarship at school by altering the number of marks opposite his name on a paper lying on the master's desk, Edward Henry had never achieved advancement by a device so simple. And he thought: " I am nothing! The Five Towns is nothing! All that one hears about Americans and the United States is true. As far as getting on goes, they can make rings round us. Still, I shall tell him about the Countess and the mule—"

" Yes," continued Mr Seven Sachs, " Wunch was very kind to me. But he was pretty well down and out, and he left, and Archibald got a new stage-manager, and I was promoted to do a bit of assistant stage-managing. But I got no increase of salary. There were two women stars in the play Archibald was doing then—'The Forty-Niners.' Romantic drama, you know! Melodrama you'd call it over here. He never did any other sort of play. Well, these two women stars were about equal, and when the curtain fell on the first act they'd both make a bee line for Archibald to see who'd get to him first and engage him in talk. They were jealous enough of each other to kill. Anybody could see that Archibald was frightfully bored, but he couldn't escape. They got him on both sides, you see, and he just *had* to talk to 'em, both at once. I used to be fussing around fixing the properties for the next act. Well, one night he comes up to me, Archibald does, and he says:

" ' Mr—what's your name? "

" ' Sachs, sir,' I says.

" ' You notice when those two ladies come up to

me after the first act. Well, when you see them talking to me, I want you to come right along and interrupt,' he says.

" ' What shall I say, sir? '

" ' Tap me on the shoulder and say I'm wanted about something very urgent. You see? '

" So the next night when those women got hold of him, sure enough I went up between them and tapped him on the shoulder. ' Mr Florance,' I said. ' Something very urgent.' He turned on me and scowled: ' What is it? ' he said, and he looked very angry. It was a bit of the best acting the old man ever did in his life. It was so good that at first I thought it was real. He said again louder, ' What is it? ' So I said, ' Well, Mr Florance, the most urgent thing in this theatre is that I should have an increase of salary! ' I guess I licked the stuffing out of him that time."

Edward Henry gave vent to one of those cordial and violent guffaws which are a specialty of the humorous side of the Five Towns. And he said to himself: " I should never have thought of anything as good as that."

" And did you get it? " he asked.

" The old man said not a word," Mr Seven Sachs went on in the same even, tranquil, smiling voice. " But next pay-day I found I'd got a rise of ten dollars a week. And not only that, but Mr Florance offered me a singing part in his new drama, if I could play the mandolin. I naturally told him I'd played the mandolin all my life. I went out and bought a mandolin and hired a teacher. He wanted to teach me the mandolin, but I only wanted him to teach me that one accompaniment. So I fired him, and practised by myself night and day for a week. I got through all the rehearsals without ever singing that song.

Cleverest dodging I ever did! On the first night I was so nervous I could scarcely hold the mandolin. I'd never played the infernal thing before anybody at all—only up in my bedroom. I struck the first chord, and found the darned instrument was all out of tune with the orchestra. So I just pretended to play it, and squawked away with my song, and never let my fingers touch the strings at all. Old Florance was waiting for me in the wings. I knew he was going to fire me. But no! 'Sachs,' he said, 'that accompaniment was the most delicate piece of playing I ever heard. I congratulate you.' He was quite serious. Everybody said the same! Luck, eh?"

" I should say so," said Edward Henry, gradually beginning to be interested in the odyssey of Mr Seven Sachs. " I remember a funny thing that happened to me—"

"However," Mr Sachs swept smoothly along, " that piece was a failure. And Archibald arranged to take a company to Europe with 'Forty-Niners.' And I was left out! This rattled me, specially after the way he liked my mandolin-playing. So I went to see him about it in his dressing-room one night, and I charged around a bit. He did rattle me! Then I rattled him. I would get an answer out of him. He said:

" ' I'm not in the habit of being cross-examined in my own dressing-room.'

" I didn't care what happened then, so I said:

" ' And I'm not in the habit of being treated as you're treating me.'

" All of a sudden he became quite quiet, and patted me on the shoulder. 'You're getting on very well, Sachs,' he said. ' You've only been at it one year. It's taken me twenty-five years to get where I am.'

"However, I was too angry to stand for that sort of talk. I said to him:

" ' I daresay you're a very great and enviable man, Mr Florance, but I propose to save fifteen years on your twenty-five. I'll equal or better your position in ten years.'

"He shoved me out—just shoved me out of the room. . . . It was that that made me turn to play-writing. Florance wrote his own plays sometimes, but it was only his acting and his face that saved them. And they were too American. He never did really well outside America except in one play, and that wasn't his own. Now I was out after money. And I still am. I wanted to please the largest possible public. So I guessed there was nothing for it but the universal appeal. I never write a play that won't appeal to England, Germany, France just as well as to America. America's big, but it isn't big enough for me. . . . Well, as I was saying, soon after that I got a one-act play produced at Hannibal, Missouri. And the same week there was a company at another theatre there playing the old man's ' Forty-Niners.' And the next morning the theatrical critic's article in the Hannibal *Courier-Post* was headed: ' Rival attractions. Archibald Florance's " Forty-Niners " and new play by Seven Sachs.' I cut that heading out and sent it to the old man in London, and I wrote under it, ' See how far I've got in six months.' When he came back he took me into his company again. . . . What price that, eh? "

Edward Henry could only nod his head. The customarily silent Seven Sachs had little by little subdued him to an admiration as mute as it was profound.

"Nearly five years after that I got a Christmas

card from old Florance. It had the usual printed
wishes—'Merriest possible Christmas and so on'—
but, underneath that, Archibald had written in pencil,
'You've still five years to go.' That made me roll
my sleeves up, as you may say. Well, a long time
after that I was standing at the corner of Broadway
and Forty-fourth Street, and looking at my own name
in electric letters on the Criterion Theatre. First time
I'd ever seen it in electric letters on Broadway. It
was the first night of 'Overheard.' Florance was
playing at the Hudson Theatre, which is a bit higher
up Forty-fourth Street, and *his* name was in electric
letters too, but further off Broadway than mine. I
strolled up, just out of idle curiosity, and there the
old man was standing in the porch of the theatre, all
alone! 'Hullo, Sachs,' he said, 'I'm glad I've seen
you. It's saved me twenty-five cents.' I asked how.
He said, 'I was just going to send you a telegram of
congratulations.' He liked me, old Archibald did.
He still does. But I hadn't done with him. I went
to stay with him at his house on Long Island in the
spring. 'Excuse me, Mr Florance,' I says to him.
'How many companies have you got on the road?'
He said, 'Oh! I haven't got many now. Five, I think.'
'Well,' I says, 'I've got six here in the United States,
two in England, three in Austria, and one in Italy.'
He said, 'Have a cigar, Sachs; you've got the goods
on me!' He was living in that magnificent house all
alone, with a whole regiment of servants!"

V

"WELL," said Edward Henry, "you're a great
man!"

"No, I'm not," said Mr Seven Sachs. "But my

income is four hundred thousand dollars a year, and rising. I'm out after the stuff, that's all."

" I say you are a great man! " Edward Henry repeated. Mr Sachs's recital had inspired him. He kept saying to himself: " And I'm a great man, too. And I'll show 'em."

Mr Sachs, having delivered himself of his load, had now lapsed comfortably back into his original silence, and was prepared to listen. But Edward Henry, somehow, had lost the desire to enlarge on his own variegated past. He was absorbed in the greater future.

At length he said very distinctly:

" You honestly think I could run a theatre? "

" You were born to run a theatre," said Seven Sachs.

Thrilled, Edward Henry responded:

" Then I'll write to those lawyer people, Slossons, and tell 'em I'll be around with the brass about eleven to-morrow."

Mr Sachs rose. A clock had delicately chimed two.

" If ever you come to New York, and I can do anything for you—" said Mr Sachs, heartily.

" Thanks," said Edward Henry. They were shaking hands. " I say," Edward Henry went on. " There's one thing I want to ask you. Why *did* you promise to back Rose Euclid and her friends? You must surely have known—" He threw up his hands.

Mr Sachs answered:

" I'll be frank with you. It was her cousin that persuaded me into it—Elsie April."

" Elsie April? Who's she? "

" Oh! You must have seen them about together

—her and Rose Euclid! They're nearly always to-gether."

" I saw her in the restaurant here to-day with a rather jolly girl—blue hat."

" That's the one. As soon as you've made her acquaintance you'll understand what I mean," said Mr Seven Sachs.

" Ah! But I'm not a bachelor like you," Edward Henry smiled archly.

" Well, you'll see when you meet her," said Mr Sachs. Upon which enigmatic warning he departed, and was lost in the immense glittering nocturnal silence of Wilkins's.

Edward Henry sat down to write to Slossons by the 3 A.M. post. But as he wrote he kept saying to himself: " So Elsie April's her name, is it? And she actually persuaded Sachs—Sachs—to make a fool of himself! "

CHAPTER VI

LORD WOLDO AND LADY WOLDO

I

THE next morning, Joseph, having opened wide the window, informed his master that the weather was bright and sunny, and Edward Henry arose with just that pleasant degree of fatigue which persuades one that one is if anything rather more highly vitalized than usual. He sent for Mr Bryany, as for a domestic animal, and Mr Bryany, ceremoniously attired, was received by a sort of jolly king who happened to be trimming his beard in the royal bathroom but who was too good-natured to keep Mr Bryany waiting. It is remarkable how the habit of royalty, having once taken root, will flourish in the minds of quite unmonarchical persons. Edward Henry first inquired after the health of Mr Seven Sachs, and then obtained from Mr Bryany all remaining papers and trifles of information concerning the affair of the option. Whereupon Mr Bryany, apparently much elated by the honour of an informal reception, effusively retired. And Edward Henry too was so elated, and his faith in life so renewed and invigorated, that he said to himself:

" It might be worth while to shave my beard off, after all! "

As in his electric brougham he drove along muddy and shining Piccadilly, he admitted that Joseph's account of the weather had been very accurate. The weather was magnificent; it presented the best features of summer combined with the salutary pungency of autumn. And flags were flying over the establishments of tobacconists, soothsayers and insurance companies in Piccadilly. And the sense of Empire was in the very air, like an intoxication. And there was no place like London. When, however, having run through Piccadilly into streets less superb, he reached the Majestic, it seemed to him that the Majestic was not a part of London, but a bit of the provinces surrounded by London. He was very disappointed with the Majestic, and took his letters from the clerk with careless condescension. In a few days the Majestic had sunk from being one of " London's huge caravanserais " to the level of a swollen Turk's Head. So fragile are reputations!

From the Majestic Edward Henry drove back into the regions of Empire, between Piccadilly and Regent Street, and deigned to call upon his tailors. A morning-suit which he had commanded being miraculously finished, he put it on, and was at once not only spectacularly but morally regenerated. The old suit, though it had cost five guineas in its time, looked a paltry and a dowdy thing as it lay, flung down anyhow, on one of Messrs Quayther & Cuthering's cane chairs in the mirrored cubicle where baronets and even peers showed their braces to the benign Mr Cuthering.

" I want to go to Piccadilly Circus now. Stop at the fountain," said Edward Henry to his chauffeur. He gave the order somewhat defiantly, because he was a little self-conscious in the new and gleaming suit, and because he had an absurd idea that the chauffeur might guess that he, a provincial from the Five Towns, was about to venture into West End theatrical enterprise and sneer at him accordingly.

But the chauffeur merely touched his cap with an indifferent and lofty gesture, as if to say:

" Be at ease. I have driven persons more moon-struck even than you. Human eccentricity has long since ceased to surprise me."

The fountain in Piccadilly Circus was the gayest thing in London. It mingled the fresh tinkling of water with the odour and flame of autumn blossoms and the variegated colours of shawled women who passed their lives on its margin engaged in the commerce of flowers. Edward Henry bought an aster from a fine bold, red-cheeked, blowsy, dirty wench with a baby in her arms, and left some change for the baby. He was in a very tolerant and charitable mood, and could excuse the sins and the stupidity of all mankind. He reflected forgivingly that Rose Euclid and her friends had perhaps not displayed an abnormal fatuity in discussing the name of the theatre before they had got the lease of the site for it. Had not he himself bought all the option without having even seen the site? The fact was that he had had no leisure in his short royal career for such details as seeing the site. He was now about to make good the omission.

It is a fact that as he turned northwards from Piccadilly Circus, to the right of the County Fire Office, in order to spy out the land upon which his theatre was to be built, he hesitated, under the delusion that all the passers-by were staring at him! He felt just as he might have felt had he been engaged upon some scheme nefarious. He even went back and pretended to examine the windows of the County Fire Office. Then, glancing self-consciously about, he discerned—not unnaturally—the words " Regent Street " on a sign.

" There you are! " he murmured, with a thrill.

" There you are! There's obviously only one name for that theatre—' The Regent.' It's close to Regent Street. No other theatre is called ' The Regent.' Nobody before ever had the idea of ' Regent ' as a name for a theatre. ' Muses ' indeed! . . . ' Intellectual '! . . . ' The Regent Theatre '! How well it comes off the tongue! It's a great name! It'll be the finest name of any theatre in London! And it took yours truly to think of it! "

Then he smiled privately at his own weakness. . . . He too, like the despised Rose, was baptizing the unborn! Still, he continued to dream of the theatre, and began to picture to himself the ideal theatre. He discovered that he had quite a number of startling ideas about theatre-construction, based on his own experience as a playgoer.

When, with new courage, he directed his feet towards the site, upon which he knew there was an old chapel known as Queen's Glasshouse Chapel, whose ownership had slipped from the nerveless hand of a dying sect of dissenters, he could not find the site and he could not see the chapel. For an instant he was perturbed by a horrid suspicion that he had been victimized by a gang of swindlers posing as celebrated persons. Everything was possible in this world and century! None of the people who had appeared in the transaction had resembled his previous conceptions of such people! And confidence-thieves always operated in the grandest hotels! He immediately decided that if the sequel should prove him to be a simpleton and gull, he would at any rate be a silent simpleton and gull. He would stoically bear the loss of two hundred pounds and breathe no word of woe.

But then he remembered with relief that he had

genuinely recognized both Rose Euclid and Seven
Sachs; and also that Mr Bryany, among other documents, had furnished him with a photograph of the
Chapel and surrounding property. The Chapel therefore existed. He had a plan in his pocket. He now
opened this plan and tried to consult it in the middle of
the street, but his agitation was such that he could
not make out on it which was north and which was
south. After he had been nearly prostrated by a taxi-
cab, a policeman came up to him and said, with all
the friendly disdain of a London policeman addressing
a provincial:

" Safer to look at that on the pavement, sir! "

Edward Henry glanced up from the plan.

" I was trying to find the Queen's Glasshouse
Chapel, officer," said he. " Have you ever heard of
it? "

(In Bursley, members of the Town Council always
flattered members of the Force by addressing them as
" officer "; and Edward Henry knew exactly the
effective intonation.)

" It *was there*, sir," said the policeman, less disdainful, pointing to a narrow hoarding behind which could
be seen the back-walls of high buildings in Shaftesbury Avenue. " They've just finished pulling it
down."

" Thank you," said Edward Henry, quietly, with a
superb and successful effort to keep as much colour
in his face as if the policeman had not dealt him a
dizzying blow.

He then walked towards the hoarding, but could
scarcely feel the ground under his feet. From a wide
aperture in the palisades a cart full of earth was emerging; it creaked and shook as it was dragged by a
labouring horse over loose planks into the roadway;

a whip-cracking carter hovered on its flank. Edward Henry approached the aperture and gazed within. An elegant young man stood solitary inside the hoarding and stared at a razed expanse of land in whose furthest corner some navvies were digging a hole. . . .

The site!

But what did this sinister destructive activity mean? Nobody was entitled to interfere with property on which he, Alderman Machin, held an unexpired option! But was it the site? He perused the plan again with more care. Yes, there could be no doubt that it was the site. His eye roved round and he admitted the justice of the boast that an electric sign displayed at the southern front corner of the theatre would be visible from Piccadilly Circus, Lower Regent Street, Shaftesbury Avenue, etc., etc. He then observed a large notice-board, raised on posts above the hoardings, and read the following:

SITE

OF THE

FIRST NEW THOUGHT CHURCH

to be opened next Spring.

Subscriptions invited.

> Rollo Wrissell: *Senior Trustee.*
> Ralph Alloyd: *Architect.*
> Dicks & Pato: *Builders.*

The name of Rollo Wrissell seemed familiar to him, and after a few moments' searching he recalled that Rollo Wrissell was one of the trustees and executors of the late Lord Woldo, the other being the widow—

and the mother of the new Lord Woldo. In addition
to the lettering the notice-board held a graphic representation of the First New Thought Church as it would
be when completed.

"Well," said Edward Henry, not perhaps unjusti-
fiably, "this really is a bit thick! Here I've got an
option on a plot of land for building a theatre, and somebody else has taken it to put up a church!"

He ventured inside the hoarding, and addressing
the elegant young man asked:

"You got anything to do with this, mister?"

"Well," said the young man, smiling humorously,
"I'm the architect. It's true that nobody ever pays
any attention to an architect in these days."

"Oh! You're Mr Alloyd?"

"I am."

Mr Alloyd had black hair, intensely black, changeful
eyes, and the expressive mouth of an actor.

"I thought they were going to build a theatre
here," said Edward Henry.

"I wish they had been!" said Mr Alloyd. "I'd
just like to design a theatre! But of course I shall
never get the chance."

"Why not?"

"I know I shan't," Mr Alloyd insisted with gloomy
disgust. "Only obtained this job by sheer accident!
. . . You got any ideas about theatres?"

"Well, I have," said Edward Henry.

Mr Alloyd turned on him with a sardonic and half-
benevolent gleam.

"And what are your ideas about theatres?"

"Well," said Edward Henry, "I should like to
meet an architect who had thoroughly got it into his
head that when people pay for seats to see a play they
want to be able to *see* it, and not just get a look at it

now and then over other people's heads and round corners of boxes and things. In most theatres that I've been in the architects seemed to think that iron pillars and wooden heads are transparent. Either that, or the architects were rascals! Same with hearing! The pit costs half-a-crown, and you don't pay half-a-crown to hear glasses rattled in a bar or motor-omnibuses rushing down the street. I was never yet in a London theatre where the architect had really understood that what the people in the pit wanted to hear was the play and nothing but the play."

" You're rather hard on us," said Mr Alloyd.

" Not so hard as you are on *us!*" said Edward Henry. " And then draughts! I suppose you think a draught on the back of the neck is good for us! . . . But of course you'll say all this has nothing to do with architecture!"

" Oh, no, I shan't! Oh, no, I shan't!" exclaimed Mr Alloyd. " I quite agree with you!"

" You *do?*"

" Certainly. You seem to be interested in theatres?"

" I am a bit."

" You come from the north?"

" No, I don't," said Edward Henry. Mr Alloyd had no right to be aware that he was not a Londoner.

" I beg your pardon."

" I come from the Midlands."

" Oh! . . . Have you seen the Russian Ballet?"

Edward Henry had not—nor heard of it. " Why?" he asked.

" Nothing," said Mr Alloyd. " Only I saw it the night before last in Paris. You never saw such dancing. It's enchanted—enchanted! The most lovely thing I ever saw in my life. I couldn't sleep for it. Not that I ever sleep very well!—I merely thought, as you were interested in theatres—and Midland people are so enterprising! . . . Have a cigarette? "

Edward Henry, who had begun to feel sympathetic, was somewhat repelled by these odd last remarks. After all the man, though human enough, was an utter stranger.

" No thanks," he said. " And so you're going to put up a church here? "

" Yes."

" Well, I wonder whether you are."

He walked abruptly away under Alloyd's riddling stare, and he could almost hear the man saying, " Well, he's a queer lot, if you like."

At the corner of the site, below the spot where his electric sign was to have been, he was stopped by a well-dressed middle-aged lady who bore a bundle of papers.

" Will you buy a paper for the cause? " she suggested in a pleasant, persuasive tone. " One penny."

He obeyed, and she handed him a small blue-printed periodical of which the title was " *Azure*, the Organ of the New Thought Church." He glanced at it, puzzled, and then at the middle-aged lady.

"Every penny of profit goes to the Church Building Fund," she said, as if in defence of her action.

Edward Henry burst out laughing; but it was a nervous, half-hysterical laugh that he laughed.

II

In Carey Street, Lincoln's Inn Fields, he descended from his brougham in front of the offices of Messrs

Slosson, Hodge, Budge, Slosson, Maveringham, Slosson & Vulto—solicitors—known in the profession by the compendious abbreviation of Slossons. Edward Henry, having been a lawyer's clerk some twenty-five years earlier, was aware of Slossons. Although on the strength of his youthful clerkship he claimed, and was admitted, to possess a very special knowledge of the law—enough to silence argument when his opponent did not happen to be an actual solicitor—he did not in truth possess a very special knowledge of the law—how should he, seeing that he had only been a practitioner of shorthand?—but the fame of Slossons he positively was acquainted with! He had even written letters to the mighty Slossons.

Every lawyer and lawyer's clerk in the realm knew the greatness of Slossons, and crouched before it, and also, for the most part, impugned its righteousness with sneers. For Slossons acted for the ruling classes of England, who only get value for their money when they are buying something that they can see, smell, handle, or intimidate—such as a horse, a motor-car, a dog, or a lackey. Slossons, those crack solicitors, like the crack nerve specialists in Harley Street and the crack fortune-tellers in Bond Street, sold their invisible, inodorous and intangible wares of advice at double, treble, or decuple their worth, according to the psychology of the customer. They were great bullies. And they were, further, great money-lenders —on behalf of their wealthier clients. In obedience to a convenient theory that it is imprudent to leave money too long in one place, they were continually calling in mortgages, and re-lending the sums so collected on fresh investments, thus achieving two bills of costs on each transaction, and sometimes three, besides employing an army of valuers, surveyors and mortgage-insurance brokers. In short, Slossons had nothing to learn about the art of self-enrichment.

Three vast motor-cars waited in front of their ancient door, and Edward Henry's hired electric vehicle was diminished to a trifle.

He began by demanding the senior partner, who was denied to him by an old clerk with a face like a stone wall. Only his brutal Midland insistence, and the mention of the important letter which he had written to the firm in the middle of the night, saved him from the ignominy of seeing no partner at all. At the end of the descending ladder of partners he clung desperately to Mr Vulto, and he saw Mr Vulto—a youngish and sarcastic person with blue eyes, lodged in a dark room at the back of the house. It occurred fortunately that his letter had been allotted to precisely Mr Vulto for the purpose of being answered.

" You got my letter? " said Edward Henry, cheerfully, as he sat down at Mr Vulto's flat desk on the side opposite from Mr Vulto.

" We got it, but frankly we cannot make head or tail of it! . . . *What* option? " Mr Vulto's manner was crudely sarcastic.

" *This* option! " said Edward Henry, drawing papers from his pocket, and putting down the right paper in front of Mr Vulto with an uncompromising slap.

Mr Vulto picked up the paper with precautions, as if it were a contagion, and, assuming eyeglasses, perused it with his mouth open.

" We know nothing of this," said Mr Vulto, and it was as though he had added: " Therefore this does not exist." He glanced with sufferance at the window, which offered a close-range view of a whitewashed wall.

" Then you weren't in the confidence of your client? "

" The late Lord Woldo? "

" Yes."

" Pardon me."

" Obviously you weren't in his confidence as regards this particular matter."

" As you say," said Mr Vulto, with frigid irony.

" Well, what are you going to do about it? "

" Well—nothing." Mr Vulto removed his eye-glasses and stood up.

" Well, good morning. I'll walk round to *my* solicitors." Edward Henry seized the option.

" That will be simpler," said Mr Vulto. Slossons much preferred to deal with lawyers than with laymen, because it increased costs and vitalized the profession.

At that moment a stout, red-faced and hoary man puffed very authoritatively into the room.

" Vulto," he cried sharply. " Mr Wrissell's here. Didn't they tell you? "

" Yes, Mr Slosson," answered Vulto, suddenly losing all his sarcastic quality, and becoming a very junior partner. " I was just engaged with Mr "— (he paused to glance at his desk)—" Machin, whose singular letter we received this morning about an alleged option on the lease of the Chapel site at Picca-dilly Circus—the Woldo estate, sir. You remember, sir? "

" This the man? " inquired Mr Slosson, ex-president of the Law Society, with a jerk of the thumb.

Edward Henry said, " This is the man."

" Well," said Mr Slosson, lifting his chin, and still puffing, " it would be extremely interesting to hear his story at any rate. I was just telling Mr Wrissell about it. Come this way, sir. I've heard some strange things in my time, but—" He stopped. " Please follow me, sir," he ordained.

" I'm dashed if I'll follow you! " Edward Henry desired to say, but he had not the courage to say it. And because he was angry with himself he determined to make matters as unpleasant as possible for the innocent Mr Slosson, who was so used to bullying, and so well paid for bullying that really no blame could be apportioned to him. It would have been as reasonable to censure an ordinary person for breathing as to censure Mr Slosson for bullying. And so Edward Henry was steeling himself: " I'll do him in the eye for that, even if it costs me every cent I've got." (A statement characterized by poetical license!)

III

Mr Slosson, senior, heard Edward Henry's story, but seemingly did not find it quite as interesting as he had prophesied it would be. When Edward Henry had finished the old man drummed on an enormous table, and said:

" Yes, yes. And then? " His manner was far less bullying than in the room of Mr Vulto.

" It's your turn now, Mr Slosson," said Edward Henry.

" My turn? How? "

" To go on with the story." He glanced at the clock. " I've brought it up to date—11.15 o'clock this morning *anno domini*." And as Mr Slosson continued to drum on the table and to look out of the window, Edward Henry also drummed on the table and looked out of the window.

The chamber of the senior partner was a very dif-

ferent matter from Mr Vulto's. It was immense. It
was not disfigured by japanned boxes inartistically
lettered in white, as are most lawyer's offices. Indeed
in aspect it resembled one of the cosier rooms in a small
and decaying but still comfortable club. It had easy
chairs and cigar boxes. Moreover, the sun got into it,
and there was a view of the comic yet stately Victorian
Gothic of the Law Courts. The sun enheartened
Edward Henry. And he felt secure in an unimpugn-
able suit of clothes; in the shape of his collar, the
colour of his necktie, the style of his creaseless boots;
and in the protuberance of his pocket-book in his
pocket.

As Mr Slosson had failed to notice the competition
of his drumming, he drummed still louder. Whereupon
Mr Slosson stopped drumming. Edward Henry gazed
amiably around. Right at the back of the room—
before a back-window that gave on the whitewashed
wall—a man was rapidly putting his signature to a
number of papers. But Mr Slosson had ignored the
existence of this man, treating him apparently as a
figment of the disordered brain or as an optical
illusion.

" I've nothing to say," said Mr Slosson.

" Or to do? "

" Or to do."

" Well, Mr Slosson," said Edward Henry, " your
junior partner has already outlined your policy of
masterly inactivity. So I may as well go. I did say
I'd go to my solicitors. But it's occurred to me that
as I'm a principal I may as well first of all see the prin-
cipals on the other side. I only came here because it
mentions in the option that the matter is to be completed here—that's all."

" You a principal! " exclaimed Mr Slosson. " It

seems to me you're a long way removed from a principal. The alleged option is given to a Miss Rose Euclid—"

" Excuse me—*the* Miss Rose Euclid."

" Miss Rose Euclid. She divides up her alleged interest into fractions, and sells them here and there, and you buy them up one after another." Mr Slosson laughed, not unamiably. " You're a principal about five times removed."

" Well," said Edward Henry, " whatever I am, I have a sort of idea I'll go and see this Mr Gristle or Wrissell. Can you—"

The man at the distant desk turned his head. Mr Slosson coughed. The man rose.

" This is Mr Wrissel," said Mr Slosson, with a gesture from which confusion was not absent.

" Good morning," said the advancing Mr Rollo Wrissell, and he said it with an accent more Kensingtonian than any accent that Edward Henry had ever heard. His lounging and yet elegant walk assorted well with the accent. His black clothes were loose and untidy. Such boots as his could not have been worn by Edward Henry even in the Five Towns without blushing shame, and his necktie looked as if a baby or a puppy had been playing with it. Nevertheless, these shortcomings made absolutely no difference whatever to the impressivness of Mr Rollo Wrissell, who was famous for having said once, " I put on whatever comes to hand first, and people don't seem to mind."

Mr Rollo Wrissell belonged to one of the seven great families which once governed—and by the way still do govern—England, Scotland and Ireland. The members of these families may be divided into two species: those who rule, and those who are too lofty in spirit even to rule—those who exist. Mr Rollo

Wrissell belonged to the latter species. His nose and mouth had the exquisite refinement of the descendant of generations of art-collectors and poet-patronizers. He enjoyed life—but not with rude activity, like the grosser members of the ruling caste—rather with a certain rare languor. He sniffed and savoured the whole spherical surface of the apple of life with those delicate nostrils, rather than bit into it. His one conviction was that in a properly-managed world nothing ought to occur to disturb or agitate the perfect tranquillity of his existing. And this conviction was so profound, so visible even in his lightest gesture and glance, that it exerted a mystic influence over the entire social organism—with the result that practically nothing ever did occur to disturb or agitate the perfect tranquillity of Mr Rollo Wrissell's existing. For Mr Rollo Wrissell the world was indeed almost ideal.

Edward Henry breathed to himself, " This is the genuine article."

And, being an Englishman, he was far more impressed by Mr Wrissell than he had been by the much vaster reputations of Rose Euclid, Seven Sachs and Mr Slosson, senior. At the same time he inwardly fought against Mr Wrissell's silent and unconscious dominion over him, and all the defiant Midland belief that one body is as good as anybody else surged up in him—but stopped at his lips.

" Please don't rise," Mr Wrissell entreated, waving both hands. " I'm very sorry to hear of this unhappy complication," he went on to Edward Henry, with the most adorable and winning politeness. " It pains me." (His martyred expression said, " And really I ought not to be pained!) " I'm quite convinced that you are here in absolute good faith—the most absolute good faith—Mr—"

" Machin," suggested Mr Slosson.

" Ah! pardon me! Mr Machin. And naturally in the management of enormous estates such as Lord Woldo's little difficulties are apt to occur. . . . I'm sorry you've been put in a false position. You have all my sympathies. But of course you understand that in this particular case . . . I myself have taken up the lease from the estate. I happen to be interested in a great movement. The plans of my church have been passed by the County Council. Building operations have indeed begun."

" Oh! chuck it! " said Edward Henry, inexcusably —but such were his words. A surfeit of Mr Wrissell's calm egotism and accent and fatigued harmonious gestures drove him to commit this outrage upon the very fabric of civilization.

Mr Wrissell, if he had ever met with the phrase— which is doubtful—had certainly never heard it ad- dressed to himself; conceivably he might have once come across it in turning over the pages of a slang dictionary. A tragic expression traversed his bewildered features—and then he recovered himself somewhat.

" I—"

" Go and bury yourself! " said Edward Henry, with increased savagery.

Mr Wrissell, having comprehended, went. He really did go. He could not tolerate scenes, and his glance showed that any forcible derangement of his habit of existing smoothly would nakedly dis- close the unyielding adamantine selfishness that was the basis of the Wrissell philosophy. His glance was at least harsh and bitter. He went in silence, and rapidly. Mr Slosson, senior, followed him at a great pace.

Edward Henry was angry. Strange though it

may seem, the chief cause of his anger was the fact
that his own manners and breeding were lower, coarser,
clumsier, more brutal than Mr Wrissell's.

After what appeared to be a considerable absence
Mr Slosson, senior, returned into the room. Edward
Henry, steeped in peculiar meditations, was re-
peating:

" So this is Slosson's! "

" What's that? " demanded Mr Slosson with a
challenge in his ancient but powerful voice.

" Nowt! " said Edward Henry.

" Now, sir," said Mr Slosson, " we'd better come
to an understanding about this so-called option. It's
not serious, you know."

" You'll find it is."

" It's not commercial."

" I fancy it is—for me! " said Edward Henry.

" The premium mentioned is absurdly inadequate,
and the ground-rent is quite improperly low."

" That's just why I look on it as commercial—
from my point of view," said Edward Henry.

" It isn't worth the paper it's written on," said Mr
Slosson.

" Why? "

" Because, seeing the unusual form of it, it ought
to be stamped, and it isn't stamped."

" Listen here, Mr Slosson," said Edward Henry,
" I want you to remember that you're talking to a
lawyer."

" A lawyer? "

" I was in the law for years," said Edward Henry.
" And you know as well as I do that I can get the
option stamped at any time by paying a penalty—
which at worst will be a trifle compared to the value of
the option."

" Ah! " Mr Slosson paused, and resumed his puffing, which exercise—perhaps owing to undue excitement—he had pretermitted. " Then further, the deed isn't drawn up."

" That's not my fault."

" Further, the option is not transferable."

" We shall see about that."

" And the money ought to be paid down to-day, even on your own showing—every cent of it, in cash."

" Here is the money," said Edward Henry, drawing his pocket-book from his breast. " Every cent of it, in the finest brand of bank-notes! "

He flung down the notes with the impulsive gesture of an artist; then, with the caution of a man of the world, gathered them in again.

" The whole circumstances under which the alleged option is alleged to have been given would have to be examined," said Mr Slosson.

" *I* shan't mind," said Edward Henry. " Others might."

" There is such a thing as undue influence."

" Miss Euclid is fifty if she's a day," replied Edward Henry.

" I don't see what Miss Euclid's age has to do with the matter."

" Then your eyesight must be defective, Mr Slosson."

" The document might be a forgery."

" It might. But I've got an autograph letter written entirely in the late Lord Woldo's hand, enclosing the option."

" Let me see it, please."

" Certainly—but in a court of law," said Edward Henry. " You know you're hungry for a good action,

followed by a bill of costs as long as from here to
Jericho."

" Mr Wrissell will assuredly fight," said Mr Slosson.
" He has already given me the most explicit instructions.
Mr Wrissell's objection to a certain class of theatres is
well known."

" And does Mr Wrissell settle everything? "

" Mr Wrissell and Lady Woldo settle everything
between them, and Lady Woldo is guided by Mr
Wrissell.   There is an impression abroad that because
Lady Woldo was originally connected—er—with the
stage, she and Mr Wrissell are not entirely at one in
the conduct of her and her son's interests.   Nothing
could be further from the fact."

Edward Henry's thoughts dwelt for a few moments
upon the late Lord Woldo's picturesque and far-
resounding marriage.

" Can you give me Lady Woldo's address? "

" I can't," said Mr Slosson, after an instant's
hesitation.

" You mean you won't! "

Mr Slosson pursed his lips.

" Well, you can do the other thing! " said Edward
Henry, insolent to the last.

As he left the premises he found Mr Rollo Wrissell,
and his own new acquaintance, Mr Alloyd, the architect, chatting in the portico.   Mr Wrissell was calm,
bland and attentive; Mr Alloyd was eager, excited
and deferential.

Edward Henry caught the words " Russian Ballet."
He reflected upon an abstract question oddly dis-
connected with the violent welter of his sensations:
" Can a man be a good practical architect who isn't
able to sleep because he's seen a Russian Ballet? "

The alert chauffeur of the electric brougham, who

had an excellent idea of effect, brought the admirable vehicle to the kerb exactly in front of Edward Henry as Edward Henry reached the edge of the pavement. Ejaculating a brief command, Edward Henry disappeared within the vehicle and was whirled away in a style whose perfection no scion of a governing family could have bettered.

IV

THE next scene in the exciting drama of Edward Henry's existence that day took place in a building as huge as Wilkins's itself. As the brougham halted at its portals an old and medalled man rushed forth, touched his cap, and assisted Edward Henry to alight. Within the groined and echoing hall of the establishment a young boy sprang out and, with every circumstance of deference, took Edward Henry's hat and stick. Edward Henry then walked a few steps to a lift, and said " smoking-room " to another menial, who bowed humbly before him, and at the proper moment bowed him out of the lift. Edward Henry, crossing a marble floor, next entered an enormous marble apartment chiefly populated by easy-chairs and tables. He sat down to a table and fiercely rang a bell which reposed thereon. Several other menials simultaneously appeared out of invisibility, and one of them hurried obsequiously towards him.

" Bring me a glass of water and a peerage," said Edward Henry.

" I beg pardon, sir. A glass of water and—"

" A peerage. P double e, r, a, g, e."

" I beg your pardon, sir. I didn't catch. Which peerage, sir? We have several."

" All of them."

In a hundred seconds, the last menial having thanked him for kindly taking the glass and the pile of books, Edward Henry was sipping water and studying peerages. In two hundred seconds he was off again. A menial opened the swing-doors of the smoking-room for him and bowed. The menial of the lift bowed, wafted him downwards and bowed. The infant menial produced his hat and stick and bowed. The old and medalled menial summoned his brougham with a frown at the chauffeur and a smile at Edward Henry, bowed, opened the door of the brougham, helped Edward Henry in, bowed, and shut the door.

" Where to, sir? "

" 262 Eaton Square," said Edward Henry.

" Thank you, sir," said the aged menial, and repeated in a curt and peremptory voice to the chauffeur, " 262 Eaton Square! " Lastly he touched his cap.

And Edward Henry swiftly left the precincts of the headquarters of political democracy in London.

v

As he came within striking distance of 262 Eaton Square he had the advantage of an unusual and brilliant spectacle.

Lord Woldo was one of the richest human beings in England—and incidentally he was very human. If he had been in a position to realize all his assets and go to America with the ready money, his wealth was such that even amid the luxurious society of Pittsburg he could have cut quite a figure for some time. He owned a great deal of the land between Oxford Street and Regent Street, and again a number of the valuable squares north of Oxford Street were his, and as for Edgware Road—just as auctioneers advertise a couple of miles of trout-stream or salmon-river as a pleasing adjunct to a country estate, so, had Lord Woldo's estate come under the hammer, a couple of miles of Edgware Road might have been advertised as among its charms. Lord Woldo owned four theatres, and to each theatre he had his private entrance and in each theatre his private box, over which the management had no sway. The Woldos in their leases had always insisted on this.

He never built in London; his business was to let land for others to build upon, the condition being that what others built should ultimately belong to him. Thousands of people in London were only too delighted to build on these terms; he could pick and choose his builders. (The astute Edward Henry himself, for example, wanted furiously to build for him, and was angry because obstacles stood in the path of his desire.) It was constantly happening that under legal agreements some fine erection put up by another hand came into the absolute possession of Lord Waldo without one halfpenny of expense to Lord Woldo. Now and then a whole street would thus tumble all complete into his hands. The system, most agreeable for Lord Woldo and about a dozen other landlords in London, was called the leasehold system; and when Lord Woldo became the proprietor of some bricks and mortar that had cost him nothing, it was said that one of Lord Woldo's leases had " fallen in," and everybody was quite satisfied by this phrase.

In the provinces, besides castles, forests and moors, Lord Woldo owned many acres of land under which was coal, and he allowed enterprising persons to dig deep for this coal, and often explode themselves to death in the adventure, on the understanding that they paid him sixpence for every ton of coal brought to the surface, whether they made any profit on it or not. This arrangement was called " mining rights," another phrase that apparently satisfied everybody.

It might be thought that Lord Woldo was, as they say, on velvet. But the velvet, if it could be so described, was not of so rich and comfortable a pile after all. For Lord Woldo's situation involved many and heavy responsibilities and was surrounded by grave dangers. He was the representative of an old order going down in the unforeseeable welter of twentieth-century politics. Numbers of thoughtful students of English conditions spent much of their time in wondering what would happen one day to the Lord Woldos of England. And when a really great strike came, and a dozen ex-artisans met in a private room of a West End hotel, and decided, without consulting Lord Woldo or the Prime Minister or anybody, that the commerce of the country should be brought to a standstill, these thoughtful students perceived that even Lord Woldo's situation was no more secure than other people's; in fact that it was rather less so.

There could be no doubt that the circumstances of Lord Woldo furnished him with food for thought— and very indigestible food too. . . . Why, at least one hundred sprightly female creatures were being brought up in the hope of marrying him. And they would all besiege him, and he could only marry one of them—at once !

Now as Edward Henry stopped as near to No. 262 as the presence of a waiting two-horse carriage permitted, he saw a grey-haired and blue-cloaked woman solemnly

descending the steps of the portico of No. 262. She
was followed by another similar woman, and watched
by a butler and a footman at the summit of the steps
and by a footman on the pavement and by the coach-
man on the box of the carriage. She carried a thick
and lovely white shawl, and in this shawl was Lord
Woldo and all his many and heavy responsibilities.
It was his fancy to take the air thus, in the arms of a
woman. He allowed himself to be lifted into the open
carriage, and the door of the carriage was shut; and
off went the two ancient horses, slowly, and the two
adult fat men and the two mature spinsters, and the
vehicle weighing about a ton; and Lord Woldo's
morning promenade had begun.

" Follow that! " said Edward Henry to the chauffeur
and nipped into his brougham again. Nobody had
told him that the being in the shawl was Lord Woldo,
but he was sure that it must be so.

In twenty minutes he saw Lord Woldo being
carried to and fro amid the groves of Hyde Park
(one of the few bits of London earth that did not belong
to him or to his more or less distant connections) while
the carriage waited. Once Lord Woldo sat on a
chair, but the chief nurse's lap was between him and
the chair-seat. Both nurses chattered to him in Kensingtonian accents, but he offered no replies.

" Go back to 262," said Edward Henry to his
chauffeur.

Arrived again in Eaton Square, he did not give
himself time to be imposed upon by the grandiosity
of the square in general, nor of No. 262 in particular. He just ran up the steps and rang the visitors'
bell.

" After all," he said to himself as he waited, " these
houses aren't even semi-detached! They're just

houses in a row, and I bet every one of 'em can hear the piano next door!"

The butler whom he had previously caught sight of opened the great portal.

" I want to see Lady Woldo."

" Her ladyship—" began the formidable official.

" Now, look here, my man," said Edward Henry, rather in desperation, " I must see Lady Woldo instantly. It's about the baby—"

" About his lordship? "

" Yes. And look lively, please."

He stepped into the sombre and sumptuous hall.

" Well," he reflected, " I *am* going it—no mistake! "

VI

He was in a large back drawing-room, of which the window, looking north, was in rich stained glass. " No doubt because they're ashamed of the view," he said to himself. The size of the chimneypiece impressed him, and also its rich carving. " But what an old-fashioned grate! " he said to himself. " They need gilt radiators here." The doorway was a marvel of ornate sculpture, and he liked it. He liked, too, the effect of the oil-paintings—mainly portraits—on the walls, and the immensity of the brass fender, and the rugs, and the leather-work of the chairs. But there could be no question that the room was too dark for the taste of any householder clever enough to know the difference between a house and a church.

There was a plunging noise at the door behind him.

" What's amiss? " he heard a woman's voice.

And as he heard it he thrilled with sympathetic vibrations. It was not a North Staffordshire voice, but it was a South Yorkshire voice, which is almost the same thing. It seemed to him to be the first un-Kensingtonian voice to soothe his ear since he had left the Five Towns. Moreover, nobody born south of the Trent would have said, " What's amiss? " A southerner would have said, " What's the matter? " Or, more probably, " What's the mattah? "

He turned and saw a breathless and very beautiful woman, of about twenty-nine or thirty, clothed in black, and she was in the act of removing from her lovely head what looked like a length of red flannel. He noticed, too, simultaneously, that she was suffering from a heavy cold. A majestic footman behind her closed the door and disappeared.

" Are you Lady Woldo? " Edward Henry asked.

" Yes," she said. " What's this about my baby? "

" I've just seen him in Hyde Park," said Edward Henry. " And I observed that a rash had broken out all over his face."

" I know that," she replied. " It began this morning, all of a sudden like. But what of it? I was rather alarmed myself, as it's the first rash he's had and he's the first baby I've had—and he'll be the last too. But everybody said it was nothing. He's never been out without me before, but I had such a cold. Now you don't mean to tell me that you've come down specially from Hyde Park to inform me about that rash. I'm not such a simpleton as all that." She spoke in one long breath.

" I'm sure you're not," said he. " But we've had a good deal of rash in our family, and it just happens that I've got a remedy—a good sound north-country remedy—and it struck me you might like to know of it.

So if you like I'll telegraph to my missis for the recipe. Here's my card."

She read his name, title and address.

" Well," she said, " it's very kind of you, I'm sure, Mr Machin. I knew you must come from up there the moment ye spoke. It does one good above a bit to hear a plain north-country voice after all this fal-lalling."

She blew her lovely nose.

" Doesn't it!" Edward Henry agreed. " That was just what I thought when I heard you say ' Bless us!' Do you know, I've been in London only a two-three days, and I assure you I was beginning to feel lonely for a bit of the Midland accent!"

" Yes," she said, " London's lonely!" And sighed.

" My eldest was bitten by a dog the other day," he went on, in the vein of gossip.

" Oh, don't!" she protested.

" Yes. Gave us a lot of anxiety. All right now! You might like to know that cyanide gauze is a good thing to put on a wound—supposing anything should happen to yours—"

" Oh, don't!" she protested. "I do hope and pray Robert will never be bitten by a dog. Was it a big dog?"

" Fair," said Edward Henry. "So his name's Robert! So's my eldest's!"

" Really now! They wanted him to be called Robert Philip Stephen Darrand Patrick. But I wouldn't have it. He's just Robert. I did have my own way *there!* You know he was born six months after his father's death."

" And I suppose he's ten months now?"

" No. Only six."

" Great Scott! He's big! " said Edward Henry.

" Well," said she, " he is. I am, you see."

" Now, Lady Woldo," said Edward Henry in a new tone, " as we're both from the same part of the country I want to be perfectly straight and above-board with you. It's quite true—all that about the rash. And I *did* think you'd like to know. But that's not really what I came to see you about. You understand, not knowing you, I fancied there might be some difficulty in getting at you—"

" Oh! no! " she said simply. " Everybody gets at me."

" Well, I didn't know, you see. So I just mentioned the baby to begin with, like! "

" I hope you're not after money," she said, almost plaintively.

" I'm not," he said. " You can ask anybody in Bursley or Hanbridge whether I'm the sort of man to go out on the cadge."

" I once was in the chorus in a panto at Hanbridge," she said. " Don't they call Bursley ' Bosley ' down there—' owd Bosley '? "

Edward Henry dealt suitably with these remarks, and then gave her a judicious version of the nature of his business, referring several times to Mr Rollo Wrissell.

" Mr Wrissell! " she murmured, smiling.

" In the end I told Mr Wrissell to go and bury himself," said Edward Henry. " And that's about as far as I've got."

" Oh, don't! " she said, her voice weak from suppressed laughter, and then the laughter burst forth uncontrollable.

" Yes," he said, delighted with himself and her. " I told him to go and bury himself! "

" I suppose you don't like Mr Wrissell? "

" Well—" he temporized.

" I didn't at first," she said. " I hated him. But I like him now, though I must say I adore teasing him. Mr Wrissell is what I call a gentleman. You know he was Lord Woldo's heir. And when Lord Woldo married me it was a bit of a blow for him! But he took it like a lamb. He never turned a hair, and he was more polite than any of them. I daresay you know Lord Woldo saw me in a musical comedy at Scarborough—he has a place near there, ye know. Mr Wrissell had made him angry about some of his New Thought fads, and I do believe he asked me to marry him just to annoy Mr Wrissell. He used to say to me, my husband did, that he'd married me in too much of a hurry, and that it was too bad on Mr Wrissell. And then he laughed, and I laughed too. ' After all,' he used to say, my husband did, ' To marry an actress is an accident that might happen to any member of the House of Lords—and it does happen to a lot of 'em—but they don't marry anything as beautiful as you, Blanche? ' he used to say. ' And you stick up for yourself, Blanche,' he used to say. ' I'll stand by you,' he said. He was a straight 'un, my husband was. They left me alone until he died. And then they began—I mean *his* folks. And when Bobbie was born it got worse. Only I must say even then Mr Wrissell never turned a hair. Everybody seemed to make out that I ought to be very grateful to them, and I ought to think myself very lucky. Me—a peeress of the realm! They wanted me to change. But how could I change? I was Blanche Wilmot—on the road for ten years—never got a show in London—and Blanche Wilmot I shall ever be—peeress or no peeress! It was no joke being Lord Woldo's wife, I can tell you,

and it's still less of a joke being Lord Woldo's mother!
You imagine it. It's worse than carrying about a
china vase all the time on a slippery floor! Am I any
happier now than I was before I married? Well, I
am! There's more worry in one way, but there's
less in another. And of course I've got Bobbie! But
it isn't all beer and skittles, and I let 'em know it, too.
I can't do what I like! And I'm just a sort of exile,
you know. I used to enjoy being on the stage and
showing myself off. A hard life, but one does enjoy
it. And one gets used to it. One gets to need it.
Sometimes I feel I'd give anything to be able to go on
the stage again—Oh—oh—!"

She sneezed; then took breath.

"Shall I put some more coal on the fire?" Edward
Henry suggested.

"Perhaps I'd better ring," she hesitated.

"No, I'll do it."

He put coal on the fire.

"And if you'd feel easier with that flannel round
your head, please do put it on again."

"Well," she said, "I will. My mother used to
say there was naught like red flannel for a cold."

With an actress's skill she arranged the flannel,
and from its encircling folds her face emerged bewitch-
ing—and she knew it. Her complexion had suffered
in ten years of the road, but its extreme beauty could
not yet be denied. And Edward Henry thought:
"All the *really* pretty girls come from the Midlands!"

"Here I am rambling on," she said. "I always
was a rare rambler. What do you want me to
do?"

"Exert your influence," he replied. "Don't you
think it's rather hard on Rose Euclid—treating her

like this? Of course people say all sorts of things about Rose Euclid—"

" I won't hear a word against Rose Euclid," cried Lady Woldo. " Whenever she was on tour, if she knew any of us were resting in the town where she was she'd send us seats. And many's the time I've cried and cried at her acting. And then she's the life and soul of the Theatrical Ladies' Guild."

" And isn't that your husband's signature? " he demanded, showing the precious option.

" Of course it is."

He did not show her the covering letter.

" And I've no doubt my husband *wanted* a theatre built there, and he wanted to do Rose Euclid a good turn. And I'm quite positive certain sure that he didn't want any of Mr Wrissell's rigmaroles on his land. He wasn't that sort, my husband wasn't. . . . You must go to law about it," she finished.

" Yes," said Edward Henry, protestingly. " And a pretty penny it would cost me! And supposing I lost, after all? . . . You never know. There's a much easier way than going to law."

" What is it? "

" As I say—you exert your influence, Lady Woldo. Write and tell them I've seen you and you insist—"

" Eh! Bless you! They'd twist me round their little finger. I'm not a fool, but I'm not very clever— I know that. I shouldn't know whether I was standing on my head or my heels by the time they'd done with me. I've tried to face them out before—about things."

" Who—Mr Wrissell, or Slossons? "

" Both? Eh, but I should like to put a spoke in Mr Wrissell's wheel—gentleman as he is. You see he's just one of those men you can't help wanting to tease. When you're on the road you meet lots of 'em."

" I tell you what you can do! "

" What? "

" Write and tell Slossons that you don't wish them to act for you any more, and you'll go to another firm of solicitors. That would bring 'em to their senses."

" Can't! They're in the will. *He* settled that. That's why they're so cocky."

Edward Henry persisted—and this time with an exceedingly impressive and conspiratorial air:

" I tell you another thing you could do—you really *could* do—and it depends on nobody but yourself."

" Well," she said with decision. " I'll do it."

" Whatever it is? "

" If it's straight."

" Of course it's straight. And it would be a grand way of teasing Mr Wrissell and all of 'em! A simply grand way! I should die of laughing."

" Well—"

At this critical point the historic conversation was interrupted by phenomena in the hall which Lady Woldo recognized with feverish excitement. Lord Woldo had safely returned from Hyde Park. Starting up, she invited Edward Henry to wait a little. A few moments later they were bending over the infant together, and Edward Henry was offering his views on the cause and cure of rash.

VII

EARLY on the same afternoon Edward Henry managed by a somewhat excessive obstreperousness to penetrate once more into the private room of Mr Slosson, senior, who received him in silence.

He passed a document to Mr Slosson.

" It's only a copy," he said. " But the original is in my pocket, and to-morrow it will be duly stamped. I'll give you the original in exchange for the stamped lease of my Piccadilly Circus plot of land. You know the money is waiting."

Mr Slosson perused the document; and it was certainly to his credit that he did so without any superficial symptoms of dismay.

" What will Mr Wrissell and the Woldo family say about that, do you think? " asked Edward Henry.

" Lady Woldo will never be allowed to carry it out," said Mr Slosson.

" Who's going to stop her? She must carry it out. She wants to carry it out. She's dying to carry it out. Moreover, I shall communicate it to the papers to-night—unless you and I come to an arrangement. And if by any chance she doesn't carry it out—well, there'll be a fine society action about it, you can bet your boots, Mr Slosson."

The document was a contract made between Blanche Lady Woldo of the one part and Edward Henry Machin of the other part, whereby Blanche Lady Woldo undertook to appear in musical comedy at any West End Theatre to be named by Edward Henry, at a salary of two hundred pounds a week for a period of six months.

" You've not got a theatre," said Mr Slosson.

" I can get half a dozen in an hour—with that contract in my hand," said Edward Henry.

And he knew from Mr Slosson's face that he had won.

VIII

THAT evening, feeling that he had earned a little re-creation, he went to the Empire Theatre—not in Hanbridge, but in Leicester Square, London. The lease, with a prodigious speed hitherto unknown at Slossons', had been drawn up, engrossed and executed. The Piccadilly Circus land was his for sixty-four years.

"And I've got the old Chapel pulled down for nothing," he said to himself.

He was rather happy as he wandered about amid the brilliance of the Empire Promenade. But after half an hour of such exercise and of vain efforts to see or hear what was afoot on the stage, he began to feel rather lonely. Then it was that he caught sight of Mr Alloyd, the architect, also lonely.

"Well," said Mr Alloyd, curtly, with a sardonic smile. "They've telephoned me all about it. I've seen Mr Wrissell. Just my luck! So you're the man! He pointed you out to me this morning. My design for that church would have knocked the West End! Of course Mr Wrissell will pay me compensation, but that's not the same thing. I wanted the advertisement of the building. . . . Just my luck! Have a drink, will you?"

Edward Henry ultimately went with the plaintive Mr Alloyd to his rooms in Adelphi Terrace. He quitted those rooms at something after two o'clock in the morning. He had practically given Mr Alloyd a definite commission to design the Regent Theatre. Already he was practically the proprietor of a first-class theatre in the West End of London!

"I wonder whether Master Seven Sachs could have bettered my day's work to-day!" he reflected as he

got into a taxi-cab. He had dismissed his electric
brougham earlier in the evening. " I doubt if even
Master Seven Sachs himself wouldn't be proud of
my little scheme in Eaton Square!" said he. . . .
" Wilkins's Hotel, please, driver."

PART II

I

ON a morning in spring Edward Henry got out of an express at Euston which had come, not from the Five Towns, but from Birmingham. Having on the previous day been called to Birmingham on local and profitable business, he had found it convenient to spend the night there and telegraph home that London had summoned him. It was in this unostentatious, this half-furtive fashion, that his visits to London now usually occurred. Not that he was afraid of his wife! Not that he was afraid even of his mother! Oh, no! He was merely rather afraid of himself—of his own opinion concerning the metropolitan, non-local, speculative and perhaps unprofitable business to which he was committed. The fact was that he could scarcely look his women in the face when he mentioned London. He spoke vaguely of "real estate" enterprise, and left it at that. The women made no inquiries; they too left it at that. Nevertheless . . .!

The episode of Wilkins's was buried, but it was imperfectly buried. The Five Towns definitely knew that he had stayed at Wilkins's for a bet, and that Brindley had discharged the bet. And rumours of his valet, his electric brougham, his theatrical supper-parties, had mysteriously hung in the streets of the

Five Towns like a strange vapour. Wisps of the strange vapour had conceivably entered the precincts of his home, but nobody ever referred to them; nobody ever sniffed apprehensively nor asked anybody else whether there was not a smell of fire. The discreetness of the silence was disconcerting. Happily his relations with that angel his wife were excellent. She had carried angelicism so far as not to insist on the destruction of Carlo; and she had actually applauded, while sticking to her white apron, the sudden and startling extravagances of his toilette.

On the whole, though little short of thirty-five thousand pounds would ultimately be involved—not to speak of a liability of nearly three thousand a year for sixty-four years for ground-rent—Edward Henry was not entirely gloomy as to his prospects. He was indubitably thinner in girth; novel problems and anxieties, and the constant annoyance of being in complete technical ignorance of his job, had removed some flesh. (And not a bad thing, either!) But on the other hand his chin exhibited one proof that life was worth living, and that he had discovered new faith in life and a new conviction of youthfulness.

He had shaved off his beard.

" Well, sir! " a voice greeted him full of hope and cheer, immediately his feet touched the platform.

It was the voice of Mr Marrier. Edward Henry and Mr Marrier were now in regular relations. Before Edward Henry had paid his final bill at Wilkins's and relinquished his valet and his electric brougham, and disposed for ever of his mythical " man " on board the *Minnetonka*, and got his original luggage away from the Hotel Majestic, Mr Marrier had visited him and made a certain proposition. And such was the influence of Mr Marrier's incurable smile and of his solid optimism and of his obvious talent for getting things done on the spot (as witness the photography), that the proposition had been accepted. Mr Marrier was now Edward Henry's "representative" in London. At the Green Room Club Mr Marrier informed reliable cronies that he was Edward Henry's "confidential adviser." At the Turk's Head, Hanbridge, Edward Henry informed reliable cronies that Mr Marrier was a sort of clerk, factotum, or maid-of-all-work. A compromise between these two very different conceptions of Mr Marrier's position had been arrived at in the word "representative." The real truth was that Edward Henry employed Mr Marrier in order to listen to Mr Marrier. He turned on Mr Marrier like a tap, and nourished himself from a gushing stream of useful information concerning the theatrical world. Mr Marrier, quite unconsciously, was bit by bit remedying Edward Henry's acute ignorance.

The question of wages had caused Edward Henry some apprehensions. He had learnt in a couple of days that a hundred pounds a week was a trifle on the stage. He had soon heard of performers who worked for "nominal" salaries of forty and fifty a week. For a manager twenty pounds a week seemed to be a usual figure. But in the Five Towns three pounds a week is regarded as very goodish pay for any subordinate, and Edward Henry could not rid himself all at once of native standards. He had therefore, with diffidence, offered three pounds a week to the aristocratic Marrier. And Mr Marrier had not refused it, nor ceased to smile. On three pounds a week he haunted the best restaurants, taxi-cabs, and other resorts, and his garb seemed always to be smarter than Edward Henry's—especially in such details as waistcoat slips.

Of course Mr Marrier had a taxi-cab waiting exactly opposite the coach from which Edward Henry descended. It was just this kind of efficient attention that was gradually endearing him to his employer.

"How goes it?" said Edward Henry, curtly, as they drove down to the Grand Babylon Hotel—now Edward Henry's regular headquarters in London.

Said Mr Marrier:

"I suppose you've seen another of 'em's got a knighthood?"

"No," said Edward Henry. "Who?" He knew that by "'em" Mr Marrier meant the great race of actor-managers.

"Gerald Pompey. Something to do with him being a sheriff in the City, you know. I bet you what you laike he went in for the Common Council simply in order to get even with old Pilgrim. In fact I know he did. And now a foundation-stone-laying has dan it."

"A foundation-stone-laying?"

"Yes. The new City Guild's building, you knaow. Royalty—Temple Bar business—sheriffs—knighthood. There you are!"

"Oh!" said Edward Henry. And then after a pause added: "Pity *we* can't have a foundation-stone-laying!"

"By the way, old Pilgrim's in the deuce and all of a haole, I heah. It's all over the Clubs." (In speaking of the Clubs Mr Marrier always pronounced them with a capital letter.) "I told you he was going to sail from Tilbury on his world-tour, and have a grand embarking ceremony and seeing-off! Just laike him! Greatest advertiser the world ever saw! Well, since that P. & O. boat was lost on the Goodwins, Cora

Pryde has absolutely declined to sail from Tilbury. Ab-so-lute-ly! Swears she'll join the steamer at Marseilles. And Pilgrim has got to go with her, too."

" Why? "

" Well, even Pilgrim couldn't have a grand embarking ceremony without his leading lady! He's furious, I hear."

" Why shouldn't he go with her? "

" Why not? Because he's formally announced his grand embarking ceremony! Invitations are out. Barge from London Bridge to Tilbury, and so on! What he wants is a good excuse for giving it up. He'd never be able to admit that he'd had to give it up because Cora Pryde made him! He wants to save his face."

" Well," said Edward Henry, absently. " It's a queer world. You've got me a room at the Grand Bab? "

" Rather! "

" Then let's go and have a look at the Regent first," said Edward Henry.

No sooner had he expressed the wish than Mr Marrier's neck curved round through the window, and with three words to the chauffeur he had deflected the course of the taxi.

Edward Henry had an almost boyish curiosity about his edifice. He would go and give it a glance at the oddest moments. And just now he had a swift and violent desire to behold it. With all speed the taxi shot down Shaftesbury Avenue and swerved to the right. . . .

There it was! Yes, it really existed, the incredible edifice of his caprice and of Mr Alloyd's constructive imagination! It had already reached a height of fifteen feet; and, dozen of yards above that, cranes dominated the sunlit air, swinging loads of bricks in the azure; and scores of workmen crawled about beneath these monsters. And he, Edward Henry, by a single act of volition, was the author of it! He slipped from the taxi, penetrated within the wall of hoardings, and gazed, just gazed! A wondrous thing —human enterprise! And also a terrifying thing! . . . That building might be the tomb of his reputation. On the other hand, it might be the seed of a new renown compared to which the first would be as naught! He turned his eyes away, in fear—yes, in fear!

"I say," he said. "Will Sir John Pilgrim be out of bed yet, d'ye think?" He glanced at his watch. The hour was about eleven.

"He'll be at breakfast."

"I'm going to see him, then. What's his address?"

"25 Queen Anne's Gate. But do you knaow him? I do. Shall I cam with you?"

"No," said Edward Henry, shortly. "You go on with my bags to the Grand Bab, and get me another taxi. I'll see you in my room at the hotel at a quarter to one. Eh?"

"Rather!" agreed Mr Marrier, submissive.

II

"Sole proprietor of the Regent Theatre."

These were the words which Edward Henry wrote on a visiting-card and which procured him immediate admittance to the unique spectacle—reputed to be one of the most enthralling sights in London—of Sir John Pilgrim at breakfast.

In a very spacious front-room of his flat (so celebrated for its Gobelins tapestries and its truly wonderful parquet-flooring) sat Sir John Pilgrim at a large hexagonal mahogany table. At one side of the table a small square of white diaper was arranged, and on this square were an apparatus for boiling eggs, another for making toast, and a third for making coffee. Sir John, with the assistance of a young Chinaman and a fox-terrier, who flitted around him, was indeed eating and drinking. The vast remainder of the table was gleamingly bare, save for newspapers and letters opened and unopened which Sir John tossed about. Opposite to him sat a secretary whose fluffy hair, neat white *chemisette*, and tender years gave her an appearance of helpless fragility in front of the powerful and ruthless celebrity. Sir John's crimson-socked left foot stuck out from the table, emerging from the left half of a lovely new pair of brown trousers, and resting on a piece of white paper. Before this white paper knelt a man in a frock-coat who was drawing an outline on the paper round Sir John's foot.

" You *are* a bootmaker, aren't you? " Sir John was saying airily.

" Yes, Sir John."

" Excuse me! " said Sir John. " I only wanted to be sure. I fancied from the way you caressed my corn with that pencil that you might be an artist on one of the illustrated papers. My mistake! " He was bending down. Then suddenly straightening himself he called across the room: " I say, Givington, did you notice my pose then—my expression as I used the word ' caresssed '? How would that do? "

And Edward Henry now observed in a corner of the room a man standing in front of an easel and sketching somewhat grossly thereon in charcoal. This man said:

" If you won't bother me, Sir John, I won't bother you."

" Ah! Givington! Ah! Givington!" murmured Sir John still more airily—at breakfast he was either airy or nothing. " You're getting on in the world. You aren't merely an A.R.A.;—you're making money! A year ago you'd never have had the courage to address me in that tone. Well, I sincerely congratulate you. . . . Here, Snip, here's my dentist's bill— worry it, worry it! Good dog! Worry it!" (The dog growled now over a torn document beneath the table.) " Miss Taft, you might see that a *communique* goes out to the effect that I gave my first sitting to Mr Saracen Givington, A.R.A., this morning. The activities of Mr Saracen Givington are of interest to the world, and rightly so! You'd better come round to the other side for the right foot, Mr Bootmaker. The journey is simply nothing."

And then, and not till then, did Sir John Pilgrim turn his large and handsome middle-aged blond face in the direction of Alderman Edward Henry Machin.

" Pardon my curiosity," said Sir John, " but who are you? "

" My name is Machin—Alderman Machin," said Edward Henry. " I sent up my card and you asked me to come in."

" Ha! " Sir John exclaimed, seizing an egg. " Will you crack an egg with me, Alderman? I can crack an egg with anybody."

" Thanks," said Edward Henry. " I'll be very glad to." And he advanced towards the table.

Sir John hesitated. The fact was that, though he dissembled his dismay with marked histrionic skill, he was unquestionably overwhelmed by astonishment. In the course of years he had airily invited hundreds of callers to crack an egg with him—the joke was one of his favourites—but nobody had ever ventured to accept the invitation.

"Chung," he said weakly, "lay a cover for the Alderman."

Edward Henry sat down quite close to Sir John. He could discern all the details of Sir John's face and costume. The tremendous celebrity was wearing a lounge-suit somewhat like his own, but instead of the coat he had a blue dressing-jacket with crimson facings; the sleeves ended in rather long wristbands, which were unfastened, the opal cuff-links drooping each from a single hole. Perhaps for the first time in his life Edward Henry intimately understood what idiosyncratic elegance was. He could almost feel the emanating personality of Sir John Pilgrim, and he was intimidated by it; he was intimidated by its hardness, its harshness, its terrific egotism, its utterly brazen quality. Sir John's glance was the most purely arrogant that Edward Henry had ever encountered. It knew no reticence. And Edward Henry thought: "When this chap dies he'll want to die in public, with the reporters round his bed and a private secretary taking down messages."

"This is rather a lark," said Sir John, recovering.

"It is," said Edward Henry, who now felicitously perceived that a lark it indeed was, and ought to be treated as such. "It shall be a lark!" he said to himself.

Sir John dictated a letter to Miss Taft, and before the letter was finished the grinning Chung had laid a place for Edward Henry, and Snip had inspected him and passed him for one of the right sort.

"Had I said that this is rather a lark?" Sir John inquired, the letter accomplished.

" I forget," said Edward Henry.

" Because I don't like to say the same thing twice over if I can help it. It *is* a lark though, isn't it? "

" Undoubtedly," said Edward Henry, decapitating an egg. " I only hope that I'm not interrupting you."

" Not in the least," said Sir John. " Breakfast is my sole free time. In another half hour I assure you I shall be attending to three or four things at once." He leant over towards Edward Henry. " But between you and me, Alderman, quite privately, if it isn't a rude question, what did you come for? "

" Well," said Edward Henry, " as I wrote on my card, I'm the sole proprietor of the Regent Theatre—"

" But there is no Regent Theatre," Sir John interrupted him.

" No. Not strictly. But there will be. It's in course of construction. We're up to the first floor."

" Dear me! A suburban theatre, no doubt? "

" Do you mean to say, Sir John," cried Edward Henry, " that you haven't noticed it? It's within a few yards of Piccadilly Circus."

" Really! " said Sir John. " You see my theatre is in Lower Regent Street and I never go to Piccadilly Circus. I make a point of not going to Piccadilly Circus. Miss Taft, how long is it since I went to Piccadilly Circus? Forgive me, young woman, I was forgetting—you aren't old enough to remember. Well, never mind details. . . . And what is there remarkable about the Regent Theatre, Alderman? "

" I intend it to be a theatre of the highest class, Sir John," said Edward Henry. " Nothing but the very best will be seen on its boards."

" That's not remarkable, Alderman. We're all like that. Haven't you noticed it? "

" Then secondly," said Edward Henry, " I am the sole proprietor. I have no financial backers, no mortgages, no partners. I have made no contracts with anybody."

" That," said Sir John, " is not unremarkable. In fact many persons who do not happen to possess my own robust capacity for belief might not credit your statement."

" And thirdly," said Edward Henry, " every member of the audience—even in the boxes, the most expensive seats—will have a full view of the whole of the stage—or, in the alternative, at *matinées*, a full view of a lady's hat."

" Alderman," said Sir John, gravely, " before I offer you another egg, let me warn you against carrying remarkableness too far. You may be regarded as eccentric if you go on like that. Some people, I am told, don't want a view of the stage."

" Then they had better not come to my theatre," said Edward Henry.

" All which," commented Sir John, " gives me no clue whatever to the reason why you are sitting here by my side and calmly eating my eggs and toast, and drinking my coffee."

Admittedly, Edward Henry was nervous. Admittedly, he was a provincial in the presence of one of the most illustrious personages in the Empire. Nevertheless, he controlled his nervousness, and reflected:

" Nobody else from the Five Towns would or could have done what I am doing. Moreover, this chap is a mountebank. In the Five Towns they would kowtow to him, but they would laugh at him. They would mighty soon add *him* up. Why should I be nervous? I'm as good as he is." He finished with the thought which has inspired many a timid man with new courage in a desperate crisis: " The fellow can't eat me."

Then he said aloud:

" I want to ask you a question, Sir John."

" One? "

" One. Are you the head of the theatrical profession, or is Sir Gerald Pompey? "

" *Sir* Gerald Pompey? "

" *Sir* Gerald Pompey. Haven't you seen the papers this morning? "

Sir John Pilgrim turned pale. Springing up, he seized the topmost of an undisturbed pile of daily papers, and feverishly opened it.

" Bah! " he muttered.

He was continually thus imitating his own behaviour on the stage. The origin of his renowned breakfasts lay in the fact that he had once played the part of a millionaire-ambassador who juggled at breakfast with his own affairs and the affairs of the world. The stage-breakfast of a millionaire-ambassador created by a playwright on the verge of bankruptcy had appealed to his imagination and influenced all the mornings of his life.

" They've done it just to irritate me as I'm starting off on my world's tour," he muttered, coursing round the table. Then he stopped and gazed at Edward Henry. "This is a political knighthood," said he. " It has nothing to do with the stage. It is not like my knighthood, is it? "

" Certainly not," Edward Henry agreed. " But you know how people will talk, Sir John. People will be going about this very morning and saying that Sir Gerald is at last the head of the theatrical profession. I came here for your authoritative opinion. I know you're unbiased."

Sir John resumed his chair.

" As for Pompey's qualifications as a head," he murmured, " I know nothing of them. I fancy his heart is excellent. I only saw him twice, once in his own theatre, and once in Bond Street. I should be inclined to say that on the stage he looks more like a gentleman than any gentleman ought to look, and that in the street he might be mistaken for an actor. . . . How will that suit you? "

" It's a clue," said Edward Henry.

" Alderman! " exclaimed Sir John, " I believe that if I didn't keep a firm hand on myself I should soon begin to like you. Have another cup of coffee. Chung! . . . Good-bye, Bootmaker, good-bye! "

" I only want to know for certain who *is* the head," said Edward Henry, " because I mean to invite the head of the theatrical profession to lay the corner-stone of my new theatre."

" Ah! "

" When do you start on your world's tour, Sir John? "

" I leave Tilbury, with my entire company, scenery and effects, on the morning of Tuesday week, by the *Kandahar*. I shall play first at Cairo."

" How awkward! " said Edward Henry. " I meant to ask you to lay the stone on the very next afternoon—Wednesday, that is! "

" Indeed! "

" Yes, Sir John. The ceremony will be a very original affair—very original! "

" A foundation-stone-laying! " mused Sir John. " But if you're already up to the first floor, how can you be laying the foundation-stone on Wednesday week? "

" I didn't say foundation-stone. I said corner-stone," Edward Henry corrected him. "An entire novelty! That's why we can't be ready before Wednesday week."

"And you want to advertise your house by getting the head of the profession to assist?"

"That is exactly my idea."

"Well," said Sir John, "whatever else you may lack, Mr Alderman, you are not lacking in nerve, if you expect to succeed in *that*."

Edward Henry smiled. "I have already heard, in a roundabout way," he replied, "that Sir Gerald Pompey would not be unwilling to officiate. My only difficulty is that I'm a truthful man by nature. Whoever officiates I shall of course have to have him labelled, in my own interests, as the head of the theatrical profession, and I don't want to say anything that isn't true."

There was a pause.

"Now, Sir John, couldn't you stay a day or two longer in London, and join the ship at Marseilles instead of going on board at Tilbury?"

"But I have made all my arrangements. The whole world knows that I am going on board at Tilbury."

Just then the door opened, and a servant announced:

"Mr Carlo Trent."

Sir John Pilgrim rushed like a locomotive to the threshold and seized both Carlo Trent's hands with such a violence of welcome that Carlo Trent's eyeglass fell out of his eye and the purple ribbon dangled to his waist.

"Come in, come in!" said Sir John. "And begin to read at once. I've been looking out of the window for you for the last quarter of an hour. Alderman,

this is Mr Carlo Trent, the well-known dramatic poet.
Trent, this is one of the greatest geniuses in London.
. . . Ah! You know each other? It's not surprising!
No, don't stop to shake hands. Sit down here, Trent.
Sit down on this chair. . . . Here, Snip, take his hat.
Worry it! Worry it! Now, Trent, don't read to *me*.
It might make you nervous and hurried. Read to
Miss Taft and Chung and to Mr Givington over
there. Imagine that they are the great and enlightened
public. You have imagination, haven't you, being a
poet? "

Sir John had accomplished the change of mood
with the rapidity of a transformation scene—in which
form of art, by the way, he was a great adept.

Carlo Trent, somewhat breathless, took a manuscript from his pocket, opened it, and announced:
" The Orient Pearl."

" Oh! " breathed Edward Henry.

For some thirty minutes Edward Henry listened
to hexameters, the first he had ever heard. The effect
of them on his moral organism was worse than he had
expected. He glanced about at the other auditors.
Givington had opened a box of tubes and was spreading
colours on his palette. The Chinaman's eyes were
closed while his face still grinned. Snip was asleep
on the parquet. Miss Taft bit the end of a pencil
with her agreeable teeth. Sir John Pilgrim lay at
full length on a sofa, occasionally lifting his legs.
Edward Henry despaired of help in his great need.
But just as his desperation was becoming too acute to
be borne, Carlo Trent ejaculated the word " Curtain."
It was the first word that Edward Henry had clearly
understood.

" That's the first act," said Carlo Trent, wiping his
face. Snip awakened.

Edward Henry rose, and, in the hush, tiptoed round to the sofa.

" Good-bye, Sir John," he whispered.

" You're not going? "

" I am, Sir John."

The head of his profession sat up. " How right you are! " said he. " How right you are! Trent, I knew from the first words it wouldn't do. It lacks colour. I want something more crimson, more like the brighter parts of this jacket, something—" He waved hands in the air. " The Alderman agrees with me. He's going. Don't trouble to read any more, Trent. But drop in any time—any time. Chung, what o'clock is it? "

" It is nearly noon," said Edward Henry, in the tone of an old friend. " Well, I'm sorry you can't oblige me, Sir John. I'm off to see Sir Gerald Pompey now."

" But who says I can't oblige you? " protested Sir John. " Who knows what sacrifices I would not make in the highest interests of the profession? Alderman, you jump to conclusions with the agility of an acrobat, but they are false conclusions! Miss Taft, the telephone! Chung, my coat! Good-bye, Trent, good-bye! "

An hour later Edward Henry met Mr Marrier at the Grand Babylon Hotel.

" Well, sir," said Mr Marrier, " you are the greatest man that ever lived! "

" Why? "

Mr Marrier showed him the stop-press news of a penny evening paper, which read: " Sir John Pilgrim has abandoned his ceremonious departure from Tilbury, in order to lay the corner-stone of the new Regent Theatre on Wednesday week. He and

Miss Cora Pryde will join the *Kandahar* at Marseilles."

"You needn't do any advertaysing," said Mr Marrier. "Pilgrim will do all the advertaysing for you."

III

Edward Henry and Mr Marrier worked together admirably that afternoon on the arrangements for the corner-stone-laying. And—such was the interaction of their separate enthusiasms—it soon became apparent that all London (in the only right sense of the word " all ") must and would be at the ceremony. Characteristically, Mr Marrier happened to have a list or catalogue of all London in his pocket, and Edward Henry appreciated him more than ever. But towards four o'clock Mr Marrier annoyed and even somewhat alarmed Edward Henry by a mysterious change of mien. His assured optimism slipped away from him. He grew uneasy, darkly preoccupied, and inefficient. At last, when the clock in the room struck four, and Edward Henry failed to hear it, Mr Marrier said:

" I'm afraid I shall have to ask you to excuse me now."

" Why? "

" I told you I had an appointment for tea at four."

" Did you? What is it? " Edward Henry demanded, with an employer's instinctive assumption that souls as well as brains can be bought for such sums as three pounds a week.

" I have a lady coming to tea here. That is, downstairs."

" In this hotel? "

" Yes."

" Who is it? " Edward Henry pursued lightly, for though he appreciated Mr Marrier, he also despised him. However, he found the grace to add: " May one ask? "

" It's Miss Elsie April."

" Do you mean to say, Marrier," complained Edward Henry, " that you've known Miss Elsie April all these months and never told me? . . . There aren't two, I suppose? It's the cousin or something of Rose Euclid? "

Mr Marrier nodded. " The fact is," he said, " she and I are joint honorary organizing secretaries for the annual conference of the Azure Society. You know— it leads the New Thought movement in England."

" You never told me that, either? "

" Didn't I, sir? I didn't think it would interest you. Besides, both Miss April and I are comparatively new members."

" Oh," said Edward Henry, with all the canny provincial's conviction of his own superior shrewdness; and he repeated, so as to intensify this conviction and impress it on others, " Oh! " In the undergrowth of his mind was the thought: " How dare this man whose brains belong to me be the organizing secretary of something that I don't know anything about and don't want to know anything about? "

" Yes," said Mr Marrier, modestly.

" I say," Edward Henry inquired warmly, with an impulsive gesture, " who is she? "

" Who is she? " repeated Mr Marrier, blankly.

" Yes. What does she do? "

" Doesn't do anything," said Mr Marrier. " Very good amateur actress. Goes about a great deal.

Her mother was on the stage. Married a wealthy wholesale corset-maker."

" Who did? Miss April? " Edward Henry had a twinge.

" No. Her mother. Both parents dead, and Miss April has an income—a considerable income."

" What do you call considerable? "

" Five or six thousand a year."

" The deuce! " murmured Edward Henry.

" May have lost a bit of it, of course," Mr Marrier hedged. " But not much, not much! "

" Well," said Edward Henry, smiling, " what about *my* tea? Am I to have tea all by myself? "

" Will you come down and meet her? " Mr Marrier's expression approached the wistful.

" Well," said Edward Henry, " it's an idea, isn't it? Why should I be the only person in London who doesn't know Miss Elsie April? "

It was ten minutes past four when they descended into the electric publicity of the Grand Babylon. Amid the music and the rattle of crockery and the gliding waiters and the large nodding hats that gathered more and more thickly round the tables, there was no sign of Elsie April.

" She may have been and gone away again," said Edward Henry, apprehensive.

" Oh, no! She wouldn't go away." Mr Marrier was positive.

In the tone of a man with an income of two hundred pounds a week he ordered a table to be prepared for three.

At ten minutes to five he said:

" I hope she *hasn't* been and gone away again! "

Edward Henry began to be gloomy and resentful. The crowded and factitious gaiety of the place actually annoyed him. If Elsie April had been and gone away again, he objected to such silly feminine conduct. If she was merely late, he equally objected to such unconscionable inexactitude. He blamed Mr Marrier. He considered that he had the right to blame Mr Marrier because he paid him three pounds a week. And he very badly wanted his tea.

Then their four eyes, which for forty minutes had scarcely left the entrance staircase, were rewarded. She came, in furs, gleaming white kid gloves, gold chains, a gold bag, and a black velvet hat.

" I'm not late, am I? " she said, after the introduction.

" No," they both replied. And they both meant it. For she was like fine weather. The forty minutes of waiting were forgotten, expunged from the records of time—just as the memory of a month of rain is obliterated by one splendid sunny day.

IV

EDWARD HENRY enjoyed the tea, which was bad, to an extraordinary degree. He became uplifted in the presence of Miss Elsie April; whereas Mr Marrier, strangely, drooped to still deeper depths of unaccustomed inert melancholy. Edward Henry decided that she was every bit as piquant, challenging and delectable as he had imagined her to be on the day when he ate an artichoke at the next table to hers at Wilkins's. She coincided exactly with his remembrance of her, except that she was now slightly more plump. Her contours were effulgent—there was no other word. Beautiful she was not, for she had a turned-up nose; but what charm she radiated! Every movement and tone enchanted Edward Henry. He was enchanted not at intervals, by a chance gesture, but all the time—when she was serious, when she smiled, when she fingered her tea-cup, when she pushed her furs back over her shoulders, when she spoke of the weather, when she spoke of the social crisis, and when she made fun, with a certain brief absence of restraint—rather in her artichoke manner of making fun.

He thought and believed:

" This is the finest woman I ever saw! " He clearly perceived the inferiority of other women, whom, nevertheless, he admired and liked, such as the Countess of Chell and Lady Woldo.

It was not her brains, nor her beauty, nor her stylishness that affected him. No! It was something mysterious and dizzying that resided in every particle of her individuality.

He thought:

" I've often and often wanted to see her again. And now I'm having tea with her! " And he was happy.

" Have you got that list, Mr Marrier? " she asked, in her low and thrilling voice. So saying, she raised her eyebrows in expectation—a delicious effect, especially behind her half-raised white veil.

Mr Marrier produced a document.

" But that's *my* list! " said Edward Henry.

" Your list? "

" I'd better tell you." Mr Marrier essayed a rapid explanation. " Mr Machin wanted a list of the raight sort of people to ask to the corner-stone-laying of his theatah. So I used this as a basis."

Elsie April smiled again:

" Ve-ry good! " she approved.

" What *is* your list, Marrier? " asked Edward Henry.

It was Elsie who replied:

" People to be invited to the dramatic soirée of the Azure Society. We give six a year. No title is announced. Nobody except a committee of three knows even the name of the author of the play that is to be performed. Everything is kept a secret. Even the author doesn't know that his play has been chosen. Don't you think it's a delightful idea? . . . An offspring of the New Thought! "

He agreed that it was a delightful idea.

" Shall I be invited? " he asked.

She answered gravely, " I don't know."

" Are you going to play in it? "

She paused. . . . " Yes."

" Then you must let me come. Talking of plays—"

He stopped. He was on the edge of facetiously relating the episode of " The Orient Pearl " at Sir John Pilgrim's. But he withdrew in time. Suppose that " The Orient Pearl " was the piece to be performed by the Azure Society! It might well be! It was (in his opinion) just the sort of play that that sort of society would choose! Nevertheless he was as anxious as ever to see Elsie April act. He really thought that she could and would transfigure any play. Even his profound scorn of New Thought (a subject of which he was entirely ignorant) began to be modified —and by nothing but the enchantment of the tone in which Elsie April murmured the words, " Azure Society! "

" How soon is the performance? " he demanded.

" Wednesday week," said she.

" That's the very day of my corner-stone-laying,"

he said. " However, it doesn't matter. My little affair
will be in the afternoon."

" But it can't be," said she, solemnly. " It would
interfere with us, and we should interfere with it.
Our Annual Conference takes place in the afternoon.
All London will be there."

Said Mr Marrier, rather shamefaced:

" That's just it, Mr Machin. It positively never
occurred to me that the Azure Conference is to be on
that very day. I never thought of it until nearly four
o'clock. And then I scarcely knew how to explain
it to you. I really don't know how it escaped me."

Mr Marrier's trouble was now out, and he had
declined in Edward Henry's esteem. Mr Marrier
was afraid of him. Mr Marrier's list of personages
was no longer a miracle of foresight; it was a mere
coincidence. He doubted if Mr Marrier was worth
even his three pounds a week. Edward Henry began
to feel ruthless, Napoleonic. He was capable of brush-
ing away the whole Azure Society and New Thought
movement into limbo.

" You must please alter your date," said Elsie
April. And she put her right elbow on the table and
leaned her chin on it, and thus somehow established
a domestic intimacy for the three amid all the blare
and notoriety of the vast tea-room.

" Oh, but I can't! " he said easily, familiarly. It
was her occasional " artichoke " manner that had
justified him in assuming this tone. " I can't! " he
repeated. " I've told Sir John I can't possibly be
ready any earlier, and on the day after he'll almost
certainly be on his way to Marseilles. Besides, I
don't *want* to alter my date. My date is in the papers
by this time."

" You've already done quite enough harm to the

Movement as it is," said Elsie April, stoutly, but ravishingly.

"Me—harm to the Movement?"

"Haven't you stopped the building of our church?"

"Oh! So you know Mr Wrissell?"

"Very well, indeed."

"Anybody else would have done the same in my place!" Edward Henry defended himself. "Your cousin, Miss Euclid, would have done it, and Marrier here was in the affair with her."

"Ah!" exclaimed Elsie April. "But we didn't belong to the Movement then! We didn't know. . . . Come now, Mr Machin. Sir John Pilgrim will of course be a great draw. But even if you've got him and manage to stick to him, we should beat you. You'll never get the audience you want if you don't change from Wednesday week. After all, the number of people who count in London is very small. And we've got nearly all of them. You've no idea—"

"I won't change from Wednesday week," said Edward Henry. This defiance of her put him into an extremely agitated felicity.

"Now, my dear Mr Machin—"

He was acutely aware of the charm she was exerting, and yet he discovered that he could easily withstand it.

"Now, my dear Miss April, please don't try to take advantage of your beauty!"

She sat up. She was apparently measuring herself and him.

"Then you won't change the day, truly?" Her urbanity was in no wise impaired.

"I won't," he laughed lightly. "I daresay you aren't used to people like me, Miss April."

(She might get the better of Seven Sachs, but

not of him, Edward Henry Machin from the Five Towns!)

" Marrier! " said he, suddenly, with a bluff, humorous downrightness, " you know you're in a very awkward position here, and you know you've got to see Alloyd for me before six o'clock. Be off with you. I will be responsible for Miss April."

(" I'll show these Londoners! " he said to himself. " It's simple enough when you once get into it.")

And he did in fact succeed in dismissing Mr Marrier, after the latter had talked Azure business with Miss April for a couple of minutes.

" I must go too," said Elsie, imperturbable, impenetrable.

" One moment," he entreated, and masterfully signalled Marrier to depart. After all he was paying the fellow three pounds a week.

She watched Marrier thread his way out. Already she had put on her gloves.

" I must go," she repeated; her rich red lips then closed definitely.

" Have you a motor here? " Edward Henry asked.

" No."

" Then if I may I'll see you home."

" You may," she said, gazing full at him. Whereby he was somewhat startled and put out of countenance.

v

" ARE we friends? " he asked roguishly.

" I hope so," she said, with no diminution of her inscrutability.

They were in a taxi-cab, rolling along the Embankment towards the Buckingham Palace Hotel, where she said she lived. He was happy. " Why am I happy? " he thought. " What is there in her that makes me happy? " He did not know. But he knew that he had never been in a taxi-cab, or anywhere else, with any woman half so elegant. Her elegance flattered him enormously. Here he was, a provincial man of business, ruffling it with the best of them! . . . And she was young in her worldly maturity. Was she twenty-seven? She could not be more. She looked straight in front of her, faintly smiling. . . . Yes, he was fully aware that he was a married man. He had a distinct vision of the angelic Nellie, of the three children, and of his mother. But it seemed to him that his own case differed in some very subtle and yet effective manner from the similar case of any other married man. And he lived, unharassed by apprehensions, in the lively joy of the moment.

" But," she said, " I hope you won't come to see me act."

" Why? "

" Because I should prefer you not to. You would not be sympathetic to me."

" Oh, yes, I should."

" I shouldn't feel it so." And then, with a swift disarrangement of all the folds of her skirt, she turned and faced him. " Mr Machin, do you know why I've let you come with me? "

" Because you're a good-natured woman," he said.

She grew even graver, shaking her head.

" No! I simply wanted to tell you that you've ruined Rose—my cousin."

" Miss Euclid? Me ruined Miss Euclid! "

" Yes. You robbed her of her theatre—her one chance."

He blushed. " Excuse me," he said. " I did no

such thing. I simply bought her option from her. She was absolutely free to keep the option or let it go."

" The fact remains," said Elsie April, with humid eyes, " the fact remains that she'd set her heart on having that theatre, and you failed her at the last instant. And she has nothing, and you've got the theatre entirely in your own hands. I'm not so silly as to suppose that you can't defend yourself legally. But let me tell you that Rose went to the United States heartbroken, and she's playing to empty houses there—empty houses! Whereas she might have been here in London, interested in her theatre, and pre-paring for a successful season."

" I'd no idea of this," breathed Edward Henry. He was dashed. " I'm awfully sorry! "

" Yes, no doubt. But there it is! "

Silence fell. He knew not what to say. He felt himself in one way innocent, but he felt himself in another way blackly guilty. His remorse for the telephone-trick which he had practised on Rose Euclid burst forth again after a long period of quiescence simulating death, and acutely troubled him. . . . No, he was not guilty! He insisted in his heart that he was not guilty! And yet—and yet—

No taxi-cab ever travelled so quickly as that taxi-cab. Before he could gather together his forces it had arrived beneath the awning of the Buckingham Palace Hotel.

His last words to her were:

" Now I shan't change the day of my stone-laying. But don't worry about your Conference. You know it'll be perfectly all right! " He spoke archly, with a brave attempt at cajolery. But in the recesses of his soul he was not sure that she had not defeated him in this their first encounter. However, Seven Sachs might talk as he chose—she was not such a persuasive creature as all that! She had scarcely even tried to be persuasive.

At about a quarter-past six when he saw his underling again he said to Mr Marrier:

" Marrier, I've got a great idea. We'll have that corner-stone-laying at night. After the theatres. Say half-past eleven. Torchlight! Fireworks from the cranes! It'll tickle old Pilgrim to death. I shall have a marquee with matchboarding sides fixed up inside, and heat it with a few of those smokeless stoves. We can easily lay on electricity. It will be absolutely the most sensational stone-laying that ever was. It'll be in all the papers all over the blessed world. Think of it! Torches! Fireworks from the cranes! . . . But I won't change the day—neither for Miss April nor anybody else."

Mr Marrier dissolved in laudations.

" Well," Edward Henry agreed with false diffidence. " It'll knock spots off some of 'em in this town! "

He felt that he had snatched victory out of defeat. But the next moment he was capable of feeling that Elsie April had defeated him even in his victory. Anyhow, she was a most disconcerting and fancy-monopolizing creature.

There was one source of unsullied gratification he had shaved off his beard.

VI

" Come up here, Sir John," Edward Henry called. " You'll see better, and you'll be out of the crowd. And I'll show you something."

He stood, in a fur coat, at the top of a short flight of rough-surfaced steps between two unplastered walls—a staircase which ultimately was to form part of an emergency exit from the dress-circle of the Regent Theatre. Sir John Pilgrim, also in a fur coat, stood near the bottom of the steps, with the glare of a Wells light full on him and throwing his shadow almost up to Edward Henry's feet. Around, Edward Henry could descry the vast mysterious forms of the building's skeleton—black in places, but in other places lit up by bright rays from the gaiety below, and showing glimpses of that gaiety in the occasional revelation of a woman's cloak through slits in the construction. High overhead two gigantic cranes interlaced their arms; and, even higher than the cranes, shone the stars of the clear spring night.

The hour was nearly half-past twelve. The ceremony was concluded—and successfully concluded. All London had indeed been present. Half the aristocracy of England, and far more than half the aristocracy of the London stage! The entire preciosity of the Metropolis! Journalists with influence enough to plunge the whole of Europe into war! In one short hour Edward Henry's right hand (peeping out from that superb fur coat which he had had the wit to buy) had made the acquaintance of scores upon scores of the most celebrated right hands in Britain. He had the sensation that in future, whenever he walked about the best streets of the West End, he would be continually compelled to stop and chat with august and renowned acquaintances, and that he would always be taking off his hat to fine ladies who flashed by nodding from powerful motor-cars. Indeed, Edward Henry was surprised at the number of famous people who seemed to have nothing to do but attend advertising rituals at midnight or thereabouts. Sir John Pilgrim had, as Marrier predicted, attended to the advertisements. But Edward Henry had helped. And on the day itself the evening newspapers had taken the bit between their teeth and run off with the affair at a great pace. The affair was on all the contents-bills hours before it actually happened. Edward Henry had been interviewed several times, and had rather enjoyed that. Gradually he had perceived that his novel idea for a corner-stone-laying had caught the facile imagination of the London populace. For that night at least he was famous—as famous as anybody!

Sir John had made a wondrous picturesque figure of himself as, in a raised corner of the crowded and beflagged marquee, he had flourished a trowel, and talked about the great and enlightened public, and about the highest function of the drama, and about the duty of the artist to elevate, and about the solemn responsibility of theatrical managers, and about the absence of petty jealousies in the world of the stage. Everybody had vociferously applauded, while reporters turned rapidly the pages of their note-books. " Ass! " Edward Henry had said to himself with much force and sincerity—meaning Sir John—but he too had vociferously applauded; for he was from the Five Towns, and in the Five Towns people are like that! Then Sir John had declared the corner-stone well and truly laid (it was on the corner which the electric sign of the future was destined to occupy), and after being thanked had wandered off, shaking hands here and there absently, to arrive at length in the office of the clerk-of-the-works, where Edward Henry had arranged suitably to refresh the stone-layer and a few choice friends of both sexes.

He had hoped that Elsie April would somehow

reach that little office. But Elsie April was absent, indisposed. Her absence made the one blemish on the affair's perfection. Elsie April, it appeared, had been struck down by a cold which had entirely deprived her of her voice, so that the performance of the Azure Society's Dramatic Club, so eagerly anticipated by all London, had had to be postponed. Edward Henry bore the misfortune of the Azure Society with stoicism, but he had been extremely disappointed by the invisibility of Elsie April at his stone-laying. His eyes had wanted her.

Sir John, awaking apparently out of a dream when Edward Henry had summoned him twice, climbed the uneven staircase and joined his host and youngest rival on the insecure planks and gangways that covered the first floor of the Regent Theatre.

" Come higher," said Edward Henry, mounting upward to the beginnings of the second story, above which hung suspended from the larger crane the great cage that was employed to carry brick and stone from the ground.

The two fur coats almost mingled.

" Well, young man," said Sir John Pilgrim, " your troubles will soon be beginning."

Now Edward Henry hated to be addressed as " young man," especially in the patronizing tone which Sir John used. Moreover, he had a suspicion that in Sir John's mind was the illusion that Sir John alone was responsible for the creation of the Regent Theatre—that without Sir John's aid as a stone-layer it could never have existed.

" You mean my troubles as a manager? " said Edward Henry, grimly.

" In twelve months from now—before I come back from my world's tour—you'll be ready to get rid of this thing on any terms. You will be wishing that you had imitated my example and kept out of Piccadilly Circus. Piccadilly Circus is sinister, my Alderman—sinister."

"Come up into the cage, Sir John," said Edward Henry. "You'll get a still better view. Rather fine, isn't it, even from here?"

He climbed up into the cage, and helped Sir John to climb.

And, standing there in the immediate silence, Sir John murmured with emotion:

"We are alone with London!"

Edward Henry thought:

"Cuckoo!"

They heard footsteps resounding on loose planks in a distant corner.

"Who's there?" Edward Henry called.

"Only me!" replied a voice. "Nobody takes any notice of me!"

"Who is it?" muttered Sir John.

"Alloyd, the architect," Edward Henry answered, and then calling loud, "Come up here, Alloyd."

The muffled and coated figure approached, hesitated, and then joined the other two in the cage.

"Let me introduce Mr Alloyd, the architect—Sir John Pilgrim," said Edward Henry.

"Ah!" said Sir John, bending towards Alloyd. "Are you the genius who draws those amusing little lines and scrawls on transparent paper, Mr Alloyd? Tell me, are they really necessary for a building, or do you only do them for your own fun? Quite between ourselves, you know! I've often wondered."

Said Mr Alloyd, with a pale smile:

"Of course everyone looks on the architect as a joke!" The pause was somewhat difficult.

" You promised us rockets, Mr Machin," said Sir John.   " My mind yearns for rockets."

" Right you are! " Edward Henry complied.   Close by, but somewhat above them, was the crane-engine, manned by an engineer whom Edward Henry was paying for overtime.   A signal was given, and the cage containing the proprietor and the architect of the theatre and Sir John Pilgrim bounded most startlingly up into the air.   Simultaneously it began to revolve rapidly on its cable, as such cages will, whether filled with bricks or with celebrities.

" Oh! " ejaculated Sir John, terror-struck, clinging hard to the side of the cage.

" Oh! " ejaculated Mr Alloyd, also clinging hard.

" I want you to see London," said Edward Henry, who had been through the experience before.

The wind blew cold above the chimneys.

The cage came to a standstill exactly at the peak of the other crane.   London lay beneath the trio. The curves of Regent Street and of Shaftesbury Avenue, the right lines of Piccadilly, Lower Regent Street and Coventry Street, were displayed at their feet as on an illuminated map, over which crawled mannikins and toy-autobuses.   At their feet a long procession of automobiles were sliding off, one after another, with the guests of the evening.   The Metropolis stretched away, lifting to the north, and sinking to the south into the jewelled river on whose curved bank rose messages of light concerning whisky, tea and beer.   The peaceful nocturnal roar of the city, dwindling every moment now, reached them like an emanation from another world.

" You asked for a rocket, Sir John," said Edward Henry.   " You shall have it."

He had taken a box of fusees from his pocket. He struck one, and his companions in the swaying cage now saw that a tremendous rocket was hung to the peak of the other crane. He lighted the fuse. . . . An instant of deathly suspense! . . . And then with a terrific and a shattering bang and splutter the rocket shot towards the kingdom of heaven and there burst into a vast dome of red blossoms which, irradiating a square mile of roofs, descended slowly and softly on the West End like a benediction.

"You always want crimson, don't you, Sir John?" said Edward Henry, and the easy cheeriness of his voice gradually tranquillized the alarm natural to two very earthly men who for the first time found themselves suspended insecurely over a gulf.

"I have seen nothing so impressive since the Russian Ballet," murmured Mr Alloyd, recovering.

"You ought to go to Siberia, Alloyd," said Edward Henry.

Sir John Pilgrim, pretending now to be extremely brave, suddenly turned on Edward Henry and in a convulsive grasp seized his hand.

"My friend," he said hoarsely, "a thought has just occurred to me. You and I are the two most remarkable men in London!" He glanced up as the cage trembled. "How thin that steel rope seems!"

The cage slowly descended, with many twists.

Edward Henry said not a word. He was too deeply moved by his own triumph to be able to speak.

"Who else but me," he reflected, exultant, "could have managed this affair as I've managed it? Did anyone else ever take Sir John Pilgrim up into the sky like a load of bricks, and frighten his life out of him?"

As the cage approached the platforms of the first story he saw two people waiting there; one he recognized as the faithful, harmless Marrier; the other was a woman.

" Someone here wants you urgently, Mr Machin! " cried Marrier.

" By Jove! " exclaimed Alloyd under his breath. " What a beautiful figure! No girl as attractive as that ever wanted *me* urgently! Some folks do have luck! "

The woman had moved a little away when the cage landed. Edward Henry followed her along the planking.

It was Elsie April.

" I thought you were ill in bed," he breathed, astounded.

Her answering voice reached him, scarcely audible:

" I'm only hoarse. My Cousin Rose has arrived to-night in secret at Tilbury by the *Minnetonka*."

" The *Minnetonka!* " he muttered. Staggering co-incidence! Mystic heralding of misfortune!

" I was sent for," the pale ghost of a delicate voice continued. " She's broken, ruined; no courage left. Awful fiasco in Chicago! She's hiding now at a little hotel in Soho. She absolutely declined to come to my hotel. I've done what I could for the moment. As I was driving by here just now I saw the rocket and I thought of you. I thought you ought to know it. I thought it was my duty to tell you."

She held her muff to her mouth. She seemed to be trembling.

A heavy hand was laid on his shoulder.

" Excuse me, sir," said a strong, rough voice, " are you the gent that fired off the rocket? It's against the law to do that kind o' thing here, and you ought to know it. I shall have to trouble you—"

It was a policeman of the C Division.

Sir John was disappearing, with his stealthy and conspiratorial air, down the staircase

CHAPTER VIII

DEALING WITH ELSIE

I

THE headquarters of the Azure Society were situate in Marloes Road—for no other reason than that it happened so. Though certain famous people inhabit Marloes Road, no street could well be less fashionable than this thoroughfare, which is very arid and very long, and a very long way off the centre of the universe.

" The Azure Society, you know! " Edward Henry added, when he had given the exact address to the chauffeur of the taxi.

The chauffeur, however, did not know, and did not seem to be ashamed of his ignorance. His attitude indicated that he despised Marloes Road and was not particularly anxious for his vehicle to be seen therein—especially on a wet night—but that nevertheless he would endeavour to reach it. When he did reach it, and observed the large concourse of shining automobiles that struggled together in the rain in front of the illuminated number named by Edward Henry, the chauffeur admitted to himself that for once he had been mistaken, and his manner of receiving money from Edward Henry was generously respectful.

Originally, the headquarters of the Azure Society had been a seminary and schoolmistress's house. The thoroughness with which the buildings had been transformed showed that money was not among the things which the Society had to search for. It had rich resources, and it had also high social standing; and the deferential commissionaires at the doors and the fluffy-aproned, appealing girls who gave away programmes in the *foyer* were a proof that the Society, while doubtless anxious about such subjects as the persistence of individuality after death, had no desire to reconstitute the community on a democratic basis. It was above such transient trifles of reform, and its high endeavours were confined to questions of immortality, of the infinite, of sex, and of art: which questions it discussed in fine raiment and with all the punctilio of courtly politeness.

Edward Henry was late, in common with some two hundred other people, of whom the majority were elegant women wearing Paris or almost-Paris gowns with a difference. As on the current of the variegated throng he drifted through corridors into the bijou theatre of the Society, he could not help feeling proud of his own presence there—and yet at the same time he was scorning, in his Five Towns way, the preciosity and the simperings of those his fellow-creatures. Seated in the auditorium, at the end of a row, he was aware of an even keener satisfaction, as people bowed and smiled to him; for the theatre was so tiny and the reunion so choice that it was obviously an honour and a distinction to have been invited to such an exclusive affair. To the evening first fixed for the dramatic soirée of the Azure Society he had received no invitation. But shortly after the postponement due to Elsie April's indisposition an envelope addressed by Marrier himself, and containing the sacred card, had arrived for him in Bursley. His instinct had been to ignore it, and for two days he had ignored it, and then he noticed in one corner the initials, " E. A."

Strange that it did not occur to him immediately that E. A. stood, or might stand, for Elsie April!

Reflection brings wisdom and knowledge. In the end he was absolutely convinced that E. A. stood for Elsie April; and at the last moment, deciding that it would be the act of a fool and a coward to decline what was practically a personal request from a young and enchanting woman, he had come to London— short of sleep, it is true, owing to local convivialities, but he had come! And, curiously, he had not communicated with Marrier. Marrier had been extremely taken up with the dramatic soirée of the Azure Society —which Edward Henry justifiably but quite privately resented. Was he not paying three pounds a week to Marrier?

And now, there he sat, known, watched, a notoriety, the card who had raised Pilgrim to the skies, probably the only theatrical proprietor in the crowded and silent audience; and he was expecting anxiously to see Elsie April again—across the footlights! He had not seen her since the night of the stone-laying, over a week earlier. He had not sought to see her. He had listened then to the delicate tones of her weak, whispering, thrilling voice, and had expressed regret for Rose Euclid's plight. But he had done no more. What could he have done? Clearly he could not have offered money to relieve the plight of Rose Euclid, who was the cousin of a girl as wealthy and as sympathetic as Elsie April. To do so would have been to insult Elsie. Yet he felt guilty, none the less. An odd situation! The delicate tones of Elsie's weak, whispering, thrilling voice on the scaffolding haunted his memory, and came back with strange clearness as he sat waiting for the curtain to ascend.

There was an outburst of sedate applause, and a

turning of heads to the right. Edward Henry looked in that direction. Rose Euclid herself was bowing from one of the two boxes on the first tier. Instantly she had been recognized and acknowledged, and the clapping had in no wise disturbed her. Evidently she accepted it as a matter of course. How famous, after all, she must be, if such an audience would pay her such a meed! She was pale, and dressed glitteringly in white. She seemed younger, more graceful, much more handsome, more in accordance with her renown. She was at home and at ease up there in the brightness of publicity. The imposing legend of her long career had survived the eclipse in the United States. Who could have guessed that some ten days before she had landed heart-broken and ruined at Tilbury from the *Minnetonka* ?

Edward Henry was impressed.

" She's none so dusty! " he said to himself in the incomprehensible slang of the Five Towns. The phrase was a high compliment to Rose Euclid, aged fifty and looking anything you like over thirty. It measured the extent to which he was impressed.

Yes, he felt guilty. He had to drop his eyes, lest hers should catch them. He examined guiltily the programme, which announced " The New Don Juan," a play " in three acts and in verse "—author unnamed. The curtain went up.

II

AND with the rising of the curtain began Edward Henry's torture and bewilderment. The scene disclosed a cloth upon which was painted, to the right, a vast writhing purple cuttle-fish whose finer tentacles were lost above the proscenium arch, and to the left an enormous crimson oblong patch with a hole in it. He referred to the programme, which said: " Act I. A castle in a forest "; and also, " Scenery and costumes designed by Saracen Givington, A.R.A." The cuttle-fish, then, was the purple forest, or perhaps one tree in the forest, and the oblong patch was the crimson castle. The stage remained empty, and Edward Henry had time to perceive that the footlights were unlit and that rays came only from the flies and from the wings.

He glanced round. Nobody had blenched. Quite confused, he referred again to the programme and deciphered in the increasing gloom: " Lighting by Cosmo Clark," in very large letters.

Two yellow-clad figures of no particular sex glided into view, and at the first words which they uttered Edward Henry's heart seemed in apprehension to cease to beat. A fear seized him. A few more words and the fear became a positive assurance and realization of evil. " The New Don Juan " was simply a pseudonym for Carlo Trent's " Orient Pearl "! . . . He had always known that it would be. Ever since deciding to accept the invitation he had lived under just that menace. " The Orient Pearl " seemed to be pursuing him like a sinister destiny.

Weakly he consulted yet again the programme. Only one character bore a name familiar to the Don Juan story, to wit " Haidee," and opposite that name was the name of Elsie April. He waited for her—he had no other interest in the evening—and he waited in resignation; a young female troubadour (styled in the programme " the messenger ") emerged from the unseen depths of the forest in the wings and ejaculated to the hero and his friend, " The Woman appears."

But it was not Elsie that appeared. Six times that troubadour-messenger emerged and ejaculated, " The Woman appears," and each time Edward Henry was disappointed. But at the seventh heralding—the heralding of the seventh and highest heroine of this drama in hexameters—Elsie did at length appear.

And Edward Henry became happy. He understood little more of the play than at the historic breakfast-party of Sir John Pilgrim; he was well confirmed in his belief that the play was exactly as preposterous as a play in verse must necessarily be; his manly contempt for verse was more firmly established than ever— but Elsie April made an exquisite figure between the castle and the forest; her voice did really set up physical vibrations in his spine. He was deliciously convinced that if she remained on the stage from everlasting to everlasting, just so long could he gaze thereat without surfeit and without other desire. The mischief was that she did not remain on the stage. With despair he saw her depart, and the close of the act was ashes in his mouth.

The applause was tremendous. It was not as tremendous as that which had greeted the plate-smashing comedy at the Hanbridge Empire, but it was far more than sufficiently enthusiastic to startle and shock Edward Henry. In fact, his cold indifference was so conspicuous amid that fever that in order to save his face he had to clap and to smile.

And the dreadful thought crossed his mind, traversing it like the shudder of a distant earthquake that presages complete destruction:

" Are the ideas of the Five Towns all wrong? Am I a provincial after all? "

For hitherto, though he had often admitted to himself that he was a provincial, he had never done so with sincerity: but always in a manner of playful and rather condescending badinage.

III

" DID you ever see such scenery and costumes? " someone addressed him suddenly, when the applause had died down. It was Mr Alloyd, who had advanced up the aisle from a back row of the stalls.

" No, I never did! " Edward Henry agreed.

" It's wonderful how Givington has managed to get away from the childish realism of the modern theatre," said Mr Alloyd, " without being ridiculous."

" You think so! " said Edward Henry, judicially. " The question is—has he? "

" Do you mean it's too realistic for you? " cried Mr Alloyd. " Well, you *are* advanced! I didn't know you were as anti-representational as all that! "

" Neither did I! " said Edward Henry. " What do you think of the play? "

" Well," answered Mr Alloyd, low and cautiously, with a somewhat shamed grin, " between you and me I think the play's bosh."

" Come, come! " Edward Henry murmured as if in protest.

The word " bosh " was almost the first word of the discussion which he had comprehended, and the honest familiar sound of it did him good. Nevertheless, keeping his presence of mind, he had forborne to welcome it openly. He wondered what on earth " anti-representational " could mean. Similar conversations were proceeding around him, and each could be very closely heard, for the reason that, the audience being frankly intellectual and anxious to exchange ideas, the management had wisely avoided the expense and noise of an orchestra. The *entr'acte* was like a conversazione of all the cultures.

"I wish you'd give us some scenery and costumes like this in *your* theatre," said Alloyd, as he strolled away.

The remark stabbed him like a needle; the pain was gone in an instant, but it left a vague fear behind it, as of the menace of a mortal injury. It is a fact that Edward Henry blushed and grew gloomy—and he scarcely knew why. He looked about him timidly, half defiantly. A magnificently-arrayed woman in the row in front, somewhat to the right, leaned back and towards him, and behind her fan said:

"You're the only manager here, Mr Machin! How alive and alert you are!" Her voice seemed to be charged with a hidden meaning.

"D'you think so?" said Edward Henry. He had no idea who she might be. He had probably shaken hands with her at his stone-laying, but if so he had forgotten her face. He was fast becoming one of the oligarchical few who are recognized by far more people than they recognize.

"A beautiful play!" said the woman. "Not merely poetic but intellectual! And an extraordinarily acute criticism of modern conditions!"

He nodded. "What do you think of the scenery?" he asked.

"Well, of course candidly," said the woman, "I think it's silly. I daresay I'm old-fashioned." . . .

"I daresay," murmured Edward Henry.

"They told me you were very ironic," said she, flushing but meek.

"They!" Who? Who in the world of London

had been labelling him as ironic? He was rather
proud.

" I hope if you *do* do this kind of play—and we're
all looking to you, Mr Machin," said the lady, making
a new start, " I hope you won't go in for these costumes
and scenery. That would never do!"

Again the stab of the needle!

" It wouldn't," he said.

" I'm delighted you think so," said she.

An orange telegram came travelling from hand to
hand along that row of stalls, and ultimately, after
skipping a few persons, reached the magnificently-
arrayed woman, who read it, and then passed it to
Edward Henry.

" Splendid! " she exclaimed. " Splendid! "

Edward Henry read: " Released. Isabel."

" What does it mean? "

" It's from Isabel Joy—at Marseilles."

" Really! "

Edward Henry's ignorance of affairs round about
the centre of the universe was occasionally distressing
—to himself in particular. And just now he gravely
blamed Mr Marrier, who had neglected to post him
about Isabel Joy. But how could Marrier honestly
earn his three pounds a week if he was occupied night
and day with the organizing and management of these
precious dramatic soirées? Edward Henry decided
that he must give Mr Marrier a piece of his mind at
the first opportunity.

" Don't you know? " questioned the dame.

" How should I? " he parried. " I'm only a
provincial."

" But surely," pursued the dame, " you knew we'd
sent her round the world. She started on the *Kandahar*, the ship that you stopped Sir John Pilgrim from

taking. She almost atoned for his absence at Tilbury. Twenty-five reporters, anyway!"

Edward Henry sharply slapped his thigh, which in the Five Towns signifies: "I shall forget my own name next."

Of course! Isabel Joy was the advertising emissary of the Militant Suffragette Society, sent forth to hold a public meeting and make a speech in the principal ports of the world. She had guaranteed to circuit the globe and to be back in London within a hundred days, to speak in at least five languages, and to get herself arrested at least three times *en route*. . . . Of course! Isabel Joy had possessed a very fair share of the newspapers on the day before the stone-laying, but Edward Henry had naturally had too many preoccupations to follow her exploits. After all, his momentary forgetfulness was rather excusable.

"She's made a superb beginning!" said the re-splendent dame, taking the telegram from Edward Henry and inducting it into another row. "And before three months are out she'll be the talk of the entire earth. You'll see!"

"Is everybody a suffragette here?" asked Edward Henry, simply, as his eyes witnessed the satisfaction spread by the voyaging telegram. . . .

"Practically," said the dame. "These things always go hand in hand," she added in a deep tone.

"What things?" the provincial demanded.

But just then the curtain rose on the second act.

IV

" Won't you cam up to Miss April's dressing-room? " said Mr Marrier, who in the midst of the fulminating applause after the second act seemed to be inexplicably standing over him, having appeared in an instant out of nowhere like a genie.

The fact was that Edward Henry had been gently and innocently dozing. It was in part the deep obscurity of the auditorium, in part his own physical fatigue, and in part the secret nature of poetry that had been responsible for this restful slumber. He had remained awake without difficulty during the first portion of the act, in which Elsie April—the orient pearl—had had a long scene of emotion and tears, played, as Edward Henry thought, magnificently in spite of its inherent ridiculousness; but later, when gentle Haidee had vanished away and the fateful troubadour-messenger had begun to resume her announcements of "The woman appears," Edward Henry's soul had miserably yielded to his body and to the temptation of darkness. The upturned lights and the ringing hosannahs had roused him to a full sense of sin, but he had not quite recovered all his faculties when Marrier startled him.

"Yes, yes! Of course! I was coming," he answered a little petulantly. But no petulance could impair the beaming optimism on Mr Marrier's features. To judge by those features, Mr Marrier, in addition to having organized and managed the soirée, might also have written the piece and played every part in it, and founded the Azure Society and built its private theatre. The hour was Mr Marrier's.

Elise April's dressing-room was small and very thickly populated, and the threshold of it was barred by eager persons who were half in and half out of the room. Through these Mr Marrier's authority forced a way. The first man Edward Henry recognized in the tumult of bodies was Mr Rollo Wrissell, whom he had not seen since their meeting at Slossons.

"Mr Wrissell," said the glowing Marrier, "let me introduce Mr Alderman Machin, of the Regent Theatah."

"Clumsy fool!" thought Edward Henry, and stood as if entranced.

But Mr Wrissell held out a hand with the perfection of urbane insouciance.

"How d'you do, Mr Machin?" said he. "I hope you'll forgive me for not having followed your advice."

This was a lesson to Edward Henry. He learnt that you should never show a wound, and if possible never feel one. He admitted that in such details of social conduct London might be in advance of the Five Towns, despite the Five Towns' admirable downrightness.

Lady Woldo was also in the dressing-room, glorious in black. Her beauty was positively disconcerting, and the more so on this occasion as she was bending over the faded Rose Euclid, who sat in a corner surrounded by a court. This court, comprising comparatively uncelebrated young women and men, listened with respect to the conversation of the peeress who called Rose "my dear," the great star-actress, and the now somewhat notorious Five Towns character, Edward Henry Machin.

"Miss April is splendid, isn't she?" said Edward Henry to Lady Woldo.

"Oh! My word, yes!" replied Lady Woldo, nicely, warmly, yet with a certain perfunctoriness. Edward Henry was astonished that everybody was not passionately enthusiastic about the charm of Elsie's performance. Then Lady Woldo added: "But what a part for Miss Euclid! What a part for her!"

And there were murmurs of approbation.

Rose Euclid gazed at Edward Henry palely and weakly. He considered her much less effective here than in her box. But her febrile gaze was effective enough to produce in him the needle-stab again, the feeling of gloom, of pessimism, of being gradually overtaken by an unseen and mysterious avenger.

" Yes, indeed! " said he.

He thought to himself: " Now's the time for me to behave like Edward Henry Machin, and teach these people a thing or two! " But he could not.

A pretty young girl summoned all her forces to address the great proprietor of the Regent, to whom, however, she had not been introduced, and with a charming nervous earnest lisp said:

" But don't you think it's a great play, Mr Machin? "

" Of course! " he replied, inwardly employing the most fearful and shocking anathemas.

" We were sure *you* would! "

The young people glanced at each other with the satisfaction of proved prophets.

" D'you know that not another manager has taken the trouble to come here! " said a second earnest young woman.

Edward Henry's self-consciousness was now acute. He would have paid a ransom to be alone on a desert island in the Indian seas. He looked downwards, and noticed that all these bright eager persons, women and men, were wearing blue stockings or socks.

" Miss April is free now," said Marrier in his ear.

The next instant he was talking alone to Elsie in another corner while the rest of the room respectfully observed.

" So you deigned to come! " said Elsie April. " You did get my card."

A little paint did her no harm, and the accentuation of her eyebrows and lips and the calculated disorder of her hair were not more than her powerful effulgent physique could stand. In a costume of green and silver she was magnificent, overwhelmingly magnificent. Her varying voice and her glance at once sincere, timid and bold, produced the most singular sensations behind Edward Henry's soft frilled shirtfront. And he thought that he had never been through any experience so disturbing and so fine as just standing in front of her.

" I ought to be saying nice things to her," he reflected. But, no doubt because he had been born in the Five Towns, he could not formulate in his mind a single nice thing.

" Well, what do you think of it? " she asked, looking full at him, and the glance too had a strange significance. It was as if she had said: " Are you a man, or aren't you? "

" I think you're splendid," he exclaimed.

" Now please! " she protested. " Don't begin in that strain. I know I'm very good for an amateur—"

" But really! I'm not joking."

She shook her head.

" What do you think of my part for Rose? Wouldn't she be tremendous in it? Wouldn't she be tremendous? . . . What a chance! "

He was acutely uncomfortable, but even his discomfort was somehow a joy.

" Yes," he admitted. " Yes."

" Oh! Here's Carlo Trent," said she.

He heard Trent's triumphant voice, carrying the end of a conversation into the room: " If he hadn't been going away," Carlo Trent was saying, " Pilgrim would have taken it. Pilgrim—"

The poet's eyes met Edward Henry's, and the sentence was never finished.

" How d'ye do, Machin? " murmured the poet.

Then a bell began to ring and would not stop.

" You're staying for the reception afterwards? " said Elsie April as the room emptied.

" Is there one? "

" Of course."

It seemed to Edward Henry that they exchanged silent messages.

v

Some time after the last hexameter had rolled forth, and the curtain had finally fallen on the immense and rapturous success of Carlo Trent's play in three acts and in verse, Edward Henry, walking about the crowded stage, where the reception was being held, encountered Elsie April, who was still in her gorgeous dress of green and silver. She was chatting with Marrier, who instantly left her, thus displaying a discretion such as an employer would naturally expect from a factotum to whom he was paying three pounds a week.

Edward Henry's heart began to beat in a manner which troubled him and made him wonder what could be happening at the back of the soft-frilled shirt front that he had obtained in imitation of Mr Seven Sachs.

" Not much elbow-room here! " he said lightly. He was very anxious to be equal to the occasion.

She gazed at him under her emphasized eyebrows. He noticed that there were little touches of red on her delightful nostrils.

" No," she answered with direct simplicity. " Suppose we try somewhere else? "

She turned her back on all the amiable and intellectual babble, descended three steps on the prompt side, and opened a door. The swish of her brocaded spreading skirt was loud and sensuous. He followed her into an obscure chamber in which several figures were moving to and fro and talking.

" What's this place? " he asked. Involuntarily his voice was diminished to a whisper.

" It's one of the discussion-rooms," said she. " It used to be a classroom, I expect, before the Society took the buildings over. You see the theatre was the general schoolroom."

They sat down unobtrusively in an embrasure. None among the mysterious moving figures seemed to remark them.

" But why are they talking in the dark? " Edward Henry asked behind his hand.

" To begin with, it isn't quite dark," she said. " There's the light of the street-lamp through the window. But it has been found that serious discussions can be carried on much better without too much light. . . . I'm not joking." (It was as if in the gloom her ears had caught his faint sardonic smile.)

Said the voice of one of the figures:

" Can you tell me what is the origin of the decay of realism? Can you tell me that? "

Suddenly, in the ensuing silence, there was a click, and a tiny electric lamp shot its beam. The hand which held the lamp was the hand of Carlo Trent.

He flashed it and flashed the trembling ray in the inquirer's face. Edward Henry recalled Carlo's objection to excessive electricity in the private drawing-room at Wilkins's.

"Why do you ask such a question?" Carlo Trent challenged the inquirer, brandishing the lamp. "I ask you why do you ask it?"

The other also drew forth a lamp and, as it were, cocked it and let it off at the features of Carlo Trent. And thus the two stood, statuesque and lit, surrounded by shadowy witnessers of the discussion.

The door creaked, and yet another figure, silhouetted for an instant against the illumination of the stage, descended into the discussion chamber.

Carlo Trent tripped towards the new-comer, bent with his lamp, lifted delicately the hem of the new-comer's trousers, and gazed at the colour of his sock, which was blue.

"All right!" said he.

"The champagne and sandwiches are served," said the new-comer.

"You've not answered me, sir," Carlo Trent faced once more his opponent in the discussion. "You've not answered me."

Whereupon, the lamps being extinguished, they all filed forth, the door swung to of its own accord, shutting out the sound of babble from the stage, and Edward Henry and Elsie April were left silent and solitary to the sole ray of the street-lamp.

All the Five Towns' shrewdness in Edward Henry's character, all the husband in him, all the father in him, all the son in him, leapt to his lips, and tried to say to Elsie:

"Shall *we* go and inspect the champagne and sandwiches, too?"

And failed to say these incantatory words of salvation!

And the romantic, adventurous fool in him rejoiced at their failure. For he was adventurously happy in his propinquity to that simple and sincere creature. He was so happy, and his heart was so active, that he even made no caustic characteristic comment on the singular behaviour of the beings who had just abandoned them to their loneliness. He was also proud because he was sitting alone nearly in the dark with a piquant and wealthy, albeit amateur actress, who had just participated in a triumph at which the spiritual aristocracy of London had assisted.

VI

Two thoughts ran through his head, shooting in and out and to and fro among his complex sensations of pleasure. The first was that he had never been in such a fix before, despite his enterprising habits. And the second was that neither Elsie April nor anybody else connected with his affairs in London had ever asked him whether he was married, or assumed by any detail of behaviour towards him that there existed the possibility of his being married. Of course he might, had he chosen, have informed a few of them that a wife and children possessed him, but then really would not that have been equivalent to attaching a label to himself: " Married "? a procedure which had to him the stamp of provinciality.

Elsie April said nothing. And as she said nothing he was obliged to say something, if only to prove to both of them that he was not a mere tongue-tied provincial. He said:

" You know I feel awfully out of it here in this Society of yours! "

" Out of it? " she exclaimed, and her voice thrilled as she resented his self-depreciation.

" It's over my head—right over it! "

" Now, Mr Machin," she said, dropping somewhat that rich low voice, " I quite understand that there are some things about the Society you don't like, trifles that you're inclined to laugh at. *I* know that. Many of us know it. But it can't be helped in an organization like ours. It's even essential. Don't be too hard on us. Don't be sarcastic."

" But I'm not sarcastic! " he protested.

" Honest? " She turned to him quickly. He could descry her face in the gloom, and the forward bend of her shoulders, and the backward sweep of her arms resting on the seat, and the straight droop of her Egyptian shawl from her inclined body.

" Honest! " he solemnly insisted.

The exchange of this single word was so intimate that it shifted their conversation to a different level— a level at which each seemed to be assuring the other that intercourse between them could never be aught but utterly sincere thenceforward, and that indeed in future they would constitute a little society of their own, ideal in its organization.

" Then you're too modest," she said decidedly. " There was no one here to-night who's more respected than you are. No one! Immediately I first spoke to you—I daresay you don't remember that afternoon at the Grand Babylon Hotel!—I knew you weren't like the rest. And don't I know them? Don't I know them? "

" But how did you know I'm not like the rest? " asked Edward Henry. The line which she was taking had very much surprised him—and charmed him. The compliment, so serious and urgent in tone, was intensely agreeable, and it made an entirely new experience in his career. He thought: " Oh! there's no mistake about it. These London women are marvellous! They're just as straight and in earnest as the best of our little lot down there. But they've got something else. There's no comparison! " The unique word to describe the indescribable floated into his head: " Scrumptious! " What could not life be with such semi-divine creatures? He dreamt of art drawing-rooms softly shaded at midnight. And his attitude towards even poetry was modified.

" I knew you weren't like the rest," said she, " by your look. By the way you say everything you *do* say. We all know it. And I'm sure you're far more than clever enough to be perfectly aware that we all know it. Just see how everyone looked at you to-night! "

Yes, he had in fact been aware of the glances.

" I think I ought to tell you," she went on, " that I was rather unfair to you that day in talking about my cousin—in the taxi. You were quite right to refuse to go into partnership with her. She thinks so too. We've talked it over, and we're quite agreed. Of course it did seem hard—at the time, and her bad luck in America seemed to make it worse. But you were quite right. You can work much better alone. You must have felt that instinctively—far quicker than we felt it."

" Well," he murmured, confused, " I don't know—"

Could this be she who had too openly smiled at his skirmish with an artichoke?

" Oh, Mr Machin! " she burst out. " You've got an unprecedented opportunity, and thank Heaven you're the man to use it! We're all expecting so much from you, and we know we shan't be disappointed."

"D'ye mean the theatre?" he asked, alarmed as it were amid rising waters.

"The theatre," said she, gravely. "You're the one man that can save London. No one *in* London can do it! . . . *You* have the happiness of knowing what your mission is, and of knowing, too, that you are equal to it. What good fortune! I wish I could say as much for myself. I want to do something! I try! But what can I do? Nothing—really! You've no idea of the awful loneliness that comes from a feeling of inability."

"Loneliness," he repeated. "But surely—" he stopped.

"Loneliness," she insisted. Her little chin was now in her little hand, and her dim face upturned.

And suddenly a sensation of absolute and marvellous terror seized Edward Henry. He was more afraid than he had ever been—and yet once or twice in his life he had felt fear. His sense of true perspective—one of his most precious qualities—returned. He thought: "I've got to get out of this." Well, the door was not locked. It was only necessary to turn the handle, and security lay on the other side of the door! He had but to rise and walk. And he could not. He might just as well have been manacled in a prison-cell. He was under an enchantment.

"A man," murmured Elsie, "a man can never realize the loneliness—" She ceased.

He stirred uneasily.

"About this play," he found himself saying. And yet why should he mention the play in his fright? He pretended to himself not to know why. But he knew

why. His instinct had seen in the topic of the play
the sole avenue of salvation.

" A wonderful thing, isn't it? "

" Oh, yes," he said. And then—most astonish-
ingly to himself—added: " I've decided to do it."

" We knew you would," she said calmly. " At
any rate I did. . . .   You'll open with it, of
course."

" Yes," he answered desperately. And proceeded,
with the most extraordinary bravery, " If you'll
act in it."

Immediately on hearing these last words issue from
his mouth he knew that a fool had uttered them, and
that the bravery was mere rashness. For Elsie's
responding gesture reinspired him afresh with the
exquisite terror which he had already begun to conjure
away.

" You think Miss Euclid ought to have the part,"
he added quickly, before she could speak.

" Oh! I do! " cried Elsie, positively and eagerly.
" Rose will do simply wonders with that part. You
see she can speak verse. I can't. I'm nobody. I
only took it because—"

" Aren't you anybody? " he contradicted. " Aren't
you anybody? I can just tell you—"

There he was again, bringing back the delicious
terror! An astounding situation!

But the door creaked. The babble from the stage
invaded the room. And in a second the enchantment was lifted from him. Several people entered.
He sighed, saying within himself to the disturbers:

" I'd have given you a hundred pounds apiece if
you'd been five minutes sooner."

And yet simultaneously he regretted their arrival.
And, more curious still, though he well remembered

the warning words of Mr Seven Sachs concerning
Elsie April, he did not consider that they were justified. . . . She had not been a bit persuasive . . . only . . .

VII

HE sat down to the pianisto with a strange and agreeable sense of security. It is true that, owing to the
time of year, the drawing-room had been, in the
figurative phrase, turned upside down by the process
of spring-cleaning, which his unexpected arrival had
surprised in fullest activity. But he did not mind
that. He abode content among rolled carpets, a
swathed chandelier, piled chairs, and walls full of pale
rectangular spaces where pictures had been. Early
that morning, after a brief night spent partly in bed and
partly in erect contemplation of his immediate past and
his immediate future, he had hurried back to his pianisto
and his home—to the beings and things that he knew
and that knew him.

In the train he had had the pleasure of reading in
sundry newspapers that " The Orient Pearl," by Carlo
Trent (who was mentioned in terms of startling respect
and admiration), had been performed on the previous
evening at the dramatic soirée of the Azure Society,
with all the usual accompaniments of secrecy and
exclusiveness, in its private theatre in Kensington,
and had been accepted on the spot by Mr E. H. Machin
(" that most enterprising and enlightened recruit to the
ranks of theatrical managers ") for production at the
new Regent Theatre. And further that Mr Machin intended to open with it. And still further that his selection of such a play, which combined in the highest degree
the poetry of Mr W. B. Yeats with the critical intel-

lectuality of Mr Bernard Shaw, was an excellent augury for London's dramatic future, and that the " upward movement " must on no account be thought to have failed because of the failure of certain recent ill-judged attempts, by persons who did not understand their business, to force it in particular directions. And still further that he, Edward Henry, had engaged for the principal part Miss Rose Euclid, perhaps the greatest emotional actress the English-speaking peoples had ever had, but who unfortunately had not been sufficiently seen of late on the London stage, and that this would be her first appearance after her recent artistic successes in the United States. And lastly that Mr Marrier (whose name would be remembered in connection with . . . etc., etc.) was Mr E. H. Machin's acting manager and technical adviser. Edward Henry could trace the hand of Marrier in all the paragraphs. Marrier had lost no time.

Mrs Machin, senior, came into the drawing-room just as he was adjusting the " Tannhäuser " overture to the mechanician. The piece was one of his major favourites.

" This is no place for you, my lad," said Mrs Machin, grimly, glancing round the room. " But I came to tell ye as th' mutton's been cooling at least five minutes. You gave out as you were hungry."

" Keep your hair on, mother," said he, springing up.

Barely twelve hours earlier he had been mincing among the elect and the select and the intellectual and the poetic and the aristocratic; among the lah-di-dah and Kensingtonian accents; among rouged lips and blue hose and fixed simperings; in the centre of the universe. And he had conducted himself with considerable skill accordingly. Nobody, on the previous night, could have guessed from the cut of his fancy

waistcoat or the judiciousness of his responses to remarks about verse, that his wife often wore a white
apron, or that his mother was—the woman she was!
He had not unskilfully caught many of the tricks of
that metropolitan environment. But now they all fell
away from him, and he was just Edward Henry—nay,
he was almost the old Denry again.

" Who chose this mutton? " he asked as he bent
over the juicy and rich joint and cut therefrom exquisite thick slices with a carving-knife like a razor.

" *I* did, if ye want to know," said his mother.
" Anything amiss with it? " she challenged.

" No. It's fine."

" Yes," said she. " I'm wondering whether you
get aught as good as that in those grand hotels as you
call 'em."

" We don't," said Edward Henry. First, it was
true; and secondly, he was anxious to be propitiatory,
for he had a plan to further.

He looked at his wife. She was not talkative, but
she had received him in the hall with every detail of
affection, if a little absent-mindedly owing to the state
of the house. She had not been caustic, like his mother,
about this male incursion into spring-cleaning. She
had not informed the surrounding air that she failed
to understand why them as were in London couldn't
stop in London for a bit, as his mother had. Moreover,
though the spring-cleaning fully entitled her to wear a
white apron at meals, she was not wearing a white
apron: which was a sign to him that she still loved
him enough to want to please him. On the whole
he was fairly optimistic about his plan of salvation.
Nevertheless, it was not until nearly the end of the
meal—when one of his mother's apple-pies was being
consumed—that he began to try to broach it.

"Nell," he said, "I suppose you wouldn't care to come to London with me?"

"Oh!" she answered smiling, a smile of a peculiar quality. It was astonishing how that simple woman could put just one tenth of one per cent. of irony into a good-natured smile. "What's the meaning of this?" Then she flushed. The flush touched Edward Henry in an extraordinary manner.

("To think," he reflected incredulously, "that only last night I was talking in the dark to Elsie April— and here I am now!" And he remembered the glory of Elsie's frock, and her thrilling voice in the gloom, and that pose of hers as she leaned dimly forward.)

"Well," he said aloud, as naturally as he could, "that theatre's beginning to get up on its hind-legs now, and I should like you to see it."

A difficult pass for him, as regards his mother! This was the first time he had ever overtly spoken of the theatre in his mother's presence. In the best bedroom he had talked of it—but even there with a certain self-consciousness and false casualness. Now, his mother stared straight in front of her with an expression of which she alone among human beings had the monopoly.

"I should like to," said Nellie, generously.

"Well," said he, "I've got to go back to town to-morrow. Wilt come with me, lass?"

"Don't be silly, Edward Henry," said she. "How can I leave mother in the middle of all this spring-cleaning?"

"You needn't leave mother. We'll take her too," said Edward Henry, lightly.

"You won't!" observed Mrs Machin.

"I *have* to go to-morrow, Nell," said Edward Henry.

" And I was thinking you might as well come with me. It will be a change for you."

(He said to himself, " And not only have I to go to-morrow, but you absolutely must come with me, my girl. That's the one thing to do.")

" It would be a change for me," Nellie agreed— she was beyond doubt flattered and calmly pleased. " But I can't possibly come to-morrow. You can see that for yourself, dear."

" No, I can't! " he cried impatiently. " What does it matter? Mother'll be here. The kids'll be all right. After all, spring-cleaning isn't the Day of Judgment."

" Edward Henry," said his mother, cutting in between them like a thin blade, " I wish you wouldn't be blasphemous. London's London, and Bursley's Bursley." She had finished.

" It's quite out of the question for me to come to-morrow, dear. I must have notice. I really must."

And Edward Henry saw with alarm that Nellie had made up her mind, and that the flattered calm pleasure in his suggestion had faded from her face.

" Oh! Dash these domesticated women! " he thought, and shortly afterwards departed, brooding, to the offices of the Thrift Club.

VIII

HE timed his return with exactitude, and, going straight upstairs to the chamber known indifferently as " Maisie's room " or " nurse's room," sure enough he found the three children there alone! They were fed, washed, night-gowned and even dressing-gowned; and this was the hour when, while nurse repaired the consequences of their revolutionary conduct in the bath-room and other places, they were left to themselves. Robert lay on the hearthrug, the insteps of his soft pink feet rubbing idly against the pile of the rug, his elbows digging into the pile, his chin on his fists, and a book perpendicularly beneath his eyes. Ralph, care-less adventurer rather than student, had climbed to the glittering brass rail of Maisie's new bedstead and was thereon imitating a recently-seen circus performance. Maisie, in the bed according to regulation, and lying on the flat of her back, was singing nonchalantly to the ceiling. Carlo, unaware that at that moment he might have been a buried corpse but for the benignancy of Providence in his behalf, was feeling sympathetic towards himself because he was slightly bored.

"Hello, kids!" Edward Henry greeted them. As he had seen them before mid-day dinner, the more formal ceremonies of salutation after absence—so hateful to the Five Towns temperament—were happily over and done with.

Robert turned his head slightly, inspected his father with a judicial detachment that hardly escaped the inimical, and then resumed his book.

("No one would think," said Edward Henry to himself, "that the person who has just entered this room is the most enterprising and enlightened of West End theatrical managers.")

"'Ello, father!" shrilled Ralph. "Come and help me to stand on this wire-rope."

"It isn't a wire-rope," said Robert from the hearthrug, without stirring, "it's a brass-rail."

"Yes, it is a wire-rope, because I can make it bend," Ralph retorted, bumping down on the thing. "Anyhow, it's going to be a wire-rope."

Maisie simply stuck several fingers into her mouth, shifted to one side, and smiled at her father in a style of heavenly and mischievous flirtatiousness.

" Well, Robert, what are you reading? " Edward Henry inquired, in his best fatherly manner—half authoritative and half humorous—while he formed part of the staff of Ralph's circus.

" I'm not reading—I'm learning my spellings," replied Robert.

Edward Henry, knowing that the discipline of filial politeness must be maintained, said, " ' Learning my spellings '—what? "

" Learning my spellings, father," Robert consented to say, but with a savage air of giving way to the unreasonable demands of affected fools. Why indeed should it be necessary in conversation always to end one's sentence with the name or title of the person addressed?

" Well, would you like to go to London with me? "

" When? " the boy demanded cautiously. He still did not move, but his ears seemed to prick up.

" To-morrow? "

" No thanks . . . father." His ears ceased their activity.

" No? Why not? "

" Because there's a spellings examination on Friday, and I'm going to be top-boy."

It was a fact that the infant (whose programmes were always somehow arranged in advance, and were in his mind absolutely unalterable) could spell the most obstreperous words. Quite conceivably he could spell better than his father, who still showed an occasional tendency to write " separate " with three " e's " and only one " a."

" London's a fine place," said Edward Henry.

" I know," said Robert, negligently.

" What's the population of London? "

" I don't know," said Robert, with curtness; though he added after a pause, " But I can spell population—p,o,p,u,l,a,t,i,o,n."

" *I'*ll come to London, father, if you'll have me," said Ralph, grinning good-naturedly.

" Will you! " said his father.

" Fahver," asked Maisie, wriggling, " have you brought me a doll? "

" I'm afraid I haven't."

" Mother said p'r'aps you would."

It was true there had been talk of a doll; he had forgotten it.

" I tell you what I'll do," said Edward Henry. " I'll take you to London, and you can choose a doll in London. You never saw such dolls as there are in London—talking dolls that shut and open their eyes and say papa and mamma, and all their clothes take off and on."

" Do they say ' father '? " growled Robert.

" No, they don't," said Edward Henry.

" Why don't they? " growled Robert.

" When will you take me? " Maisie almost squealed.

" To-morrow."

" Certain sure, fahver? "

" Yes."

" You promise, fahver? "

" Of course I promise."

Robert at length stood up, to judge for himself this strange and agitating caprice of his father's for taking Maisie to London. He saw that, despite spellings, it would never do to let Maisie alone go. He was about to put his father through a cross-examination, but Henry Edward dropped Ralph (who had been climbing up him as up a telegraph pole) on to the bed and went over to the window, nervously, and tapped thereon.

Carlo followed him, wagging an untidy tail.

" Hello, Trent! " murmured Edward Henry, stooping and patting the dog.

Ralph exploded into loud laughter.

"Father's called ' Carlo '—' Trent,' " he roared. " Father, have you forgotten his name's ' Carlo '? " It was one of the greatest jokes that Ralph had heard for a long time.

Then Nellie hurried into the room, and Edward Henry, with a " Mustn't be late for tea," as hurriedly left it.

Three minutes later, while he was bent over the lavatory basin, someone burst into the bathroom. He lifted a soapy face.

It was Nellie, with disturbed features.

" What's this about your positively promising to take Maisie to London to-morrow to choose a doll? "

" I'll take 'em all," he replied with absurd levity. " And you too! "

" But really—" she pouted, indicating that he must not carry the ridiculous too far.

" Look here, d—n it," he said impulsively, " I *want* you to come. And I want you to come to-morrow. I knew it was the confounded infants you wouldn't leave. You don't mean to tell me you can't arrange it —a woman like you! "

She hesitated.

" And what am I to do with three children in a London hotel? "

" Take nurse, naturally."

" Take nurse? " she cried.

He imitated her, with a grotesque exaggeration,

yelling loudly, " Take nurse? " Then he planted a soap-sud on her fresh cheek.

She wiped it off carefully, and smacked his arm. The next moment she was gone, having left the door open.

" He *wants* me to go to London to-morrow," he could hear her saying to his mother on the landing.

" Confound it! " he thought. " Didn't she know that at dinner-time? "

" Bless us! " His mother's voice.

" And take the children—and nurse! " His wife continued, in a tone to convey the fact that she was just as much disturbed as her mother-in-law could possibly be by the eccentricities of the male.

" He's his father all over, that lad is! " said his mother, strangely.

And Edward Henry was impressed by these words, for not once in seven years did his mother mention his father.

Tea was an exciting meal.

" You'd better come to, mother," said Edward Henry, audaciously. " We'll shut the house up."

" I come to no London," said she.

" Well, then, you can use the motor as much as you like while we're away."

" I go about gallivanting in no motor," said his mother. " It'll take me all my time to get this house straight against you come back."

" I haven't a *thing* to go in! " said Nellie, with a martyr's sigh.

After all (he reflected), though domesticated, she was a woman.

He went to bed early. It seemed to him that his wife, his mother and the nurse were active and whispering up and down the house till the very middle of the night. He arose not late; but they were all three afoot before him, active and whispering.

IX

HE found out, on the morning after the highly complex transaction of getting his family from Bursley to London, that London held more problems for him than ever. He was now not merely the proprietor of a theatre approaching completion, but really a theatrical manager with a play to produce, artistes to engage, and the public to attract. He had made two appointments for that morning at the Majestic—(he was not at the Grand Babylon, because his wife had once stayed with him at the Majestic, and he did not want to add to his anxieties the business of accustoming her to a new and costlier luxury)—one appointment at nine with Marrier, and the other at ten with Nellie, family and nurse. He had expected to get rid of Marrier before ten.

Among the exciting mail which Marrier had collected for him from the Grand Babylon and elsewhere, was the following letter:

" BUCKINGHAM PALACE HOTEL.

" DEAR FRIEND,—We are all so proud of you. I should like some time to finish our interrupted conversation. Will you come and have lunch with me one day here at 1.30? You needn't write. I know how busy you are. Just telephone you are coming. But don't telephone between 12 and 1, because at that time I *always* take my constitutional in St James's Park.—Yours sincerely, E. A."

" Well," he thought, " that's a bit thick, that is! She's stuck me up with a dramatist I don't believe in, and a play I don't believe in, and an actress I don't believe in—and now she—"

Nevertheless, to a certain extent he was bluffing himself. For, as he pretended to put Elsie April back into her place, he had disturbing and delightful visions of her. A clever creature! Uncannily clever! Wealthy! Under thirty! Broad-minded! No provincial prejudices! . . . Her voice, that always affected his spine! Her delicious flattery! . . . She was no mean actress either! And the multifariousness of her seductive charm! In fact, she was a regular woman of the world, such as you would read about— if you did read! . . . He was sitting with her again in the obscurity of the discussion-room at the Azure Society's establishment. His heart was beating again.

Pooh! . . .

A single wrench and he ripped up the letter, and cast it into one of the red-lined waste-paper baskets with which the immense and rather shabby writing-room of the Majestic was dotted.

Before he had finished dealing with Mr Marrier's queries and suggestions—some ten thousand in all— the clock struck, and Nellie tripped into the room. She was in black silk, with hints here and there of gold chains. As she had explained, she had nothing to wear, and was therefore obliged to fall back on the final resource of every woman in her state. For in this connection " nothing to wear " signified " nothing except my black silk "—at any rate in the Five Towns.

" Mr Marrier—my wife. Nellie, this is Mr Marrier."

Mr Marrier was profuse: no other word would

describe his demeanour. Nellie had the timidity of a young girl. Indeed she looked quite youthful, despite the ageing influences of black silk.

"So that's your Mr Marrier! I understood from you he was a clerk!" said Nellie, tartly, suddenly retransformed into the shrewd matron, as soon as Mr Marrier had profusely gone. She had conceived Marrier as a sort of Penkethman! Edward Henry had hoped to avoid this interview.

He shrugged his shoulders in answer to his wife's remark.

"Well," he said, "where are the kids?"

"Waiting in the lounge with nurse, as you said to be." Her mien delicately informed him that while in London his caprices would be her law, which she would obey without seeking to comprehend.

"Well," he went on, "I expect they'd like the parks as well as anything. Suppose we take 'em and show 'em one of the parks? Shall we? Besides, they must have fresh air."

"All right," Nellie agreed. "But how far will it be?"

"Oh!" said Edward Henry, "we'll crowd into a taxi."

They crowded into a taxi, and the children found their father in high spirits. Maisie mentioned the doll. . . . In a minute the taxi had stopped in front of a toy-shop surpassing dreams, and they invaded the toy-shop like an army. When they emerged, after a considerable interval, nurse was carrying an enormous doll, and Nellie was carrying Maisie, and Ralph was lovingly stroking the doll's real shoes. Robert kept a profound silence—a silence which had begun in the train.

"You haven't got much to say, Robert," his father remarked, when the taxi set off again.

" I know," said Robert, gruffly. Among other things, he resented his best clothes on a week-day.

" What do you think of London? "

" I don't know," said Robert.

His eyes never left the window of the taxi.

Then they visited the theatre—a very fatiguing enterprise, and also, for Edward Henry, a very nervous one. He was as awkward in displaying that inchoate theatre as a newly-made father with his first-born. Pride and shame fought for dominion over him. Nellie was full of laudations. Ralph enjoyed the ladders.

" I say," said Nellie, apprehensive for Maisie, on the pavement, " this child's exhausted already. How big's this park of yours? Because neither nurse nor I can carry her very far."

" We'll buy a pram," said Edward Henry. He was staring at a newspaper placard which said : " Isabel Joy on the war-path again. Will she win? "

" But—"

" Oh, yes. We'll buy a pram! Driver—"

" A pram isn't enough. You'll want coverings for her—in this wind."

" Well, we'll buy the necessary number of eider-downs and blankets, then," said Edward Henry. " Driver—"

A tremendous business! For in addition to making the purchases he had to feed his flock in an A.B.C. shop, where among the unoccupied waitresses Maisie and her talkative, winking doll enjoyed a triumph. Still there was plenty of time.

At a quarter past twelve he was displaying the varied landscape beauties of the park to his family. Ralph insisted on going to the bridge over the lake, and Robert silently backed him. And therefore the entire party went. But Maisie was afraid of the water and cried. Now the worst thing about Maisie was that when once she had begun to cry it was very difficult to stop her. Even the most remarkable dolls were powerless to appease her distress.

"Give me the confounded pram, nurse," said Edward Henry. "I'll cure her."

But he did not cure her. However, he had to stick grimly to the perambulator. Nellie tripped primly in black silk on one side of it. Nurse had the wayward Ralph by the hand. And Robert, taciturn, stalked alone, adding up London and making a very small total of it.

Suddenly Edward Henry halted the perambulator, and, stepping away from it, raised his hat. An excessively elegant young woman leading a Pekinese by a silver chain stopped as if smitten by a magic dart and held spellbound.

"How do you do, Miss April?" said Edward Henry, loudly. "I was hoping to meet you. This is my wife. Nellie—this is Miss April." Nellie bowed stiffly in her black silk. (Naught of the fresh maiden about her now!) And it has to be said that Elsie April in all her young and radiant splendour and woman-of-the-worldliness was equally stiff. "And there are my two boys. And this is my little girl—in the pram."

Maisie screamed, and pushed an expensive doll out of the perambulator. Edward Henry saved it by its boot as it fell.

"And this is her doll. And this is nurse," he finished. "Fine breezy morning, isn't it?"

In due course the processions moved on.

"Well, that's done!" Edward Henry muttered to himself. And sighed.

CHAPTER IX

THE FIRST NIGHT

I

IT was upon an evening in June—and a fine evening, full of the exquisite melancholy of summer in a city —that Edward Henry stood before a window, drumming thereon as he had once, a less-experienced man with hair slightly less grey, drummed on the table of the mighty and arrogant Slosson. The window was the window of the managerial room of the Regent Theatre. And he could scarcely believe it—he could scarcely believe that he was not in a dream—for the room was papered, carpeted and otherwise furnished. Only its electric light fittings were somewhat hasty and provisional, and the white ceiling shewed a hole and a bunch of wires—like the nerves of a hollow tooth —whence one of Edward Henry's favourite chandeliers would ultimately depend.

The whole of the theatre was at least as far advanced towards completion as that room. A great deal of it was more advanced; for instance, the auditorium, *foyer*, and bars, which were utterly finished, so far as anything ever is finished in a changing world. Wonders, marvels and miracles had been accomplished. Mr Alloyd, in the stress of the job, had even ceased to bring the Russian Ballet into his conversations. Mr Alloyd, despite a growing tendency to prove to Edward Henry by authentic anecdote, about midnight, his general proposition that women as a sex treated him with shameful unfairness, had gained the high esteem of Edward Henry as an architect. He had fulfilled his word about those properties of the auditorium which had to do with hearing and seeing—in so much that the auditorium was indeed unique in London. And he had taken care that the Clerk of the Works took care that the builder did not give up heart in the race with time.

Moreover, he had maintained the peace with the terrible London County Council, all of whose inspecting departments seemed to have secretly decided that the Regent Theatre should be opened, not in June as Edward Henry had decided, but at some vague future date towards the middle of the century. Months earlier Edward Henry had ordained and announced that the Regent Theatre should be inaugurated on a given date in June, at the full height and splendour of the London season, and he had astounded the theatrical world by adhering through thick and thin to that date, and had thereby intensified his reputation as an eccentric; for the oldest inhabitant of that world could not recall a case in which the opening of a new theatre had not been promised for at least three widely different dates.

Edward Henry had now arrived at the eve of the dread date, and if he had arrived there in comparative safety, with a reasonable prospect of avoiding complete shame and disaster, he felt and he admitted that the credit was due as much to Mr Alloyd as to himself. Which only confirmed an early impression of his that architects were queer people—rather like artists and poets in some ways, but with a basis of bricks and mortar to them.

His own share in the enterprise of the Regent had in theory been confined to engaging the right people

for the right tasks and situations; and to signing
cheques. He had depended chiefly upon Mr Marrier,
who, growing more radiant every day, had gradually
developed into a sort of chubby Napoleon, taking an
immense delight in detail and in choosing minor hands
at round-sum salaries on the spur of the moment. Mr
Marrier refused no call upon his energy. He was helping Carlo Trent in the production and stage-manage-
ment of the play. He dried the tears of girlish neo-
phytes at rehearsals. He helped to number the stalls.
He showed a passionate interest in the tessellated
pavement of the entrance. He taught the managerial
typewriting girl how to make afternoon tea. He went
to Hitchin to find a mediæval chair required for the
third act, and found it. In a word, he was fully equal
to the post of acting manager. He managed! He
managed everything and everybody except Edward
Henry, and except the press-agent, a functionary
whose conviction of his own indispensability and importance was so sincere that even Marrier shared it
and left him alone in his Bismarckian operations.
The press-agent, who sang in musical comedy chorus
at night, knew that if the Regent Theatre succeeded it
would be his doing and his alone.

And yet Edward Henry, though he had delegated
everything, had yet found a vast amount of work to
do; and was thereby exhausted. That was why he
was drumming on the pane. That was why he was
conscious of a foolish desire to shove his fist through
the pane. During the afternoon he had had two scenes
with two representatives of the Libraries (so called
because they deal in theatre-tickets and not in books)
who had declined to take up any of his tickets in advance. He had commenced an action against a firm
of bill-posters. He had settled an incipient strike in

the ' limes ' departments, originated by Mr Cosmo
Clark's views about lighting. He had dictated answers
to seventy-nine letters of complaint from unknown
people concerning the supply of free seats for the first
night. He had responded in the negative to a request
from a newspaper critic who, on the score that he was
deaf, wanted a copy of the play. He had replied
finally to an official of the County Council about the
smoke-trap over the stage. He had replied finally
to another official of the County Council about the
electric sign. He had attended to a new curiosity on
the part of another official of the County Council about
the iron curtain. But he had been almost rude to
still another official of the County Council about the
wiring of the electric light in the dressing-rooms. He
had been unmistakably and pleasurably rude in writing
to Slossons about their criticisms of the lock on the
door of Lord Woldo's private entrance to the theatre.
Also he had arranged with the representative of the
Chief Commissioner of Police concerning the carriage
regulations for " setting-down and taking-up."

And he had indeed had more than enough. His
nerves, though he did not know it, and would have
scorned the imputation, were slowly giving way.
Hence, really, the danger to the pane! Through the
pane, in the dying light, he could see a cross-section
of Shaftesbury Avenue, and an aged newspaper-lad
leaning against a lamp-post and displaying a poster
which spoke of Isabel Joy. Isabel Joy yet again!
That little fact of itself contributed to his exasperation.
He thought, considering the importance of the Regent
Theatre and the salary he was paying to his press-
agent, that the newspapers ought to occupy their
pages solely with the metropolitan affairs of Edward
Henry Machin. But the wretched Isabel had, as it

were, got London by the throat. She had reached
Chicago from the West, on her triumphant way home,
and had there contrived to be arrested, according to
boast, but she was experiencing much more difficulty
in emerging from the Chicago prison than in entering it. And the question was now becoming acute
whether the emissary of the Militant Suffragettes
would arrive back in London within the specified period
of a hundred days. Naturally, London was holding
its breath. London will keep calm during moderate
crises—such as a national strike or the agony of the
House of Lords—but when the supreme excitation is
achieved London knows how to let itself go.

" If you please, Mr Machin—"

He turned. It was his typewriter, Miss Lindop,
a young girl of some thirty-five years, holding a tea-
tray.

" But I've had my tea once! " he snapped.

" But you've not had your dinner, sir, and it's
half-past eight! " she pleaded.

He had known this girl for less than a month, and
he paid her fewer shillings a week than the years of
her age—and yet somehow she had assumed a worship-
ping charge of him, based on the idea that he was incapable of taking care of himself. To look at her
appealing eyes one might have thought that she would
have died to ensure his welfare.

" And they want to see you about the linoleum
for the gallery stairs," she added timidly. " The
County Council man says it must be taken up."

The linoleum for the gallery stairs! Something
snapped in him. He almost walked right through
the young woman and the tea-tray.

" I'll linoleum them! " he bitterly exclaimed, and
disappeared.

II

HAVING duly "linoleumed them," or rather having very annoyingly quite failed to "linoleum them," Edward Henry continued his way up the right-hand gallery staircase, and reached the auditorium, where to his astonishment a good deal of electricity, at one penny three farthings a unit, was blazing. Every seat in the narrow and high-pitched gallery, where at the sides the knees of one spectator would be on a level with the picture-hat of the spectator in the row beneath, had a perfect and entire view of the pro-scenium opening. And Edward Henry now proved this unprecedented fact by climbing to the topmost corner seat and therefrom surveying the scene of which he was monarch. The boxes were swathed in their new white dust-sheets; and likewise the higgledy-piggledy stalls, not as yet screwed down to the floor, save three or four stalls in the middle of the front row, from which the sheet had been removed. On one of these seats, far off though it was, he could descry a paper bag—probably containing sandwiches—and on another a pair of gloves and a walking-stick. Several alert ladies with sketch-books walked uneasily about in the aisles. The orchestra was hidden in the well provided for it, and apparently murmuring in its sleep. The magnificent drop-curtain, designed by Saracen Givington, A.R.A., concealed the stage.

Suddenly Mr Marrier and Carlo Trent appeared through the iron door that gave communication—to initiates—between the wings and the auditorium; they sat down in the stalls. And the curtain rose with a violent swish, and disclosed the first " set " of "The Orient Pearl."

"What about that amber, Cosmo?" Mr Marrier

cried thickly, after a pause, his mouth occupied with sandwich.

" There you are! " came the reply.

" Right! " said Mr Marrier. " Strike! "

" Don't strike! " contradicted Carlo Trent.

" Strike, I tell you! We must get on with the second act." The voices resounded queerly in the empty theatre.

The stage was invaded by scene-shifters before the curtain could descend again.

Edward Henry heard a tripping step behind him. It was the faithful typewriting girl.

" I say," he said. " Do you mind telling me what's going on here? It's true that in the rush of more important business I'd almost forgotten that a theatre is a place where they perform plays."

" It's the dress-rehearsal, Mr Machin," said the woman, startled and apologetic.

" But the dress-rehearsal was fixed for three o'clock," said he. " It must have been finished three hours ago."

" I think they've only just done the first act," the woman breathed. " I know they didn't begin till seven. Oh! Mr Machin, of course it's no affair of mine, but I've worked in a good many theatres, and I do think it's such a mistake to have the dress-rehearsal quite private. If you get a hundred or so people in the stalls then it's an audience, and there's much less delay and everything goes much better. But when it's private a dress-rehearsal is just like any other rehearsal."

" Only more so—perhaps," said Edward Henry, smiling.

He saw that he had made her happy; but he saw also that he had given her empire over him.

" I've got your tea here," she said, rather like a hospital-nurse now. " Won't you drink it? "

" I'll drink it if it's not stewed," he muttered.

" Oh! " she protested, " of course it isn't! I poured it off the leaves into another teapot before I brought it up."

She went behind the barrier, and reappeared balancing a cup of tea with a slice of sultana cake edged on to the saucer. And as she handed it to him —the sustenance of rehearsals—she gazed at him and he could almost hear her eyes saying: " You poor thing! "

There was nothing that he hated so much as to be pitied.

" You go home! " he commanded.

" Oh, but—"

" You go home! See? " He paused, threatening. " If you don't clear out on the tick I'll chuck this cup and saucer down into the stalls."

Horrified, she vanished.

He sighed his relief.

After some time the leader of the orchestra climbed into his chair, and the orchestra began to play, and the curtain went up again, on the second act of the masterpiece in hexameters. The new scenery, which Edward Henry had with extraordinary courage insisted on Saracen Givington substituting for the original incomprehensibilities displayed at the Azure Society's performance, rather pleased him. Its colouring was agreeable, and it did resemble something definite. You could, though perhaps not easily, tell what it was meant to represent. The play proceeded, and the general effect was surprisingly pleasant to Edward Henry. And then Rose Euclid as Haidee came on for the great scene of the act. From the distance of the gallery she looked quite passably youthful, and beyond question she had a dominating presence in her resplendent costume. She was incomparably and amazingly better than she had been at the few previous rehearsals which Edward Henry had been unfortunate enough to witness. She even reminded him of his earliest entrancing vision of her.

" Some people may *like* this! " he admitted, with a gleam of optimism. Hitherto, for weeks past, he had gone forward with his preparations in the most frigid and convinced pessimism. It seemed to him that he had become involved in a vast piece of machinery, and that nothing short of blowing the theatre up with dynamite would bring the cranks and pistons to a stop. And yet it seemed to him also that everything was unreal, that the contracts he signed were unreal, and the proofs he passed, and the posters he saw on the walls of London, and the advertisements in the newspapers. Only the cheques he drew had the air of being real. And now, in a magic flash, after a few moments gazing at the stage, he saw all differently. He scented triumph from afar off, as one sniffs the tang of the sea. On the morrow he had to meet Nellie at Euston, and he had shrunk from meeting her, with her terrible remorseless, provincial, untheatrical common sense; but now, in another magic flash, he envisaged the meeting with a cock-a-doodle-doo of hope. Strange! He admitted it was strange.

And then he failed to hear several words spoken by Rose Euclid. And then a few more. As the emotion of the scene grew, the proportion of her words audible in the gallery diminished. Until she became, for him, totally inarticulate, raving away there and struggling in a cocoon of hexameters.

Despair seized him. His nervous system—every separate nerve of it—was on the rack once more.

He stood up in a sort of paroxysm, and called loudly across the vast intervening space:

"Speak more distinctly, please."

A fearful silence fell upon the whole theatre. The rehearsal stopped. The building itself seemed to be staggered. Somebody had actually demanded that words should be uttered articulately!

Mr Marrier turned towards the intruder, as one determined to put an end to such singularities.

"Who's up theyah?"

"I am," said Edward Henry. "And I want it to be clearly understood in my theatre that the first thing an actor has to do is to make himself heard. I daresay I'm devilish odd, but that's how I look at it."

"Whom do you mean, Mr Machin?" asked Marrier in a different tone.

"I mean Miss Euclid of course. Here I've spent heaven knows how much on the acoustics of this theatre, and I can't make out a word she says. I can hear all the others. And this is the dress-rehearsal!"

"You must remember you're in the gallery," said Mr Marrier, firmly.

"And what if I am? I'm not giving gallery seats away to-morrow night. It's true I'm giving half the stalls away, but the gallery will be paid for."

Another silence.

Said Rose Euclid, sharply, and Edward Henry caught every word with the most perfect distinctness:

"I'm sick and tired of people saying they can't make out what I say! They actually write me letters about it! Why *should* people make out what I say?"

She quitted the stage.

Another silence. . . .

"Ring down the curtain," said Mr Marrier in a thrilled voice.

III

Shortly afterwards Mr Marrier came into the managerial office, lit up now, where Edward Henry was dictating to his typewriter and hospital-nurse, who, having been caught in hat and jacket on the threshold, had been brought back and was tapping his words direct on to the machine.

It was a remarkable fact that the sole proprietor of the Regent Theatre was now in high spirits and good humour.

"Well, Marrier, my boy," he saluted the acting-manager, "how are you getting on with that rehearsal?"

"Well, sir," said Mr Marrier, "I'm not getting on with it. Miss Euclid refuses absolutely to proceed. She's in her dressing-room."

"But why?" inquired Edward Henry with bland surprise. "Doesn't she *want* to be heard—by her gallery-boys?"

Mr Marrier showed an enfeebled smile.

"She hasn't been spoken to like that for thirty years," said he.

"But don't you agree with me?" asked Edward Henry.

"Yes," said Marrier, "I *agree* with you—"

"And doesn't your friend Carlo want his precious hexameters to be heard?"

"We baoth agree with you," said Marrier. "The fact is, we've done all we could, but it's no use. She's splendid, only—" He paused.

" Only you can't make out ten per cent. of what she says," Edward Henry finished for him. " Well, I've got no use for that in my theatre." He found a singular pleasure in emphasizing the phrase, " my theatre."

" That's all very well," said Marrier. " But what are you going to *do* about it? I've tried everything. *You*'ve come in and burst up the entire show, if you'll forgive my saying saoh! "

" Do? " exclaimed Edward Henry. " It's perfectly simple. All you have to do is to act. God bless my soul, aren't you getting fifteen pounds a week, and aren't you my acting-manager? Act, then! You've done enough hinting. You've proved that hints are no good. You'd have known that from your birth up, Marrier, if you'd been born in the Five Towns. Act, my boy."

" But haow? If she won't go on, she won't."

" Is her understudy in the theatre? "

" Yes. It's Miss Cunningham, you know."

" What salary does she get? "

" Ten pounds a week."

" What for? "

" Well—partly to understudy, I suppose."

" Let her earn it, then. Go on with the rehearsal. And let her play the part to-morrow night. She'll be delighted, you bet."

" But—"

" Miss Lindop," Edward Henry interrupted, " will you please read to Mr Marrier what I've dictated? " He turned to Marrier. " It's an interview with myself for one of to-morrow's papers."

Miss Lindop, with tears in her voice if not in her eyes, obeyed the order and, drawing the paper from the machine, read its contents aloud.

Mr Marrier started back—not in the figurative but in the literal sense—as he listened.

"But you'll never send that out!" he exclaimed.

"Why not?"

"No paper will print it!"

"My dear Marrier," said Edward Henry, "don't be a simpleton. You know as well as I do that half-a-dozen papers will be delighted to print it. And all the rest will copy the one that does print it. It'll be the talk of London to-morrow, and Isabel Joy will be absolutely snuffed out."

"Well," said Mr Marrier, "I never heard of such a thing!"

"Pity you didn't, then!"

Mr Marrier moved away.

"I say," he murmured at the door, "don't you think you ought to read that to Rose first?"

"I'll read it to Rose like a bird," said Edward Henry.

Within two minutes—it was impossible to get from his room to the dressing-rooms in less—he was knocking at Rose Euclid's door. "Who's there?" said a voice. He entered and then replied: "I am."

Rose Euclid was smoking a cigarette and scratching the arm of an easy-chair behind her. Her maid stood near by with a whisky-and-soda.

"Sorry you can't go on with the rehearsal, Miss Euclid," said Edward Henry very quickly. "However, we must do the best we can. But Mr Marrier thought you'd like to hear this. It's part of an interview with me that's going to appear to-morrow in the press."

Without pausing, he went on to read: "' I found Mr Alderman Machin, the hero of the Five Towns and the proprietor and initiator of London's newest and

most up-to-date and most intellectual theatre, surrounded by a complicated apparatus of telephones
and typewriters in his managerial room at the Regent.
He received me very courteously. " Yes," he said in
response to my question, " the rumour is quite true.
The principal part in ' The Orient Pearl ' will be played
on the first night by Miss Euclid's understudy, Miss
Olga Cunningham, a young woman of very remarkable talent. No, Miss Euclid is not ill or even indisposed. But she and I have had a grave difference of
opinion. The point between us was whether Miss
Euclid's speeches ought to be clearly audible in the
auditorium. I considered they ought. I may be
wrong. I may be provincial. But that was and is
my view. At the dress-rehearsal, seated in the gallery,
I could not hear her lines. I objected. She refused
to consider the objection or to proceed with the rehearsal. *Hinc illae lachrymae!* " . . . " Not at all,"
said Mr Machin in reply to a question, " I have the
highest admiration for Miss Euclid's genius. I should
not presume to dictate to her as to her art. She has
had a very long experience of the stage, very long,
and doubtless knows better than I do. Only, the
Regent happens to be my theatre, and I'm responsible
for it. Every member of the audience will have a
complete uninterrupted view of the stage, and I intend
that every member of the audience shall hear every
word that is uttered on the stage. I'm odd, I know.
But then I've a reputation for oddness to keep up.
And by the way, I'm sure that Miss Cunningham will
make a great reputation for herself." ' "

" Not while I'm here, she won't! " exclaimed Rose
Euclid, standing up, and enunciating her words with
marvellous clearness.

Edward Henry glanced at her, and then continued

to read: " Suggestions for headlines. ' Piquant quarrel between manager and star-actress.' ' Unparalleled situation.' ' Trouble at the Regent Theatre.' "

" Mr Machin," said Rose Euclid, " you are not a gentleman."

" You'd hardly think so, would you? " mused Edward Henry, as if mildly interested in this new discovery of Miss Euclid's.

" Maria," said the star to her maid, " go and tell Mr Marrier I'm coming."

" And I'll go back to the gallery," said Edward Henry. " It's the place for people like me, isn't it? I daresay I'll tear up this paper later, Miss Euclid— we'll see."

IV

On the next night a male figure in evening dress and a pale overcoat might have been seen standing at the corner of Piccadilly Circus and Lower Regent Street, staring at an electric sign in the shape of a shield which said, in its glittering, throbbing speech of incandescence:

THE REGENT

———

ROSE EUCLID

IN

" THE ORIENT PEARL "

The figure crossed the Circus, and stared at the sign from a new point of view. Then it passed along Coventry Street, and stared at the sign from yet another point of view. Then it reached Shaftesbury Avenue and stared again. Then it returned to its original station. It was the figure of Edward Henry Machin, savouring the glorious electric sign of which he had dreamed. He lit a cigarette, and thought of Seven Sachs gazing at the name of Seven Sachs in fire on the façade of a Broadway Theatre in New York. Was not this London phenomenon at least as fine? He considered it was. The Regent Theatre existed—there it stood! (What a name for a theatre!) Its windows were all illuminated. Its entrance-lamps bathed the pavement in light, and in this radiance stood the commissionaires in their military pride and their new uniforms. A line of waiting automobiles began a couple of yards to the north of the main doors and continued round all sorts of dark corners and up all manner of back streets towards Golden Square itself. Marrier had had the automobiles counted and had told him the number, but such was Edward Henry's condition that he had forgotten. A row of boards reared on the pavement against the walls of the façade said: " Stalls Full," " Private Boxes Full," " Dress Circle Full," " Upper Circle Full," " Pit Full," " Gallery Full." And attached to the ironwork of the glazed entrance canopy was a long board which gave the same information in terser form: " House Full." The Regent had indeed been obliged to refuse quite a lot of money on its opening night. After all, the inauguration of a new theatre was something, even in London! Important personages had actually begged the privilege of buying seats at normal prices, and had been refused. Unimportant personages—such as those whose boast in the universe was that they had never missed a first night in the West End for twenty, thirty, or even fifty years—had tried to buy seats at abnormal prices, and had failed: which was in itself a tragedy. Edward

Henry at the final moment had yielded his wife's stall to the instances of a Minister of the Crown, and at Lady Woldo's urgent request had put her into Lady Woldo's private landowner's-box, where also was Miss Elsie April, who " had already had the pleasure of meeting Mrs Machin." Edward Henry's first night was an event of magnitude. And he alone was responsible for it. His volition alone had brought into being that grand edifice whose light yellow walls now gleamed in nocturnal mystery under the shimmer of countless electric bulbs.

" There goes pretty nigh forty thousand pounds of my money! " he reflected excitedly.

And he reflected:

" After all, I'm somebody."

Then he glanced down Lower Regent Street and saw Sir John Pilgrim's much larger theatre, now sub-let to a tenant who was also lavish with displays of radiance. And he reflected that on first nights Sir John Pilgrim, in addition to doing all that he himself had done, would hold the great *rôle* on the stage throughout the evening. And he admired the astounding, dazzling energy of such a being, and admitted ungrudgingly:

" He's somebody too! I wonder what part of the world he's illuminating just now! "

Edward Henry did not deny to his soul that he was extremely nervous. He would not and could not face even the bare possibility that the first play presented at the new theatre might be a failure. He had meant to witness the production incognito among the crowd in the pit or in the gallery. But, after visiting the pit a few moments before the curtain went up, he had been appalled by the hard-hearted levity of the pit's remarks on things in general. The pit did not seem to be in any way chastened or softened by the fact that a fortune, that reputations, that careers were at stake. He had fled from the packed pit. (As for the gallery, he decided that he had already had enough of the gallery.) He had wandered about corridors, and to and fro in his own room and in the wings, and even in the basement, as nervous as a lost cat or an author, and as self-conscious as a criminal who knows himself to be on the edge of discovery. It was a fact that he could not look people in the eyes. The reception of the first act had been fairly amiable, and he had suffered horribly as he listened for the applause. Catching sight of Carlo Trent in the distance of a passage, he had positively run away from Carlo Trent. The first *entr'acte* had seemed to last for about three months. Its nightmarish length had driven him almost to lunacy. The "feel" of the second act— so far as it mystically communicated itself to him in his place of concealment—had been better. And at the second fall of the curtain the applause had been enthusiastic. Yes, enthusiastic! Curiously, it was the revulsion caused by this new birth of hope that, while the third act was being played, had driven him out of the theatre. His wild hope needed ozone. His breast had to expand in the boundless prairie of Piccadilly Circus. His legs had to walk. His arms had to swing.

Now he crossed the Circus again to his own pavement and gazed like a stranger at his own posters. On several of them, encircled in a scarlet ring, was the sole name of Rose Euclid—impressive! (And smaller, but above it, the legend, "E. H. Machin, Sole Proprietor.") He asked himself impartially, as his eyes uneasily left the poster and slipped round the Circus—deserted save by a few sinister and idle figures at that hour—"Should I have sent that interview to the papers, or shouldn't I? . . . I wonder. I expect some folks would say that on the whole I've been rather hard on Rose since I first met her! . . . Anyhow, she's speaking up all right to-night!" He laughed shortly.

A newsboy floated up from the Circus bearing a poster with the name of Isabel Joy on it in large letters.

He thought:

" Be blowed to Isabel Joy! "

He did not care a fig for Isabel Joy's competition now.

And then a small door opened in the wall close by, and an elegant cloaked woman came out on to the pavement. The door was the private door leading to the private box of Lord Woldo, owner of the ground upon which the Regent Theatre was built. The woman he recognized with confusion as Elsie April, whom he had not seen alone since the Azure Society's night.

" What are you doing out here, Mr Machin? " she greeted him with pleasant composure.

" I'm thinking," said he.

" It's going splendidly," she remarked. " Really! . . . I'm just running round to the stage-door to meet dear Rose as she comes off. What a delightful woman your wife is! So pretty, and so sensible! "

She disappeared round the corner before he could compose a suitable husband's reply to this laudation of a wife.

Then the commissionaires at the entrance seemed to start into life. And then suddenly several pre-occupied men strode rapidly out of the theatre, buttoning their coats, and vanished phantom-like. . . . Critics, on their way to destruction!

The performance must be finishing. Hastily he followed in the direction taken by Elsie April.

v

HE was in the wings, on the prompt side. Close by stood the prompter, an untidy youth with imperfections of teeth, clutching hard at the red-scored manuscript of "The Orient Pearl." Sundry players, of varying stellar degrees, were posed around in the opulent costumes designed by Saracen Givington, A.R.A. Miss Lindop was in the background, ecstatically happy, her cheeks a race-course of tears. Afar off, in the centre of the stage, alone, stood Rose Euclid, gorgeous in green and silver, bowing and bowing and bowing—bowing before the storm of approval and acclamation that swept from the auditorium across the footlights. With a sound like that of tearing silk, or of a gigantic contralto mosquito, the curtain swished down, and swished up, and swished down again. Bouquets flew on to the stage from the auditorium (a custom newly imported from the United States by Miss Euclid, and encouraged by her, though contrary to the lofty canons of London taste). The actress already held one huge trophy, shaped as a crown, to her breast. She hesitated, and then ran to the wings, and caught Edward Henry by the wrist impulsively, madly. They shook hands in an ecstasy.

It was as though they recognized in one another a fundamental and glorious worth; it was as though no words could ever express the depth of appreciation, affection and admiration which each intensely felt for the other; it was as though this moment were the final consecration of twin-lives whose long, loyal comradeship had never been clouded by the faintest breath of mutual suspicion. Rose Euclid was still the unparalleled star, the image of grace and beauty and dominance upon the stage. And yet quite clearly Edward Henry saw close to his the wrinkled, damaged, daubed face and thin neck of an old woman; and it made no difference.

" Rose! " cried a strained voice, and Rose Euclid wrenched herself from him and tumbled with half a sob into the clasping arms of Elsie April.

" You've saved the intellectual theatah for London, my boy! That's what you've done! " Marrier now was gripping his hand. And Edward Henry was convinced that he had.

The strident vigour of the applause showed no diminution. And through the thick, heavy rain of it could be heard the monotonous, insistent detonations of one syllable:

" 'Thor! 'Thor! 'Thor! 'Thor! 'Thor! "

And then another syllable was added:

" Speech! Speech! Speech! Speech! "

Mechanically Edward Henry lit a cigarette. He had no consciousness of doing so.

" Where is Trent? " people were asking.

Carlo Trent appeared up a staircase at the back of the stage.

" You've got to go on," said Marrier. " Now, pull yourself together. The Great Beast is calling for you. Say a few wahds."

Carlo Trent in his turn seized the hand of Edward Henry, and it was for all the world as though he were seizing the hand of an intellectual and poetic equal, and wrung it.

" Come now! " Mr Marrier, beaming, admonished him, and then pushed.

" What must I say? " stammered Carlo.

" Whatever comes into your head."

" All right! I'll say something."

A man in a dirty white apron drew back the heavy mass of the curtain about eighteen inches, and Carlo Trent stepping forward, the glare of the footlights suddenly lit his white face. The applause, now multiplied fivefold and become deafening, seemed to beat him back against the curtain. His lips worked. He did not bow.

" Cam back, you fool! " whispered Marrier.

And Carlo Trent stepped back into safe shelter.

" Why didn't you say something? "

" I c-couldn't," murmured weakly the greatest dramatic poet in the world, and began to cry.

" Speech! Speech! Speech! Speech! "

" Here! " said Edward Henry, gruffly. " Get out of my way! I'll settle 'em! Get out of my way! " And he riddled Carlo Trent with a fusillade of savagely scornful glances.

The man in the apron obediently drew back the curtain again, and the next second Edward Henry was facing an auditorium crowded with his patrons. Everybody was standing up, chiefly in the aisles and crowded at the entrances, and quite half the people were waving, and quite a quarter of them were shouting. He bowed several times. An age elapsed. His ears were stunned. But it seemed to him that his brain was working with marvellous perfection. He perceived that he had been utterly wrong about " The Orient Pearl." And that all his advisers had been splendidly right. He had failed to catch its charm and to feel its power. But this audience—this magnificent representative audience drawn from London in the brilliant height of the season—had not failed.

It occurred to him to raise his hand. And as he raised his hand it occurred to him that his hand held a lighted cigarette. A magic hush fell upon the magnificent audience, which owned all that endless line of automobiles outside. Edward Henry, in the hush, took a pull at his cigarette.

"Ladies and gentlemen," he said, pitching his voice well—for municipal politics had made him a practised public speaker, " I congratulate you. This evening you—have succeeded! "

There was a roar, confused, mirthful, humorously protesting. He distinctly heard a man in the front row of the stalls say: " Well, for sheer nerve—! " And then go off into a peal of laughter.

He smiled and retired.

Marrier took charge of him.

" You merit the entire confectioner's shop! " exclaimed Marrier, aghast, admiring, triumphant.

Now Edward Henry had had no intention of meriting cake. He had merely followed in speech the secret train of his thought. But he saw that he had treated a West End audience as a West End audience had never before been treated, and that his audacity had conquered. Hence he determined not to refuse the cake.

" Didn't I tell you I'd settle 'em? " said he.

The band played " God Save the King."

VI

ONE hour later, in the double-bedded chamber at the Majestic, as his wife lay in bed and he was methodically folding up a creased white tie and inspecting his chin in the mirror, he felt that he was touching again, after an immeasurable interval, the rock-bottom of reality. Nellie, even when he could only see her face—and that in a mirror!—was the most real phenomenon in his existence, and she possessed the strange faculty of dispelling all unreality round about her.

" Well," he said, " how did you get on in the box? "

" Oh! " she replied, " I got on very well with the Woldo woman. She's one of our sort. But I'm not so set up with your Elsie April."

" Dash this collar! "

Nellie continued:

"And I can tell you another thing, I don't envy Mr Rollo Wrissell."

" What's Wrissell got to do with it? "

" She means to marry him."

" Elsie April means to marry Wrissell? "

" He was in and out of the box all night. It was as plain as a pikestaff."

" What's amiss with my Elsie April? " Edward Henry demanded.

" She's a thought too *pleasant* for my taste," answered Nellie.

Astonishing, how pleasantness is regarded with suspicion in the Five Towns, even by women who can at a pinch be angels!

VII

OFTEN during the brief night he gazed sleepily at the vague next bed and mused upon the extraordinariness of women's consciences. His wife slept like an innocent. She always did. It was as though she gently expired every evening and returned gloriously to life every morning. The sunshiny hours between three and seven were very long to him, but it was indisputable that he did not hear the clock strike six: which was at any rate proof of a little sleep to the good. At five minutes past seven he thought he heard a faint rustling noise in the corridor, and he arose and tiptoed to the door and opened it. Yes, the Majestic had its good qualities! He had ordered that all the London morning daily papers should be laid at his door as early as possible—and there the pile was, somewhat damp, and as fresh as fruit, with a slight odour of ink. He took it in.

His heart was beating as he climbed back into bed with it and arranged pillows so that he could sit up, and unfolded the first paper. Nellie had not stirred.

Once again he was disappointed in the prominence given by the powerful London press to his London enterprise. In the first newspaper, a very important one, he positively could not find any criticism of the Regent's first night. There was nearly a page of the offensive Isabel Joy, who was now appealing, through the newspapers, to the President of the United States. Isabel had been christened the World-Circler, and the special correspondents of the entire earth were gathered about her carpeted cell. Hope still remained that she would reach London within the hundred days. An unknown adherent of the cause for which she suffered had promised to give ten thousand pounds to that cause if she did so. Further, she was receiving over sixty proposals of marriage a day. And so on and so on! Most of this he gathered in an instant from the headlines alone. Nauseating! Another annoying item in the paper was a column and a half given to the foundation-stone-laying of the First New Thought

Church, in Dean Street, Soho—about a couple of hundred yards from its original site. He hated the First New Thought Church as one always hates that to which one has done an injury.

Then he found what he was searching for: " Regent Theatre. Production of poetical drama at London's latest playhouse." After all, it was well situated in the paper, on quite an important page, and there was over a column of it. But in his nervous excitation his eyes had missed it. His eyes now read it. Over half of it was given up to a discussion of the Don Juan legend and the significance of the Byronic character of Haidee—obviously written before the performance. A description of the plot occupied most of the rest, and a reference to the acting ended it. " Miss Rose Euclid, in the trying and occasionally beautiful part of Haidee, was all that her admirers could have wished." . . . . " Miss Cunningham distinguished herself by her diction and bearing in the small part of the Messenger." The final words were, " The reception was quite favourable."

" Quite favourable " indeed! Edward Henry had a chill. Good heavens, was not the reception ecstatically, madly, foolishly enthusiastic? " Why! " he exclaimed within, " I never saw such a reception! " It was true, but then he had never seen any other first night. He was shocked, as well as chilled. And for this reason: for weeks past all the newspapers, in their dramatic gossip, had contained highly sympathetic references to his enterprise. According to the paragraphs, he was a wondrous man, and the theatre was a wondrous house, the best of all possible theatres, and Carlo Trent was a great writer, and Rose Euclid exactly as marvellous as she had been a quarter of a century before, and the prospects of the intellectual-poetic drama in London so favourable as to amount to a certainty of success.   In those columns of dramatic gossip there was no flaw in the theatrical world.   In those columns of dramatic gossip no piece ever failed, though sometimes a piece was withdrawn, regretfully and against the wishes of the public, to make room for another piece.   In those columns of dramatic gossip theatrical managers, actors, and especially actresses, and even authors, were benefactors of society, and therefore they were treated with the deference, the gentleness, the heartfelt sympathy which benefactors of society merit and ought to receive.

The tone of the criticism of the first night was different—it was subtly, not crudely, different.   But different it was.

The next newspaper said the play was bad and the audience indulgent.   It was very severe on Carlo Trent, and very kind to the players, whom it regarded as good men and women in adversity—with particular laudations for Miss Rose Euclid and the Messenger. The next newspaper said the play was a masterpiece —and would be so hailed in any country but England. England, however—!   Unfortunately this was a newspaper whose political opinions Edward Henry despised.   The next newspaper praised everything and everybody, and called the reception tumultuously enthusiastic.   And Edward Henry felt as though somebody, mistaking his face for a slice of toast, had spread butter all over it.   Even the paper's parting assurance that the future of the higher drama in London was now safe beyond question did not remove this delusion of butter.

The two following newspapers were more sketchy or descriptive, and referred at some length to Edward Henry's own speech, with a kind of sub-hint that Edward

Henry had better mind what he was about. Three illustrated papers and photographs of scenes and figures, but nothing important in the matter of criticism. The rest were "neither one thing nor the other," as they say in the Five Towns. On the whole, an inscrutable press, a disconcerting, a startling, an appetite-destroying, but not a hopeless press!

The general impression which he gathered from his perusals was that the author was a pretentious dullard, an absolute criminal, a genius; that the actors and actresses were all splendid and worked hard, though conceivably one or two of them had been set impossible tasks—to wit, tasks unsuited to their personalities; that he himself was a Napoleon, a temerarious individual, an incomprehensible fellow; and that the future of the intellectual-poetic drama in London was not a topic of burning actuality. . . . He remembered sadly the superlative-laden descriptions, in those same newspapers, of the theatre itself, a week or two back, the unique theatre in which the occupant of every seat had a complete and uninterrupted view of the whole of the proscenium opening. Surely that fact alone ought to have ensured proper treatment for him!

Then Nellie woke up and saw the scattered newspapers.

" Well," she asked, " what do they say? "

" Oh! " he replied lightly, with a laugh. " Just about what you'd expect. Of course you know what a first-night audience always is. Too generous. And ours was, particularly. Miss April saw to that. She had the Azure Society behind her, and she was determined to help Rose Euclid. However, I should say it was all right—I should say it was quite all right. I told you it was a gamble, you know."

When Nellie, dressing, said that she considered she ought to go back home that day, he offered no objection. Indeed he rather wanted her to go. Not that he had a desire to spend the whole of his time at the theatre, unhampered by provincial women in London. On the contrary, he was aware of a most definite desire not to go to the theatre. He lay in bed and watched with careless curiosity the rapid processes of Nellie's toilette. He had his breakfast on the dressing-table (for he was not at Wilkins's, neither at the Grand Babylon). Then he helped her to pack, and finally he accompanied her to Euston, where she kissed him with affectionate common sense and caught the twelve five. He was relieved that nobody from the Five Towns happened to be going down by that train.

As he turned away from the moving carriage the evening papers had just arrived at the bookstalls. He bought the four chief organs—one green, one yellowish, one white, one pink—and scanned them self-consciously on the platform. The white organ had a good heading: " Re-birth of the intellectual drama in London. What a provincial has done. Opinions of leading men." Two columns altogether! There was, however, little in the two columns. The leading men had practised a sagacious caution. They, like the press as a whole, were obviously waiting to see which way the great elephantine public would jump. When the enormous animal had jumped they would all exclaim: " What did I tell you? " The other critiques were colourless. At the end of the green critique occurred the following sentence: " It is only fair to state, nevertheless, that the play was favourably received by an apparently enthusiastic audience."

" Nevertheless! " . . . " Apparently! "

Edward Henry turned the page to the theatrical advertisements.

> " REGENT THEATRE. (Twenty yards from Piccadilly Circus.) 'The Orient Pearl,' by Carlo Trent. Miss ROSE EUCLID. Every evening at 8.30. Matinées every Wednesday and Saturday at 2.30. Box-office open 10 to 10. Sole Proprietor—E. H. Machin."

Unreal! Fantastic! Was this he, Edward Henry? Could it be his mother's son?

Still—" Matinées every Wednesday and Saturday." " *Every* Wednesday and Saturday." That word implied and necessitated a long run—anyhow a run extending over months. That word comforted him. Though he knew as well as you do that Mr Marrier had composed the advertisement, and that he himself was paying for it, it comforted him. He was just like a child.

VIII

" I SAY, Cunningham's made a hit! " Mr Marrier almost shouted at him as he entered the managerial room at the Regent.

" Cunningham? Who's Cunningham? "

Then he remembered. She was the girl who played the Messenger. She had only three words to say, and to say them over and over again; and she had made a hit!

" Seen the notices? " asked Marrier.

" Yes. What of them? "

" Oh! Well! " Marrier drawled. " What would you expect? "

" That's just what *I* said! " observed Edward Henry.

" You did, did you? " Mr Marrier exclaimed, as if extremely interested by this corroboration of his views.

Carlo Trent strolled in; he remarked that he happened to be just passing. But discussion of the situation was not carried very far.

That evening the house was nearly full, except the pit and the gallery, which were nearly empty. Applause was perfunctory.

" How much? " Edward Henry inquired of the box-office manager when figures were added together.

" Thirty-one pounds, two shillings."

" Hem! "

" Of course," said Mr Marrier, " in the height of the London season, with so many counter-attractions—! Besides, they've got to get used to the idea of it."

Edward Henry did not turn pale. Still, he was aware that it cost him a trifle over sixty pounds " to ring the curtain up " at every performance—and this sum took no account of expenses of production nor of author's fees. The sum would have been higher, but he was calculating as rent of the theatre only the ground-rent plus six per cent. on the total price of the building.

What disgusted him was the duplicity of the first-night audience, and he said to himself violently, " I was right all the time, and I knew I was right! Idiots! Chumps! Of course I was right! "

On the third night the house held twenty-seven pounds and sixpence.

" Naturally," said Mr Marrier, " in this hot weathah! I never knew such a hot June! It's the open-air places that are doing us in the eye. In fact I heard to-day that the White City is packed. They simply can't bank their money quick enough."

It was on that day that Edward Henry paid salaries. It appeared to him that he was providing half London with a livelihood: acting-managers, stage-managers, assistant ditto, property men, stage-hands, electricians, prompters, call-boys, box-office staff, general staff, dressers, commissionaires, programme-girls, cleaners, actors, actresses, understudies, to say nothing of Rose Euclid at a purely nominal salary of a hundred pounds a week. The tenants of the bars were grumbling, but happily he was getting money from them.

The following day was Saturday. It rained—a succession of thunderstorms. The morning and the evening performances produced together sixty-eight pounds.

" Well," said Mr Marrier, " in this kind of weathah you can't expect people to come out, can you? Besides, this cursed week-ending habit—"

Which conclusions did not materially modify the harsh fact that Edward Henry was losing over thirty pounds a day—or at the rate of over ten thousand pounds a year.

He spent Sunday between his hotel and his club, chiefly in reiterating to himself that Monday began a new week and that something would have to occur on Monday.

Something did occur.

Carlo Trent lounged into the office early. The man was for ever being drawn to the theatre as by an invisible but powerful elastic cord. The papers had a worse attack than ever of Isabel Joy, for she had been convicted of transgression in a Chicago court of law, but a tremendous lawyer from St Louis had loomed over Chicago and, having examined the documents in the case, was hopeful of getting the conviction quashed. He had discovered that in one and the same document " Isabel " had been spelt " Isobel " and—worse—Illinois had been deprived by a careless clerk of one of its " l's." He was sure that by proving these grave irregularities in American justice he could win an appeal.

Edward Henry glanced up suddenly from the newspaper. He had been inspired.

" I say, Trent," he remarked, without any warning or preparation, " you're not looking at all well. I want a change myself. I've a good mind to take you for a sea-voyage."

" Oh! " grumbled Trent. " I can't afford sea-voyages."

" *I* can! " said Edward Henry. " And I shouldn't dream of letting it cost you a penny. I'm not a philanthropist. But I know as well as anybody that it will pay us theatrical managers to keep you in health."

" You're not going to take the play off? " Trent demanded suspiciously.

" Certainly not! " said Edward Henry.

" What sort of a sea-voyage? "

" Well—what price the Atlantic? Been to New York? . . . Neither have I! Let's go. Just for the trip. It'll do us good."

" You don't mean it? " murmured the greatest dramatic poet, who had never voyaged further than the Isle of Wight. His eyeglass swung to and fro.

Edward Henry feigned to resent this remark.

" Of course I mean it. Do you take me for a blooming gas-bag? " He rose. " Marrier! " Then more loudly: " Marrier! " Mr Marrier entered. " Do you know anything about the sailings to New York?"

"Rather!" said Mr Marrier, beaming. After all, he was a most precious aid.

"We may be able to arrange for a production in New York," said Edward Henry to Carlo, mysteriously.

Mr Marrier gazed at one and then at the other, puzzled.

CHAPTER X

ISABEL

I

THROUGHOUT the voyage of the *Lithuania* from Liverpool to New York, Edward Henry, in common with some two thousand other people on board, had the sensation of being hurried. He who in a cab rides late to an important appointment, arrives with muscles fatigued by mentally aiding the horse to move the vehicle along. Thus were Edward Henry's muscles fatigued, and the muscles of many others; but just as much more so as the *Lithuania* was bigger than a cab.

For the *Lithuania*, having been seriously delayed in Liverpool by men who were most ridiculously striking for the fantastic remuneration of one pound a week, was engaged on the business of making new records. And every passenger was personally determined that she should therein succeed. And, despite very bad June weather towards the end, she did sail past the Battery on a grand Monday morning with a new record to her credit.

So far Edward Henry's plan was not miscarrying. But he had a very great deal to do, and very little time in which to do it, and whereas the muscles of the other passengers were relaxed as the ship drew to her berth, Edward Henry's muscles were only more tensely tightened. He had expected to see Mr Seven Sachs on the quay, for in response to his telegram from Queenstown the illustrious actor-author had sent him an agreeable wireless message in full Atlantic; the which had inspired Edward Henry to obtain news by Marconi both from London and New York, at much expense; from the east he had had daily information of the dwindling receipts at the Regent Theatre, and from the west daily information concerning Isabel Joy. He had not, however, expected Mr Seven Sachs to walk into the *Lithuania's* music-saloon an hour before the ship touched the quay. Nevertheless, this was what Mr Seven Sachs did, by the exercise of those mysterious powers wielded by the influential in democratic communities.

" And what are you doing here? " Mr Seven Sachs greeted Edward Henry with geniality.

Edward Henry lowered his voice.

" I'm throwing good money after bad," said he.

The friendly grip of Mr Seven Sachs's hand did him good, reassured him, and gave him courage. He was utterly tired of the voyage, and also of the poetical society of Carlo Trent, whose passage had cost him thirty pounds, considerable boredom, and some sick-nursing during the final days and nights. A dramatic poet with an appetite was a full dose for Edward Henry; but a dramatic poet who lay on his back and moaned for naught but soda-water and dry land amounted to more than Edward Henry could conviently swallow.

He directed Mr Sachs's attention to the anguished and debile organism which had once been Carlo Trent, and Mr Sachs was so sympathetic that Carlo Trent began to adore him, and Edward Henry to be somewhat disturbed in his previous estimate of Mr Sachs's common sense. But at a favourable moment Mr

Sachs breathed humorously into Edward Henry's ear the question:

"What have you brought *him* out for?"

"I've brought him out to lose him."

As they pushed through the bustle of the enormous ship, and descended from the dizzy eminence of her boat-deck by lifts and ladders down to the level of the windy, sun-steeped rock of New York, Edward Henry said:

"Now, I want you to understand, Mr Sachs, that I haven't a minute to spare. I've just looked in for lunch."

"Going on to Chicago?"

"She isn't at Chicago, is she?" demanded Edward Henry, aghast. "I thought she'd reached New York!"

"Who?"

"Isabel Joy."

"Oh! Isabel's in New York, sure enough. She's right here. They say she'll have to catch the *Lithuania* if she's going to get away with it."

"Get away with what?"

"Well—the goods."

The precious word reminded Edward Henry of an evening at Wilkins's and raised his spirits even higher. It was a word he loved.

"And I've got to catch the *Lithuania*, too!" said he. "But Trent doesn't know! . . . And let me tell you she's going to do the quickest turn-round that any ship ever did. The purser assured me she'll leave at noon to-morrow unless the world comes to an end in the meantime. Now what about a hotel?"

"You'll stay with me—naturally."

"But—" Edward Henry protested.

"Oh, yes, you will. I shall be delighted."

" But I must look after Trent."

" He'll stay with me too—naturally. I live at the Stuyvesant Hotel, you know, on Fifth. I've a pretty private suite there. I shall arrange a little supper for to-night. My automobile is here."

" Is it possible that I once saved your life and have forgotten all about it? " Edward Henry exclaimed. " Or do you treat everybody like this? "

" We like to look after our friends," said Mr Sachs, simply.

In the terrific confusion of the quay, where groups of passengers were mounted like watch-dogs over hillocks of baggage, Mr Sachs stood continually between the travellers and the administrative rigour and official incredulity of a proud republic. And in the minimum of time the fine trunk of Edward Henry and the modest packages of the poet were on the roof of Mr Sachs's vast car. The three men were inside, and the car was leaping, somewhat in the manner of a motor-boat at full speed, over the cobbles of a wide mediæval street.

" Quick! " thought Edward Henry. " I haven't a minute to lose! "

His prayer reached the chauffeur. Conversation was difficult; Carlo Trent groaned. Presently they rolled less perilously upon asphalt, though the equipage still lurched. Edward Henry was for ever bending his head towards the window aperture in order to glimpse the roofs of the buildings, and never seeing the roofs.

" Now we're on Fifth," said Mr Sachs, after a fearful lurch, with pride.

Vistas of flags, high cornices, crowded pavements, marble, jewellery behind glass—the whole seen through a roaring phantasmagoria of competing and menacing vehicles!

And Edward Henry thought:

" This is my sort of place! "

The jolting recommenced. Carlo Trent rebounded limply, groaning between cushions and upholstery. Edward Henry tried to pretend that he was not frightened. Then there was a shock as of the concussion of two equally unyielding natures. A pane of glass in Mr Seven Sachs's limousine flew to fragments and the car stopped.

" I expect that's a spring gone! " observed Mr Sachs with tranquillity. " Will happen, you know, sometimes! "

Everybody got out. Mr Sachs's presumption was correct. One of the back wheels had failed to leap over a hole in Fifth Avenue some eighteen inches deep and two feet long.

" What is that hole? " asked Edward Henry.

" Well," said Mr Sachs, " it's just a hole. We'd better transfer to a taxi." He gave calm orders to his chauffeur.

Four empty taxis passed down the sunny magnificence of Fifth Avenue and ignored Mr Sachs's urgent waving. The fifth stopped. The baggage was strapped and tied to it: which process occupied much time. Edward Henry, fuming against delay, gazed around. A nonchalant policeman on a superb horse occupied the middle of the road. Tram-cars passed constantly across the street in front of his caracoling horse, dividing a route for themselves in the wild ocean of traffic as Moses cut into the Red Sea. At intervals a knot of persons, intimidated and yet daring, would essay the voyage from one pavement to the opposite pavement; there was no half-way refuge for these adventurers, as in decrepit London; some apparently arrived; others seemed to disappear for ever in the feverish welter of confused motion and were never heard of again. The policeman, easily accommodating himself to the caracolings of his mount, gazed absently at Edward Henry, and Edward Henry gazed first at the policeman, and then at the high decorated grandeur of the buildings, and then at the Assyrian taxi into which Mr Sachs was now ingeniously inserting Carlo Trent. He thought:

" No mistake—this street is alive. But what cemeteries they must have! "

He followed Carlo, with minute precautions, into the interior of the taxi. And then came the supremely delicate operation—that of introducing a third person into the same vehicle. It was accomplished; three chins and six knees fraternized in close intimacy; but the door would not shut. Wheezing, snorting, shaking, complaining, the taxi drew slowly away from Mr Sachs's luxurious automobile and left it forlorn to its chauffeur. Mr Sachs imperturbably smiled. (" I have two other automobiles," said Mr Sachs.) In some sixty seconds the taxi stopped in front of the tremendous glass awning of the Stuyvesant. The baggage was unstrapped; the passengers were extracted one by one from the cell, and Edward Henry saw Mr Sachs give two separate dollar bills to the driver.

" By Jove! " he murmured.

" I beg your pardon," said Mr Sachs, politely.

" Nothing! " said Edward Henry.

They walked into the hotel, and passed through a long succession of corridors and vast public rooms surging with well-dressed men and women.

" What's all this crowd for? " asked Edward Henry.

" What crowd? " asked Mr Sachs, surprised.

Edward Henry saw that he had blundered.

" I prefer the upper floors," remarked Mr Sachs as they were being flung upwards in a gilded elevator, and passing rapidly all numbers from 1 to 14.

The elevator made an end of Carlo Trent's manhood. He collapsed. Mr Sachs regarded him, and then said:

" I think I'll get an extra room for Mr Trent. He ought to go to bed."

Edward Henry enthusiastically concurred.

" And stay there! " said Edward Henry.

Pale Carlo Trent permitted himself to be put to bed. But, therein, he proved fractious. He was anxious about his linen. Mr Sachs telephoned from the bedside, and a laundry-maid came. He was anxious about his best lounge-suit. Mr Sachs telephoned, and a valet came. Then he wanted a siphon of soda-water, and Mr Sachs telephoned, and a waiter came. Then it was a newspaper he required. Mr Sachs telephoned and a page came. All these functionaries, together with two reporters, peopled Mr Trent's bedroom more or less simultaneously. It was Edward Henry's bright notion to add to them a doctor—a doctor whom Mr Sachs knew, a doctor who would perceive at once that bed was the only proper place for Carlo Trent.

" Now," said Edward Henry, when he and Mr Sachs were participating in a private lunch amid the splendours and the grim, silent service of the latter's suite at the Stuyvesant, " I have fully grasped the fact that I am in New York. It is one o'clock and after, and as soon as ever this meal is over I have just *got* to find Isabel Joy. You must understand that on this trip New York for me is merely a town where Isabel Joy happens to be."

" Well," replied Mr Sachs, " I reckon I can put you on to that. *She's going to be photographed at two o'clock by Rentoul Smiles.* I happen to know because Rent's a particular friend of mine."

" A photographer, you say? "

Mr Sachs controlled himself. " Do you mean to say you've not heard of Rentoul Smiles? . . . Well, he's called ' Man's photographer.' He has never photographed a woman! Won't! At least, wouldn't! But he's going to photograph Isabel. So you may guess that he considers Isabel *some* woman, eh? "

" And how will that help me? " inquired Edward Henry.

" Why! I'll take you up to Rent's," Mr Sachs comforted him. " It's close by—corner of Thirty-ninth and Five."

" Tell me," Edward Henry demanded, with immense relief, " she hasn't got herself arrested yet, has she? "

" No. And she won't! "

" Why not? "

" The police have been put wise," said Mr Sachs.

" Put wise? "

" Yes. *Put wise !* "

" I see," said Edward Henry.

But he did not see. He only half saw.

" As a matter of fact," said Mr Sachs, " Isabel can't get away with the goods unless she fixes the police to lock her up for a few hours. And she'll not succeed in that. Her hundred days are up in London next Sunday. So there'll be no time for her to be arrested and bailed out either at Liverpool or Fishguard. And that's her only chance. I've seen Isabel, and if you ask me my opinion she's down and out."

" Never mind! " said Edward Henry with glee.

" I guess what you're after her for," said Mr Seven Sachs, with an air of deep knowledge.

" The deuce you do! "

" Yes, sir! And let me tell you that dozens of 'em have been after her already. But she wouldn't! Nothing would tempt her."

" Never mind! " Edward Henry smiled.

II

WHEN Edward Henry stood by the side of Mr Sachs in a doorway half shielded by a *portière*, and gazed unseen into the great studio of Mr Rentoul Smiles, he comprehended that he was indeed under powerful protection in New York. At the entrance on Fifth Avenue he and Sachs had passed through a small crowd of assorted men, chiefly young, whom Sachs had greeted in the mass with the smiling words, " Well, boys! " Other men were within. Still another went up with them in the elevator, but no further. They were reporters of the entire world's press, to each of whom Isabel Joy had been specially " assigned." They were waiting; they would wait.

Mr Rentoul Smiles having been warned by telephone of the visit of his beloved friend, Seven Sachs, Mr Sachs and his English *protegé* had been received at Smiles's outer door by a clerk who knew exactly what to do with them, and did it.

" Is she here? " Mr Sachs had murmured.

" Yep," the clerk had negligently replied.

And now Edward Henry beheld the objective of his pilgrimage, her whose personality, portrait and adventures had been filling the newspapers of two hemispheres for three weeks past. She was not realistically like her portraits. She was a little, thin, pale, obviously nervous woman, of any age from thirty-five to fifty, with fair untidy hair, and pale grey-blue eyes that showed the dreamer, the idealist and the harsh fanatic. She looked as though a moderate breeze would have overthrown her, but she also looked, to the enlightened observer, as though she would recoil before no cruelty and no suffering in pursuit of her vision. The blind dreaming force behind her apparent frailty would strike terror into the heart of any man intelligent enough to understand it. Edward Henry had an inward shudder. " Great Scott! " he reflected. " I shouldn't like to be ill and have Isabel for a nurse! "

And his mind at once flew to Nellie, and then to Elsie April. " And so she's going to marry Wrissell! " he reflected, and could scarcely believe it.

Then he violently wrenched his mind back to the immediate objective. He wondered why Isabel Joy should wear a bowler hat and a mustard-coloured jacket that resembled a sporting man's overcoat; and why these garments suited her. With a whip in her hand she could have sat for a jockey. And yet she was a woman, and very feminine, and probably old enough to be Elsie April's mother! A disconcerting world, he thought.

The " man's photographer," as he was described in copper on Fifth Avenue and in gold on his own doors, was a big, loosely-articulated male, who loured over the trifle Isabel like a cloud over a sheep in a great field. Edward Henry could only see his broad bending back as he posed in athletic attitudes behind the camera.

Suddenly Rentoul Smiles dashed to a switch, and Isabel's wistful face was transformed into that of a drowned corpse, into a dreadful harmony of greens and purples.

" Now," said Rentoul Smiles, in a deep voice that was like a rich unguent, " we'll try again. We'll just play around that spot. Look into my eyes. Not *at* my eyes, my dear woman, *into* them! Just a little more challenge—a little more! That's it. Don't wink, for the land's sake! Now."

He seized a bulb at the end of a tube and slowly squeezed—squeezed it tragically and remorselessly, twisting himself as if suffering in sympathy with the bulb, and then in a wide, sweeping gesture he flung the bulb on to the top of the camera and ejaculated:

" Ha! "

Edward Henry thought:

" I would give ten pounds to see Rentoul Smiles photograph Sir John Pilgrim." But the next instant the forgotten sensation of hurry was upon him once more. Quick, quick, Rentoul Smiles! Edward Henry's scorching desire was to get done and leave New York.

" Now, Miss Isabel," Mr Smiles proceeded, exasperatingly deliberate, " d'you know, I feel kind of guilty? I have got a little farm out in Westchester County and I'm making a little English pathway up the garden with a gate at the end. I woke up this morning and began to think about the quaint English form of that gate, and just how I would have it." He raised a finger. " But I ought to have been thinking about you. I ought to have been saying to myself, ' To-day I have to photograph Isabel Joy,' and trying to understand in meditation the secrets of your personality. I'm sorry! Now, don't talk. Keep like that. Move your head round. Go on! Go on! Move it. Don't be afraid. This place belongs to you. It's yours. Whatever you do, we've got people here who'll straighten up after you. . . . D'you know why I've made money? I've made money so that I can take *you* this afternoon, and tell a two-hundred-dollar client to go to the deuce. That's why I've made money. Put your back against the chair, like an Englishwoman. That's it. No, don't *talk*, I tell you. Now look joyful, hang it! Look joyful. . . . No, no! Joy isn't a contortion. It's something right deep down. There, there!"

The lubricant voice rolled on while Rentoul Smiles manipulated the camera. He clasped the bulb again and again threw it dramatically away.

" I'm through!" he said. " Don't expect anything very grand, Miss Isabel. What I've been trying to do this afternoon is my interpretation of you as I've studied your personality in your speeches. If I believed wholly in your cause, or if I wholly disbelieved in it, my work would not have been good. Any value that it has will be due to the sympathetic impartiality of my spiritual attitude. Although "—he menaced her with the licensed familiarity of a philosopher— " although, lady, I must say that I felt you were working against me all the time. . . . This way!"

(Edward Henry, recalling the comparative simplicity of the London photographer at Wilkins's, thought: " How profoundly they understand photography in America!")

Isabel Joy rose and glanced at the watch in her bracelet, then followed the direction of the male hand and vanished.

Rentoul Smiles turned instantly to the other doorway.

" How do, Rent? " said Seven Sachs, coming forward.

" How do, Seven? " Mr Rentoul Smiles winked.

" This is my good friend, Alderman Machin, the theatre-manager from London."

" Glad to meet you, sir."

" She's not gone, has she? " asked Sachs, hurriedly.

" No, my housekeeper wanted to talk to her. Come along."

And in the waiting-room, full of permanent examples of the results of Mr Rentoul Smiles's spiritual attitude towards his fellow-men, Edward Henry was presented to Isabel Joy. The next instant the two men and the housekeeper had unobtrusively retired, and he was alone with his objective. In truth, Seven Sachs was a notable organizer.

III

SHE was sitting down in a cosy-corner, her feet on a footstool, and she seemed a negligible physical quantity as he stood in front of her. This was she who had worsted the entire judicial and police system of Chicago, who spoke pentecostal tongues, who had circled the globe, and held enthralled—so journalists computed—more than a quarter of a million of the inhabitants of Marseilles, Athens, Port Said, Candy, Calcutta, Bangkok, Hong Kong, Tokio, Hawaii, San Francisco, Salt Lake City, Denver, Chicago, and lastly, New York! This was she!

" I understand we're going home on the same ship! " he was saying.

She looked up at him, almost appealingly.

" You won't see anything of me, though," she said.

" Why not? "

" Tell me," said she, not answering his question, " what do they say of me, really, in England? I don't mean the newspapers. For instance, well—the Azure Society. Do you know it? "

He nodded.

" Tell me," she repeated.

He related the episode of the telegram at the private first performance of " The Orient Pearl."

She burst out in a torrent of irrelevant protest:

" The New York police have not treated me right. It would have cost them nothing to arrest me and let me go. But they wouldn't. Every man in the force —you hear me, every man—has had strict orders to leave me unmolested. It seems they resent my dealings with the police in Chicago, where I brought about the dismissal of four officers, so they say. And so I'm to be boycotted in this manner! Is that argument, Mr Machin? Tell me. You're a man, but honestly, is it argument? Why, it's just as mean and despicable as brute force."

" I agree with you," said Edward Henry, softly.

" Do they really think it will harm the militant cause? Do they *really* think so? No, it will only harm me. I made a mistake in tactics. I trusted—fool!— to the chivalry of the United States. I might have been arrested in a dozen cities, but I on purpose re- served my last two arrests for Chicago and New York, for the sake of the superior advertisement, you see! I never dreamt—! Now it's too late. I am defeated! I shall just arrive in London on the hundredth day. I shall have made speeches at all the meetings. But I shall be short of one arrest. And the ten thousand pounds will be lost to the cause. The militants here—such as they are—are as disgusted as I am. But they scorn me. And are they not right? Are they not right? There should be no quarter for the vanquished."

" Miss Joy," said Edward Henry, " I've come over from London specially to see you. I want to make up the loss of that ten thousand pounds as far as I can.

I'll explain at once. I'm running a poetical play of the highest merit, called 'The Orient Pearl,' at my new theatre in Piccadilly Circus. If you will undertake a small part in it—a part of three words only—I'll pay you a record salary, sixty-six pounds thirteen and fourpence a word—two hundred pounds a week!"

Isabel Joy jumped up.

"Are you another of them, then?" she muttered. "I did think from the look of you that you would know a gentlewoman when you met one! Did you imagine for the thousandth part of one second that I would stoop—"

"Stoop!" exclaimed Edward Henry. "My theatre is not a music-hall—"

"You want to make it into one!" she stopped him.

"Good day to you," she said. "I must face those journalists again, I suppose. Well, even they—! I came alone in order to avoid them. But it was hopeless. Besides, is it my duty to avoid them—after all?"

It was while passing through the door that she uttered the last words.

"Where is she?" Seven Sachs inquired, entering.

"Fled!" said Edward Henry.

"Everything all right?"

"Quite!"

Mr Rentoul Smiles came in.

"Mr Smiles," said Edward Henry, "did you ever photograph Sir John Pilgrim?"

"I did, on his last visit to New York. Here you are!"

He pointed to his rendering of Sir John.

"What did you think of him?"

"A great actor, but a mountebank, sir."

During the remainder of the afternoon Edward

Henry saw the whole of New York, with bits of the Bronx and Yonkers in the distance, from Seven Sachs's second automobile. In his third automobile he went to the theatre and saw Seven Sachs act to a house of over two thousand dollars. And lastly he attended a supper and made a speech. But he insisted upon passing the remainder of the night on the *Lithuania*. In the morning Isabel Joy came on board early and irrevocably disappeared into her berth. And from that moment Edward Henry spent the whole secret force of his individuality in fervently desiring the *Lithuania* to start. At two o'clock, two hours late, she did start. Edward Henry's farewells to the admirable and hospitable Mr Sachs were somewhat absent-minded, for already his heart was in London. But he had sufficient presence of mind to make certain final arrangements.

" Keep him at least a week," said Edward Henry to Seven Sachs, " and I shall be your debtor for ever and ever."

He meant Carlo Trent, still bedridden.

As from the receding ship he gazed in abstraction at the gigantic inconvenient word—common to three languages—which is the first thing seen by the arriving, and the last thing seen by the departing, visitor, he meditated:

" The dearness of living in the United States has certainly been exaggerated."

For his total expenses, beyond the confines of the quay, amounted to one cent, disbursed to buy an evening paper which had contained a brief interview with himself concerning the future of the intellectual drama in England. He had told the pressman that " The Orient Pearl " would run a hundred nights. Save for putting " The Orient Girl " instead of " The Orient Pearl," and two hundred nights instead of one hundred nights, this interview was tolerably accurate.

IV

Two entire interminable days of the voyage elapsed before Edward Henry was clever enough to encounter Isabel Joy—the most notorious and the least visible person in the ship. He remembered that she had said: " You won't see anything of me." It was easy to ascertain the number of her state-room—a double-berth which she shared with nobody. But it was less easy to find out whether she ever left it, and if so, at what time of day. He could not mount guard in the long corridor; and the stewardesses on the *Lithuania* were mature, experienced and uncommunicative women, their sole weakness being an occasional tendency to imagine that they, and not the captain, were in supreme charge of the steamer. However, Edward Henry did at last achieve his desire. And on the third morning, at a little before six o'clock, he met a muffled Isabel Joy on the D deck. The D deck was wet, having just been swobbed; and a boat—chosen for that dawn's boat-drill—ascended past them on its way from sea-level to the dizzy boat-deck above; on the other side of an iron barrier, large crowds of early-rising third-class passengers were standing and talking and staring at the oblong slit of sea which was the only prospect offered by the D deck; it was the first time that Edward Henry aboard had set eyes on a steerage passenger; with all the conceit natural to the occupant of a costly state-room, he had unconsciously assumed that he and his like had sole possession of the ship.

Isabel responded to his greeting in a very natural way. The sharp freshness of the summer morning at sea had its tonic effect on both of them; and as for Edward Henry, he lunged and plunged at once into the subject which alone preoccupied and exasperated him. She did not seem to resent it.

" You'd have the satisfaction of helping on a thing that all your friends say ought to be helped," he argued. " Nobody but you can do it. Without you there'll be a frost. You would make a lot of money, which you could spend in helping on things of your own. And surely it isn't the publicity that you're afraid of! "

" No," she agreed. " I'm not afraid of publicity." Her pale grey-blue eyes shone as they regarded the secret dream that for her hung always unseen in the air. And she had a strange, wistful, fragile, feminine mien in her mannish costume.

" Well then—"

" But can't you see it's humiliating? " cried she, as if interested in the argument.

" It's not humiliating to do something that you can do well—I know you can do it well—and get a large salary for it, and make the success of a big enterprise by it. If you knew the play—"

" I do know the play," she said. " We'd lots of us read it in manuscript long ago."

Edward Henry was somewhat dashed by this information.

" Well, what do you think of it? "

" I think it's just splendid! " said she with enthusiasm.

" And will it be any worse a play because you act a small part in it? "

" No," she said shortly.

" I expect you think it's a play that people ought to go and see, don't you? "

" I do, Mr Socrates," she admitted.

He wondered what she could mean, but continued:

" What does it matter what it is that brings the audience into the theatre, so long as they get there and have to listen? "

She sighed.

" It's no use discussing with you," she murmured. " You're too simple for this world. I daresay you're honest enough—in fact, I think you are—but there are so many things that you don't understand. You're evidently incapable of understanding them."

" Thanks! " he replied, and paused to recover his self-possession. " But let's get right down to business now. If you'll appear in this play I'll not merely give you two hundred pounds a week, but I'll explain to you how to get arrested and still arrive in triumph in London before midnight on Sunday."

She recoiled a step and raised her eyes.

" How? " she demanded, as with a pistol.

" Ah! " he said. " That's just it. How? Will you promise? "

" I've thought of everything," she said musingly. " If the last day was any day but Sunday I could get arrested on landing and get bailed out and still be in London before night. But on Sunday—no—! So you needn't talk like that."

" Still," he said, " it can be done."

" How? " she demanded again.

" Will you sign a contract with me if I tell you? . . . Think of what your reception in London will be if you win after all! Just think! "

Those pale eyes gleamed; for Isabel Joy had tasted

the noisy flattery of sympathetic and of adverse crowds, and her being hungered for it again; the desire of it had become part of her nature.

She walked away, her hands in the pockets of her ulster, and returned.

" What is your scheme? "

" You'll sign? "

" Yes, if it works."

" I can trust you? "

The little woman of forty or so blazed up. " You can refrain from insulting me by doubting my word," said she.

" Sorry! Sorry! " he apologized.

v

THAT same evening, in the colossal many-tabled dining-saloon of the *Lithuania* Edward Henry sat as usual to the left of the purser's empty chair, at the purser's table, where were about a dozen other men. A page brought him a marconigram. He opened it and read the single word " Nineteen." It was the amount of the previous evening's receipts at the Regent, in pounds. He was now losing something like forty pounds a night —without counting the expenses of the present excursion. The band began to play as the soup was served, and the ship rolled politely, gently, but nevertheless unmistakably, accomplishing one complete roll to about sixteen bars of the music. Then the entire saloon was suddenly excited. Isabel Joy had entered. She was in the gallery, near the orchestra, at a small table alone. Everybody became aware of the fact in an instant, and scores of necks on the lower

floor were twisted to glimpse the celebrity on the upper.
It was remarked that she wore a magnificent evening-
dress.

One subject of conversation now occupied all the
tables. And it was fully occupying the purser's table
when the purser, generally a little late, owing to the
arduousness of his situation on the ship, entered and
sat down. Now the purser was a northerner, from
Durham, a delightful companion in his lighter moods,
but dour, and with a high conception of authority and
of the intelligence of dogs. He would relate that
when he and his wife wanted to keep a secret from
their Yorkshire terrier they had to spell the crucial
words in talk, for the dog understood their every
sentence. The purser's views about the cause represented by Isabel Joy were absolutely clear. None
could mistake them, and the few clauses which he
curtly added to the discussion rather damped the discussion, and there was a pause.

" What should you do, Mr Purser," said Edward
Henry, " if she began to play any of her tricks here? "

" If she began to play any of her tricks in this ship,"
answered the purser, putting his hands on his stout
knees, " we should know what to do? "

" Of course you can arrest? "

" Most decidedly. I could tell you things—" The
purser stopped, for experience had taught him to be
very discreet with passengers until he had voyaged
with them at least ten times. He concluded: " The
captain is the representative of English law on an
English ship."

And then, in the silence created by the resting
orchestra, all in the saloon could hear a clear, piercing
woman's voice, oratorical at first and then quickening:

" Ladies and gentlemen, I wish to talk to you to-

night on the subject of the injustice of men to women."
Isabel Joy was on her feet and leaning over the gallery
rail. As she proceeded a startled hush changed to
uproar. And in the uproar could be caught now and
then a detached phrase, such as " For example, this
man-governed ship."

Possibly it was just this phrase that roused the
northerner in the purser. He rose and looked towards
the captain's table. But the captain was not dining
in the saloon that evening. Then he strode to the
centre of the saloon, beneath the renowned dome
which has been so often photographed for the illustrated papers, and sought to destroy Isabel Joy with
a single marine glance. Having failed, he called out
loudly:

" Be quiet, madam. Resume your seat."

Isabel Joy stopped for a second, gave him a glance
far more homicidal than his own, and resumed her
discourse.

" Steward," cried the purser, " take that woman
out of the saloon."

The whole complement of first-class passengers was
now standing up, and many of them saw a plate descend
from on high and graze the purser's shoulder. With
the celebrity of a sprinter the man of authority from
Durham disappeared from the ground-floor and was
immediately seen in the gallery. Accounts differed,
afterwards, as to the exact order of events; but it is
certain that the leader of the band lost his fiddle,
which was broken by the lusty Isabel on the purser's
head. It was known later that Isabel, though not
exactly in irons, was under arrest in her state-room.

" She really ought to have thought of that for
herself, if she's as smart as she thinks she is," said
Edward Henry, privately.

THOUGH he was on the way to high success his anxieties and solicitudes seemed to increase every hour. Immediately after Isabel Joy's arrest he became more than ever a crony of the Marconi operator, and began to dispatch vivid and urgent telegrams to London, without counting the cost. On the next day he began to receive replies. (It was the most interesting voyage that the Marconi operator had had since the sinking of the *Catherine of Siena,* in which episode his promptness through the air had certainly saved two hundred lives.) Edward Henry could scarcely sleep, so intense was his longing for Sunday night—his desire to be safe in London with Isabel Joy! Nay, he could not properly eat! And then the doubt entered his mind whether after all he would get to London on Sunday night. For the *Lithuania* was lagging. She might have been doing it on purpose to ruin him. Every day, in the auction-pool on the ship's run, it was the holder of the lower field that pocketed the money of his fellow-men. The *Lithuania* actually descended below five hundred and forty knots in the twenty-four hours. And no authoritative explanation of this behaviour was ever given. Upon leaving New York there had been talk of reaching Fishguard on Saturday evening. But now the prophesied moment of arrival had been put forward to noon on Sunday. Edward Henry's sole consolation was that each day on the eastward trip consisted of only twenty-three hours.

Further, he was by no means free from apprehension about the personal liberty of Isabel Joy. Isabel had exceeded the programme arranged between them. It had been no part of his scheme that she should cast plates, nor even break violins on the shining crown of an august purser. The purser was angry, and he had the captain, a milder man, behind him. When Isabel Joy threatened a hunger-strike if she was not immediately released, the purser signified that she might proceed with her hunger-strike; he well knew that it would be impossible for her to expire of inanition before the arrival at Fishguard.

The case was serious, because Isabel Joy had created a precedent. Policemen and Cabinet Ministers had for many months been regarded as the lawful prey of militants, but Isabel Joy was the first of the militants to damage property and heads which belonged to persons of neither of those classes. And the authorities of the ship were assuredly inclined to hand Isabel Joy over to the police at Fishguard. What saved the situation for Edward Henry was the factor which saves most situations—namely, public opinion. When the saloon clearly realized that Isabel Joy had done what she had done with the pure and innocent aim of winning a wager, all that was Anglo-Saxon in the saloon ranged itself on the side of true sport, and the matter was lifted above mere politics. A subscription was inaugurated to buy a new fiddle, and to pay for shattered crockery. And the amount collected would have purchased, after settling for the crockery, a couple of dozen new fiddles. The unneeded balance was given to Seamen's Orphanages. The purser was approached. The captain was implored. Influence was brought to bear. In short, the wheels that are within wheels went duly round. And Miss Isabel Joy, after apologies and promises, was unconditionally released.

But she had been arrested.

And then early on Sunday morning the ship met a storm that had a sad influence on divine service; a storm of the eminence that scares even the brass-buttoned occupants of liners' bridges. The rumour went round the ship that the captain would not call at Fishguard in such weather. Edward Henry was ready to yield up his spirit in this fearful crisis, which endured two hours. The captain did call at Fishguard, in pouring rain, and men came aboard selling Sunday newspapers that were full of Isabel's arrest on the steamer, and of the nearing triumph of her arrival in London before midnight. And newspaper correspondents also came aboard, and all the way on the tender, and in the sheds, and in the train, Edward Henry and Isabel Joy were subjected to the journalistic experiments of hardy interviewers. The train arrived at Paddington at 9 P.M. Isabel had won by three hours. The station was a surging throng of open-mouthed curiosities. Edward Henry would not lose sight of his priceless charge, but he sent Marrier to despatch a telegram to Nellie, whose wifely interest in his movements he had till then either forgotten or ignored.

And even now his mind was not free. He saw in front of him still twenty-four hours of anguish.

VII

THE next night, just before the curtain went up, he stood on the stage of the Regent Theatre, and it is a fact that he was trembling—not with fear but with simple excitement.

Through what a day he had passed! There had been the rehearsal in the morning; it had gone off very well, save that Rose Euclid had behaved impossibly, and that the Cunningham girl, the hit of the piece but ousted from her part, had filled the place with just lamentations and recriminations.

And then had followed the appalling scene with Rose Euclid. Rose, leaving the theatre for lunch, had beheld workmen removing her name from the electric sign and substituting that of Isabel Joy! She was a woman and an artist, and it would have been the same had she been a man and an artist. She would not submit to this inconceivable affront. She had resigned her *rôle*. She had ripped her contract to bits and flung the bits to the breeze. Upon the whole Edward Henry had been glad. He had sent for Miss Cunningham, who was Rose's understudy, had given her her instructions, called another rehearsal for the afternoon, and effected a saving of nearly half Isabel Joy's fantastic salary. Then he had entered into financial negotiations with four evening papers and managed to buy, at a price, their contents-bills for the day. So that all the West End was filled with men and boys wearing like aprons posters which bore the words: " Isabel Joy to appear at the Regent to-night." A great and an original stroke!

And now he gazed through the peep-hole of the curtain upon a crammed and half-delirious auditorium. The assistant stage-manager ordered him off. The curtain went up on the drama in hexameters. He waited in the wings, and spoke soothingly to Isabel Joy, who, looking juvenile in the airy costume of the Messenger, stood flutteringly agog for her cue. . . . He heard the thunderous crashing roar that met her entrance. He did not hear her line. He walked forth to the glazed balcony at the front of the house, where in the *entr'actes* dandies smoked cigarettes baptized with girlish names. He could see Piccadilly Circus, and he saw Piccadilly Circus thronged with a multitude of loafers who were happy in the mere spectacle of Isabel Joy's name glowing on an electric sign. He went back at last to the managerial room. Marrier was there, hero-worshipping.

" Got the figures yet? " he asked.

Marrier beamed.

" Two hundred and sixty pounds. As long as it keeps up it means a profit of getting on for two hundred a naight! "

" But, dash it, man, the house only holds two hundred and thirty."

" But my good sir," said Marrier, " they're paying ten shillings a piece to stand up in the dress-circle."

Edward Henry dropped into a chair at the desk. A telegram was lying there, addressed to himself.

" What's this? " he demanded.

" Just cam."

He opened it and read:

" I absolutely forbid this monstrous outrage on a work of art.—TRENT."

" Bit late in the day, isn't he? " said Edward Henry, showing the telegram to Marrier.

" Besides," Marrier observed, " he'll come round when he knows what his royalties are."

" Well," said Edward Henry, " I'm going to bed." And he gave a devastating yawn.

VIII

ONE afternoon Edward Henry sat in the king of all the easy-chairs in the drawing-room of his house in Trafalgar Road, Bursley. Although the month was

September, and the weather warm even for September, a swansdown quilt lay spread upon his knees. His face was pale—his hands were paler; but his eye was clear and his visage enlightened. His beard had grown to nearly its original dimensions. On a chair by his side were a number of letters to which he had just dictated answers. At a neighbouring table a young clerk was using a typewriter. Stretched at full length on the sofa was Robert Machin, engaged in the perusal of the second edition of that day's *Signal*. Of late Robert, having exhausted nearly all available books, had been cultivating during his holidays an interest in journalism, and he would give great accounts, in the nursery, of events happening in each day's instalment of the *Signal's* sensational serial. His heels kicked idly one against the other.

A powerful voice resounded in the lobby, and Dr Stirling entered the room with Nellie.

" Well, doc.! " Edward Henry greeted him.

" So you're in full blast again! " observed the doctor, using a metaphor invented by the population of a district where the roar of furnaces wakens the night.

" No! " Edward Henry protested, as an invalid always will. " I'm only just keeping an eye on one or two pressing things."

" Of course he's in full blast! " said Nellie with calm conviction.

" What's this I hear about ye ganging away to the seaside, Saturday? " asked the doctor.

" Well, can't I? " said Edward Henry.

" Ye can," said the doctor. " Let's have a look at ye, man."

" What was it you said I've had? " Edward Henry questioned.

" Colitis."

" Yes, that's the word. I thought I couldn't have got it wrong. Well, you should have seen my mother's face when I told her what you called it. She said, ' He may call it that if he's a mind to, but we had another name for it in my time.' You should have heard her sniff! . . . Look here, doc., do you know you've had me down now for pretty near three months? "

" Nay," said Stirling, " it's yer own obstinacy that's had ye down, man. If ye'd listened to yer London doctor at first, mayhap ye wouldn't have had to travel from Euston in an invalid's carriage. If ye hadn't had the misfortune to be born an obstinate simpleton ye'd ha' been up and about six weeks back. But there's no doing anything with you geniuses. It's all nerves with you and your like."

" Nerves! " exclaimed Edward Henry, pretending to scorn. But he was delighted at the diagnosis.

" Nerves," repeated the doctor, firmly. " Ye go gadding off to America. Ye get yeself mixed up in theatres. . . . How's the theatre? I see yer famous play's coming to an end next week."

" And what if it is? " said Edward Henry, jealous for reputations, including his own. " It will have run for a hundred and one nights. And right through August too! No modern poetry play ever did run as long in London, and no other ever will. I've given the intellectual theatre the biggest ad. it ever had. And I've made money on it. I should have made more if I'd ended the run a fortnight ago, but I was determined to pass the hundredth night. And I shall do! "

" And what are ye for giving next? "

" I'm not for giving anything next, doc. I've let the Regent for five years at seven thousand five hundred pounds a year to a musical comedy syndicate, since you're so curious. And when I've paid the ground rent and taxes and repairs, and something towards a sinking-fund, and six per cent. on my capital, I shall have not far off two thousand pounds a year clear annual profit. You may say what you like, but that's what I call business! "

It was a remarkable fact that, while giving unde-manded information to Dr Stirling, Edward Henry was in reality defending himself against the accusa-tions of his wife—accusations which, by the way, she had never uttered, but which he thought he read some-times in her face. He might of course have told his wife these agreeable details directly, and in private. But he was a husband, and, like many husbands, apt to be indirect.

Nellie said not a word.

" Then you're giving up London? " The doctor rose to depart.

" I am," said Edward Henry, almost blushing.

" Why? "

" Well," the genius answered. " Those theatrical things are altogether too exciting and risky! And they're such queer people— Great Scott! I've come out on the right side, as it happens, but—well, I'm not as young as I was. I've done with London. The Five Towns are good enough for me."

Nellie, unable to restrain a note of triumph, in-discreetly remarked, with just the air of superior sagacity that in a wife drives husbands to fury and to foolishness:

" I should think so indeed! "

Edward Henry leaped from his chair, and the swans-down quilt swathed his slippered feet.

" Nell," he exploded, clenching his hand. " If you

say that once more in that tone—once more, mind!—
I'll go and take a flat in London to-morrow! "

The doctor crackled with laughter. Nellie smiled.
Even Robert, who had completely ignored the doctor's
entrance, glanced round with creased brows.

" Sit down, dearest," Nellie quietly enjoined the
invalid.

But he would not sit down, and, to show his in-
dependence, he helped his wife to escort Stirling into
the lobby.

Robert, now alone with the ignored young clerk
tapping at the table, turned towards him, and in his
deliberate, judicial, disdainful, childish voice said to
him:

" Isn't father a funny man? "